Keeper's Prophecy

The Final Keeper Trilogy

Book Three

Chronicles from Alku

Recommended Reading Order

The Final Keeper Trilogy

Contents

Foreword

"Everything happens for a reason, young one. Though I understand what you've all endured has been painful, trust that it was deemed necessary for whatever path the fates have placed before you all."

Wow, I can't believe we've arrived at book three already.

You hold within your hands the final entry in The Final Keeper Trilogy and the wrap-up of Onnie's first adventure. It won't be her last, though, I promise. When I began writing, I never thought I'd write three books or publish them. Apparently, I was wrong.
I'm very glad I was.

Sharing the town of Alku, our world of magic, and all of the amazing people residing within both has been an honor, and it's one I cannot wait to continue with. Which is good, considering Xayn has been busy whispering in my ear with Marco behind him in line. Even sweet Mrs. Radcliff has been making plans for a newcomer to join the Alku residents.

Thank you for sharing a piece of your life and time with us here in Alku.
Welcome to the Alku Chosen Family.
We're very glad you're here.

From my world to yours,
Eliza

.

For the girl who believed her only option was to stop feeling anything.
You kept yourself safe.
It's time to come back now.

Acknowledgements

At this point, I could fill a book with all of the wonderful people who have assisted me, listened to me rant or rave, stood by me when I wanted to quit, and even scolded me when I needed it.
Thank you to each and every one of you and the many more that didn't make it onto the list this time. I couldn't have done this without you. #AlkuChosenFamily

Alpha Readers:
Donnette Goldsmith

Beta Readers:
Ander Van
Diana Marshall
Daisy

ARC Team:
Marhen DeNoble
Therese Walleri
Grace Pollard-Smith
Val Jackson
Abby R.
Kaci Rehkemper

Additional Cheerleaders:
Vincent Leone, Aaron Goldsmith, Stephen Goldsmith, Mama Mary Lynn, Adam Bassett, Chris Agel, Samantha Pearson, Martin Jackson, Maria Ocanas

Pronunciation Guide & Glossary

Names/Characters:
Eliza Leone (e-lie-za lee-o-knee)

Abbot Moore (ab-ot more) Keeper: The previous Keeper and owner of The Book Nook in Alku.

Anton Sove (so-vuh) Qondo: Owner of A Shot in the Dark, the local Alku coffee shop.

Danella Vansand (dan-ella van-sand) Human: Onnie's best friend, Gabe's sister, and Elaric's girl friend. The Alku Librarian and Head Sister for the Scholarly Light.

Elanor Radcliff (el-an-or rad-cliff) nymph: Alku's local florist, an elder nymph, and town gossip.

Elaric Rickson (e-lar-ick rick-son) Transmogromorph: Old friend to many in Alku, past romantic partner to Marco, and current boyfriend to Dany.

Gabriel Vansand (gay-bree-el van-sand) Guardian: Local school physical education teacher, brother to Dany, and boyfriend to Onnie.

Jakob Vansand (jay-cob van-sand) former guardian: Former guardian to Abbot, father to Gabe and Dany, and now known as the rogue guardian to the residents of Alku.

Kushima (caw-she-ma) Keeper/Entity: The first Keeper and being that became the entity that is the archive.

Marco Nezera (mar-co neh-zer-ah) Sanguiste: Night manager for the Day Night Cafe and best friend to Elaric.

Maldwyn Link (maald-win) Link: A Russian Blue feline who is a manifested portion of the entity that is the archive.

Onnie Moore (on-ee more) Keeper: The current Keeper residing in Alku, owner of the local bookshop, and Granddaughter to the late Abbot Moore, the previous Keeper.

Rebecca Link (re-be-caw) Link: An older woman who is a manifested portion of the entity that is the archive.

Sam Athan (ah-thahn) Day Walker: Son to Vanessa and Stephan, and chosen family to Marco. Best friend to Gabe, Xayn, and others.

Stephan Athan (ah-thahn) Sanguiste: Owner of the Day Night Cafe, father to Sam, husband to Vanessa, and chosen family to Marco.

Vanessa Athan (ah-thahn) Day Walker: Owner of the Day Night Cafe, mother to Sam, wife to Vanessa, and chosen family to Marco.

Xayn Ellwood (zuh-ay-n l-wood) Green Witch: Gabe's best friend and Dany's chosen brother.

Zamio (zay-me-oh) herbalist familiar: A raven and Xayn's familiar.

Locations:

Alku (al-coo): A sanctuary city for those of the magical world located in the forests of Washington State, USA. The current location of the Keeper and the world's archive.

Nisi Dakry (nye-sigh dack-ry): A sanctuary city for those of the magical world. A past location of the Keeper and the world's archive.

Tiefen Hool (tee-fen whooo-l): A sanctuary city for those of the magical world. A past location of the Keeper and the world's archive.

Species / Races:

Angel of Death: Humanoid beings with differing traits depending on which direction they ferry a soul after life.

Atarga (ah-tar-guh): The broad term for humans who can transmorph into an underwater creature.

Ceirnes (see-sins): A species of creature found mostly in Europe that uses its voices to lead unsuspecting prey to those sanguiste in residence nearby.

Day Walker: A group of humans that have been cursed by a group of sanguiste to suffer for eternity for murdering the non-immortals in their village over 1000 years ago.

Green Witch: Humans with an evolutionary aspect allowing them to connect to the earth and its magic. Also known as Hedge Witch or Herbalist

Guardian: A protector of the Keeper and the world's archive.

Keeper: A being chosen to protect the world's knowledge in an endless archive.

Link: A physical manifestation of a portion of the knowledge archive that the Keeper protects.

Mechanite (meh-caw-night): A human who has evolved with the capability to speak with mechanical objects and machines.

Nymph (nim-pfh): A being who has an affinity with nature and becomes part of it at death.

Paranam (pair-ah-nam): Human with two souls: one human and one animal. Can shift into the soul's animal form.

Qondo (con-doe): A being who can manipulate the sleep and dreams of another.

Sanguiste (sang-whist): An immortal being once human but traded their soul to a demon upon death. Consumers of blood, emotions, or bodily fluids for sustenance.

Transmogromorph (trans-mog-row-morph): A group of beings that can shift their physical form into that of another human if acquired first. Naturally good, relatively rare, and highly secretive.

Zwerkalt (zwer-cult): A species of beings that are short of stature, prefer living beneath the earth, and... they are dwarves. Onnie said it best.

Other:

Custos regni (cus-toes wren-ee): The book is known as The Keeper's Reign or the recorded history and line of Keepers, their Links, and Guardians.

Outsider: A human ignorant of the magical world and its inhabitants.

Blood Link: The ritual in which a sanguiste will carve their personal crest into the flesh of another, binding them together for eternity or until the demon retakes the sanguiste's soul.

Do you know about Campfire?

Campfire is a website and ebook storefront with a novel addition to standard ebooks. (Sorry, I couldn't resist.) Campfire allows the author to provide readers with extras that unlock as they read or can be purchased separately.

Character bios and backstories, location descriptions, recipes, maps, magic, species, and item encyclopedias exist. And that's just the start!

Check out all three books for updated and different information as the series progresses!

https://campfi.re/keepers-prophecy

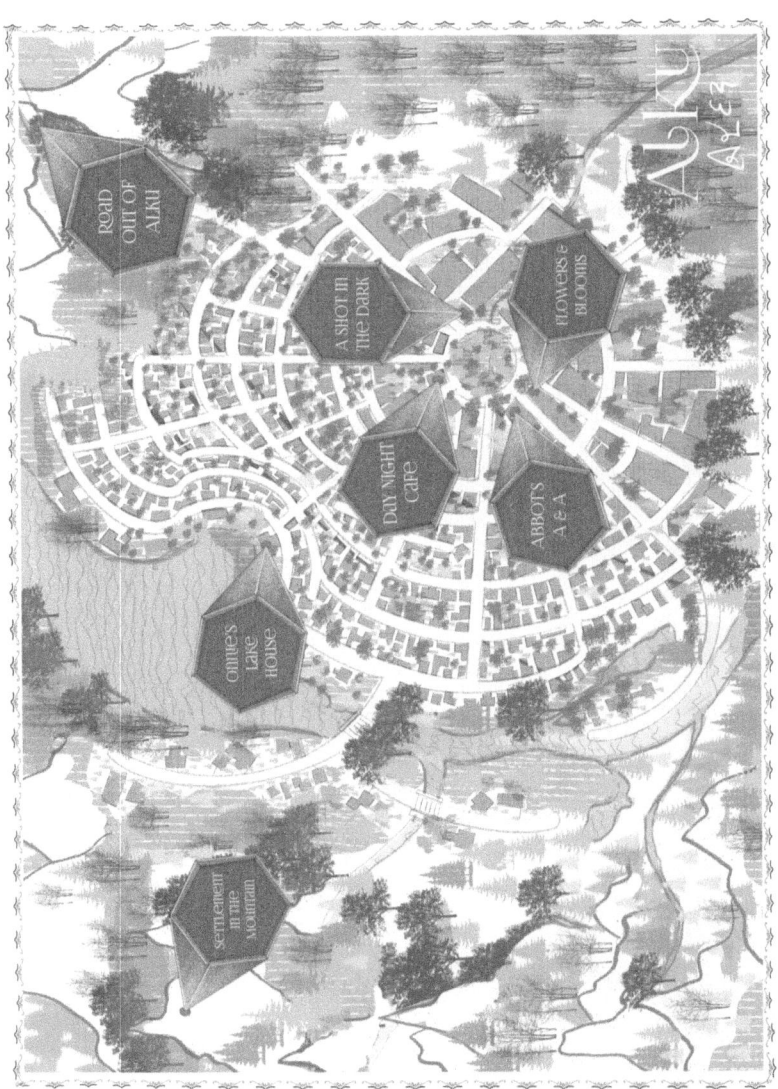

ALKU
ALEX

ROAD OUT OF ALKU

A SHOT IN THE DARK

FLOWERS & BLOOMS

DAY NIGHT CAFE

ABBOTS A&A

ONTAE'S LAKE HOUSE

SETTLEMENT IN THE MOUNTAIN

The story so far...

October 2021

A young woman named Onnie moves to Alku, a quaint town nestled in the forested mountains of the Pacific Northwest where her Grandfather requested that she inherit his bookshop.

Over the next few weeks, her days are filled with happy tourists, dinner at her grandfather's, and her nights watching the clock until she can return to the shop. She meets many residents of Alku, including Dany, a spirited chameleon of a woman who doesn't give Onnie the option of not being her friend.

One stormy afternoon, the local PE teacher, Gabriel, braves the rain to ask Onnie for help in finding a book he's desperate to obtain. After hours of searching, Onnie finds a book matching the description, and when both she and Gabriel touch the book, everything changes.

Onnie learns she's not just inheriting a bookshop but has also been chosen by the entity that is the world's knowledge archive to become the next Keeper or protector of said knowledge. Gabriel has been chosen to be her Guardian and watch over her, and she finds out that they are emotionally connected via glowing strands called the Bond.

One night, a pain sears through Onnie and Gabriel, bringing them to their knees, and they find the bookshop broken into and vandalized. Mal, Onnie's cat, appears in her arms with bad news. The damage done to the shop was too much for a weakened Keeper, and her grandfather was killed in the attack.

The morning after the break-in, Onnie sees the attacker and chases after him into the woods, but he disappears from within her grasp, and she's left with more questions than answers.

While Gabriel and Mal finalize the funeral arrangements, Onnie moves into her grandfather's home, inviting Gabriel to join her and Mal. On the day of the funeral, Onnie is met with a group of people from around the world who travel to pay their respects to the fallen Keeper and witness the Transference of power.

Onnie is shocked and betrayed when Gabriel stabs her in the heart, but they complete the ritual and return to their bodies, and the transfer is complete. An icy feeling washes over Onnie, but now she's more powerful and able to freeze the skulking man in black in place to confront him. Gabe and Mal take the man back to the bookshop, where they learn who is behind everything. Jakob, Gabe and Dany's father, and Abbot's former Guardian.

After a chaotic start to a new life in Alku, Onnie finally feels like she's found the place she belongs, and when a soft feminine voice in her mind agrees, Onnie knows her new life has only begun.

March 2022

A few months after Abbot's funeral, Onnie and the others find themselves under constant attack from the rogue guardian's minions. We learn that Onnie has grown in strength and can now manipulate the Bond on a detailed level and is using that capability to store the souls of the minions she's had to fend off. However, there are side effects of playing with souls, especially corrupted ones, and Onnie is not immune to them.

Not everything in the past few months has been negative, though. The shop has created a new room for the children of Alku where they learn magic history from Onnie in the form of storytime. On the day that Onnie chooses to teach the young ones about the history of transmogromorphs, a stranger enters the shop raising Onnie's curiosity.

At dinner, Onnie relays what she saw to Gabe and Dany only to be interrupted by a knock on the front door. A new stranger is there, speaking of letters from Abbot and admitting he is, indeed, that same transmogromorph from the shop. He's returned to Alku at Abbot's request to help her and has already begun formulating a plan.

As the days begin to grow longer, Elaric reconnects with those he'd left behind in Alku while getting to know the new Keeper and those she keeps closest to her. When Jakob escalates their conflict on the night of a storm, Elaric is determined to go undercover into the former guardian's operation to see what he can learn.

While Elaric is earning the rouge guardian's trust, Onnie learns more about the shop and the First Keeper who has now become a permanent companion to her. As Onnie and Dany try to learn as much as they can, Elaric begins feeding Jakob false information about the Keeper until an opportunity to stage an interaction presents itself. Not all goes as planned though, and Onnie ends up hurt and nearly breaking Elaric's cover with Jakob.

Months later, it's time for Elaric to return, but there's one more piece of information they need before he does. In her outrage at Elaric being in harm's way even more, Dany storms off, leaving the group to decide on what to do next.

Only they find Dany missing the next morning. After determining that the rouge guardian has her, Elaric and Gabe attempt to get her back, both failing and falling into Jakob's clutches. After a heated confrontation between the twisted man and Onnie, Elaric sees an opportunity to hopefully rid themselves of Jakob forever and takes it, leading to his assumed death.

After Onnie ensures everyone's safety, she heads to Marco's apartment to tell him what happened, but the First Keeper interrupts them, and they learn that Marco may have saved Elaric after all.

Keeper's Prophecy

The Final Keeper Trilogy
Book 3

Chapter 1: Mid-night Hope

July 2022 - Alku | Onnie Moore

Onnie woke with a start, sitting bolt upright in bed, her breath ragged in the dark room. She quickly glanced around and got her bearings, her heart rate calming once her eyes adjusted, and she recognized her bedroom.

Breathe, young one. You're safe, Kushima soothed along their Bond. *Sorry, I had a nightmare, but something woke me up. I felt something. Tell me.*

Onnie rubbed her face roughly and was surprised to find herself covered in a layer of cold sweat. She shivered violently before she threw back her covers. When she saw Mal asleep at the foot of the bed, she froze and waited to see if she'd accidentally woken him up in her haste. Relief washed over her when he continued to breathe deeply, and she moved as carefully as possible to the edge of the bed and swung her legs over. She stuck her feet into a pair of slippers and roughly pulled a sweatshirt over her head before tip-toeing out of her bedroom.

She peeked down the hallway towards Gabe's room and used her Bond with him to scan his emotions. When she saw the typical combination that indicated that he was still asleep, she couldn't suppress her smile.

I never thought I'd be so grateful for the summer sports season. While

*football, field hockey, and volleyball just after dawn sound horrible to me,
Gabe having to be at work so early is extremely convenient. Lucky for me,
he agreed to sleep separately. If he hadn't been in his room, and I woke him
up, he'd have a million questions, and I don't feel like explaining.*

Keeper, Kushima spoke formally, causing Onnie to trip over her
own feet.

What is it?

Tell me of the dream, Kushima paused, *please.*

*Sure, I meant that I didn't want to explain to Gabe, not you. You and
I have somewhere to be.*

Kushima chuckled, and Onnie felt the First Keeper's excitement
vibrate along their Bond. *That's what I was hoping you'd say.*

Onnie grinned. *These two will be pissed if they find out. We need to
hurry.*

Agreed.

Her jacket hung from a hook in the entryway, and she slung it over
her arm before retrieving her cell phone from the charger beside it and
quickly texting Marco.

I'll be there in 15.

With the message sent, she shoved her phone into her pocket and
instantly relocated herself to the bookshop and into her late
grandfather's study.

I need to change, and then I'll go get Marco.

Explain while you dress.

Onnie dashed to the trunk in the corner of Abbot's study, where
she stored extra clothes, draping her coat over the couch as she passed
it. Kushima lit the candles on the wall sconces and in the chandelier
hanging in the center of the room for her, and it wasn't more than a
few seconds before the calming effects of Xayn's spelled candles began
to ease Onnie's anxiety.

*It felt like something...ripped. I don't think it was Elaric's Bond. It
reminds me of the tattered souls after Jakob tried to replace them, but not
quite. I think we were right, though. He did get away, but I don't think*

he'll be in the cemetery waiting for us. At least, I don't think he'll be in a physical body. I'm really hoping the stone we planted worked.

Interesting. It would take immense power to remove one's soul from one's physical being. It's more likely that Jakob did it, and Elaric got away somehow.

Onnie shivered as the nightmare she'd awoken from resurfaced, merging with the memories of her last interaction with the man who was Gabe and Dany's father, Abbot's former Guardian, and who they now referred to as the rogue guardian.

I don't like either of those options, but I want to reserve judgment until we get there. I can't get my hopes up or risk Marco doing the same.

Wise. I shall as well.

Now that Onnie was wearing jeans, thick socks, and a bra, she yanked her sweatshirt back over her head and shoved her feet into a pair of running shoes stashed at the bottom of the trunk. She finger-combed her near-waist-length raven hair before rotely braiding it and flinging it over her shoulder.

Ready.

She retrieved her phone from her pajamas and put it in her pocket. Then she shrugged on her coat and relocated again, this time into the hallway leading to Marco's apartment, which was at the top of a flight of stairs on the second floor of the Day Night Cafe.

Marco had been waiting for her as usual, and before she could raise her hand to knock, he threw the door open. His face was hopeful for the first time in a month, and his eyes glittered with anticipation, not agony and grief.

"Onnie!" Marco rushed forward, caught her in his arms, and swung her in a circle.

She laughed and squeezed him back. "Hey, Marco."

"You're sure you felt him?"

Onnie nodded but held both his cheeks in her palms and gave him a stern look. "I did, but I want you to remember. It might not turn out how we want it to. I don't want you to get hurt, so please, please, keep your expectations low." She practically whined at him, but she couldn't bear to see him anywhere close to the state he'd been in the night Elaric had died. "I have no idea what we're going to find."

Thankfully, Marco nodded, but the light in his eyes didn't dull even a fraction.

"Understood."

He placed her back on her feet, reached into his apartment, and pulled a long black trench coat off a hook before slipping it on. Marco's pale skin, dark eyes, and slender build made him strikingly handsome, but when he added the trench coat over his standard work suit, sans jacket, Onnie couldn't help thinking he looked more like a mob boss than a pacifist empath.

"I promise I'm fine, and I'll keep my head." Marco smiled and pulled his front door closed with a soft click.

"Alright," Onnie said, bundling her coat tighter around herself.

Like its residents, the town seemed to mourn Abbot's passing, and its sorrow had kept winter around for a few more months than usual. Eventually, spring did arrive, though *extremely* late, and the nights were still rather chilly, especially after clear days like the one they'd had earlier that day.

Okay, I think we're ready. Cross your fingers, she said to Kushima.

Be safe, Onnie.

Onnie looked at Marco. "Ready? We don't have time to walk."

To his credit, the sanguiste's eyes only widened briefly before he repressed his fear of being relocated. Then he cleared his throat. "Yes. Let's go."

Onnie moved them immediately, not giving him much time to worry about what was coming. The next moment, they were standing side by side on a hill overlooking the only cemetery in Alku. Marco stumbled over to a nearby tree as he leaned on it, and took a few deep breaths.

"Sorry," he said meekly. "I'm not sure why that's so," he coughed, "unsettling."

Onnie shook her head and smiled. "Don't be sorry. I don't do that very often." She rubbed his back gently, "I'm the one who should be sorry. I'll practice."

Marco smirked and took a few more breaths before straightening his spine and then his coat. Then he gazed out over the cemetery below them. Onnie studied his profile, his expression blank, and her heart ached for him. Marco had refused to attend Elaric's service or visit his grave in the month since he'd been presumed dead. Marco used the justification that since he knew Elaric wasn't truly gone, he didn't want to pretend in front of the others. But Onnie was pretty sure he simply loathed cemeteries. Not that she could blame him, considering he probably knew most, if not all, of the beings buried in the valley below them. If she'd been in his position, she'd likely hate cemeteries, too.

Onnie slipped her hand into his and squeezed it gently. "Are you ready?"

Marco held on to her a bit tighter before swallowing hard and finally nodding.

Here we go, Onnie relayed before projecting what she could see of the valley below them into the void for Kushima to see.

Remember, you are not alone.

Onnie smiled to herself and began to lead Marco down the hill and directly to the hedge maze that protected the Keeper's mausoleum and the resting places of their families in the gardens just outside of it. Onnie had Elaric's headstone placed among the section set aside for her family, and whether it was a charade or not, he would have that space until it truly was needed. She'd left his years of life off of the headstone deliberately, and either no one appeared to have noticed, or they assumed that because he was a transmogromorph and they had exceptionally long lives that she was protecting that information by omitting it in case an Outsider saw it. The only reaction she'd gotten was a sidelong glance from Stephan, who probably thought she hadn't noticed it.

Marco shivered beside her, and Onnie increased their pace along the verdant paths. He'd been matching her strides since she was a few inches shorter than he was, but she neither wanted to relocate them to the grave and upset Marco's body again nor linger any longer than they needed to and harm his mind.

Left next, young one, Kushima advised.

Onnie had only been within the maze a few times and never at two in the morning, so she was incredibly grateful for the woman's assistance.

Left again.

"Please tell me you know where you're going, Onnie," Marco asked quietly.

"No idea, to be honest. It's too dark, but the First Keeper does. She's giving me directions."

Right.

"Oh, can she see us?"

Onnie shook her head. "Nope, but I can show her what I see, and we talk a lot."

Skip the following two branches and continue forward.

Marco chuckled, "Built in companionship."

Onnie peeked over at him and was relieved to see he looked amused, not depressed.

"Yup. But we give each other privacy as well, thankfully. I'm sure there are certain situations she really doesn't want to receive running updates on as they occur."

Kushima chuckled, *Indeed a truth. Two more rights and one last left, Onnie.*

Got it, thank you.

Of course.

"Two more rights and a left," Onnie relayed to Marco, who seemed to quicken his pace now that their goal was so close. "Remember, Marco. Low expectations. Please."

Onnie was essentially begging, but she couldn't bear Marco breaking down again. The first time, he literally took her legs from under her when he'd lost control momentarily and regressed to his most basic sanguiste instincts. Even more than that, though, she couldn't handle the guilt.

Again, it is not your guilt to carry.

Onnie sighed mentally but said nothing. She and Kushima had had many conversations about the topic of guilt in the last month.

"I can't believe how intense the smell of flowers is," Onnie said, closing her eyes and taking a deep breath.

Marco chuckled, and she cracked her eyes open and glanced up at his soft smile.

"What?"

He shook his head, "Nothing. You're right."

"And...?"

He rolled his eyes. "My sense of smell is better than yours. I was just thinking you'd probably be fascinated by the nuances in the fragrance with each step we take."

Onnie snorted. "Yup, and now I'm sad I can't. Thanks for that."

As they passed through the last opening in the hedge maze and stepped into the center portion of the cemetery, the courtyard and stone mausoleum stood before them. They both stopped to stare at it, their conversation silenced.

"Wow, it's...eerie at night," Onnie voiced aloud unintentionally.

"Mmm hmm," Marco mumbled beside her.

Onnie noticed his gaze was fixed straight ahead, his facial expression blank, and his jaw was clenched so tightly that his muscles flexed.

"Marco," she squeezed his hand. "Come on. Let's go."

She smiled, and when the corners of his mouth turned upward slightly, she took her small win and led him to the section where Elaric's headstone was located. As she approached the tree near his grave that she, Dany, and Ana had sat under on the day of his service, Marco stopped walking, and Onnie jerked backward at its abruptness.

"Marco?"

She rotated to see what had happened, noticed his wide-eyed stare, and didn't require aura reading to see his fear.

Kushima, he's...terrified.

I'd imagine so.

"Hey, Marco?" Onnie said, returning to where he'd planted his feet.

The distance between where his body had stopped and the grave was probably right before Marco would have been able to read the lettering. Chances are, it was instinctual more than a conscious choice —one that his body and mind had made for him.

"Can you stay here?"

He blinked a few times and then looked down at her. "I'm sorry, I can—"

"No," she shook her head. "Sorry, let me rephrase. I'd like it if you could help me and stand watch. From here, you can see me and the entrance from the hedge maze. Would you watch my back while I go check on things?"

Marco hesitated momentarily before nodding and releasing her hand. "Do what you need to. I'll keep you safe."

Well done, Keeper, Kushima said with pride.

I'm glad it worked.

"I'll be right back."

She smiled one more time and hurried over to the dark headstone, alone in a section by itself. The first of her family to have fallen. Because there hadn't been a body, there was no disturbance to the grass in front of the granite slab, and she dropped to her knees on its plushness. There were a few bunches of flowers and a potted plant placed around the stone, and she was relieved to see the vase of flowers she'd asked Dany to deliver weeks prior was still there. Onnie had tucked a small stone into the stems of Elanor's magic blooms—hiding, waiting. A gamble or a lifeline, depending on how you looked at it.

"Hey, Elaric. I brought Marco with me. He misses you. He wanted to tell you himself, but I asked him to keep watch for me. I hope you're not mad."

While Onnie whispered to Elaric, she knew Marco's enhanced hearing could still hear her, so she kept her comments short. She sniffled and took a deep breath.

"Okay, I have a job to do."

Kushima, ready?

I am. Do you know what you're looking for?

Not really.

Onnie closed her eyes, inhaled a few more deep breaths laced with the smell of earth and blooms, and evened her breathing. When she felt calmer and more in control of herself, she put her mental walls up and blocked Mal, Gabe, and Dany out.

Just in case.

I'll pay attention to Mal while you're focused.

Thank you. Onnie took one more breath and clenched her fists on her knees. *Here goes nothing. Please be here, Elaric.*

Onnie believed she'd been prepared for anything, but the moment she reached for the Bonds around her to see what was nearby, she yelped and lurched backward. Her eyes flew open, but she kept the Bonds around her visible over the world rather than viewing them in the void. Marco hurried to her side, his earlier trepidation forgotten.

"Onnie, what's wrong?" He knelt beside her, his suit pants becoming muddy and damp in the morning dew. "Are you alright?"

Kushima.... Onnie projected what she saw to the other Keeper.

I can see it.

"Onnie?" Marco said again and then shook her shoulder slightly.

She placed her hand over his but didn't look away from the vase of flowers sitting to the side of the headstone.

"I'm fine. Just surprised."

Marco hesitated, "Can I ask...."

Before he could finish, she interrupted him. "Watch your eyes."

"What?"

She projected what she saw to Marco along their shared Bond, Elaric's mutated thread woven between them. Marco hissed and covered his eyes with his free arm but lowered it hesitantly a second later. From the corner of her eye, she saw as his understanding began to knit together at what he was seeing and the implications of its existence.

Onnie's tears flowed freely now, and she was grinning like a maniac.

"Marco?"

"I see it." He shifted beside her and scrutinized the light more closely. "Please," his voice hitched as his emotions dangled by a thread. "Please tell me that's what I think it is."

All she could do was nod repeatedly.

Before the pair, only possible because of Onnie's strength, the First Keeper's teaching, and Marco and Dany's love for Elaric, tucked away in the bottom of a vase of flowers was a piece of amber that pulsated and blazed a brilliant golden color. It was a perfect color match for the Bond Marco and Elaric shared when connected by their blood link.

"It's Elaric's soul," Onnie whispered. "He's still here, Marco."

"He...he made it home." Marco's voice cracked, and then his silent tears joined hers.

Chapter 2: Returning Home

July 2022 - Alku | Onnie Moore

Onnie, we should get you home before the others wake up, Kushima reminded Onnie gently. *Unless you plan on sharing what happened tonight.*

No, you're right.

"Marco?" she asked the man beside her, holding a small fragment of amber in his palm as if it were the earth's most precious object, not simply his.

He turned to focus on her and nodded, "I know. We have to go."

"We do. It will be light soon, and you need to get to bed. Not to mention," she chuckled, "if I'm out of mine when Gabe and Mal wake up, there'll be hell to pay."

"Understood." Marco carefully placed the stone in her palm and closed her hands around it. "Please, keep him safe."

"Of course."

Onnie sighed deeply and stared at their hands. "I know this isn't fair, but please, can you help me keep this from Dany, Gabe, and everyone else? Just until we've figured out what to do."

"Onnie," Marco shifted to one knee, his hands still clasping hers, holding the stone. "No," he shook his head, "Keeper," he smiled sweetly at her. "You hold my world in your hands. If you told me to give my eternity for his, you would have it. So, if you want me to keep this between the First Keeper and us, you need say no more."

Once again, Onnie's eyes filled with tears. "Thank you, Marco. I will do whatever I can to bring him back. I appreciate your understanding."

Marco nodded and got to his feet, helping her to hers before tugging her into his side and wrapping his arm around her shoulder. "Shall we head out? I'll walk you home."

Onnie giggled, "You sure you don't want me just to move—"

"No!" Marco blurted but then cleared his throat. "Let's walk."

Unable to contain it, Onnie clutched her side and laughed far too loudly for a cemetery. "Alright, you win. I'd love it if you walked me home."

I see why Elaric feels the way he does. I genuinely enjoy this version of Marco.

I agree, Kushima said. *It's lovely to see him able to be more faithful to himself.*

"Hey, Marco?" Onnie said, unable to keep her opinions to herself.

"Hmm?"

"Please don't take this the wrong way," she hesitated, and he turned to meet her gaze, one eyebrow raised. "I really like this version of Marco."

He didn't react for a moment, but eventually, he smirked and returned his eyes to the path in front of them. "Please don't take this as narcissism," he mimicked her comment, "but you're one of only a handful of people who have ever gotten to see it."

"I'm honored."

She smiled, and when she shivered, he drew her nearer to his side, his body blocking some of the wind's chill.

"Oh, I have a question for you."

"Ask away," Marco replied.

Actually, I'm going to ask here, she said to Kushima and Marco.

What is it, young one?

Did you two know each other? I mean, when the First Keeper was alive?

Marco chuffed and Onnie felt Kushima's amusement through their Bond.

We did, Kushima answered, and Marco nodded.

It was a very long time ago, he added.

Extremely.

Oh, did you recognize the First Keeper's library from the night I brought you there?

Ah, no. I never had the pleasure when she was among the living.

Indeed, Kushima agreed and then added privately to Onnie, *Young one, just as few get to enjoy Marco's more...truthful persona, even fewer have stepped foot in my library—past or present.*

Oh.... Onnie hadn't expected it was a frequent hot spot or anything, but she didn't realize it had been so...secret. *Oh shit, when I first found it...I let Dany and Gabe in. Should I have not done that?*

It was fine. I wouldn't have allowed them in if it were not.

Is that why Elaric couldn't see the door until I bound his powers and connected him to me?

Correct.

Wait, does Marco know your name, then?

He does. I can't imagine he's forgotten it, though I suppose it's possible.

Yeah, knowing him, he likely remembers.

Indeed. Even when I was human, he always used my title, though, so I doubt that will change.

"Has Elaric seen the inside of the library?" Marco asked casually.

Onnie shook her head, "Nope." She felt her cheeks heat and hoped Marco didn't notice. "Um, the morning after the storm...he helped Gabe and Dany at the shop when I...uh...."

Struggled a bit, Kushima added delicately to them both.

"I remember. Mal appeared out of nowhere to check on the cafe since Elaric was helping you." Marco chuffed. "Well, that's what he said he was doing, but considering he came directly to see me in my apartment, his excuse was thin at best."

Onnie snorted, but then her smile dropped. "Yeah, I was scared that I'd hurt that room, and while I was unconscious, Elaric helped Dany and Gabe take care of me. At one point, he asked them what door everyone was talking about, and that's when they realized he couldn't see it."

I hope he will see a lot more of it in the future, Kushima said.

Onnie saw Marco smile from the corner of her eyes, and her heart warmed. In her pocket, she clutched the small stone a little tighter, and her spirits felt lighter than they had in weeks.

She and Marco had hope—they all had hope, even if the others weren't aware of it yet.

Earlier that day...
Elaric Rickson

Elaric's soul traveled up the structure he'd plummeted down when he'd attempted to end the rogue guardian's life once and for all. When Elaric reached the top of the stone shaft, he was once again in the chamber where Dany had been tortured. If he'd had a stomach still, it would have turned at the memory. Unwilling to spend any longer than needed, he made his way through the rooms beyond and out into the forest. Not having a corporeal form was unsettling, and Elaric felt the urge to shiver, except there wasn't anything for him to shiver with.

He needed to get back to Alku and find Onnie. The Keeper would figure something out, even if all she could accomplish were to put his soul to rest. Anything was better than wandering the world as a soul alone for eternity. Marco's face the night Elaric had told him their plan surfaced in his memories, and Elaric was overcome with grief and guilt. He prayed to whoever was listening that Marco was alright and would make it through. Eventually.

When Elaric saw a way to protect Dany, but only by breaking his promise to return home to Marco to do it, Elaric nearly stayed silent. It had only taken a handful of seconds to change his mind. If he'd had the opportunity to save Dany and instead chose Marco's happiness over her life, it wouldn't matter if Elaric had made it home. It would have destroyed Marco either way.

A breeze blew past Elaric, and he watched as leaves spun in its wake. He followed their path, and when he reached a nearby rock, a raven was perched upon it and staring directly at him. The bird tipped its head to the side, one dark eye evaluating him, and then it took to the sky. When it looked back at Elaric and waited, he reasoned he was dead, so why not try following the mystery bird on his way back down the mountain? It wasn't the strangest thing he'd done. Hell, not even the strangest thing in the last twenty-four hours.

Elaric willed his essence to follow the slipstream the raven made, and together, they gradually descended into the valley. No paths required, instead traveling simply as the crow, or in this case, raven, flew. As they wove between trees and shrubs, Elaric noticed the forest was not the same as it had been that morning. Leaves were more vibrant, the ground less saturated, and young plants pushed through the soil.

When the raven landed on a tree branch, Elaric looked to where it gazed and saw Alku's cemetery a ways further down the mountain. This time, Elaric's incorporeal stomach did actually sink. How long had he been gone?

Beside him, the raven chirped and flew off back in the direction they'd come from, leaving Elaric alone once more. He pivoted back to the cemetery, and when he scrutinized the area below him, he saw a soft glow emanating from one corner of the Keeper's section. The light pulsed softly, and he felt it was calling him. He didn't resist it, allowing himself to float past the evergreens with spring bird nests in their branches and the maze with rabbits in their hidden warrens beneath the hedges as he made his way to the center. He'd been right.

The warm light was in the family plots of the Keeper's portion of the cemetery. When he approached, he saw an area with a single headstone in a corner. It was overrun with flowers and offerings to the deceased, and the glow seemed to be radiating from a vase of flowers tucked near the rear of the grouping.

When Elaric read his name inscribed upon the stone, he froze.

As he hovered before his own grave, he suddenly felt extremely lost. There was no way for anyone to have erected a marker for him the same day he'd plunged down the well. Instead, that slab of stone confirmed his earlier suspicions.

Elaric had been tortured for far longer than he'd realized.

Elaric floated above his grave for hours. The sun had set for the night, and the sky had turned dark before he came to terms with what had happened. The glow in the vase of flowers pulsed brighter in the night than it had during the day, and he finally approached it to take a closer look. He felt the moment the stone realized that his soul was within reach, and Elaric was suddenly being dragged towards it. It only took a few seconds, but that's all the stone needed as it drew him inside.

He was trapped.

Again, Elaric prayed that this was the Keeper's plan and decided to wait and see what happened. Not that he had much of a choice.

Thankfully, his wait was worth it.

A short while later, Elaric watched as Onnie and Marco entered the cemetery section where his gravestone was. Had souls been capable of weeping, his would have been a blubbering mess.

When he saw Marco stop, his body locking, and he refused to get close to Elaric's grave, he realized how foolish he'd been. There was no way Marco was going to recover from his death. He'd been an idiot to think he would. Elaric's only choice was to get his body back somehow.

Onnie approached his grave and kneeled in the grass, and Elaric did everything he could think of. He tried to shout and connect with her in his head as he had before, and he even tried to visualize the Bonds she'd often spoken about, even though he had only witnessed them once, during the ritual to bind his powers. None of it seemed to be working, though.

Onnie spoke in a hushed whisper, "Hey, Elaric. I brought Marco with me. He misses you. He wanted to tell you he missed you, but I asked him to keep watch for me. I hope you're not mad."

Elaric knew that Marco could hear her, and Elaric was stunned to see that even with something so simple, yet with a huge impact, Onnie allowed Marco to have the space he needed, and she didn't push him. From that small action alone, Elaric knew she'd respected his last request to take care of Marco for him. They'd undoubtedly gotten closer if their body language was anything to judge by, and relief flowed through Elaric.

The Keeper sniffled and took a deep breath. "Okay, I have a job to do."

He watched her close her eyes, and Elaric figured this might be his only opportunity. If souls could speak, his would have been screaming at the top of its lungs. Evidently, it worked because Onnie was knocked backward, and Marco rushed to her side.

"Onnie, what's wrong?" Marco asked as he knelt beside her. "Are you alright?" When Onnie didn't reply, Elaric began shouting again, and Marco jostled her shoulder. "Onnie?"

She never took her eyes off the stone Elaric was in, and he knew she'd heard him. "I'm fine. Just surprised."

Marco hesitated, "Can I ask...."

"Watch your eyes."

"What?"

Elaric sensed when Marco and Onnie's Bonds reached out to the stone he was inside. At that moment, Elaric decided he would do whatever his Keeper asked of him for the remainder of his life—no questions asked. Now that he had renewed hope, he would get to experience the remainder of his life.

Tears streaked down Onnie's face, and she and Marco continued to talk. "It's Elaric's soul," Onnie said softly. "He's still here, Marco."

"He...he made it home."

Onnie carefully extracted the flowers from the vase his stone was in and pulled the amber out. Elaric felt warm the moment she touched it, but when she passed him to Marco, it felt like Elaric had been lit on fire. He burned but with a feeling of cleansing rather than pain.

A calm settled over Elaric, and his weary soul relaxed.

He had hope now. Onnie would find a way.

After Marco had escorted Onnie back to her house and saw her safely inside the front entry, she removed Elaric's stone from her pocket and smiled at it. The next instant, Elaric saw they were in Abbot's study at the bookshop. He was grateful he didn't have a body at that moment, for if he had, he undoubtedly would have been sick.

Onnie had remained silent, so Elaric assumed she was speaking with the First Keeper while she carried his stone to the door leading into the library. She pulled it open, and Elaric was in awe of the room once Onnie stepped into it and he was able to get a better look around.

The walls, floor, and ceiling were carved stone blocks, and in some areas, the floor was practically worn smooth. Heavy bookcases lined some of the walls, with tables, chairs, and a few trunks scattered around the room, making the space look like a medieval lecture hall. There were so many books, and even with just a glance, he could see they were ancient. No wonder Marco knew the First Keeper. The sanguiste was just as old as those books, likely older.

Aside from that, the most impressive part of the space was the braziers with blue fire burning within them. The same fire ran up the walls and across the ceiling in thin channels. The center of the room's ceiling had some crest or sigil made from the lines of flame, and Elaric was overcome with a feeling of honor to be able to see the space at all.

Elaric watched as Onnie closed her eyes. When she re-opened them, a young woman stood beside them, and both women's eyes glowed Keeper blue. They raised their hands and placed them palm to palm, but Elaric caught the newcomer's hand passing inside Onnie's ever so slightly.

"I'm so happy to see you," Onnie said with a silly grin. She raised Elaric's stone to the other woman, who bent her face closer to him. "What do you think?"

The woman was pale-skinned, dark-haired, and with ice-blue eyes. Elaric knew immediately that this had to be the First Keeper, but more shocking was the uncanny resemblance between her and Onnie.

"Wait, really?" Onnie blurted out, drew the stone away from the First Keeper, and began to examine it again. The blue glow of Onnie's eyes was captivating up close, and he found himself tracing the flecks of color with his gaze. "No harm in trying, I suppose."

Elaric was struggling, the one-sided dialogue being difficult to follow, but he waited for whatever Onnie was planning. Except, when she spoke, he found himself the speechless one.

"Elaric? Can you hear me?"

Once he snapped out of his stunned stupor, Elaric began shouting and screaming just as he had in the cemetery. He immediately stopped when Onnie winced and held him further away.

"Okay, I'm going to take that as a yes," she chuckled and looked at the other woman. "You're right. He had to have been able to hear us. Also, ouch."

Onnie turned to squint at his stone again. "Elaric, I'm not sure what you're doing, but um…a little less, please? Your Bond glows incredibly bright, and when you do whatever you just did, I'm pretty sure you'll do lasting damage to my eyes if you keep it up." She grinned.

He attempted to whisper, hoping the glow would flicker or pulse or something, but at a lesser brightness.

"Oh, for fucks sake." Onnie suddenly sank into the chair behind her and squeezed the bridge of her nose with her eyes shut. "That was better, Elaric. Thank you."

There was silence between the two women for a few minutes, and Elaric figured he was intentionally being excluded from their conversation. Onnie moaned and carefully settled his stone on a pile of blankets in the center of an antique research table.

"Elaric, I have to go, but you'll be safe here. Long story short, you're in the void. The First Keeper is here with you, and tomorrow, I'll see if I can figure out a way for you to talk to the three of us or at least make it so you can hear her."

Onnie stood, pressed her palm to the First Keeper's again, and then glanced back at him.

"No one but us and Marco knows you're here, and we are the only three who knew you were still...alive."

She hesitated, and he could see the regret written all over her face. What she hadn't said was that they had lied to Dany and the others, and even though Elaric knew she wouldn't have done so without justification, he could see it weighed on her conscience.

Onnie cleared her throat. "I'm sorry, I seriously have to go. I'll be back tomorrow. Today? Later," she smiled. "I promise."

She quickly retreated to the door, but before she pushed it open, Onnie looked back over her shoulder. "Elaric, welcome home."

Then she was gone.

The First Keeper watched her leave, then rotated to look at his stone. She smiled softly, nodded once, and then disappeared.

Elaric was alone again.

For now.

Chapter 3: Drawn and Quartered

July 2022 - Alku | Onnie Moore

"Cat," Gabe whispered in Onnie's ear. She groaned and tugged a pillow over her head to block him out.

Cat, that doesn't work. Gabe chuckled and gently pulled the pillow away from her face. "Did you not sleep well?"

Onnie yawned. "What time is it?" her raw voice croaked.

"Just after five. I saw your note. When did you get up?"

Onnie's eyes shot open, and everything that had ensued the night before rushed back to her. She took a breath and calmed down, not wanting to draw attention to the situation with her odd behavior. Gabe was sitting on the side of their bed, dressed for work in jeans and a sweatshirt. His brown hair was combed neatly, he smelled of his soap and toothpaste, and his cheeks were slightly flushed from a shower. By the looks of it, he was ready to walk out the door.

"Oh," she said as calmly as she could and tried to recover from her outburst, but she could already feel Gabe's suspicions rising. "Sorry, I woke up and couldn't sleep. I made some tea."

"Why didn't you wake me up?" Gabe asked affectionately as he brushed her hair behind her ear.

"You had to get up early. I just did a few things and then went back to bed."

Onnie tried to push contented emotions through their Bond to mask her guilt for lying to him again. She paired it with a smile for extra assurance.

It is not truly a lie, young one. It's for the greater good. Cease the guilt, Kushima scolded, once again acting as the voice of reason within Onnie's head.

"What made you change your mind about getting up early? Didn't I sleep in my room so you could sleep in?"

Gabe brushed her cheek and leaned in to kiss her forehead before he got to his feet.

"Yeah," she nodded, "But I didn't realize I had something I wanted to do today." She threw back the blankets and skipped to the bathroom to start the shower.

"Alright," Gabe said from where he now leaned on the doorway. "I'm sorry, I have to run. I can't wait for you. I wish I'd seen your note sooner." He frowned, and disappointment rumpled his forehead.

Onnie strode back over to him and stood on her tip-toes to drape her arms around his neck. She was truly happy after everything that had happened the night prior, and she wanted Gabe to share the excitement with her, even if he didn't know why.

"It's fine. I'm going to get ready, grab a coffee, and then head into the shop. Would you like me to bring you lunch?"

"Oh," Gabe raised his eyebrows and bent to kiss her lips gently. "That would be a nice surprise."

Onnie giggled, "It's not a surprise if I've already told you, you goof." She kissed him once more and then attempted to shove him out of the bathroom—not that he moved more than an inch. His size compared to hers meant there wasn't a chance she'd win unless he let her. "Now, off to work with you. I'll text you later."

"Yes, ma'am," Gabe said, kissing her cheek again before he left the bedroom and closed the door behind himself.

This is going to get complicated, Onnie said to Kushima as she yawned so hard her jaw popped.

I agree. You cannot be awake all night, nor will you be able to hide the exhaustion.

Agreed.... Onnie yawned again and blinked her watering eyes. *Alright, thinking later. Shower and coffee first.*

Kushima chuckled as Onnie dragged her weary body into the shower.

Mal, where you at? Onnie called to her Link as she wandered down the cobbled streets of Alku toward their local coffee shop, A Shot in the Dark.

Even though it was the middle of summer and would probably be warm later in the day, Onnie wore a dark, thin-fabric long-sleeve shirt, jeans, ankle boots, and her typical braid over her shoulder. As with the night before, she had no bag or purse and only her cell phone tucked into her back pocket.

A Russian Blue feline appeared at her feet, falling in step beside her. His yellow eyes stared up at her, and he grinned slightly.

"Morning," Mal said.

"Hey. Where were you this morning? You were gone when I woke up."

She had been surprised he wasn't on the bed but assumed he'd left for the other room when Gabe came in to wake her. Only when she finally made it into the kitchen did she discover Mal wasn't in the house at all.

Mal scrutinized the ground, and Onnie narrowed her eyes at him. "Mal, are you being shifty?"

When he didn't answer, Onnie quit walking and crossed her arms in front of her chest. Mal stopped and looked up at her, though his eyes didn't quite meet hers.

"I was at Dany's."

"Oh, okay?" That was not what she had expected, and she cocked her head to the side. "Why do you feel guilty about it?"

Mal sighed before indicating to her arms with a paw. "Up?"

Onnie uncrossed them, and he leapt into her arms, where she snuggled him before resuming their walk. "Talk to me?"

"It's not bad," Mal said, his voice at a lower volume now that they were closer to the center of town. "I've been going to check on her. She still has nightmares."

"Okay, that's wonderful, but what's the part making you clam up? It's not like you committed a crime or anything."

Mal slowly met her gaze. "Dany doesn't know, so don't tell her."

Onnie's eyes widened a bit, but she nodded. "Sure. Can you tell me the whole story? If you're comfortable," she asked.

"There's not much more. Dany tends to have nightmares in the early morning. I noticed when I stayed with her the first few days after she went home. I tried to wake her the first time, but she grabbed me and gave me snugs. It seemed to help, and she went back to sleep."

"Aw, Mal, that's so sweet." Onnie stopped in her tracks. "Wait, have you been doing this every morning since she left the house?"

Mal nodded.

"Oh, my." Onnie giggled, "I'm a bit jealous."

Shit, Kushima, we were really close last night.

So it seems.

Onnie smooched Mal's head and scratched under his chin. "Why don't you head to the shop? I'll grab you a hot cocoa and be right behind you."

Mal's eyes lit up when she mentioned chocolate and whipped cream. "Don't have to tell me twice." He licked the tip of her nose and then was gone from Onnie's arms.

She shook her head, grinning, as she removed her cell phone from her pocket and quickly texted Dany.

Gonna bring Gabe lunch later. You free after?

It wasn't even seven yet, and there was no way Dany would be awake, so Onnie switched to her text with Marco without waiting for Dany to answer.

Have something to tell you. It's not bad. :-) Text me when you're up.

Onnie put her phone away and slipped through the door to A Shot in the Dark when someone held it open for her. While she stood in line, she struggled to keep her happiness within herself and found she was grinning. Gabe's acknowledgment of her emotions flowed along their Bond, and her smile grew even wider.

It seemed like things were finally looking up, and maybe all of them would be able to move on from the dark and depressing crap that had been tormenting them for nearly a year.

Onnie peeked at the clock on the wall in the bookshop, rolled her eyes, and groaned.

"How is it only eleven thirty?"

She slumped over the front counter and rested her head on her arms. The chill of the marble counter radiated through her light shirt, causing her to shiver. Kushima must have noticed because the marble began to warm up unnaturally quickly.

"What's with you today?" Mal asked, resting his paw on the back of Onnie's head. "You're a total zombie."

She whined, the sound echoing off the marble countertop and into her ear. "Didn't get much sleep."

"Wanna take a nap? I can watch the shop and wake you up if someone comes in."

Onnie rolled her head back and forth, not wasting the energy to raise it first or reply audibly. She may have dozed on her feet because when the shop's phone rang from underneath the counter, she shrieked and leapt backward before catching herself on a nearby bookcase.

"For fucks sake, Onnie!" Mal cursed as he tumbled off the counter and reappeared back on top of it before even striking the floor.

Cat? Gabe asked her along their Bond.

Fine, sorry. The phone startled me.

She felt Gabe's concern recede as she answered the phone.

"Abbot's, how can I help you?"

She waited for a few heartbeats, but no one responded.

"Hello? Can I help you?"

When there was still no reply, she hung up and shrugged. "No one there."

"You scared me half to death for a prank call?" Mal whined.

Onnie giggled and scratched under his chin. "You and me both. I guess I should get ready to head over to the schoo—"

Before she had finished her sentence, the phone rang again, and this time, she glowered at it before picking it up and answering in a clipped tone.

"Abbot's. Can I help you?"

This time, someone answered.

"Yessss, you can…."

Onnie hung up the phone and slammed it on the counter, the battery cover flying in one direction and the batteries in another.

Gabe! Dany!

Onnie would recognize that voice until the day she died.

What is it, Cat? Gabe's Bond was soaked with fear, panic, and confusion, even if his mental voice was subdued.

Onnie? Dany asked hastily.

Calm, Keeper, Kushima cautioned privately.

Onnie ratcheted her emotions back to a more normal level and put a barrier between herself and the others. She took a deep breath before answering them all.

We need to talk. Change of plans, both of you need to come here as soon as possible. We can order lunch.

Mal's eyes were wide, and he gaped at her like she'd finally snapped, but he said nothing.

I'll be there in fifteen, Gabe said, and Dany agreed to the same. *Are you alright until then, Cat?*

Yes, I have Mal. Onnie scooped the feline into her arms and clutched him tight enough that he squeaked. *Oh, actually, I'm going to go into the First Keeper's library for a few minutes. I need to find an answer to something.*

Fine, Gabe replied. *We'll see you in fifteen. Come out by then, or we'll come in to get you.*

Got it, Onnie said, tipping Mal back onto the counter and heading directly to the First Keeper's library.

Kushima, can you please lock the front door? Also, I won't be summoning you today. I don't have the time right now.

Done, and agreed.

Sorry, Mal, Onnie apologized as she walked. *Can you watch the shop? I'll be right back. The door's locked.*

You'll explain when they get here, Mal stated, not asked.

I will.

Onnie yanked open the library door, swiftly stepping inside and pulling the door closed behind her. She then raced to Elaric's stone on the table and sat down to get closer to eye level with it.

"Elaric, I need to ask you a question. I'm not sure if this will work, but I need you to try."

She closed her eyes and examined his Bond from within the void, relieved to see it was still as vibrant as the night before.

"If you can hear me, can you make your Bond pulse twice? Mid-level brightness, please?"

When she saw the glow of Elaric's Bond strengthen and lessen twice, she exhaled and dropped her head to the table with a soft thunk.

"Oh, I'm so glad that worked."

No time to waste, Keeper, Kushima scolded, and Onnie's head shot back up.

"Right. Elaric," Onnie hesitated, "I can't imagine how you got into this state, and we'll deal with that later, but I need you to answer this for me. Pulse twice if the answer is yes and once for no." She took a deep breath. "Is he still alive?"

For a few heartbeats, Onnie was sure Elaric would answer with a single pulse, but when the glow flashed not once but then a second time, all she could do was focus on not freaking out.

"I had a feeling you'd say that."

She stood and paced a few times, leaving her view of the Bond visible and overlaying the world around her. From the corner of her eye, she saw Elaric flashing, and she frowned down at his stone.

"I'm sorry, Elaric, I don't know how to hear you yet. I planned to figure that out tonight, but something's come up."

He continued to brighten, and she sighed and plunked back into her chair. "Jakob just called the shop, and you confirmed it wasn't a prank or coincidence."

Elaric's glow seemed to flicker, and Onnie looked around her, panicked but unable to think of how to help him.

Perhaps, picking him up, Onnie. I imagine he has some sense of emotional connection while in that form.

"Oh, that's a good idea," Onnie said, reaching out carefully and taking the stone into her palm. "Elaric, it will be okay. We'll figure it out. You're safe here, and Dany and Gabe are on their way to the shop. I have to explain to them what happened when he called, so I won't be able to come back here until tonight, but I will try to come back again once Mal and Gabe are sleeping. Okay?"

Elaric's Bond ceased its fluttering and distinctly pulsed twice, and Onnie couldn't help but smile down at him.

"Good. Are you alright in here, relatively speaking, that is?"

Two flickers.

"Alright. Let me talk to the others, and I'll return as soon as possible."

Onnie gently placed the amber stone back on the blankets and got to her feet.

"First Keeper, keep him safe, alright?"

Of course. Always.

"Thank you," she said audibly, more for Elaric's sake than hers. She knew Kushima would protect him, but after his reaction earlier, she reasoned being overly communicative with him wouldn't hurt.

I think the first thing we should address is to see if I can communicate with him. It may help him feel less isolated and help us answer a few questions, especially if we can't figure out how to get him to talk to you at first.

Onnie made her way back to the door. *Great idea. Baby steps, but they're still steps.*

She pushed open the door and saw Dany sitting on the couch while Gabe paced the floor in front of the fire. Onnie stepped out of the frigid room and shut the door.

"Hey, sorry about that."

"What the hell is going on, Cat?" Gabe asked, striding over and pulling her into his arms.

"Yeah, what did the phone do to deserve to be drawn and quartered?" Dany sniggered as she stroked Mal, who was draped over her lap like a mink stole.

Dany's hair was still blue-black, and today, it was braided into loose pigtails that rested on her shoulders and the thin black straps of her corset top. She wore dark jeans and strappy flats, everything matching her perfectly applied smoky black makeup with various pieces of silver jewelry.

"Ah...well...." Onnie drew back from Gabe. "Gabe, go sit by Dany."

Onnie could see his hesitancy, and she would have bet that he wouldn't do as she asked, but he nodded and took a seat beside his sister.

Gabe, I need you to keep a poker face when I tell you this. Emotions as well.

...alright....

I will freeze you if you cannot. Do you understand?

You're scaring me, Cat.

Swear it. Onnie was relieved to see Gabe's face was still neutral, even while they spoke, because she was absolutely making him freak out. She could feel it.

I swear. What's going on?

Jakob is alive.

Onnie walked around the couch to sit before the fire, drawing Dany's gaze while Gabe processed the information in advance. To his credit, he quickly slammed up his mental walls, and his face barely flinched. Since Dany's eyes were on her, she didn't seem to notice the shift in her brother.

I have questions, Gabe said.

Onnie could see how hard his jaw was clenched. *I know, but I'm more worried about Dany right now.*

Gabe's body relaxed a bit, and she knew he understood why she had only told him, not to mention the odd demands she'd made.

"What's up, Onnie?" Dany said. "You scared the crap out of us earlier. I winced so bad I dropped a box of Nancy Drew novels."

Onnie chuffed. "Sorry about that. It happened so fast I was caught off guard."

Dany's eyes contracted and then shifted between her and Gabe and then down to Mal. "Alright, what don't I know? You're all acting strange."

Gabe cleared his throat, "Ah, Dany...."

Any suggestions, Kushima? Onnie asked privately.

No, only that you may need to prepare for the worst.

Onnie sighed, and it caused Dany to refocus on her. "Enough. Spit it out."

Onnie nodded once. "Rip the band-aid off?"

Dany crossed her arms, her cheeks rosy, her anxiety and panic elevating as the seconds passed. "Yes. Now."

Onnie raised walls around Dany's Bond with the others, leaving only hers connected to her best friend.

"The rogue guardian is alive."

For what felt like an eternity, all Onnie could hear was the clock ticking from deeper within the shop. Dany didn't move. Her face didn't change, and her body didn't tense. She looked like a statue of herself. It was as if someone had pressed her pause button.

Kushima? Onnie was growing more concerned that her friend didn't react at all.

Kushima hesitated, *I'm not su—*

Dany's brain must have caught up with Onnie's words because suddenly, it felt like someone had plunged Onnie into an ice bath. She shivered, and her teeth began to chatter violently. When she went to speak, her breath escaped in a visible cloud of vapor, and the sound of cracking broke the silence as ice began forming on the floor and walls.

Onnie! Lock her in! Kushima shouted, and Onnie reacted instantly.

She thrust walls up around Dany's mind and pressed her to sleep. The same way she had done when Gabe lost control after Dany had been kidnapped.

Everything had occurred in less than thirty seconds. Gabe had vaulted to his feet to sprint over to Onnie's side when she'd begun to shiver, but he pivoted when he saw Dany collapse onto the couch.

"What the fuck, Cat!" He bellowed, his control finally running out as he rushed to his sister and checked her pulse.

Mal appeared on Onnie's lap, staring up and searching her face. "Girl, what the hell just happened?"

Onnie stroked her palms along her upper arms in an attempt to get rid of the chill, but the shop remained frozen. Thankfully, the ice had stopped spreading.

"She lost control. She's only sleeping, Gabe."

His head swiveled to her, but his features were slightly more relaxed than his voice. "Did you do what you did to me?"

She nodded, and thankfully, Gabe's tension eased.

"Okay, well, she's gonna be pissed, but it didn't hurt."

He got to his feet again and stepped toward Onnie, but his foot hit a patch of ice and slipped from beneath him.

"Gabe!" Onnie froze him mid-air on reflex before she swiftly set him down and released him. "Sorry, I just reacted."

Gabe shook his head and placed his feet more carefully. "It's fine. Thank you."

"Good catch, Onnie," Mal said, nuzzling his head against her torso.

Gabe sat beside her on the hearth, put his arm around her, and attempted to warm her with his body heat. "I think I missed a few things. Start at the beginning, please."

"Yeah," Onnie nodded. "He called the shop this afternoon."

Gabe looked at her, one eyebrow lifted in disbelief. "As in...used the phone?"

"Yes, duh."

"So, that's why you axed it," Mal chortled with a goofy grin. "Harsh. It wasn't the phone's fault."

Onnie chuckled and poked the feline's nose. "It freaked me out. I recognized his voice, and my first instinct was to get it away from me as fast as possible."

"Fair. Can't argue with that. What did he say?" Gabe asked, his face now inquisitive as he believed her.

"I answered and asked if I could help him. He just said yes."

"And you're sure it was him?" Gabe questioned.

Onnie tensed, and she couldn't help but become peeved at his question. She tore away from him and glowered. "Do you really think I would have risked *this,*" she gestured to the ice, Dany, and her own shivering, "without being one hundred percent positive?"

Gabe raised both hands in surrender. "You're right. I'm sorry. I guess I was hoping it wasn't true."

Don't we all? Onnie said to Kushima.

"Now explain why the shop is experiencing an ice age," Mal asked.

"Ah, sorry, Mal. I actually told Gabe about the phone call a minute before I told Dany."

Mal hissed at her and turned away, and Onnie was sure if the feline had arms, they would have been crossed, and his lower lip would have been out in a pout.

"I'm sorry. I had to warn him in case something like this happened."

"Yeah, trust me. You lucked out," Gabe whined, massaging his eyes. She forced me to keep a straight face, or she'd freeze me. Not sure how I managed that, to be honest."

"Dude, harsh," Mal said, grinning at Onnie.

"Yeah…well, I blocked Dany's Bond from you both just in case."

"Makes sense," Mal said.

"Yeah. So that's why it felt like she didn't react at all," Gabe added.

Onnie shook her head. "No. At first, she didn't react. I left my

Bond with her open to keep an eye on her, but she went from unphased to *literally ice* so fast that I nearly didn't make it."

Gabe's eyes went wide, "Wait, you're saying Dany did this?"

Mal jumped off Onnie's lap to the floor, where he quickly slid a few inches, vanished, and relocated onto the couch next to Dany.

"Damn, I take back making fun of you, man. That ice is no joke."

Gabe chuckled, "I know." He looked back at Onnie. "How did she do this?"

First Keeper, Onnie prompted so that everyone could hear the explanation, *You wanna take this one? My jaw hurts.*

The shivering was starting to make her muscles ache, so Onnie relocated to the basket of blankets on the other side of the room, grabbed one, and then relocated back to the hearth and wrapped herself in it.

Of course. As Onnie said, Dany didn't react at first. I assume she was processing, as I can't imagine that was easy for her to hear.

"Agreed." Worry crinkled on Gabe's brow as he frowned at his sleeping sister.

"No shit," Mal added, curling up on Dany's lap.

When she finally did react, her emotions were so intense and...wild that when they flowed through her Bond with Onnie and then down Onnie's and mine, the outcome was the creation of the physical representation of her emotion.

"Ice," Onnie stated. "Thankfully, the fact that he's alive isn't what she's angry about, or I'd assume we'd have burned down."

"Small mercies," Gabe sighed.

"So, what's with the ice then?" Mal asked.

It was Onnie's turn to scoff, and she scanned her best friend, who was in so much pain that she manipulated the shop herself. "Remember Dante's Inferno?"

"Yeah..." Gabe answered.

The lowest of hell are not burned but frozen, Kushima remarked.

Onnie nodded, "Your sister is out for blood. His blood, and when she gets it...."

Gabe winced, "I can only imagine."

"Never thought I'd say this," Mal said, rubbing his head on Dany's arm, "I kind of feel bad for the bastard. He should have stayed dead."

Onnie thought about the stone hidden in the other room and felt her eyes flare blue.

"Nope. I'm with Dany. There will be blood, and it won't be one of ours this time."

Chapter 4: Hard Conversations are Easier with Friends

July 2022 - Alku | Onnie Moore

Dany, you need to calm down. I know what you're thinking. None of what you're feeling is wrong, but I cannot let you out until you stabilize. Your emotions are physically affecting the shop.

Onnie was kneeling on the icy floor in front of the couch, where Dany was still trapped within her own mind. When Onnie tried to release her, Dany's emotions lashed out immediately, and Onnie was forced to lock her back in.

She held one of Dany's hands in hers and rubbed the back of it gently. Carefully, Onnie lowered the mental walls she'd erected around her friend a fraction, but only enough to test Dany's current mental state. When sensations of vengeance didn't smack her, Onnie sighed and dropped the walls a bit more.

Dany, the guys, and the shop are cut off from you for right now. It's just you and me. Let's talk. Tell me what you're thinking.

Do I really need to explain it? Her low and primal mental voice was nearly a growl, searing through Onnie's heart.

Fine, don't explain. You're right. I know exactly what you're feeling, and I will make sure he's destroyed. If I have to rip him limb from limb or sever his soul and crush it in my fist, we will not let him harm another person.

Dany stayed silent, and Onnie took the opportunity to try and draw her farther back into reality.

I'm sure you're pissed that I locked you in here. I did it to Gabe when you went missing. I'm sorry, but I need you to understand why I had no choice.

I'm listening.

You froze the shop—literally. As in, both Gabe and Mal went ice skating in Abbot's study, and I nearly have hypothermia.

Dany went quiet again, and it was another few minutes before she finally spoke. Thankfully, her voice was significantly more relaxed, and her emotions mirrored its tone.

Thank you for doing what you did, then. I'm glad no one was seriously hurt. Can you please let me out now? I...I really need a hug....

Dany's emotions were back to levels that wouldn't create local polar ice caps, so Onnie freed her consciousness and assisted her back to her body. When Dany opened her eyes, she shifted on the couch and peeked down at Onnie.

"I'm so sorry."

Onnie climbed to her feet, pulled back the blanket she'd thrown over Dany, and slipped under it, curling up into her best friend's side.

"Warm me up," Onnie demanded with a smile.

Dany giggled and clung tighter to her.

Gabe and Mal were making tea in the backroom, and Onnie told them, *She's fine.*

Good, we'll be back in a few, Mal replied.

Dany's eyes darted around Abbot's study, and Onnie loathed the guilt plainly displayed on her best friend's face when she frowned at the water dripping from the ceiling and the steam coming from the hearth.

"I really did this?"

In a way, Sister, Kushima answered softly.

"Oh, hello, First Keeper. I'm...so sorry." Dany looked down in shame.

Onnie squeezed her harder. "Stop that. It'll be fine. Water can be dried."

Indeed, and you achieved something I have never seen, not in all my lifetimes as this entity.

"Huh?" Dany asked, looking up with her head cocked to the side.

"Like I said. *You* did this. Not me."

Correct. Before Onnie told you of the rogue, she blocked your emotions from the others. So when you reacted, your emotions flowed solely through her before spilling over to me.

Onnie watched as Dany's incredible mind worked through what she was hearing. When her eyes widened and she grinned, Onnie knew her best friend would be fine.

"Did you just realize how much work we have to do to experiment and then replicate this?"

Dany nodded and would have gotten up from the couch to begin working right then had Onnie not been weighing her down.

"Oh my gods, do you know what this means?!"

"Tell me," Onnie beamed.

She'll be fine, young one.

Thank you, and I'm sorry about before. I should have been paying more attention.

Nonsense, but we'll talk later. For now, focus on your Sister.

"What if we could funnel emotions to you, and you could mix them with the shop's power?" Dany said, speaking incredibly fast.

Gabe walked around the corner, Mal on his shoulder, and stopped short when they saw Dany theorizing at an impressive pace. Life had returned to her eyes, and passion had returned to her voice.

I told you she'd be okay, Onnie said to Gabe and Mal. *Now, bring me that tea. I'm fucking freezing.*

Gabe began laughing, and Dany twisted to look at him. "Gabe! Did she tell you how this happened?"

Gabe handed each of them a cup before he went to sit in front of the fire, Mal moving to his side.

Did she say anything about Jakob, Cat? Gabe asked along their Bond, never breaking eye contact with his sister as she continued to theorize.

We talked a bit before I woke her up. She's stabilized, so you needn't worry.

I always worry.

I know you do. Onnie let some of her love flow toward him, and when Gabe smiled, she knew it was in response to her and not Dany's explanation. *For now, let her talk. It's good for her, and you know how brilliant she is. Chances are she'll discover something we can use from this situation.*

I'm sure she will.

Oh, Gabe, I forgot. I'd like to have Dany move in for a while. Or have Mal stay with her.

Gabe's brows came together, but he quickly restored his smiling facade. *I can assume, but why?*

Don't tell her or Mal this. Mal's been going to see her every morning. She has nightmares, but apparently, when he gets there, she reaches for him, and then she can go back to sleep.

She has no idea?

Nope, and Mal doesn't want her to know he's been doing it. He thinks she's afraid that she'll look weak.

Got it. Yes, whichever she chooses. Though, considering the last time, I think I'd prefer her with us.

Agreed.

Onnie had been sipping her tea, the warmth of the liquid essentially gone as her skin had absorbed it through the cup while she had been speaking with Gabe. Thankfully, when they'd finished, Dany hadn't seemed to notice her prolonged silence. When the energetic woman paused to take a breath and a sip of her tea, it gave Onnie the opportunity to slip into the conversation.

"Hey, Dany, I have a request."

"Sure, shoot."

"Will you move in with us for a little while? I…" Onnie studied the remaining liquid in her cup. "I've been having trouble sleeping, and I would really like it if you were with me. Gabe's been going to work so early because of the stupid summer sports league...."

Liar, Mal hissed, his eyes narrowed at her as he glared from across the room, *but good job...and thank you.*

Onnie smiled behind her tea cup as Dany was considering her request. After a few minutes, she nodded.

"Alright. I can do that." Dany turned and looked at Mal and Gabe. "If it's okay with you two, obviously."

Mal nodded, and Gabe crossed his arms and scowled. "As if it wouldn't be okay for you to help Cat. Whatever I can do to help her. Even if that's letting *you* help her when *I* can't."

Dany's smile was small, but Onnie felt her friend's relief at Gabe's response. "Thanks, brother," she murmured.

That's one thing handled, Onnie said to Kushima. *Remind me to tell Elaric later. I'm sure he's going crazy with worry.*

I'm sure he is.

Gabriel Vansand

Gabe knocked lightly on the small cottage door, then shoved his hands into his jeans pockets. He took a deep breath and closed his eyes, inhaling the fragrances of Alku's summer and the myriad of plants that Xayn had planted in front of his home.

There was rustling inside the house, and then the door opened.

"Gabe?" Xayn asked concern and surprise in his voice.

Gabe opened his eyes, and when he met his best friend's lime-green ones, they widened, and Xayn stepped aside.

"Come in."

Gabe nodded robotically and entered the warm living space, which smelled of soil, greenery, and spices. He wandered over to the couch along one wall and dropped into it.

Xayn followed but settled on the coffee table, leaning on his knees, his shoulder-length brown hair falling forward against his cheeks.

"Gabe? What's going on?"

"Sorry, I should have called—"

"Stop it. Talk to me. Is Dany alright? Onnie?"

Gabe nodded. "Yes. Well, mostly. Jakob called the shop this afternoon."

Xayn sucked in his breath and flinched backward. "He's alive?"

"Apparently."

Both of them were quiet for a minute, but then Xayn sighed. "And Elaric?"

Gabe managed to shake his head but then rested it back on the couch and shoved the heels of his palms into his eyes.

"Cat told Dany, Mal, and I about an hour ago. Apparently, he called the shop, and Cat recognized his voice."

"And Dany...."

"She didn't take it very well."

"Can't imagine so."

Gabe groaned behind his palms. "Her emotional reaction was so strong that she overpowered Cat and froze the shop."

"Literally?"

"Yup."

Xayn got to his feet, and Gabe felt when he was no longer beside him. When he opened his eyes, Xayn had gone into the kitchen and was searching around in his fridge before returning with a bottle of cider for each of them.

"I assume you're not going back to school this afternoon?" he asked Gabe while holding a bottle out to him.

"No," he said, accepting the drink. "Was done with the kids before lunch. I can catch up on paperwork from home later."

Xayn flopped down on the couch beside him, and they both took a few gulps from their bottles.

"How can I help?" Xayn asked after a few minutes.

Gabe took a deep breath and shook his head. "I don't want you anywhere near this."

"Gabe, I can—"

"No," Gabe snarled. "You're not made for this shit, and I can't go through losing you, too."

Xayn sighed, and Gabe felt him lean into his side just a bit.

"So what are you going to do?"

"I have no idea," Gabe confessed and laid his head back again. "We know nothing. We have nothing to go on, and he's far more destructive than we expected."

"I'll see if Grandma has any ideas."

"How is she?"

When Xayn didn't answer after a minute, Gabe glanced over at him and wasn't surprised to see a tortured expression.

"She's fine."

"Xayn…."

"She told me to thank you for bringing Onnie over for tea." A slight smile crept into Xayn's features. "She likes her."

Gabe chuckled, "Well, that's good, though I'd have been surprised if she hadn't."

"Me too. Pretty hard not to like Onnie."

Xayn's grandmother was practically Gabe and Dany's, too, and the older woman's opinion mattered to him more than he'd outwardly admit. If he was honest with himself, that was why he'd waited so long to take Cat to see her—not that he was worried they wouldn't get along, but that Grandma Yvonne would think she was too good for him.

"Hey, Gabe?"

"Hmm?"

"Thanks for coming over."

Gabe glanced over at his chosen brother and noticed Xayn staring down at where his fingers held the neck of his cider bottle.

"Thanks for listening, though I didn't actually intend on coming here. I just started walking and ended up at your door."

Xayn nodded the slightest amount. "Doesn't matter. I'm just glad you did."

"Me too," Gabe admitted candidly.

"Gabe?" Dany asked from where she stood, holding her apartment door open for him. "What are you doing here?"

"I stopped to see Xayn and figured I'd check and see if you'd left for the house yet."

"Oh, how is he?"

Dany shut the door behind him and walked back into the bedroom that had been his before he had passed her his lease when moving in with his two cats.

"About the same." Gabe hesitated, but before he could decide whether to tell Dany about their conversation, she noticed his silence.

"What is it?"

Gabe sat on her bed and began folding one of the shirts she'd piled on the end of it. When he realized everything she'd pulled out to pack was black, his heart broke a little more for his sister.

"Gabe?"

"He offered to help us."

"With wha—" Dany stopped, and when she met Gabe's eyes, they were cold and still. "No, absolutely not. There's no way—"

"I told him the same, Dany. He gets it."

Dany scrutinized him for a few more seconds, and then her shoulders slackened, and she nodded. "Good." She turned around to dig through her dresser drawers, but when she spoke again, her voice was low and with unmistakable suffering in it. "I'm not like you, Gabe. I…I wouldn't be able to bring you back like you did for me."

Gabe squeezed his eyes closed, squeezing the shirt in his hands. His emotions must have spiked more than he thought because he felt Onnie checking on him. He took a deep breath, set down the shirt he'd rumpled and went to stand behind his sister before gently rotating her around and enfolding her in his arms. She sniffled, and he could hear her battling back tears.

"I know. Xayn's nearly as important to me as you are, and if he were to end up hurt, or worse, I…."

Dany nodded against him and sniffled again.

"It doesn't matter. I told him to leave it alone. He's going to ask Grandma if she has any suggestions, but other than that and stocking up on supplies, I told him I'd kick his ass myself if he got any closer to this."

"I will kill him, Gabe."

He knew she was talking about their father, but he forced himself to laugh softly. "Xayn?"

"No," Dany said, pinching his upper arm. "Jakob. If I have the chance, I will do it myself."

"Dany—"

"Don't." Dany stepped away from him and dashed the tears from her cheeks. When she looked up and met his eyes, hers were stone again.

Gabe sighed but managed to nod. "Have you talked to Marco?"

When his sister physically flinched, he wanted to retract his question. They'd always considered Marco a friend, and Dany wasn't one to avoid people.

"Ah, no. I haven't." Dany grabbed a few more things and shoved them in the bag that lay open on her bed.

"That's surprising. You know he'd probably be a good person to talk to."

"No."

"Dany?"

She turned to face him and shoved her fists on her hips. "And what would I say, Gabe? Hey, Marco. How are you after your best friend died to save me? Oh, and by the way, he did it for nothing because the bastard is still alive, and El...aric is not."

Dany's voice caught, and she stomped her foot. Then, she bolted into the attached bathroom, where he heard her turn on the sink.

Gabe groaned, sat back on the bed, and continued folding. A month ago, Dany blamed him for Elaric's death. Now, she apparently blamed herself. He wished she still blamed him instead.

A few minutes later, Dany reemerged from the bathroom with a small bag in her hands and slightly rosy cheeks. She didn't look at him.

She simply settled the smaller bag within the larger one and then accepted the folded pile of clothes he offered her.

"Thanks," she mumbled, tucked everything away, and zipped up the bag.

"I'll carry it," Gabe said, taking it from her. "Anything else?"

Dany shook her head and he followed her out the front door and they began their walk back to the lake house in silence.

Onnie Moore

Onnie relocated directly outside Marco's door like she had the night before, and in an odd sense of deja vu, he pulled the door open and greeted her with a smile, fangs and all.

"Hey, Onnie."

Tonight, he wasn't in his work suit and instead wore a less formal pair of slacks and a really soft-looking long-sleeve shirt. When he pulled her in for a hug, he felt warm, and his whole body looked better than it had in months. His muscles were less tense, and there was more color to his skin.

Since Onnie had first connected herself to Marco along with his blood link to Elaric, she could see people's auras if she concentrated a little harder when looking at their Bond. When she saw Marco's dreary, guilty, and grief-ridden blue aura was, instead, bright and fiery red today, she felt like she'd won the lottery.

He truly is doing better, Kushima said happily.

Wait until we get him to Elaric, Onnie chuckled.

"How are you today?" Marco asked, stepping back into his apartment to retrieve his coat from the hook.

"Long day. I'll explain, but not here. Actually," she took a few steps over his threshold and closed the door behind her. "I'd like to try something real quick. You mind?"

He smiled. "Sure, what do you need me to do?"

"I want to look at your Bond and maybe show you something. Will you close your eyes?"

Without hesitation, Marco did as requested, and she took his hand. Then, she relocated them into Abbot's study. When Marco didn't react, she released his hand and beamed.

"Perfect, you can open them."

"I didn't see—" When his eyes opened, and he realized he'd been tricked, Marco laughed and shook his head. "Thank you. That was much easier."

She shrugged. "I wasn't sure if it would help, but my guess is that maybe your brain struggles to catch up to your body, and your eyes are what triggers the vertigo."

Marco draped his now unnecessary coat over the arm of the sofa. "It makes sense to me, though I never would have thought of it."

Brilliant, young one. He's right. That was very clever.

I try, Onnie said with a laugh. "Alright, come on, I have a lot to tell you, and I'm gonna be screwed if I get caught missing."

She led him to the door tucked in the corner of the study and pulled it open for him to enter first. As soon as she stepped inside, she viewed the Bonds in the room and left them overlaying the world around her. As predicted, Elaric's stone flashed and flittered when they entered. She closed the door behind them and ushered Marco to the center table.

"Good, I figured seeing him would make you happy."

"Always," Marco answered, and Onnie couldn't help but smirk.

"I was talking to Elaric." Onnie slipped her hands into her sweatshirt pocket and watched Marco's understanding grow as he stared at her.

"Wait! Can he hear us?"

The joy on Marco's face made Onnie blush. She'd expected he'd be happy, but between his excitement and Elaric's pulsing Bond, she had miscalculated just how much.

She nodded. "I'm going to go summon the First Keeper. Take a few minutes. I can help you translate a bit later."

Marco turned around slowly, and Onnie watched his back as he cautiously approached Elaric's stone. When she saw it pulse happily, she walked to the farthest wall to give the two men some privacy while she manifested Kushima's projection.

I'm envious of the connection they have, Kushima. Does that make me horrible?

Why would that make you horrible?

Onnie shrugged. *I have so many people who care about me, friends, and loved ones, but there's just something about what they have that's...different.*

They were quiet for a while, and when Kushima finally spoke, her eyes were soft and motherly. Not for the first time, Onnie thought about the older Keeper's children and what had happened to them.

You're correct. What they have is different...but I wouldn't give up yet, young one. You are just that, young. One day, you'll find the mate for your soul.

Onnie closed her eyes, leaned on the wall behind her, and listened to the flames that crackled as they ran up the stones only a few feet from her. She wasn't sure how long she stood like that, but when Marco cleared his throat, Onnie jumped.

"Shit, sorry."

He chuckled and pulled a chair out for her beside the table Elaric was on. "Come sit. You look exhausted."

Onnie yawned and followed Marco's advice. "Yeah, I'm sorry, I won't be able to do this every night. Eventually, they'll notice."

"Of course," Marco said, taking a chair opposite her, but only after pulling one out for the First Keeper as well. "How are you keeping this from them?"

Onnie smirked, "Oh, it was a whole thing. Let me give you the short version, but trigger warning. I need you to control your base instincts, don't panic, and trust me when I say Elaric is safe here."

Marco's eyes widened, and then he smirked. "Hell of a lead-up, but I understand. Please continue."

"You, too," Onnie said to Elaric, whose Bond pulsed twice in response. "Good." She sighed. "Jakob is still alive. I found out today, and when I told the others, Dany...didn't react well."

Understatement, Kushima added. *She lost control, and we nearly did, too.*

Onnie nodded. "True."

Elaric's Bond flared, and she blinked at the spots in her eyes.

"Oh, shit. Sorry," she giggled. "The First Keeper said Dany didn't react badly. She lost control, and because of that, I nearly did as well."

Elaric's soul flashed so bright that Onnie winced and turned away.

"Hey! Didn't I tell you not to overreact!"

Marco glanced back and forth from the stone to her, and she groaned.

"Ug, I'm going to need to sleep for a week after this." Then she closed her eyes and manipulated the Bond in Elaric's stone so Marco could visualize it again. "There, now you can see him too, but I warn you," she glared at Elaric, "Dude will blind you if you're not careful."

When his Bond pulsed faintly, Onnie chuffed. "You're forgiven."

"Okay," Marco said, rubbing his eyes before blinking and then looking back at the stone. "Keep going."

"Yeah, so Dany's better, but I told a partial lie that I was having trouble sleeping and wanted her to stay with me. Gabe's leaving early in the morning right now, so she agreed. So, currently, she's in my bed with Mal, and both are exhausted from today. Tomorrow, though…it won't be as easy to slip away."

Marco took a deep breath and sat back in his chair but didn't take his eyes off Elaric's stone. "Understood."

Onnie yawned again.

"Alright. Elaric, tomorrow, I will work with the First Keeper and see if we can make it so that you and she can communicate. I think it may be easier to connect you to her than to me." Onnie shrugged, "But that's a hunch."

Elaric's stone pulsed twice.

"Was that a yes?" Marco asked.

"It was. Two for yes." Onnie smiled and yawned a third time, this time her jaw straining from the extent of it. "Shesh."

I think it's time you retired, Kushima said.

Please tell me if you're uncomfortable with this, but...could I leave Marco here for a few hours? I could return before dawn and get him home, but then he could talk to Elaric a little.

Do you trust him that much? Kushima asked, meeting Onnie's eyes.

I greatly trust Elaric and Marco, but this is your decision, not mine.

I will keep his Bond visible, but I cannot leave, so they will have no privacy.

I'm sure they won't mind. Onnie smiled, "Thank you."

Marco looked at her and raised an eyebrow. "Having secret conversations again?" he teased.

She grinned. "Yes, and as Elaric once told me, having a conversation where people don't have the ability to eavesdrop is rude, and I was being rude."

Elaric's stone fluttered, and Onnie decided to believe he was laughing.

"Sounds like E," Marco said with a sweet smile.

"But yes, we were. Marco, would you like to stay here for a while?"

"Wait, what?"

"I need to get back to bed, but the First Keeper has agreed to let you remain here until I return and get you before dawn. She'll still be here, so there's no privacy, but if you wanted more time to talk...."

Marco looked over at Elaric's stone. "E, what do you think?"

Elaric's stone pulsed twice, and Onnie nodded. "Alright." She got to her feet and stretched. "I'll come back and get you home just before dawn. Technically, you can leave on your own, but I'd like to keep these meetings under wraps."

"Of course," Marco stood, hugged her, and whispered in her ear. "You have no idea...."

She squeezed him tighter. "It's good to see you with life in your eyes again, Marco." She pulled back and kissed him on the cheek. "Enjoy your conversation. It may be a few nights before we can do this again."

Marco nodded, and Elaric pulsed twice.

Kushima, you have trouble. Wake my ass up. I'll be here in less than five seconds.

Kushima laughed. *Of course. Sleep well, young one. I'm proud of you.*

Onnie lifted her palm to match Kushima's, and then she waved to the other two before slipping out the heavy door and relocating home.

Within two minutes, Onnie was back in bed and sound asleep, snuggled into Dany's side.

Elaric Rickson

Elaric watched Onnie leave the First Keeper's library with one last sleepy wave. The First Keeper was still visible, and Marco had swiveled in his chair to talk to her. They must have been talking along the Bond because, after a minute or two, the First Keeper turned and looked at Elaric's stone, smiled, and, with a nod, was gone.

Marco turned back to him and ran his hand through his hair. "Honestly, this world doesn't deserve those two."

Elaric agreed and pulsed twice.

Marco pushed the blanket Elaric's stone was resting on, further back into the center of the table so he could rest his chin on his arms in front of him.

"Are you okay, E? Relatively, I suppose."

Worry creased Marco's brow, and Elaric quickly pulsed twice. He *was* okay, relatively speaking. Hopefully, he wouldn't have to spend the rest of his existence as a rock, but it sure as shit was better than being dead. Or tortured. His soul did that shiver-like thing, and Marco noticed.

"What was that?" He asked and then shook his head with a grin. "Sorry, yes or no only. Crap.... Um, was that a bad reaction?"

Elaric wasn't sure how to reply, so he pulsed once and waited for Marco.

"Is that a no?"

He pulsed twice.

"Okay, once for no, twice for yes, and little flickers are

amusement."

Elaric laughed, and sure enough, his stone flickered, and Marco grinned.

"Was I right?"

Elaric pulsed twice.

Marco smiled and stared into space, and after a minute, Elaric knew Marco was in his head too much. He pulsed a few times but tried to make it more distinct, and it seemed to snap Marco out of his introspections.

"Sorry, we only have a short amount of time, and I'm brooding."

Elaric agreed, and Marco smiled, though it didn't quite reach his eyes.

"She's going to fix this…right?" Marco asked quietly.

Even only knowing the Keeper the short while he did, he still replied with a yes. She would, Elaric wasn't sure how, but if anyone could, it was Onnie.

"You used the blood link."

That blood link saved his life and his soul. Elaric laughed and then replied. He originally had asked Marco to bind them together only to calm Marco's fears. It turned out that his fears were justified, and Marco was just as much responsible for saving Elaric's life as Onnie was.

"E, I heard about what he did to Dany…."

Elaric watched Marco struggle to complete his question, so he pulsed twice.

"Did he…to you?" Marco's eyes were glassy, but Elaric watched them closely as he answered with two pulses. Marco squeezed his eyes closed and clenched his fist on the table. After a few deep breaths, he opened his eyes, and Elaric was relieved to see him still in control of his instincts.

"Did he do this to your soul?"

Elaric pulsed once, and Marco's eyes went wide.

"Wait, if he didn't, who did?" Marco shook his head again when he realized Elaric couldn't answer his question. "Was it someone else?"

Elaric paused, the answer was both yes and no, but he opted for a no.

Marco looked confused, but Elaric understood why. What had happened to him shouldn't have been possible, and Elaric didn't know how he'd done it either.

"Did...you do it?" Marco asked tentatively.

Elaric pulsed twice.

Marco shifted in his chair and pointedly looked away from Elaric's stone. He sat so still that Elaric was concerned he was struggling with his instincts again, but Marco bent forward and put his head in his hands. Elaric pulsed a few times to get his attention, but with his eyes closed, Marco didn't notice. Elaric tried to wait patiently while Marco worked through his thoughts, but the longer he waited, the more he worried about him.

When Marco eventually glanced up again, Elaric had an idea, and he began pulsing in a pattern.

Dash, dot dot dot dot, dot dash, dash dot, dash dot dash. He paused slightly longer, then added. Dash dot dash dash, dash dash dash, dot dot dash.

"Wait," Marco refocused on his stone. "Start over."

Elaric repeated the pattern, and Marco's lips curled up slightly. "Why are you thanking me?"

He began again.

Dot dot dot, dot dash, dot dot dot dash, dot, dash dot dot. Pause. Dash dash, dot.

Marco sighed and shook his head, his smile gone. "E, are you sure? What if I didn't save you...what if...I am the reason you're like this...."

Elaric pulsed twice, and he desperately needed Marco to understand. Without him and his blood link, and without him by his side now, Elaric would have gone mad. He owed Marco everything.

Marco was still frowning, so Elaric tried one last time.

Dot dot dot dot, dot dot dash, dash dash dot.

"I don't understand, E," Marco said with a sad shake of his head.

Elaric repeated his message.

"You want me to hug you?" Marco asked. His voice was weary, and his whole body showed it.

Elaric pulsed twice.

Marco sighed. "I'd give anything to, but how can I touch a soul? Not without Onnie's help."

Before Elaric could say anything else, Marco looked at the ceiling and chuckled. "Really?"

Elaric realized that Marco must be talking to the First Keeper again.

"It couldn't hurt to try, I guess." Marco looked back at Elaric's stone, leaned forward, and carefully lifted it into his palm.

As with the night before, Elaric felt the same fire flash through him, and he pulsed twice. Marco's eyes widened, and he had apparently doubted what the First Keeper had recommended. When he saw Elaric fluttering, he finally gave in to his emotions, and the tears Marco had been holding back finally broke free.

"Thank you. Again," Marco said, looking up before he pressed his forehead to Elaric's stone, and Elaric did the only thing he could. He fluttered his entire soul as hard as he could, hoping he could return the warmth he felt from Marco in one form at least.

"Fuck, E," Marco whispered. "I miss you."

Elaric pulsed twice and continued to flutter.

They spent the next few hours talking as they could, and as the night turned into morning and dawn approached, Marco relaxed a bit more, though he never returned Elaric's stone to the blankets.

When Onnie quietly opened the door just before dawn, Marco had his head on the table, Elaric still in his palm.

Onnie was still in her pajamas, her hair not even brushed, and Elaric felt a sudden pang of guilt, knowing she was lying to Dany and the others because of him.

Onnie looked at his stone suddenly and glared. "No guilt, Elaric. Stop." He pulsed twice, and she confirmed his suspicions shortly after.

"I can read auras now that I'm bonded with you and Marco. You're soaked with guilt, and I want you to stop that."

Marco shifted, their one-sided exchange drawing him from his head. Onnie gently touched his shoulder, and when he flinched and closed his fist, Elaric's world went black. He could still hear their conversation, just a bit muffled. As Onnie apologized for startling him, Marco opened his hand and carefully put the stone back on the blankets.

"I'm sorry, it's nearly dawn," Onnie said with a frown.

"It's fine, and we understand."

She nodded but still looked upset.

"Morse code," Marco said to Onnie, and after a fraction of a second, she grinned.

"Of course, you both know Morse code." She rolled her eyes and looked at Elaric, "I'll brush up for next time, okay?"

Elaric fluttered and then pulsed twice.

Marco chuckled, and Onnie shook her head.

"I'm glad I left you here. You did well." She hugged Marco and kissed his cheek, "But I am sorry, I need to get you home now." She looked at Elaric's stone, "Do you need to say goodbye?"

Marco looked at Elaric, smirked, and then shook his head. "No. I'll see him soon. Right?"

Elaric pulsed twice.

"Good. No more goodbyes." Marco glanced up and probably said thank you and goodbye to the First Keeper and then looked at Onnie and took a deep breath. "Eyes closed?"

Onnie giggled through a yawn. "Yeah, but we can't relocate from in here." She slipped her arm around his and turned to wave to Elaric as they left. "See you soon, Elaric."

With one last smile, Marco and Onnie exited the library, the door closing behind them, and Elaric was alone again.

Only today, he didn't feel alone at all.

Chapter 5: Unfamiliar Feelings

July 2022 - Alku | Onnie Moore

"Thanks, Gabe," Onnie said, kneeling on the passenger seat so she could lean over the center console to kiss his cheek. "See you after school."

Gabe smiled, caught the back of her neck before she backed away, and captured her lips. *Dinner tonight? I have to work late, but the Day Night Cafe should be open by the time I'm done.*

Sure.

I'll pick you up. Let me know if you are still at the shop or go home. Gabe released her, and his eyes glittered.

Someone smacked Onnie's backside, which was half in the car and half out.

"Hurry up, you two. Caffeine. Needs. Mandatory." Dany grumbled through a yawn.

"Bye, Cat," Gabe said as Onnie fully exited the car and closed the door. "Bye, Dany!" he called out the open window, and both women waved as he pulled away from the curb in front of A Shot in the Dark.

Onnie tugged her long t-shirt down further over her yoga pants and skipped through the door Dany held open for her.

"How much longer does Gabe have to go in so…" Dany yawned,

"...early?"

"Not sure, but seriously, Dany. Thanks for staying. I slept well last night."

Onnie removed her cell phone from the pocket on her thigh and pulled up her credit card, hiding her eyes from her best friend because, once again, she wasn't exactly lying, but she was pretty damn close. Onnie was positive her sleep quality was more because of her two middle-of-the-night excursions than Dany's presence beside her.

"Hey, if I helped, I'm glad." Dany smiled and reached for her wallet, but Onnie stopped her.

"It's on me. Why don't you grab a table? I don't have to be at the shop for a while yet."

Dany nodded and stifled another yawn with her hand. "Perf and thanks."

Onnie watched Dany's back and the sway of the fabric of her black dress as the gorgeous woman wound her way through the mismatched chairs and tables and found one to claim for them. It was in the same corner from the first day Onnie arrived in Alku and when Dany came over to introduce herself. It felt to Onnie like that was only yesterday, but when she realized she'd been in Alku for over ten months, she was slightly taken aback.

Wow. Grandfather and Rebecca's deaths. Meeting you, Gabe, Dany, Marco, Elaric, Xayn, and everyone else. Fighting Jakob's roaches and then...Elaric's death. Finding him again, all of it. A lot's happened.

Indeed, young one.

Onnie quickly reached the front of the line and ordered her and Dany's coffees and two muffins. While she waited for their order, she fiddled with her phone and saw that she'd missed a text from Marco earlier.

Thank you.

Onnie took a deep breath and clutched tighter to her phone.

Kushima, how did last night go? Please don't give specifics unless absolutely necessary. I want to try to give them as much privacy as we can.

Of course, I am in agreement. I also did my best not to listen in. I do think Marco has…come to terms with the situation. It sounds like Elaric got through to him, and he carries a bit less guilt.

Good. I don't want Marco to feel guilty. He has no reason. Kushima didn't say anything, and Onnie felt like there was something she'd not mentioned. *Kushima…*

I did hear how Elaric ended up in the state he's in.

Oh?

It seems he did it to himself.

Onnie squeezed her eyes shut. The implication of someone forcibly removing their soul from their own body was something that she needed far more caffeine to even contemplate. Thankfully, their order was ready, and she collected everything and wandered over to Dany.

"Grabbed muffins, too," Onnie said, placing everything on the table. Dany's cup had barely hit the wood before she had it under her nose.

"You're a goddess." Dany closed her eyes and purred, a contented smile on her lips. Onnie flinched at how absent that smile had been on her best friend's face in the last month.

She settled into her chair, picked off a piece of her muffin, and popped it into her mouth.

"How'd you sleep? I didn't bother you, right?"

Dany shook her head. "No, you never do. I slept great, actually."

Mission accomplished, Onnie informed Gabe. *It looks like Dany didn't have any nightmares last night, or they were mild enough that I didn't notice them, and she's hiding them from me.*

Gabe's warmth and affection for his sister and his love for Onnie's support of Dany pressed along their Bond in silent gratitude.

"I'm glad. If I ever bug you, kick me," Onnie smirked.

They quietly ate and sipped their coffee, gazing out the shop's front window. Onnie listened to the chatter around her and smiled as she picked up stray details. Since it was rather early, most parents were still at home with their kids getting ready for daycare or summer activities, so the primary clientele within the shop was the early-rising singles. Discussions around them flit from complaints about having to go to work to being thankful that the weather was finally shifting to summer. One young woman was on her cell phone, gushing about a date she'd gone on the night before, and Onnie smiled at the vibrant aura that enveloped the woman.

Out of nowhere, Onnie felt a surge of shock, then fear, then pain, deep within her. She winced, and they were gone before she could figure out what the feelings meant or where they had come from.

What was that? Kushima, did you feel it, too?

I did.

"Onnie?" Dany questioned after witnessing Onnie's physical reaction to what seemed like nothing from Dany's perspective.

Gabe, Mal, you all alright? Onnie asked them and included Dany.

Sleeping, Mal answered with a yawn.

Gabe was, predictably, now on alert. *What is it?*

Nothing, I just shivered, I think. I'm fine.

Dany frowned at her but didn't say anything to the group.

When everyone had receded away from Onnie once again, she carefully grazed against Marco's Bond but was fairly certain he was sleeping.

"Are you okay?" Dany asked in a hushed whisper.

Onnie managed to nod and took a gulp of her coffee, requiring more effort to keep her hand steady than she'd like to admit.

Kushima, what the hell was that?

Onnie peeked at Dany, who frowned but returned to her phone. She was undoubtedly not the cause of the oddity, and evidently, neither was Gabe or Mal.

I'm not quite sure, but I'm more concerned as to why only you and I felt it, Kushima stated, her tone filled with anxiety.

Me too.

"You ready?" Dany asked, pointing at Onnie's empty muffin wrapper on the table.

"Yup. Are you coming to the shop or headed to the library?" Onnie asked as she collected their trash and stepped a few feet away to dispose of it, trying to act as if nothing odd had happened a minute earlier.

"Library today. I'll ask around for any information that we might find helpful when we research what happened yesterday." Dany grinned, took one last drink from her coffee, and tossed the empty cup into the trash.

"Sounds good. Let me know if you need anything or if you're ready to go through whatever you find."

Onnie followed Dany onto the sidewalk, both of them tipping their smiling faces to the sky and the sun that warmed their skin. Dany glanced at her from the corner of her eye, giggled, and then drew Onnie into a hug.

"Will do. See you later!" Dany waved as she headed off in the opposing direction from Onnie and the bookshop.

I'm glad she seems to be doing alright, Onnie said to Kushima.

Me too.

Oh, Mal. Dany said she slept well. Did she?

Hey. Yeah, it seemed like it. I'm not sure if that's because she nearly strangled me all night or if she just didn't have any nightmares.

Onnie chuckled, and Kushima stole the words from her mind. *Don't talk as if you did not enjoy it,* she teased the feline.

I admit to nothing.

Coming to the shop, Mal?

Later. Nap time.

Onnie sniggered and skipped across the street and into City Center Park.

The weather is fantastic. I'll be honest, I thought people were lying. I don't understand how the winter can be so...dreary, but then summer is like this.

Summer in Washington is very lovely, from what I've gathered.

A bit wet still, but I don't think I mind it much. I've grown rather fond of boots.

Kushima chuckled but was cut off when Onnie heard a fire truck's siren as it approached, eventually passed her, and continued on its way.

Huh…that's odd. That's the first siren I've heard since moving here.

Onnie's gut nagged at her, and her eyes darted around the park. When she was confident no one was around, she quickly relocated into the shop and turned the lights on using the Bond as she headed into the First Keeper's library.

Can you cover for me? I want to poke my head in. Two minutes tops.

I can tell you he's fine, but I understand you want to see him for yourself.

Onnie grinned up at the ceiling. *Thank you. I know it's silly, but still, it'll make me feel better.*

She opened the door, quickly shut it behind her, and rushed to Elaric's stone.

"Hey, you okay?" Onnie paused for his response, and when he pulsed twice, she collapsed into the chair in front of him and groaned. She glimpsed Elaric, flashing a pattern, and attempted to follow it but couldn't and ended up shaking her head. "Shit. Can you translate Morse code, First Keeper?"

I can. He asked why you were asking.

"Oh, I was just making sure. Something strange happened, and I wanted to check on you."

She rubbed her face and relaxed her shoulders, her adrenaline calming but not altogether gone. Hearing a siren after nearly a year of not hearing one had thrown her more than she would have guessed. Alku truly was a sanctuary city. A lack of fires, car accidents, and crime were some of the many benefits and differentiating features from purely human cities.

He'd like to know what happened.

Onnie explained her bizarre feelings in the coffee shop and then about the firetruck she'd heard while in the park. Elaric replied to the First Keeper, who quickly translated.

He asks you not to ignore it.

Onnie stared at the stone, a bit dumbfounded. "I wouldn't—I won't, but why do you say that?"

She observed as he beep-booped out whatever his message to

Kushima was, and Onnie was overwhelmingly grateful for his extended life experiences and age.

"Don't let your guard down. It's not a coincidence."

Onnie sighed but nodded. "You're right. Of course." She got to her feet. "I have to go. I didn't tell them I was coming in here."

Elaric began replying, and Kushima chuckled. *He said, "Don't get caught."*

Onnie laughed as she strode to the door. "Easier said than done, but so far so good. Be back soon."

He pulsed twice, and she quickly exited the library. When she closed the door, Onnie waited for the impending scolding, but after a few seconds of silence, she exhaled dramatically.

"Made it."

So it would seem. Do you feel better?

I do. Thank you.

Of course. What do you intend to do next?

Onnie entered the back room and set the kettle to boil. "Tea, open the shop, and then I hit the books. Or at least what I can find out here." She switched to speaking along their Bond. *I'm thankful for the progress Marco made with Elaric, but I don't want to delay this any longer than I have to.*

Then may I suggest you start in this section?

She felt a subtle tug to her Bond and followed where Kushima guided her. Onnie removed a book from the shelf and laughed so hard she began crying.

"Really? Morse code for dummies?" she snorted.

Kushima laughed with her, and Onnie had the urge to wrap herself in the warmth of its soothing sound.

I'm kidding.

Onnie stuck the book back on the shelf and began walking back to the small room behind the counter. "You're hilarious."

Okay, for real, try this shelf.

Kushima directed Onnie again, this time to another shelf crammed with new-age books documenting out-of-body experiences.

A few of these encounters were written by people who had their forms taken by transmogromorphs but were unaware of what had occurred.

"Oh, that's interesting. So, they just thought they were…I don't know, high or dying or something?" Onnie asked, running her fingers along the spines as she skimmed the titles.

Essentially.

"Well, I've got plenty of time before dinner with Gabe tonight, so why not?"

Onnie beamed and started loading her arms with texts to bring to Abbot's study before she opened the shop for the day.

I'm here. Want me to come in? Gabe asked Onnie along their Bond.
Damn, no. I'll be right there. Give me five to tidy up.

Onnie jumped up from the chair behind her grandfather's desk and rushed to stack the piles of books around her into organized groupings. After everything was orderly enough that she'd know where she'd left off in the morning, Onnie rinsed her teacup and the pot. She tucked her phone into her pocket, checked her hair in the back room's mirror, and retrieved her eyeliner from a small pouch beside it. She didn't feel particularly dressed for a date, but a bit of makeup on her eyes helped—a little.

"Mal, I'm going to dinner with Gabe. Can you keep Dany company?" Onnie called over her shoulder as she switched off lamps and put the store's new phone on the charger.

"No prob, but we're ordering sushi," Mal said while stretching on the couch behind her.

Onnie chuckled, "You two can have whatever you want. Have her use my card."

Mal padded along after her before jumping up onto the front counter. "Got it, girly."

"Thanks, Mal." Onnie gave him a loud smacking kiss and squished his cheeks. "I appreciate it."

"Duh," he pushed her hand away with his paw. "Now get before he comes charging in here. I'll go find Dany at the library."

"Love you!" Onnie said as she hurried to the front door.

Love you, too, Mal voiced in her head, and when she spun around, he was already gone.

Take care of Elaric, Kushima. Onnie requested as she stepped outside and drew the door closed behind her.

Of course. Enjoy your dinner, Kushima assured, and Onnie heard the Keeper lock the shop's door before Onnie had a chance to do it herself.

She hurried to the small parking lot beside the shop and slid into Gabe's car.

"Hey, Cat," he smiled before leaning over to kiss her gently. When he drew away, he's eyes sparkled with mischievousness, making Onnie smirk.

"Finishing what you started this morning?"

"Not yet," he said in nearly a growl, and she felt her face heat.

She playfully pinched his bicep and grinned. "Oy you, Dany's staying over."

Gabe groaned and shifted the car into gear before pulling out of the parking lot. "I'm suddenly regretting saying yes."

Onnie glimpsed his slight smile and knew he was teasing, but she tsked at him anyway. "How'd sports camp go?"

Gabe chuffed and shook his head. "Damn, I don't know where those kids get the energy, but I'd like some of it."

Onnie scoffed, "As if you're not just as bad as they are."

"Not even close." Gabe glanced at her sideways, "I had to rescue one of the middle schoolers from the top of the fire pole today. Got all the way up and froze."

She winced. "Wow, that sounds horrible. I'll keep to my books, thank you."

Gabe snorted and captured her hand with his free one, lacing their fingers together. "That's fine. I like you with your nose in your books." He winked and returned his focus to driving the short distance across town.

When they reached the Day Night Cafe, Gabe parked in the rear lot, and he reclaimed her hand as they walked around the building and to the front entrance. It was just after dark when they arrived, and multiple groups of people were at the podium waiting to check in since the restaurant had only recently reopened for the night's business after its decor transformation.

Due to the summer's long daylight hours, the night portion of the cafe opened later since the sanguistes who staffed it could not leave for work until after the sun went down. The shorter nights balanced out with the winter hours when the day cafe, which was run by day walkers and various other species, had to be home before the sun set. In the summer, the day crew swapped the restaurant into its other face, and the night crew took care of it in the winter. Both seasons had outside help, mainly in the form of young high schoolers needing some fun money.

Onnie and Gabe went to stand in line, and Marco was at the podium smiling, his usual calm and professional persona in place. When he glimpsed the two of them near the back of the line, his eyes brightened, and for a second, Onnie glimpsed genuine Marco slip past the mask he always wore.

Gabe glanced at her, his eyebrow raised as Marco waved them forward.

"Evening, you two, come with me."

He pivoted, and they had no choice but to follow after him as he threaded his way through the tables and brought them to the same table in the back where Onnie had had dinner with Stephan the last time she'd been there.

"Please," he pulled out a chair for Onnie and gestured for her to sit.

"Um," Onnie began to say but followed his request anyway.

Marco bent and kissed her cheek before shaking Gabe's hand. "Stephan says hello." Marco placed two menus on the table and smiled again. "I'll come to chat again when I can. Enjoy your meal."

Gabe pulled out his chair and sat down. "What was that?"

"No idea? I'll have to message Stephan later and ask."

Gabe's forehead creased, and he lifted his menu, effectively ending the discussion. Onnie inspected their Bond and felt an unfamiliar mix of emotions emanating from him.

"Are you...mad?" she asked. The word didn't feel entirely accurate, but it was the most correct one she could think of.

Gabe shook his head but didn't look up or lower his menu. She pursed her lips but let the topic go until after they had ordered and the waiter had left them alone again. Onnie watched the violinist seated in the center of the room before she closed her eyes to listen to the soft music. It felt...sad, and she opened her eyes and refocused on Gabe. He still felt off, and she adjusted how she viewed their Bond and, instead, scanned his aura. When it started to pulse around him, she recognized the odd emotion she'd been incapable of identifying through emotion alone.

"Are you jealous?" Onnie blurted out without thinking.

Gabe's eyes widened briefly, but he hastily recovered and turned his face away. "Of who?"

"I don't know. That's why I asked." She reached across the table and took his hand, twining their fingers together.

He sighed but didn't say more than that.

Talk to me?

Gabe shifted in his chair, sipped his wine, and then began to draw small circles on the back of her hand with his pointer finger.

Sorry, it's stupid. It's just...the look Marco gave you earlier.

Onnie had picked that moment to take a sip of her wine, and she instantly regretted it as she choked on it and coughed it back up from her lungs.

You...you do remember he's gay, right?

Gabe cracked a smile, and Onnie felt better when he rolled his eyes at her or, more likely, himself. *Yes, which is why I wasn't going to say anything. I'm being stupid.*

You are not, and honestly, you're not...exactly incorrect. You're just on the wrong path. She felt his hand tense, and she pinched the skin between his thumb and pointer finger. *Stop that, and let me finish.*

Gabe cleared his throat and sheepishly looked away again. *Sorry. Continue.*

You know how close Marco was to Elaric. When I met with Stephan before—before we lost him—he told me more about their relationship. After I brought Ana to the house that day, I came to see Marco.

Gabe turned to look at her again, and she saw his aura transition from jealous and suspicious to saddened and empathetic. *Mal told me you had gone to see him, but I was....*

Preoccupied. Onnie smiled. *Yes, it's okay. I came and told Marco what happened, and it was...bad.*

Onnie instinctively shivered as her body recalled the threat of an unrestrained sanguiste with his fixation exclusively on her.

What happened? Gabe's tone was concerned, but now she felt his worry over her discomfort after her involuntary reaction.

Nothing happened, but I was also at my emotional limit by then, and we sat and cried together. I've been checking in on him and trying to be a friend to him right now. She swallowed roughly and sniffled. *Elaric.... It was the last thing he asked me to do. Take care of Marco.*

Gabe lowered his gaze and mumbled, "I'm sorry."

"For what?"

"I was so focused on Dany and wasn't there for you when you needed me to be."

Onnie smiled and leaned across the table to poke his nose with her free pointer finger.

"You have nothing to apologize for. You were where you needed to be, doing what you needed to be doing. I can't rely on *only* you, and I needed to be the one to see Marco."

Gabe's frown deepened, and she realized that her meaning hadn't come across as intended.

"Let me rephrase. I *was* relying on you—to take care of Dany while I looked after Marco and helped Ana. Gabe, you're far more to me as my Guardian than just a sword and shield. Try not to forget how important all that other stuff is to me, too, okay?"

Before Gabe could respond, their waiter delivered their dinner, and Marco came over to check on them.

"How does it look?"

"Amazing as usual," Onnie said, beaming. "Thank you."

"How are you, man?" Gabe asked, and Onnie was pleased to hear that his usual cheery and concerned nature was back in his voice.

Marco grinned even larger, but he quickly recovered and reduced his enthusiasm. "Getting better."

Gabe nodded, "I'm glad. Thank you for taking care of Cat."

Marco peeked at her, and she shrugged before he answered, "You're welcome, though I'm pretty sure she's been doing more of that than I have."

"If you need anything, just ask, alright?" Gabe said, and Marco's eyes widened a fraction.

Onnie quickly told Marco, *I told him I've been helping you grieve... I had to say something.*

"I promise, thank you," Marco said, resting his hand on Gabe's shoulder, and Gabe nodded, content with the exchange. "Oh," Marco said abruptly, "Did you two hear about the accident today?"

It was Onnie's turn to tense. "What accident?"

"No, I didn't," Gabe said simultaneously.

Marco frowned. "From what I gather, there was an accident at the tunnel right before the border into Alku. A car lost control and hit a delivery truck that was on its way out of town."

"Wait, what?" Onnie asked, shocked, but then she felt the blood drain from her face. "Wait, was it this morning? About eight?"

"Sounds right. I was asleep, but Sam told me it was bad enough that the fire truck was needed."

Onnie's brow furrowed, and Gabe nudged her foot under the table. "Cat, what's wrong?"

She shook her head and forced a smile back onto her face. "Nothing. I'm just not used to hearing about that type of thing happening in Alku."

"It normally doesn't," Marco stated solemnly.

"Yeah, the wards tend to protect us from things like that. Freak accidents and stuff," Gabe added.

"Do you know anything else about what happened, Marco?" Onnie asked, her gut sinking with every word she said. Which then drew Kushima's attention to their conversation.

Marco shook his head. "Not much, just that the delivery driver and the people in the car were killed. The only one to survive was the driver who lost control, and he had no idea where he was or what had happened."

Onnie closed her eyes and crossed her metaphorical fingers, "Because he hit his head?"

"Not sure." Marco frowned and then glanced back to the front of the restaurant. "I'm sorry. I have to get back," he tilted forward in a polite bow as Onnie shooed him off with a very false smile.

"Go. Thanks, Marco," Gabe said with a genuine one.

When they were alone again, Gabe narrowed his eyes at her, and his smile was replaced with worry lines and a frown.

"What are you thinking, Cat?"

Onnie shook her head. "Nothing. Yet. Let me think."

Gabe hesitated but nodded. "Alright," he said, picking up his wine and pointing to her plate. "Eat before it gets cold."

Onnie did as suggested but simultaneously asked Kushima, *Where's the warding line located near the tunnel leading into Alku?*

Oh…young one….

Yes, exactly.

Onnie sighed, stuck a piece of pasta in her mouth, chewing what now tasted like ash, and threatened to turn her stomach.

Chapter 6: Brainstorm

July 2022 - Alku | Onnie Moore

By the time Onnie and Gabe had returned home, she was so far in her head that when Gabe spoke, she barely even realized it. He pulled the car into the driveway and turned off the engine before shifting in his seat to look at her.

"Cat?"

Gabe placed his hand on her left knee, which startled her, and she jumped out of her thoughts.

"Sorry, what?"

He sighed and squeezed her knee gently. "Come on. Let's go in."

Onnie blinked and glanced out the window, surprised to be home already. "Oh. Yeah, sorry."

She heard Gabe sigh again as he climbed out of the car, walked around, and offered his hand to help her out.

"Thanks," she smiled and took it gladly.

The warmth of his skin felt good in contrast with her cold palm, and after he shut the car door, she reached up, wrapped her arms around his neck, and kissed his cheek.

"I'm sorry, that was probably not the best date."

Gabe kissed her lips lightly. "Cat, all our dates are the best."

Onnie felt her ears grow hot. She rested her head on his chest and gave him a good squeeze as he wrapped his arms around her.

"Gabe?"

"Yeah?"

"I love you."

Gabe shifted, tilted her face to look up at his, and then kissed her until they were both breathless. "I love you, too."

She rubbed her nose on his and then stepped back, taking one of his hands and leading him to the front door.

"Come on, I need to talk to Dany, and the sooner I get this crap out of my brain, the better."

Thankfully, Gabe chuckled and followed where she pulled him. Onnie unlocked the front door and hollered into the kitchen.

"Dany? Mal?"

"I'm gonna change," Gabe said, kissing her cheek and heading straight for his bedroom to grab clothes.

"Onnie!" Dany cheered as she poked her head around the doorway that led into the kitchen.

Onnie pulled off her shoes with her toes and wandered into the kitchen after her best friend, where she wasn't at all surprised to see a spread of sushi on the counter. Mal lifted his head as she walked in, a piece of salmon sashimi hanging from his mouth.

"Hey, Ofni," he slurred around the piece of fish.

"Don't talk with your mouth full," Dany scolded, poking his belly as she returned to her chair at the kitchen bar.

Onnie chuckled, stole a piece of edamame from one of the containers, and leaned on the counter across from Dany.

"How was dinner?" Dany asked, then used her chopsticks to put a piece of sushi in her mouth.

Onnie frowned and shook her head, then shrugged, "Fine."

Dany narrowed her eyes and then covered her full mouth before speaking. "Not convincing."

"Mouth full!" Mal teased, and Dany grabbed his plate with her chopsticks and began sliding it away from him. It only made it a few inches before he stuck his paw on it and pulled it back towards himself.

"Did you hear the fire truck this morning?" Onnie asked Dany, who nodded while she chewed. "Marco said there was an accident in the tunnel."

Dany's eyes widened, and she swallowed roughly. "Casualties, I assume."

Onnie hummed in agreement and picked up another soybean pod as Gabe entered the kitchen.

"Yeah, a few," he added to Onnie's response before filling the kettle and putting it on the electric base to boil.

Thanks, Onnie said, along her Bond with Gabe. He came over to lean on the counter next to her and brushed a light kiss over her temple.

"Outsiders?" Dany clarified as she set down her chopsticks.

"Yeah…but I think there's something else to it." Onnie started picking at the bean husk between her fingers and ripping it into tiny pieces.

"Okay…" Dany said hesitantly. "You've got me worried. I'm assuming this has to do with the rogue?"

Gabe's eyes flit between Dany and then Onnie, and his brows crinkled. "Really, that's what's got you in knots?"

"She's right, but I think it's worse than that." Onnie sighed, pushed herself up from the counter, and went to prep her teacup with Keeper's Tea, her back to the other three in the room. "Remember when I asked you all if you were okay this morning?"

"Oh," Gabe said, "that was the time of the accident, wasn't it?"

Onnie nodded without turning around. "If I'm right, I think Jakob was testing the warding around Alku. I…I felt the emotions of one of the drivers as they hit the wards."

No one said anything, and she didn't turn around. She knew their expressions would only make her feel worse—they always did. Everyone thought everything she was dealing with was unfair, and it may be, but it was what it was, and she wished they'd stop looking at her with pity in their eyes.

"I thought it was one of you at first, which is why I asked, but when it wasn't, I got sidetracked and forgot about it. Until Marco mentioned it."

She methodically filled her tea strainer, resealed the mason jar of the unique blend, and pushed it back against the wall. When the kettle beeped, she pulled out a teacup and poured the hot water over the strainer into it. She watched the color bloom and billow outward from the mesh in whispy patterns. It reminded her of breath on a cold night. Or blood in water.

"Cat?" Gabe asked, his voice calm as if he were confronting a scared animal ready to bolt.

Once the liquid's color was correct, she removed the strainer and set it aside before pivoting around to face the others again. The three expressions staring back at her were indeed as she'd imagined—a mix of concern, fear, and pity.

I really wish they didn't always look at me like that, Kushima. Onnie mentally sighed at her friend, thankful she couldn't see her face at that moment, too.

They worry about you, and in this case, I think I agree with their concern. This could be catastrophic.

"Onnie, I assume you've checked the warding," Mal asked crisply.

"Of course. The moment I pieced it together. Everything's fine. Whatever Jakob was trying to achieve, I don't think it worked."

"This time," Dany mumbled, thrusting her plate away. "Now I understand why your dinner was fine."

"What are you thinking, Cat?"

Onnie sipped her tea and observed the steam curling as it rose from the cup. After a minute or two, she responded.

"Nothing."

"Nothing?" Mal mimicked and cocked his head to the side.

"I need more information. I don't know enough about the wards around Alku yet." She met Dany's eyes. "Help me?"

Her best friend's stiff posture relaxed, and she stood up and walked over to Onnie, seizing her teacup and setting it on the counter. Then, she pulled Onnie into her arms.

"You don't ever need to ask, but I'm glad you did." *I'm glad you didn't try to do this alone, Onnie.* Dany added so that only they could hear it.

"Thank you." Onnie buried her face in Dany's neck and held her tightly, savoring her best friend's warmth and calming scent. *There's just so…much.*

I know.

And so much at stake.

I know.

Dany squeezed her once, then returned her teacup to her hands, making Onnie laugh.

"Thank you."

Dany went to the kettle and poured herself a cup using the jasmine green tea in the jar next to the Keeper's Tea.

"As much as I still don't like how much you're drinking, you need it right now, and I won't argue with the First Keeper."

Kushima laughed softly, and Onnie smirked at the exchange between the two of them.

Gabe and Mal were watching her and Dany, and Onnie would bet they were talking about her along the Bond.

"Can I make a suggestion?" Dany asked while she waited for her tea to steep.

"Course," Onnie said, sipping the warm, soothing liquid in her cup.

"For tonight, let's bake cookies, drink tea, and ignore it all. Tomorrow, I'll go with you to the shop, and I can start teaching you more about the warding."

Gabe snorted. "Always cookies."

"Hey," Mal said, smacking Gabe's arm with his paw. "Shut it. I want cookies."

Onnie giggled and felt the tension in her shoulders ease up a little.

"I think that's a brilliant plan."

She knocked back the remainder of her tea and set down the cup before going to the freezer, where she had dough already prepped for such an occasion.

Onnie glanced over at the clock on the nightstand and then at Dany, who was sleeping soundly beside her. Mal was at the foot of the bed, draped over both of their legs, softly snoring. They'd been asleep for an hour, and when Onnie checked her Bond with Gabe, she concluded that he was also sleeping.

Can we talk? Onnie asked as she closed her eyes.

Of course, Kushima replied.

Onnie evened out her breathing and followed her Bond into the void. After a minute of focus, she saw a projection of herself standing in the endless black space.

Are you not going to sleep tonight? Kushima's voice hummed from all around her.

When Onnie was in the void, Kushima felt closer to her than when they spoke solely using their Bond, and tonight, she needed that extra layer of connection.

Not yet. Can we talk about Elaric?

Indeed. What's on your mind?

Onnie paced within the void, her anxious energy working its way out of her the only way it could. *I can feel whatever is coming is close. Can't you?*

In a way. I can feel what you share, so yes, I feel it, too.

We need to get Elaric back and fast. I think we are running out of time.

Understood.

Onnie clicked her nails together as she paced, the expected sound silent in her projection form.

I need to figure out how to communicate with him faster. Morse code is great, but it relies on you translating, and even then, without Marco or me, it's one way.

You are thinking if I could speak with him, you could communicate without entering my library.

Exactly. It would be a game of telephone, but better than nothing.

Onnie stopped her movement and squinted, focusing on the space in front of her within the void. Like she would project images of the actual world to Kushima, she tried projecting the couch from Abbot's study into the darkness. Unexpectedly, it actually appeared, and she flopped her body onto it and giggled.

I didn't think that would work. I can't feel the couch beneath me but didn't fall through it, so I'm good with this.

Kushima remained silent, and Onnie sat up and cocked her head to the side. *Kushima?*

Apologies. It amazes me sometimes how far you've come. That's all.

Onnie beamed and laid back on the couch, draping her arms over her head.

So, how do we make this happen? Connecting your Bond with Elaric's directly won't work since I should be able to talk to him already if that were the solution.

Or Marco. Agreed. I think the Bond isn't the answer. At least not directly.

We need a way to magnify the Bond. What about a ritual similar to the one we utilized when I bound Elaric's powers? We were able to talk to Grandfather. Could that work?

Hmm, amplifying the connection.

Yeah, except in your library, only you and I can see the Bond, and it's limited at that. If I don't manipulate it into view for the others, they see nothing.

It is... Kushima trailed off, and Onnie paused to let her think. After a minute, Kushima continued. *The only Bonds that are accessible in my library are the ones that are part of the library itself or of those currently residing within it.*

Onnie's eyes snapped open, staring up into the void. *Wait, can we make him part of the library? Well, not him, per se, but what about his stone?*

Ah…actually, I think there's merit to that. Keep going.

Okay, Onnie returned to her feet and resumed pacing as her brain processed. *Theoretically, if we made him part of the library…maybe I could manifest his form as I do yours? If I did that, I could speak to him as I do you, and then perhaps you two could talk Bond to Bond.*

It's possible.

So, we have to anchor him somehow. He needs to be a part of the room, not just in it.

I think it is worth experimenting with. However, I find your base logic sound.

Onnie stopped pacing, plopped back down on the void couch, and put her head in her hands. *Kushima, can I really do this? It's his soul I'm experimenting with.*

Keeper, Kushima said forcefully, and Onnie stared up. *If there is one thing I have learned about Elaric throughout this ordeal, it's that he trusts you. He trusts you so completely that he's given you power over his soul. So has Marco. They have lived long lives, seen many things, and known many Keepers. If they trust you with this, you must trust you with this.*

Onnie swallowed roughly and nodded. *You're right.*

Young one, you should get some rest. From what I understand, you'll be rather busy with Dany tomorrow.

Onnie groaned but couldn't hold back the small smile that crept into her lips. *Yeah, and I should probably call Marco and have him meet us tomorrow night. I want to try helping Elaric as soon as possible.*

Then you most certainly need rest. Sleep well, daughter of my blood.

Onnie nodded and retreated from the void back to her body, nearly instantly slipping into a deep, restorative sleep.

Chapter 7: Absorbing

July 2022 - Alku | Onnie Moore

"Thank you. Enjoy your stay in Alku."

Onnie smiled as she handed a paper bag with three novels in it across the counter to a tourist. The middle-aged woman grinned and thanked her before exiting the shop, gushing over her new purchases to her friend beside her.

When the door shut behind them, Onnie stretched her arms over her head and bent her back as she returned to Abbot's study. Dany was still on the floor, as she had been when Onnie left to assist her customers. Piles of books encircled the woman, looking like miniature battlements standing tall and ready to protect her.

"Another satisfied tourist?" Dany asked without looking up from the heavy-looking text in her lap.

"A handful of novels and a friendly smile. I live to serve." Onnie said sarcastically as she flopped on the couch. *This version is far more comfortable,* Onnie added to Kushima, who laughed softly.

"Okay," Dany said, still scrutinizing the book she had opened but pointing at Onnie. "How many layers of warding does Alku have?"

"Individual wards, or ward types?"

Dany smirked at the pages in her lap. "Sure."

"Thirty-six and nine, respectively."

Onnie retrieved her cell phone from her pocket and texted Marco. *If you're free tonight, text me when you wake up.*

"Perfect," Dany praised. "What are the nine types?"

Onnie tucked her phone away and pinched the bridge of her nose as if that would help her magically remember the information Dany had been cramming into her brain all morning.

"Spiritual—both in and out."

"One and two," Dany said, holding up one finger after another.

"Memory manipulation."

"Three," she raised another finger.

"Enforcement of banishments."

A fourth finger. "Four."

"Power containment and filtering."

"Five, keep going."

"Reflection slash camouflage."

"Six." Dany's hand switched, her pointer finger touching her thumb, the American Sign Language sign for six.

"Natural disaster dampener."

"Seven," her middle finger switched to touch her thumb.

"The Outsider wards as a bunch."

"Nearly done, eight," her ring finger swapped with her middle one. Onnie groaned and rubbed her temples. "Um…."

"Come on, you got this," Dany encouraged.

"The aura-ish one…."

"Close. What can auras show you…." Dany finally raised her gaze as she prodded Onnie closer to the answer without giving it away.

"Intention. The ninth is intention warding!" Onnie grinned and then pulled a pillow over her face.

"Yes!" Dany cheered.

Fantastic job, young ones, Kushima said to both of them.

"Ug…" Onnie groaned through her smile into the pillow. "My brain hurts."

"You did great," Dany said, and Onnie moved the pillow just enough to see her best friend grinning ear to ear.

"Good teacher," Onnie mumbled as she began to yawn.

Dany closed the book on her lap and added it to the tallest stack beside her. "Question."

"Answer?" Onnie replied as Dany got to her feet.

"If you had to guess, which ward was hit yesterday?"

Dany lifted Onnie's legs, sat on the couch beside her, and draped them over her lap.

"Oh," Onnie frowned and entirely removed the pillow from her face. "That's a good question."

Indeed.

"My uneducated guess would be that he didn't target any specific one, so I would assume all of them. If I had to pick one, though, my limited knowledge and logic would say…intention?"

"Interesting," Dany said, narrowing her eyes as if squinting across the room would reveal the correct answer.

"Don't think so?"

Dany shook her head. "Actually, I think I agree. I'm wondering if the driver was possessed or something. Maybe influenced, not sure, but either way, I think the ward they tried to puncture wasn't the point."

"What do you think was the point then," Onnie asked, propping herself up on her elbows.

"I'm not sure, but I think he was experimenting." Dany stared into space and then shook her head clear, a smile replacing her tight frown. "Thankfully, whatever it was, it didn't work."

"True," Onnie sat up and began absentmindedly braiding her long raven hair. *I really hope whatever he was doing didn't work. We have no real way of knowing at this point though, do we?*

I think not, young one, but keep watching and learning.

"I think all we can do is keep watch and keep learning," Onnie quoted Kushima, and Onnie felt as their Bond warmed.

"Agreed," Dany said, shifting Onnie's legs so she could stand up and stretch. "I better get back to it."

Onnie was about to offer to assist her when she felt the tingle indicating that someone was entering the shop. "Oh, be right back."

She wandered back to the front room as half a dozen patrons entered the shop. The entire group resembled one another, and Onnie smiled at what had to have been a group of people having a family reunion.

"Hello, welcome to Abbot's," she said with a genuine smile.

Sometimes, I like dealing with naive travelers.

Kushima laughed. *There's something calming in the mundane. I couldn't have said it better myself.*

Onnie was curled up in a quilt on one of the chairs in the First Keeper's library. Kushima and Marco sat watching her, and technically, Elaric as well, from his stone. Onnie had relayed the idea she and Kushima had discussed the night before to the pair, and now they awaited the men's opinions.

"Okay, so that's what we were thinking. What do you think?"

Marco elegantly sat in one of the spindly chairs with his arms crossed in front of him, his brow furrowed. He had taken the night off from the cafe again and wore a simple black sweater and pinstripe slacks. Ever the dapper sanguiste, even outside of a suit on his day off.

Onnie was pleased to see him more comfortable and behaving nearer to his true self than he had in the past. Every time they met, he became less his persona and more *just* Marco.

Onnie glimpsed a series of flashes in her peripheral vision as Elaric responded, and she waited for Kushima to translate. Onnie had tried learning what she could, but trying to study Morse code on top of the wards with Dany, Onnie's brain was quickly becoming goo. Since she couldn't tell Dany why she was suddenly interested in Morse code, Onnie's best option was to look up each letter individually, which was far too slow to be helpful.

He's okay with it. Willing to try, Kushima conveyed for Elaric.

"Marco?" Onnie prompted gently.

Marco stared at Elaric's stone, but his frown was so deep that it could have been etched onto his face. "Ultimately, it's up to E, but in general, I think it's worth the try."

Elaric's stone flared and then began to flash, making Marco smirk. Onnie glanced over to Kushima, who was trying to suppress a smile. *Elaric wants to know why Marco looks like he 'sucked on a lemon,' as he put it.*

Onnie snorted. "He's got a point. If you're worried about something, I'd like to know about it. Even if you say it's Elaric's choice, you can still ask."

Marco pinched the bridge of his nose, and Onnie mentally laughed, having now found where she'd picked up the habit of doing the same.

"It's nothing exactly. The whole situation is difficult. That's all."

Onnie reached over and touched Marco's knee before squeezing it gently. "Marco, look at me." When he did, she spoke only to him along the Bond and didn't break their eye contact. *You have my word. I will fix this. I told you that. I will bring him back to you, Marco.*

Marco turned away first, and Onnie settled back in her chair as Kushima looked at her quizzically.

It's nothing, Onnie told Kushima only. *Rather, it's nothing you don't already know.*

I see.

"Are we ready? Or would you prefer to try another night? Nothing says we have to do this today," Onnie asked, rubbing her palms together before blowing on her chilled fingers, desperately trying to warm them up.

Again, Kushima translated Elaric's response. *He says, 'If you're okay, let's do it.' I think he's concerned for you in this instance, Onnie.*

"Wait, you're worried about me?"

Elaric's stone pulsed twice as he agreed with Kushima's observation.

"Thank you for the concern, Elaric. I'm fine. I assumed we would do this tonight, so I was conservative with my activities today." She chuckled softly, "Well, I tried to be. I think Dany may be trying to drown me in ward history."

Elaric's stone flickered in amusement, and even Kushima nodded in agreement. When Marco took a deep breath, it brought Onnie's focus back to him, but her shoulders eased a bit when he nodded.

"Alright. Then let's do this," he agreed.

"Thank you, Marco. Would you mind doing me one favor before we start?"

"Tell me," he declared stiffly.

"I'm going to prep a few things in here. Would you mind going back out into the shop and making me some of the Keeper's Tea from the red tin in the back room? There's a thermos back there, too."

"Sure." Marco stood and headed towards the door.

"Feel free to make yourself tea, coffee, or something else. You're welcome to anything," she added.

"Appreciated," he said with a small smile before exiting the room.

What was that about? Kushima questioned.

"Elaric, there's one more thing I want to tell you about this. If you decide to share it with Marco later, that's your choice, and I have no objections. I simply want it to be your decision and not make it for you."

Elaric's stone fluttered in acknowledgment, and she continued.

"By merging your Bond with the shop's, and this room specifically, you will essentially become an extension of the shop. What that means in a practical sense could be complicated. There are many things I can't answer in advance, for example, if the shop can no longer support this room…if this room goes back into stasis, I'm not sure how that will affect you." Onnie frowned and waited for Kushima's translation.

He understands.

"Um, there's one more thing. I think?" Onnie winced. "I think your blood link with Marco has already…altered your lifespan, but I'm pretty positive that even if it hadn't, tying you to the shop will. Theoretically, you might be able to…end it, but it wouldn't be easy."

When Elaric's stone didn't change, Onnie glanced at Kushima, who shook her head.

"I know Marco's is endless, and I know yours was already long, but this will fundamentally change you. At least, I think it will, but it's a potential risk. If that's the way you choose to look at it."

Onnie let Elaric digest everything she'd conveyed to him, and she waited patiently, tracing the stitching on her quilt with her fingertip. After a few minutes, she saw the stone flashing from the corner of her eye and looked up. Whatever Elaric was saying was long, and Onnie's eyes broadened as she watched the seemingly unending flickers of light.

After he finished, Kushima smiled fondly at him and nodded before addressing Onnie. *He said he's still willing to do this. He's sensitive that you're Dany's best friend and doesn't want you to misunderstand, but Dany is human, and if he has the opportunity to return and remain by Marco's side when his time with Dany ends, he will take the gift being offered.*

"Hey, Elaric, please, don't be concerned about your relationship with Dany. At least not with me, or her for that matter. She and I talked, and Stephan gave me some of the history between you and Marco. Dany is indeed human. Time cares nothing of your relationship or anyone else's. Just because you love someone today does not mean you aren't allowed to love someone else after they're gone."

Elaric's stone flashed a few times, and Kushima reached over to press her projected palm over it. Then she removed it and translated his reply for Onnie.

'Thank you, Keeper. Thank you, Onnie.'

"You're welcome. I've spent a lot of time with Marco lately, and honestly, he's lucky to have you. Though I wish you and Dany a long, happy life, I am relieved to know Marco will still have you after the rest of us are gone."

'Always,' Kushima restated just as Marco opened the door to the library, carrying a thermos in each hand.

"Marco, you are my hero," Onnie said, shivering as if it were summoned by the idea of warm tea walking towards her. "I get cold easily when I'm tired, and this room does not help." She took a thermos from him with a thank you. "Besides, an extra kick of power wouldn't hurt."

"Of course. Let me know if you need anything else." Marco returned to his chair and placed the second container on the table before him. "Did you complete what you needed?"

Onnie poured a cup of the tea into the thermos lid and breathed its steam in before speaking. "I did. Perfect timing, too. I just finished."

"Can I do anything to assist you with all of this?" he requested formally.

Onnie sipped her tea and hummed her affirmation. "Yes, though you'll find it boring," she grinned. "I need you to watch. I'll have my eyes closed, and while there shouldn't be much that you should see with the naked eye, it would really help if you told me if something changes, no matter how small."

"Consider it done. Anything else?"

"I'm not sure to tell you the truth."

"Fair enough," Marco said, and Elaric's stone flashed as he spoke. When Elaric finished, Marco glowered at the stone and rolled his eyes. "Someone has to be. You're taking this too lightly, E."

Onnie glanced from Kushima to Marco and back.

Not for our ears, Kushima said with a slight head shake.

Onnie nodded and observed Marco from the corner of her eye as she sipped her tea. When he tensed up, she remained still, but he quickly slackened and sighed.

"You know I can't argue with you." Marco turned back to her, "Apologies, we're ready when you are."

"No apologies needed. Are you sure?"

"Yes," Marco said, so Onnie drained her tea and set the empty lid on the table.

"Alright," she said, addressing Elaric specifically. "Ready?"

After his two pulses, she pivoted to Kushima. "You're next. Ready for this?"

Kushima nodded but answered so solely Onnie could hear her. *Be careful, Onnie. Take your time, check things twice, and have faith. You can do this, Keeper.*

You'll be at my side?

Never anywhere else, daughter of my blood, Kushima said with affection.

"Alright, Marco and Elaric. Would you like me to talk as I work, or would you rather I just do my thing, and you'd rather not know what's happening?"

"Do what you need to do, Keeper," Marco said, and Elaric agreed with a quick yes.

"Alright." Onnie took a deep breath and grinned at the stone a few feet away. "Well, see you soon, Elaric."

She saw him pulse twice before she shut her eyes.

Onnie began by concentrating on taking a few more deep breaths. She relaxed her hands loosely on her legs, which were curled beneath her in the chair, the quilt draped over them. Then, she cleared her mind, and only after she felt even and stable did she project herself into the void.

Kushima?

Here, Keeper.

Alright. I think we tie him into the center of your sigil on the ceiling. Thoughts?

I'd like to hear your reasoning.

Of course.

Onnie projected the sigil from the library's ceiling into the void before her. The only difference was that it was vertical, as if on a wall, not above her. She approached it and indicated to a point in the center.

Like the other souls, I believe the fire will hide and anchor his soul and the stone. This point has a high concentration of flame, and being at the center point of the circle and the intersection points of the other elements means it should be more stable from an energy perspective.

I see no faults with that. Proceed.

Onnie swallowed roughly and pushed the sigil to hover above her, into the same position it was outside the void, blazing above her physical body. The projection of herself walked to stand directly under the center of it, and then she drew the Bonds around her body into view.

Marco's Bond and the slight glow of his aura that became visible wavered like a flame made of fear and anxiety but also hope. She gently pressed on it and sent him warmth until she heard him gasp beside her. When she let go, she watched as his aura calmed a little.

Next to Marco, Onnie saw Kushima seated beside her and Elaric's stone on the table nearby. Onnie surveyed the stone closer and located the Bond for the stone as an object, along with the one that was Elaric's specifically. She selected the one not leading to Elaric's soul and then spoke aloud. "Marco, I am going to move the stone. Don't be alarmed."

"Understood," his voice wavered negligibly, but she still caught it.

Onnie carefully pulled on the stone's Bond and drew it over to where she stood with the sigil above her in the void, mirrored where the mark was upon the ceiling in the library.

"Onnie..." Marco asked, his voice and aura now noticeably fearful.

"Don't worry. I'm going to hide it among the flames. He'll be fine."

She pressed the stone to the projected image of the sigil, and in the real world, it rested against the stone ceiling. When she felt it was situated where she wanted it to be, she began pulling one fiber of the stone's Bond apart at a time. Once she had one freed from the rest, she wove it together with the threads from the stone bricks in the ceiling. As she worked, she spidered out the threads from the amber stone's center, and it slowly became covered by its own Bond and those of the bricks around it. The amber became increasingly a part of the original room's foundation as she went, and even when she occasionally tugged it, the amber didn't shift.

Kushima, everything look alright?

You're doing wonderfully.

Onnie refocused on her task, feeling more confident with a second opinion. After what she was sure must have felt like an eon for Marco, Onnie was positive the stone wouldn't be able to move, fall, or be separated from the ceiling without extreme force and intention—or her delicate removal of it.

She rotated her neck, and even in the void, she could tell her body was becoming stiff in her chair.

"Marco, would you mind pouring me another cup of tea and placing it in my palm?"

Marco's chair screeched along the floor when he stood to do as she'd requested. Once the cup was in her hand, she took a small sip and a deep breath.

"Thank you. The stone's attached to the ceiling. Now I have to merge Elaric's Bond with the library's."

Marco seemed to hesitate but then spoke regardless. "How—" he paused, and when he tried again, his voice was more stable than before. "Going well so far?"

Onnie smiled. "Perfectly."

Marco moved around her, and she watched his Bond as he drank from the second thermos, the aroma of coffee tickling her nose. She gulped down her tea and then asked Marco to return the lid to the thermos.

"Alright. Going to start again."

"Please be careful, Keeper. Not just for E's sake."

"I promise."

Onnie returned to the amber stone hovering above her in the void, now tangled amongst a web of Bond fibers onto a projection of the stone bricks above it. This time, she ignored the stone's Bond and instead concentrated on Elaric's.

Kushima, would it be bad if I were to admit that I'm afraid?

I would be disappointed if you weren't. Being afraid means you understand the gravity and importance of your task. That said, take a deep breath and continue. You can do this.

Onnie did as she was told, and then she began again.

Elaric's soul was vastly more complicated than the amber's. The fibers were mismatched and discolored, some of which she attributed to his transmogromorph nature and others to his blood link. None of those were alarming, and she carefully attended to them first, pulling the threads apart and entwining them with the shop, the library's Bonds, and, ultimately, her own.

You alright, Kushima?

I am.

Onnie repeated the same process with each of the standard threads. She isolated a portion of Elaric's Bond, found a suitable match from the library, gently coaxed them together, and incorporated the fibers into one thread. When she was about eighty percent finished, her body shivered violently in her chair.

"Onnie?" Marco questioned, and she caught his aura flash to one filled with concern.

"I'm alright. Just tired, but I'm nearly finished."

She resumed, but Elaric's remaining threads were fractured and jagged, making her job more challenging and tenuous.

I assume these wounds are from when he ripped himself free.

I think that's probably accurate. Are you alright?

I am. I'm just being extra careful. Perhaps I should have done these first when I was less worn out.

You're almost there.

Onnie slowed down even further, her movements precise and methodical as she refused to make a mistake and put Elaric's existence in jeopardy. When she finished the last thread, she felt a rush of energy and emotion wash over her.

Elaric?

Hello, Keeper.

Onnie erupted into tears instantly when she heard his mental voice.

Oh, my gods, it's so good to hear your voice.

"Onnie!?" Marco was beside her body in less than a second, and she sensed his palm on her cheek.

I'm sorry. Let me do one last thing, she said to Elaric and Kushima.

Onnie followed the same process she used to project Kushima into the library, this time with Elaric's soul. After a failed attempt due to her rampant tears and emotions, she tried once more. Even in the void, she knew when she'd succeeded and gradually blinked open her eyes. Marco was kneeling at her feet, gazing up at her, worry in every line on his face.

"Onnie, are you alright? What's wrong?"

All she managed to do was sniffle and then focused over Marco's shoulder. He followed her gaze and sucked in his breath, covering his mouth with one trembling hand.

Elaric stood a few feet away, his hands clasped behind his back and a slight smile on his lips. Onnie recognized his true base form with ta nned skin, short-cropped hair, and sparkling eyes. He wore jeans and a long-sleeved shirt, with the piercings in his ear and eyebrow glinting in the firelight.

Onnie looked at Kushima, who still sat beside her, and the First Keeper glowed with pride as she, too, studied Elaric's incorporeal form.

Marco's hand on Onnie's knee began to shake, and she placed her palm over it. She could see in his profile that he hadn't looked away from Elaric.

Elaric? she said to only him.

Yeah. I know.

"Marco," she nearly whispered, but he didn't register her words at all. She chuckled and tried again. "Marco."

"Yes?" he asked without blinking, moving, or lowering his hand from his face.

"I'm going to step out of the library for a few minutes—"

His head whipped around to look at her, and his eyes went wide in fear.

She shook her head and rested her free palm on his cheek, brushing a few tears from under his eyes. "Don't worry. Elaric will still be here. The First Keeper will help."

I will, indeed.

Marco swallowed hard and nodded, then struggled to his feet and helped her to hers. They walked together to stand in front of Elaric, Marco's hand still clutching hers.

She smiled at Elaric. "We have lots to talk about now that it won't take me ten years to translate one sentence."

Elaric laughed with a wide grin.

"But we have *plenty* of time." She peeked from him to Marco and back. *Be careful, Elaric, but I'll give you some privacy,* she said privately. *Thank you, Onnie.*

She squeezed Marco's hand and then slipped herself from his hold. She walked past Elaric and over to the door. Before she left, she witnessed Marco fall to his knees, his shoulders shuddering, as Elaric knelt beside him, unable to touch him but likely speaking with him. Onnie yanked open the door and closed it behind her, where she leaned against it before sliding to the floor and burying her head in her arms.

Her position mimicked Marco's, but she knew the grief and relief she felt was a drop in the bucket compared to his.

She had no idea how he'd held it together for so long. Then she, too, sobbed in relief.

Elaric Rickson

As Marco fell to his knees once Onnie was across the room, Elaric could only watch. He quickly knelt beside his only family and tried to soothe him with the only thing he could—his words.

Marco, it's alright. I'm right here. Elaric desperately wanted to reach out and touch him, but that wasn't possible yet, so he clenched his fists at his sides instead.

I shall make myself scarce. Call on me if you need anything, the First Keeper said before she disappeared.

Appreciated, Elaric replied for both he and Marco.

Elaric sat on the floor in front of Marco, his knees on either side of the other man's. Even though he couldn't comfort him through touch, Elaric could get as close to him as possible.

Marco. Please, Elaric pleaded. His heart was breaking, and even though he'd witnessed the grief Marco had carried when Elaric was in the amber stone, he had underestimated how much the stoic sanguiste was keeping hidden.

I will never be able to repay you, Marco, Elaric said softly. *When I activated the blood link, I...I didn't do it, thinking it would save me. I just, I hoped you'd know that you were the last—*

"Stop!" Marco shouted, dropping his hands to his knees, his eyes dark and dilated. "I don't want to hear it, E. Do you have any idea what it felt like when you activated it? I swear, I thought everything..." his voice caught, "...was gone. I knew you'd only activate it if there were no other options. Then, when I couldn't feel you at the other end of the link." Marco squeezed his eyes closed.

Elaric sighed, *I'm sorry.*

"When Onnie showed up at my door, I felt her emotions. The agony. The guilt. The...anger. E, I nearly lost control right then and there. I'm fairly positive I did for a second or two."

Elaric clenched his jaw and forced his eyes shut. For Marco to lose control completely in front of a human and the Keeper of Prophecy at that....

I really screwed up, First Keeper.

Peace, child. He'll recover. You all will. It just takes time.

What can I do? Elaric whispered, staring down at Marco's upturned palms and desperately wanting to grab them.

After a few minutes, Marco sighed. "Nothing. You already did it."

Elaric focused on Marco's eyes and was pleased to find they were back to normal.

Enlighten me? Elaric requested with a smirk.

"All of it. Activating the blood link. Saving Dany. Coming back. That's what you needed to do." Marco squeezed his eyes closed. "Everything occurs for a reason, and while I wish all of this could have been avoided...you did the right thing." Marco opened his eyes and smiled, moisture visibly collecting at the corners. "I'm proud of you, E. Dany's safe because of you. You did well."

Elaric said nothing. There was nothing to say. Marco was right. Dany was safe, and at that moment, that was what mattered.

Thankfully, he made it back to everyone, but if it happened again...
he'd make the very same choice.

Elaric peeked up at Marco, relieved to see genuine Marco sitting
before him. Something Elaric would never take for granted again.

This time, Elaric would make sure he stuck around. Abbot had
been correct again.

Always? he asked hesitantly.

A single tear ran down Marco's damp cheek. "Forever."

Chapter 8: Under the Mountain

July 2022 - Alku | Onnie Moore

Onnie ended her call with her brother Tyler, a massive grin on her face from where she sat on the shop's backroom couch. She'd only called to ask him a question about a cookie recipe, but somehow, they'd talked for over an hour and she had laughed so hard her sides ached. She missed her brothers, but talking to them always relieved some of her anxiety over their safety. So far, very few knew who she was outside of Alku, but with Jakob's scheming, she didn't want to give him the benefit of the doubt and then end up the cause of her family's pain. Or something worse.

Did you enjoy your conversation with your brother?

Onnie smiled at the ceiling. *I did. I miss them, but they seem to be doing fine. It makes it easier not to have them to worry about.*

Understandable.

How's Elaric?

Just fine, young one. I will say it's nice to have someone to talk with when you're unavailable.

Onnie growled playfully up at the ceiling. *I am never unavailable for you, Kushima.*

The Keeper's laugh was light, and Onnie returned to smiling.

My apologies. That wasn't what I meant.

Good. Onnie groaned and dropped her head back on the couch. *I guess I better get this over with then.*

She retrieved her water bottle from beside her on the couch, took a swig, and reached out to Gabe and Mal.

Hey, Gabe?

What's up, Cat?

Do you have classes this afternoon?

Not after one, why?

I need my Guardian's help, Link's too, Mal.

Mal appeared on the couch next to her and sat down beside her thigh. *What's up, girly?*

Is everything alright? Gabe asked, and Onnie felt his unease and panic flare in response to the unknown situation.

Both of you, calm down. Nothing's wrong. I need to do something, and if I do it alone, you'll both flay me alive. So, I'm asking for help.

Gabe's emotions settled down, and Mal nodded before he bumped her bicep with his nose. *You got it,* Mal said. *Meet us here when you can, big guy.*

See you in a bit. Gabe paused. *Hey, Cat…thanks.*

Onnie smiled. *Yeah yeah. Don't say I never listen to you.* She snorted and began scratching under Mal's chin.

"Any chance you'll tell me now what's going on?" Mal asked, and the end of his question blended into a loud pur when she found a good spot to scratch.

"I want to go get Elaric's body."

His purring ceased instantly, and he stared at her, unblinking. "Explain."

Onnie chuffed. "Why are you so…" she gestured to him, "whatever this is?"

"Shocked. Suspicious. Confused," Mal informed her.

"Yeah, why? It's Elaric. We weren't able to get him when it happened, and I'd like to be able to tell Dany his body is where it belongs."

Mal gave her a heavy dose of side-eye but seemed pacified by her answer and didn't press her further.

Damn, Kushima. I didn't think he'd react like that. I figured he'd be angry or something, not suspicious.

I am also confused, young one, but I believe you've proven your point. You should be able to accomplish your goal.

"Onnie," Mal said abruptly, moving to sit on her knees and look directly at her.

"Hm?" She tried to stay calm and smile.

"You know it wasn't your fault, right?"

Ah, I think I understand now, young one. He's suspicious because he's worried your intentions are out of guilt and doesn't want you to put yourself in any emotional or physical danger because of it.

Onnie lowered her nose to the feline's and gently bonked them together. "I'm aware. Do I still feel guilt? Yes. I will for the remainder of my life. However, that's not why I'm doing this. Believe me?"

Mal purred, brushing his face against her nose and cheek. "I'm glad. Love you, Onnie."

"Okay, it's time for snuggles!" Onnie cheered, scooped him into her arms, peppered him with kisses, and squeezed him gently before nibbling on his ear and smooshing her face into his fur. "I love you, too, Mal. Thanks for worrying about me."

Mal laughed, purred, and tried to push her away and squirm out of her grasp, but all in mock annoyance. He could have disappeared instantly if he wanted to, but Onnie knew he was a big softy with a weakness for cuddles.

After their snug fest, they sat together and enjoyed the shop's quiet and the day's calm for a while. When it was a quarter to one, Onnie stood up and stretched. When she moved, Mal opened one eye from where he was napping on the couch and watched her.

"Going somewhere?" he asked with a glance at the clock on the wall.

"Yeah, I need to run into the First Keeper's library for a few minutes. Mind watching the shop for me?"

Mal yawned but got up and stretched before jumping off the couch and padding past her into the shop's main room. She followed behind him when he jumped up onto the counter and began to bathe.

"Fine, but I can't guarantee I can keep Gabe from coming to get you."

Onnie gave Mal a good full-body stroke on her way past him. "Thanks."

She heard Mal grunt in acknowledgment as she headed into the back of the shop.

Gabe, I'm popping into the First Keeper's library for a few minutes before you get here. Mal's watching the shop.

Alright, see you soon. Twenty-ish.

Perfect. Be safe.

Onnie nabbed a sweatshirt off the back of the desk chair in Abbot's study and pulled it over her head as she opened the library's door and quickly closed it behind her.

"Hey, you two," she said as her head popped out of the sweatshirt's neck, and she fixed her wild hair.

Hey, Onnie, Elaric replied, followed by Kushima's hello.

"I don't have long, so I'm not going to manifest either of you, but I wanted to ask you a few things, Elaric."

Course. What's up?

"I am going to go retrieve your body. What can you tell me about where it is?" Onnie flopped into a chair and draped the nearby quilt over her knees. She understood why the room was always so cold, but she didn't have to like it.

You're going alone? Elaric's voice questioned with delicacy.

Onnie chuckled. "You're no better than the other three. No, I'm taking Mal and Gabe. I told them I wanted to put your body where it belongs. I plan on relocating it to the shop, but I'll tell them I placed it in your grave."

Elaric sighed. *I hate that you're lying for me.*

"Ah," Onnie said, holding up her finger. "I am not lying for you. I am lying for me. I *could* tell them everything, but it would make my life harder. This is purely me being selfish. Don't borrow guilt."

Silence stifled the conversation, and then Elaric laughed. *Fine, fine. You win. Alright, down the well, you find a very long shaft. I'm not even sure what it was for, to be honest, but it was definitely man-made. I'm actually only assuming it was a well.*

"First Keeper, any idea what it could be or alternate entrances? Maps of Alku, old mining shafts, I don't know. Anything?"

I'll see what I can find.

"Thanks. Anything else you can tell me, Elaric?"

I think there was water at the bottom, but not a lake or a large body of water. Also, not just a puddle. It was enough to see....

"Please, that's enough," Onnie said softly. "Thank you, your information was helpful. If you remember anything, tell the First Keeper, and she'll let me know."

Indeed. Also, I believe you are correct. There is a mining entrance that could be linked to where Elaric described. It's a way down the mountain, and you've probably passed by it.

"Oh, that's great! Is there a map or something I can show the others?"

Elaric, are you perhaps aware of the abandoned cabin on the mountain? Kushima asked.

As always, nothing gets past you, Keeper, Elaric said with amusement. *I am, indeed. It's the location where I used to shift forms when I was within his ranks.*

"Alright..."Onnie paused. "That's...convenient."

You sound upset, Elaric asked.

"Not upset. Just...this feels too easy. Too many coincidences."

Hmm, I see what you mean.

I would not worry, young one. You won't be alone, and I don't think you'll have any issues. While he may be vile, the rogue guardian is not stupid. He will have moved locations by now.

"I guess you're right." Onnie sighed and stood up. "Alright, I'm sure Gabe's nearly here, and I can only trust his restraint to a very tiny degree when it comes to this room."

Elaric laughed. *Be safe, Keeper.*

"Always am. Thanks to you both. See you soon."

Onnie draped the blanket over the chair and headed to the door. When she put her hands on the wood to push it open, it gave way with little effort, and she stumbled forward and fell into Gabe with a grunt.

"Why, hello, Cat," he said, grinning down at her before he righted her on her feet again.

"Gabe?" Onnie straightened her clothes and nudged him out of the way before closing the door behind her. "Were you about to break my rule?" She looked at him with narrowed eyes and a scowl.

"No, I was going to ring the bell to let you know I was here, but I figured I'd help open the door for you since it's so heavy."

Onnie shook her head. "What a wonderful lying gentleman you are." She winked at him before pulling her sweatshirt over her head and putting it back on the chair.

"Are you going to explain?" Gabe said, crossing his arms and watching her flit around the room, tidying up.

"I said I would. Mal?" she called, and the feline appeared on Gabe's shoulder.

"Here."

Onnie smiled and drank the remaining tea from the cup she'd left on the desk that morning. She grimaced as the duration it had been left unattended had turned it bitter. Not to mention, the cold made it even worse. When Gabe chuckled, she shot him a look, and he continued laughing.

"Yeah, I gave Mal a bit of a pre-read, but I want to go get Elaric's body."

Gabe tensed, and his eyes darkened. "No."

To her surprise, Mal smacked him on the head with his paw. "She's doing it whether we like it or not, my man, so suck it up and hear her out."

Onnie's eyes went wide, but she thanked Mal along their Bond.

"He's right, Gabe. I'm going to get it and put it where it belongs one way or another. You can either go with Mal and me or brood and stay here?"

Gabe stood unmoving, and Onnie shifted her posture to mimic his.

"Your choice, love," Onnie said with sarcastic sweetness.

He must have realized he would lose their staring contest because he sighed and ran his fingers through his hair before growling, "Fine."

Onnie smiled and crossed the room to kiss his cheek. "Thank you. I'd feel much better with you at my side than without."

"Tell me everything," he said before sitting heavily on the couch.

"The First Keeper found an abandoned mineshaft a way down the mountain. There's a cabin near it that Elaric used to use for his shifting." Onnie noticed Gabe's raised eyebrow but ignored it. "We are thinking that if we follow that shaft, it should lead us to about where the well's bottom should be."

"And how are you so sure there is another way in?" Gabe asked.

"According to the maps, there should be, but you're right. We won't know until we get there."

Mal poked Gabe's cheek. "Let's hit the road then, Jack."

Onnie smiled, her hope rising as she watched Gabe's demeanor shift to his slightly more playful one.

"Sure thing, *Jill,*" he said and poked Mal in the belly.

Onnie sniggered into her hand but wandered to the trunk in the corner and began pulling out more suitable clothing for a hike. "Need to change, Gabe? I can send you home if you'd like."

"Nope, this is fine." She heard him get up from the couch as she chucked two sturdy running shoes over her shoulder and onto the floor behind her. "We'll watch the front while you get ready."

She turned, and they were both gone.

Well, I'm glad that worked.

Stay vigilant, young one.

I promise, besides, you're coming, too.

Onnie grinned, quickly swapped her casual attire for hiking gear, and put on her shoes. She pulled out her phone, saw nothing important, and slipped it back into her pocket before joining the guys in the front of the shop.

When she approached the counter, Gabe handed her a bottle of water. "Ready for our *run*," he said pointedly before adding along the Bond, *Cover story just in case he's got any roaches left in town watching us.*

Works for me, Onnie agreed. *We're only a couple out for a run in the woods.*

Mal scoffed. *Sure, a couple who brings their cat with them on their jogging date. Who jogs for a date?*

Onnie glared at him but rolled her eyes at his protest and then addressed Gabe. "I am. It's been too long since we've gone on one. Shall we?"

Mal snorted at their poorly acted cover story, which was needless within the shop, but they quickly stepped out onto the cobbled street, and Onnie locked up.

"Mountain run today?" Gabe asked as he bent, stretching to the side.

"Sure, that sounds great. It's a nice day for it, too."

Onnie stretched her calves out. No false cover story needed. It really had been a while since they'd gone for a run.

They both warmed up and then took off at a jog toward the mountains behind Alku. Once they were away from town, Mal joined them, and they shifted to a slower walking pace. It hadn't taken long for her lungs to begin burning. She glanced at Gabe, who looked fresh as a daisy and scowled.

So not fair sometimes, she whined to Kushima in jest.

Kushima laughed, and Onnie could hear the smile in her voice. *Yes, but you have your own skills, some of which he also thinks are unfair.*

Onnie chuckled, and Gabe glanced at her sideways. "Everything alright over there?"

"Yeah, just lamenting the limits of my physical skills compared to yours."

"Why the hell would you compare yourself to him?" Mal asked, surprised.

"I wasn't really," Onnie said but gently placed her hand on Gabe's arm for stability while she closed her eyes and looked at the Bonds around them. *Almost there,* she relayed, opened her eyes, and then removed her hand.

The forest was lively around them, and Onnie was relieved to feel everything was peaceful and as it should be. With the sun out and the clouds tucked away, the dew and excess spring moisture that pooled on the ground and napped upon the leaves all glittered in the sunlight. She took a deep breath and couldn't restrain her smile.

"We should go visit Xayn soon," Onnie blurted out before thinking.

"We should," Gabe said curtly.

Onnie dropped the subject, knowing that Xayn was in a delicate place after his Grandmother had fallen and injured herself. He was barely talking to Dany and Gabe, so likely, she wasn't on his list of priorities to take a walk with.

What's the plan when we get there, Cat?

Don't really have one. I'm reasonably confident that everything will be abandoned, but I'll check before we go in anyway.

Want me to do some recon? Mal asked.

Sure, that would be a big help, Onnie agreed.

Mal, can you check his old hideout? Make sure nothing will surprise us from above if we do make it to the bottom of the well? Gabe asked, and Mal disappeared in response.

Only a few minutes later, Mal returned and retched a few times. *That was disgusting, but I can confirm that it has been abandoned.*

Good. Thanks, Mal.

Gabe stopped abruptly, and Onnie followed his stare. She also halted when she saw the roof of a cabin amidst the trees ahead of them.

She continued their ruse and commented, "Neat. I didn't know there was a cabin out here."

"I didn't either." Gabe peeked at her and grinned, the only thing giving away his lie of excitement being his genuine anxiety along their Bond. "Should we go explore it?"

Onnie skipped in place. "I'm down!"

She pulled her view of the Bond up over the environment around them, and when she determined they were alone, she waved at Gabe and Mal to join.

"Hurry up!" *All clear. No heartbeats.*

Gabe jogged behind her to catch up, and when they'd passed a few copses of trees, a tiny, one-room cabin stood before her. It was closer to a shed than a cabin, but Onnie projected its image to Kushima.

Can you double-check with Elaric to ensure we are in the right place?

Onnie wandered around the side of the cabin and found a very old, very rusty spigot and an iron bucket with a hole in the bottom. A few antique-looking mining tools were leaning against the back of the structure, and from behind it, she could see a gap in the shaker-style roof.

That's the correct location. According to my maps, if you walk directly North, you'll come to the side of the mountain in less than one-quarter of a mile. There you should find an entrance.

You're both fantastic. Thank you.

"What have you found?" Gabe asked as he came around the corner, Mal trotting along behind him.

"Mining tools! I wonder if there's an old mine nearby? Should we look?" *North, a quarter of a mile.*

"I'm up for another adventure. Lead the way, Cat." Gabe said with a smile, and Mal dashed out from behind him and started running in their intended direction.

Onnie giggled and chased after the feline. "Wait up!"

The three of them ran among the trees, taking slightly different paths as they laughed. Mal would slither under low branches and relocate to the other side of boulders while Onnie slipped sideways between trees and vaulted over rocks and fallen logs. Gabe was no less effective or graceful, but where the other two left no trace of themselves behind, Gabe left crushed leaves and broken sticks in his wake.

After a good jog, Onnie saw the trees thinning ahead of them, and when she reached the other side, she gasped. She tilted her head back nearly all the way, and her eyes traveled upward at the sight of the mountain looming over her. Most of the rockface was still in its natural state, but portions were sheered off for support beams, cables, and lamps on hooks to be embedded in it. At the mountain's base was a small opening, all three sides braced by wooden beams that looked weathered but stable. A rope was threaded through eye hooks midway up the wall to act as a sort of handrail or guideline.

Gabe slowed to a stop behind her, and his gaze slowly followed the same path hers had.

"Incredible, isn't it?" she said with genuine glee.

"It really is." A grin pulled at Gabe's lips, and Onnie took his free hand and squeezed it.

"We got a problem, love birds," Mal interjected, and Onnie noticed him sitting by the mine entrance.

"Oh." When she looked at him, she giggled, "I see." She turned to get Gabe's attention, which was still focused above them. When he noticed her staring, he finally looked in Mal's direction and groaned.

"Well, shit."

"Yeah," Onnie agreed. "I don't think you'll be going with us after all."

Mal sat beside the entrance, and his size relative to the opening was nearly one-third. Onnie would fit, probably crouched, but there was no way on this earth that Gabe's build would fit through that opening.

"Well, guess we go home cuz you're not going without me," Gabe said, crossing his large arms in front of his broad chest. He'd be intimidating if he weren't so in love with her.

"May I make a suggestion?" Onnie said, putting her palm on Gabe's forearm. "Hear me out."

He nodded, and Mal appeared on his shoulder. "What is it?" Gabe replied.

"You and *my body* stay out here, and Mal and my astral form can go look. If we find a place large enough, I can move us both there. Or, if we don't find anything…exciting…we can leave."

Gabe stared at her, but Mal grinned. "Sounds solid to me, my dude."

"Ug," Gabe groused. "Yeah, it does. Fine."

"Yes!" Onnie said and released his arm. "Where do you feel most comfortable guarding me while you wait?"

Gabe looked around the space and squinted at a small hollow at the mountain's base. He walked over to it, rubbed the stone wall, and then dug the toe of his shoe into the ground. Apparently satisfied, he pointed to the place by his feet, "Here."

"Alright, you got it." Onnie walked over, stood on her tip-toes, and kissed his cheek. "Thank you."

"Mhm," he said as Mal jumped to the ground and returned to the mine entrance.

"Do you need me to do anything specific, Gabe?" Onnie asked as she sat on the soft ground, her back to the mountain.

"Be careful," he said, looking down at her, his eyes gentle.

"Promise. Besides, I'll keep in contact." She shifted a little and laid her hands in her lap comfortably. "Shall we, Mal?"

"Time for a field trip," Mal said, disappearing into the darkened entrance.

Onnie closed her eyes and projected herself just inside the opening and behind Mal.

Lead on, Mal. I assume you can see?

Mostly, but you might wanna pull up the Bond for the walls around us just to double-check me.

On it.

Onnie did as he suggested, and the walls and floor of the tunnel appeared before her eyes. She grinned and wished she could touch the rope that ran along the rock beside her. The natural light was extremely low, and the further they got from the entrance, the darker it got.

This wasn't a half-bad idea. It's so dark that if I were corporeal without the Bond, I'd have scalped myself multiple times by now.

Ew, gross mental image, Mal whined from in front of her.

Focus, Cat, Gabe scolded, but his tone gave away his amusement.

She and Mal continued down the tunnel for nearly twenty minutes before they reached their first branching path. Mal sniffed the air in both directions and suggested they go right.

Why? Onnie asked. *Just curious, not second-guessing you.*

It smells like his lair.

Blegh, Onnie thought.

Can't say I remember its smell, Gabe added.

Lucky, both Mal and Onnie replied at the same time and then laughed.

Gabe sighed. *I was a bit preoccupied the last time....*

It's fine, Gabe, Onnie said and pressed his Bond gently with feelings of peace.

The smell is getting stronger, Mal informed and then abruptly stopped walking. *Onnie, Elaric's body has been down here a long time....*

Onnie's chest warmed at her Link's care and concern for her mental well-being. *I know. Don't worry. I'm prepared.*

If you're sure.

Mal continued down the tunnel, and after another five minutes, they turned left and then made another right. Finally, the shaft opened into an expansive, brightly lit room.

Onnie stepped in a circle, looking above her, her mouth open in awe. *This is....*

Cat? Gabe asked tentatively.

All around the walls of the carved-out cave were scaffolds and walkways built of wooden beams and dug into the rock. Lanterns lined the walls around the paths, and hanging down in the center of the multi-story room was a cluster of lanterns and a large red gemstone at its center. Smaller hallways branched off in all directions, and as the room went up, it became increasingly narrow. Beside each opening and various other places, the stone looked carved with clusters of lines and faded pigment.

Cat.... Gabe growled this time, breaking her ogling.

Sorry, let me come back to get you. Be right back, Mal.

He nodded, and she pulled herself back to her body and opened her eyes. Gabe offered her a hand and dragged her to her feet. She brushed off her backside and grinned.

"I just can't even. You have to see this."

"Alright, let's go," Gabe said, taking one of her hands as she relocated them back inside the mountain.

They appeared right where her astral form had been, and she watched Gabe's face flash through multiple expressions, one after the other. His eyebrows raised in shock, then he squinted at something across the space and grinned. When he continued to wander with his eyes, his brows pinched.

"Question...." he said, releasing her hand and looking down at her. "Any idea who built this mine?"

First Keeper? Thoughts?

A few, but right now, it's not essential. Focus. It's getting late.

Onnie laughed. "Looks like we need to wait for that answer. We should get going."

Gabe raised one eyebrow, and Mal snorted. "Master K, scold you?"

"Nope, but she did remind me we're here for a reason, and Dany will be home soon." Onnie shivered and rubbed her bare arms. "Damn, it's much colder in here."

"It's all the stone. We're pretty far in," Mal said.

Onnie turned to look at all the different path options, and before she could ask which direction they should go, her nose wrinkled.

"Oh, gods, it's so foul." She covered her nose with her free hand and pointed down a hallway with the other. "It's one hundred percent, this direction."

Gabe snorted, seemed unphased by the odor, and kissed her forehead before taking the lead. "Mal, watch the back?"

"Yup," Mal said, stepping behind Onnie as their expedition train of three entered a larger tunnel.

Gabe's body fit fine in the larger space, but Onnie began to shiver more with each step.

We're close, Onnie said to Kushima. *I can feel it.*

Good. We're both anxious for you to be out of there.

Onnie coughed, the foul smell becoming sticky on her tongue. She examined the Bonds around them and saw they were coming to the end of the tunnel and what looked to be the bottom of the well room. Before they stepped into the open room, Gabe stopped and turned to look at her.

"Are you sure you want to see this?" His frown and a gentle squeeze of her upper arm accompanied his feelings of concern.

She nodded, unwilling to open her mouth and let more of the vile air into her lungs. *Yes, but I would like to hurry. This odor...isn't normal.*

I can't smell anything.

Rub it in some more, Mal said from the ground where he was stretched forward, butt in the air, both is paws pressed over his nose.

Seriously, Gabe. I already looked. There's nothing living in that room. Let me pass so I can move him, and we can get out. Hell, I won't even get close . Once I can see any portion of him, I'll relocate him.

She thought Gabe was going to argue, but he stepped aside. "Make it quick. Move the body, then take us home. Got it?"

She nodded vigorously and quickly hurried into the room at the bottom of the well. Elaric was correct. There was a small water basin at the base of the opening, but the water looked like obsidian in its undisturbed stillness. She could see the reflection of the stone shaft above it, and she shivered. On the far side, tucked behind the reservoir on the floor, was Elaric's body. Onnie recognized his base form, and she smiled before immediately regretting it as she started coughing.

Incoming, she warned Kushima before relocating Elaric's body to the back room of the shop, directly in front of the First Keeper's door.

Received. Hurry now, young one.

Done, she said to the guys and then quickly warned, *Hold on, taking us home,* before relocating the three of them onto the deck behind the house.

She ripped her arm from in front of her face and took a deep breath of fresh air but regretted it instantly when she began to vomit on the deck in front of her.

"Onnie!" Mal said, instantly at her side.

Chapter 9: Comforting Relationships

July 2022 - Alku | Onnie Moore

Onnie's stomach rolled a second time as her hands began to shake.

"Cat!" Gabe rushed over and pulled her hair back and away from her sick. "Mal, what's happening?"

"I think it was the air. You really did luck out not being able to smell that." Mal retched but was able to hold back his sick.

"Is that all it was, Cat?" Gabe asked, and Onnie saw him bend over out of the corner of her eye to see her face.

Yeah. Water. Shower, was all she could manage, but it was enough. Gabe scooped her into his arms and carried her into the house. When Dany saw them, she jumped up from the couch in the living room.

"What the hell, when did— Onnie!" Dany shouted and raced over to her.

"She's fine, Dany," Mal answered as he appeared beside her on a small table. "I'll explain, but she threw up. She just needs a shower."

I'm fine—Mal's right. Talk after, Onnie reassured her worried friend as Gabe whisked her away and into the bathroom.

He pushed open the door with his foot and clicked on the light with his elbow. "What do you need, Cat?"

Shower is fine. Put me down. Please?

She felt him fighting his instincts not to let her go, but he did as she asked and set her on her feet. When she proved stable, he released her and moved over to turn the shower on to begin warming up.

"Gabe, I can…do this alone." She felt just a second of hurt along their Bond, and she lowered her eyes as he came over and kissed the top of her head.

"Of course. I'll go talk to Dany and figure out dinner. I know you probably don't feel like food right now, but—"

Onnie gripped one of his hands. "That's perfect. Thank you." When he saw her smile, he looked more relaxed than she'd expected, making her feel better about her reasoning behind pushing him away.

"Alright. Let us know if you need anything." Then he smiled and left, pulling the bathroom door shut behind him.

Onnie waited until she heard the bedroom door close as well, and then she quickly undressed, ignoring the still unpleasant feeling in her stomach.

Kushima, um…can you uh…ask Elaric to close his eyes?

What are you planning? Oh, Kushima chuckled. *Yes.*

Thanks.

Onnie stepped under the water and thoroughly wet her hair. Then she squeezed out as much of it as possible and relocated herself into Abbot's study at the shop. She shivered in the cool air and then frowned at the puddle she was leaving at her feet.

Never thought I'd be hauling corpses around a bookstore in my birthday suit.

Kushima exploded into laughter, and Onnie couldn't help but grin along with her as she ran to the door leading into the library and opened it as wide as it would go. Then she returned to Elaric's body and was relieved that their hypothesis had been correct. His body showed no signs of decay, rigor mortis, or blood loss. He just looked happily asleep.

Onnie relocated him as close as she could to the doorway, and then she grabbed both his wrists and began pulling him into the library.

"Good gods! Why does it have to be so fucking cold in here!" she hissed as the void-chilled stones hit her bare feet and the frigid air accosted her wet, naked skin. "You better have your eyes closed, Elaric. I swear."

Elaric's laughter was as abrupt as Kushima's, and the two of them filled the silence while Onnie struggled to pull Elaric a few more feet past the doorway. When he was far enough that she could close the door, she gently placed his arms on the floor and began switching feet in place while rubbing her arms.

"Okay, I'm out. I'll be back tonight, hopefully."

Take your time, he struggled to say through another laugh, and for the second time, Onnie hoped spirits and bookshops could turn around.

And, Keeper...thank you again.

"Oy, shush you," she stated, waving him off as she ran to the door. "Toodles!"

The moment she closed the door, she relocated back into the shower and underneath the warm water. The drastic difference in temperature burned her now thoroughly frozen body, and her teeth began to clatter. She was only in the shower for a minute before she heard a soft knock on the door.

"Onnie, it's me," Dany said from the bedroom. "Can I come in?"

Onnie clenched her jaw and tried to stop her uncontrollable shivering before Dany saw the oddity and asked questions. "Come in," she said, nearly biting her tongue.

The bathroom door opened and then closed, and Onnie could see Dany's feet as she sat on the edge of the bathtub. Thankfully, the shower wall blocked each other's view, which gave Onnie a chance to get her body under control.

"Mal told me what you guys did," Dany's voice said softly, and Onnie's continued teeth chattering kept her from responding. "Why... why did you go without me?"

It wasn't that they had gone without Dany in order to exclude her. It was more that Onnie knew Elaric wouldn't have wanted her to go through that. It was the same reason she hadn't asked Marco to assist her. Instead, she asked for Gabe and Mal's help. Unfortunately, while

Onnie was trying to figure out how to explain that and didn't answer immediately, Dany took her silence inaccurately.

"Is it because I would have been dead weight? I know I don't have magic or anything, and I don't have Gabe's muscle—"

"Stop it," Onnie cut her off and quickly turned off the taps, her chill forgotten. She grabbed a towel from outside the shower, quickly wrapped herself in it, and stopped in front of Dany. "I don't want to hear that. Ever."

Dany didn't look up at her, and Onnie sighed but then giggled and squished her wet body against Dany's dry one in a hug.

"You deserve a wet hug."

As she'd expected, Dany laughed back and wrapped her arms around Onnie's shoulders.

"Dany, you are the furthest thing from dead weight. Leaving aside your status as a Sister, look at your physical capabilities. You're right. You don't look jacked like Gabe, but Dany…you're just as capable as he is, and where we've needed you and likely will again in the future, I wouldn't think twice about having you at my back."

Dany sniffled, mostly, but there was a small laugh within it, and Onnie released her, a wet splotch down her friend's side. She sat on the bathtub's edge beside her but refrained from sharing her shower water any further.

"Really, Dany. Please don't ever think that again. The only reason I didn't ask you to come with us was that I didn't want to get your hopes up. Or…for you to see anything you don't need to build a memory off of."

Dany nodded and looked up. "Mal said he didn't know the uh… state of his body."

"No, I moved him too quickly. It's where it belongs now, and everything is fine. It showed no signs of…nefarious activity or anything similar."

Dany sniffled again. "Thank you."

"Of course, I'm glad I was able to help." Onnie rested her head on Dany's shoulder and smiled.

Almost, she thought to Kushima. *I can almost take all the pain she's feeling from her.*

Oh, young one. I think I speak for Dany when I say it's not your pain to take.

I'm going to do it anyway.

Kushima sighed, but Onnie ignored it. She lifted her head and pushed herself away from the bathtub.

"Alright, let me get dressed, and we can eat."

Dany rubbed her face and got to her feet. "Okay, I'll meet you out there then."

She quickly slipped from the bathroom, and Onnie hastily dressed and braided her hair to the side. After being sick, her teeth felt gross, so she brushed them and followed Dany into the kitchen.

"How are you feeling, Cat?" Gabe asked, getting up from the dining table, pulling her into his arms, and kissing her forehead.

"Better. Thank you," she reached up and gave him a quick peck on the lips before going to make some tea. The kettle was already heating up, and she looked over her shoulder and saw Dany shrug.

"Figured you might want some."

Onnie crossed the kitchen, wrapped her arms around Dany's waist, one side still damp, and buried her face in the woman's deep blue-black hair. "Thanks, Dany."

"Duh," Dany hugged her back and gave her a soft squeeze. "Do you know what made you sick?"

"Had to be the air," Mal said from the counter, where he gagged again.

"Yeah...Mal's right."

Gabe frowned. "I wonder why I couldn't smell it."

Onnie extricated herself from Dany and dealt with the now attention-seeking kettle.

"Whatever it was, it probably had something to do with what was behind the last door in the mountain that I skipped."

"What?" Gabe said sharply, and Onnie saw Dany flinch.

Onnie flicked her gaze to Dany, whose eyes were staring at the floor. "Sorry...I...well, a lot happened that day, but before I brought Ana home, the First Keeper and I quickly looked around his base."

Dany shivered, and then she clenched her fists at her sides.

"Dany, do you want me to—"

"No. It's fine. I'm fine."

Dany swallowed roughly and went to sit at the dining table. She'd boiled a whole kettle, so Onnie started making Dany a cup of her favorite tea before continuing.

"Long story short, there was one room where when I touched the door, the First Keeper and I both felt...gross."

"Gross," Gabe said with a slight smirk on his lips.

She delivered Dany her tea and took the chair beside her to drink her own.

"Yes. We both decided to leave it be."

It was Onnie's turn to shiver, and Kushima laughed. *I agree.*

"Master K, have any ideas?" Mal asked and then jumped up to sit on Dany's lap. Dany sniggered at his nickname and softly ran her palm down the feline's back. "What is she, a breakfast cereal?"

"Packed with stuff to make your brain grow big and strong," Mal teased.

Do you? Onnie asked Kushima while they both tried not to laugh at Mal and give the sass the satisfaction of it.

Yes, but I do not think it is a conversation for this audience, especially at the present moment.

"She's told me nothing," Onnie stated honestly.

"Well, that's frightening," Dany mumbled.

"Can't disagree," Gabe added, leaning back in his chair and crossing his arms. Worry lined his brows while sadness and grief marred his sister's.

The four of them sat for a while, each in their heads, until Onnie's stomach growled so loudly that they all looked at her before bursting into laughs.

"Well, then," Onnie said with a blush.

"Message received," Gabe snickered, getting to his feet and kissing her cheek before stopping in front of Dany. "Help me with dinner?"

Much to Onnie's relief, Dany smiled and nodded before taking the hand he'd held out to her, and Mal relocated off somewhere without a word.

"Sure."

"I think I'll lay down while you cook if that's alright? Still a bit...blegh." Onnie's earlier revisitation of her lunch had made her feel weak and shaky, but she needed to get it under control before she returned to the shop later.

Perhaps the cause was dragging a corpse, not the upset digestion, Kushima sassed, catching Onnie off guard enough that she nearly choked on her last sip of tea.

"Cat?"

Onnie waved her hand as she coughed up the liquid and managed to squeak out, "Fine. Swallowed wrong."

"Go rest. We'll come to get you when it's ready," Dany said, taking Onnie's empty teacup and shooing her out of the kitchen.

You are spending far too much time with Elaric, Onnie teased while she made her way to her bedroom.

She felt Kushima's fondness for Elaric rush through their Bond. *He found that quite amusing.*

Onnie softly closed the bedroom door and ungracefully flopped onto her bed's fluffy blankets and pillows. Once snuggled into them adequately enough, she closed her eyes and entered the void. When she was there and saw herself, she projected the couch from Abbot's study into the void again and sank into it.

Hello, young one. I thought you were to be resting?

Onnie smirked but glared up at the void—*Hush you.*

What's weighing on you, Onnie?

Is Elaric alright? I'm sorry I had to just drop his body in there. At the very least, it must be...odd to see it.

Kushima was quiet for a moment before responding. *He said for you not to worry,* she laughed softly. *He said he's rarely in his base form, and part of him doesn't associate it with his own body.*

...I can't even comprehend that, Onnie giggled.

I assume he feels much like I did when you first summoned me into the library.

Onnie's giggles stopped, and she sat up stiffly. *Wait, why?*

It had been thousands of years since I'd seen myself, and the age I manifest as is not the age at which I became what I am now.

Oh, I guess I'd never thought about that. I wonder why, then.

I imagine because that is what I looked like when I was made the Keeper, not the entity. Perhaps whatever I was becoming had frozen me at that age.

Onnie flopped back onto the couch, and her forehead creased as her mind raced in a thousand directions. It wasn't long until she heard Mal calling her for dinner from somewhere near her body.

I'm going to eat your portion.

Brat, Onnie said with a grin and then got up from the void couch.

Enjoy your meal, young one. Eat well. You will need the sustenance for this evening.

Agreed. Tonight, we put things back where they belong.

Kushima's warmth spread through Onnie. She opened her eyes in her room and found Mal sitting on her chest, his eyes reflecting in the darkness.

"Talking to the First Keeper?"

"Yeah. Food ready?" Onnie said, scratching Mal before gently nudging him off her so she could sit up.

"It is. Let's go."

Onnie's stomach growled again, and they returned to the kitchen, giggling together at her vocal tummy.

Elaric Rickson

Elaric couldn't help but stare at his soul-less body on the First Keeper's floor. With his soul integrated into the room itself, it was like he was watching a security camera feed of the room nonstop, without blinking.

What's on your mind, young one? the First Keeper's now familiar voice asked along their connected Bond.

Nothing specific, mostly my mind was wandering.

He heard the First Keeper's delicate laugh, which reminded Elaric of another woman from his past. *Yes, that's a pretty common occurrence for mine as well.*

Is this what it's like for you? The unending view into the shop.

Partly. While you are limited to seeing within this room, I can see the entirety of the shop—even the rooms and segments within stasis. I can also hear what Onnie does, and if I choose to, I can speak with her and Mal. But in general, yes. This is my every day, if you can call them that at this point.

Would it be too intrusive of me to ask...are you okay like this?

Elaric waited when the First Keeper did not answer him, and he became concerned he'd overstepped, but he'd grown fond of her and was starting to tell what the subtle changes in her voice implied. Before he was able to apologize, though, she finally spoke.

Indeed, it matters not. However, I can say the time I have spent with Onnie and you other young ones has been the most fulfilling in all my many years, whether human or entity.

I'm relieved, Elaric said genuinely. *If...if Onnie—no,* Elaric laughed, *When Onnie returns me to my body, I will still be connected to you, correct?*

I believe so.

Is that alright with you?

Elaric, I would not have allowed her to do this, were it not. As I've told her, while you've only recently met me, I have known you and Marco for a long time. I had no hesitation in allowing her to do this.

I thank you for that, then. Do you know if we'll still be able to talk? Elaric snorted. *Like this, I mean, not just me shouting at the ceiling.*

I am unsure. However, I would be surprised if we were not. I would actually like to make a request of you if that's alright.

The First Keeper's voice was filled with a smile, and he knew whatever she would ask of him wasn't something to be taken lightly.

Anything.

The First Keeper sighed, and Elaric heard when discomfort infected her voice and pushed aside the contentment.

I am not infallible, and I seem to have overlooked something when I created Mal as her companion.

A filter?

That, too, and a stomach with a bottom. They laughed together at the statement of fact. *Along that line of thought, though, I overlooked Onnie's unending dedication and...unbreakable focus.*

Well, that's an understatement. That woman is worse than Dany when she latches on to something.

All too true, and together, they will undoubtedly drive us all mad.

Can't help but agree, but I'm sorry I keep interrupting.

It's no problem. I enjoy our conversations and am in no rush to end it. Related to that, I'd like to ask if you'd be willing to assist Onnie in caring for the shop.

Oh, well...that's not what I expected. May I ask why? Wait...Mal. Got it.

Precisely. While Onnie need not work every day, and for the most part, she doesn't, she truly has no one on whom to rely when she's ill, out of Alku, or simply needs a day of rest. While the others can assist in rudimentary ways, none can communicate with me, and relying on Mal for an interface isn't always an option, especially when Outsiders are involved.

Understood, and I'd be honored. I assume you'll both want me to keep my ability to talk to you private, though.

At least for now. While we both trust you implicitly, without the traditional Keeper, Guardian, and Link elements, you would be made vulnerable if anyone were to learn of the capability.

Not to mention you and Onnie, Elaric agreed

Also, correct.

You have my word. Though I warn you, I'll try, but I'm sure Marco will eventually figure it out.

Understandable, she laughed softly, *and you are correct, once again. He'll likely notice sooner rather than later. Thank you, young one.*

Elaric chuckled. *It still feels strange to have someone call me that.*

Compared to me, you are.

Fair. Even to Marco, I'm basically a child. Not to mention Stephan.

Elaric would have sworn he could feel the First Keeper's amusement at his remarks.

I believe they are the only two beings within Alku who would be able to address me as the young one.

Did you know either of them from your time before being Keeper?

I did, both of them, though unrelated to one another. I don't believe Marco had met Stephan at that point.

Elaric hadn't really thought about it, but he knew Stephan had brought Marco to Alku nearly a thousand years before. After the angels had given Marco's second father his true death. Elaric had never asked *how* Stephan knew to find Marco.

Did I say something that alarmed you?

Ah, no. Sorry. I realized that I never learned how Stephan had known to find Marco and bring him to Alku. I'd always thought they were strangers until that point.

Apologies, let me clarify. Marco hadn't met Stephan yet...but Stephan knew of Marco.

Are you comfortable telling me how?

I think that is a question better asked of Stephan. However, I will tell you this. Marco's life has been long, and only recently was it...healthy, but information about his struggles was not kept within his blood family.

Elaric sighed. *Yeah, I know about some of it. I don't think Marco knows I'm aware of it, though. If he knew I did....*

I can't help but agree, and I, too, think he would change his behavior. Not because you'd actually think differently of him, but because he would assume that you would.

You have known him for a long time, Elaric said fondly of the complicated and fragile sanguiste. *I will admit I'm once more thankful to*

Onnie. I'd pretty much given up on ever seeing Marco drop his mask around anyone but me.

Yes, she seems to have that effect on people. You, too, have changed since returning to Alku, young one.

Elaric groaned. *It's probably a stupid question, but how much do you know about my past?*

Enough that I will say this and nothing more. I will always be here if you need me. I'll also extend that to Onnie on her behalf because if I didn't, she'd lecture me.

Even though Elaric wanted to shrink into nothing, he couldn't curb the laugh the First Keeper had freed from him.

She probably would. I remember when Gabe told me not to call her Keeper. Said she had an entire speech about the subject.

She does. I've received it. The First Keeper's statements were clipped but full of restrained amusement.

Really? That's...somehow unsurprising.

It certainly surprised me at that moment, the First Keeper giggled. *I don't think I'd been that taken aback in a few centuries, if not longer.*

I can imagine. All three of them, Dany and Gabe included, often say things that catch me off guard.

They do.

Elaric hesitated. *So, can I assume that you know the true origins of my kind?*

I do.

Right. Okay.

Does that make you uncomfortable?

Not exactly, Elaric said honestly.

While I cannot say for sure, I believe Stephan may also, but beyond him and myself, no one else in Alku does.

Elaric was quiet, and he must have worried the First Keeper, for she eventually spoke, though her voice was tentative and careful.

Elaric, Abbot considered you one of his own, and while he was unaware of the specifics, he always felt that you were concealing yourself from others.

I was. Am.

I am not saying you should say anything to anyone. However, I'd like to ask you a question.

…Sure.

You agreed that if Marco knew what you knew of his past, he'd assume you thought less of him, but you do not, correct?

Of course not.

Then, do you honestly believe if you were to tell Marco or Onnie the truth, they would love you any less?

Elaric thought back to when Onnie had manifested him the night before and the look on both of their faces when they saw him. The grief, relief, and unwavering devotion. He'd expected it from Marco, but Onnie's had shocked him.

I do not.

This time, he knew what he'd felt was the First Keeper's warmth as it washed over him.

I'm glad, for they would not. You have my word that unless it were imperative and there were no different options, I will not speak of it to Onnie or anyone else. But I think you should remember your answer. Maybe one day, you'll feel safe to speak of it with them.

I understand. Thank you.

The First Keeper laughed softly. *Besides, were it ever to become an issue, you could always remind Onnie of her nude body-dragging escapades.*

Elaric snorted. *She never ceases to entertain me with her thoughts and actions.*

Nor I, young one. Nor I.

Together, he and the First Keeper spent the evening waiting for Onnie and Marco as they laughed at the strange and remarkable woman who was their Keeper. More importantly, though, she was Onnie.

Chapter 10: Back in Place

July 2022 - Alku | Onnie Moore

Onnie relocated herself and Marco into Abbot's study, where she immediately stepped into a puddle of water.

"Damn."

She grabbed a towel from the trunk and began to dry the floor while Marco looked down at her, his hands in his pockets and one eyebrow raised.

"Don't ask," Onnie snapped before quickly adding, "And if you ask Elaric, I will hunt you both down until the day I die."

Marco's eyes widened, and then he erupted in laughter. When Kushima joined him, Onnie looked at the ceiling and glared. "Hush you. I don't wanna hear you laughing either."

"Can I at least assist in cleaning up this…unmentionable water?" Marco offered with a grin.

Onnie got to her feet, chucked the towel into the last puddle, and quickly smeared it around with her foot.

"There," she dusted her palms off, "done." She strode over to the door and grabbed the handle but hesitated. "Ah, Marco," she said, turning around, shifting her tone from grumbling and playful to careful and concerned. "Don't forget, his body looks unharmed. Like he's sleeping, but…."

"Onnie," Marco said, walking to her side and resting his palm on her shoulder. "I'm fine. I promise. You've proven I can trust you—he and I both can. Thank you for the warning, though."

She smiled, her ears warming a little. "Yeah. You're welcome. Oh, and Elaric's clothes, um, they reek of the air in the mountain. Hopefully, it's dissipated a little, but I warn you, it made me physically ill earlier."

Marco frowned but nodded. "Alright."

"Okay, let's go."

She began to heave the heavy door towards herself when Marco grabbed the loop beside her hand and smiled down at her.

"It's about time I do something helpful, isn't it? Even if it's only opening an obnoxiously heavy door." He chuckled, and she couldn't help but do the same.

"I'll take you up on that offer." She stepped back and out of the way while Marco easily pulled the door open. "Besides," she said, entering the room and gesturing at Elaric's body on the floor a foot from the door, "I've got another thing you could move for me."

Marco shut the door behind them, and she saw his eyes follow the water trail that ended beside Elaric's dry body. The touch of a smile crept into his lips.

"I must admit, I *really* want to ask about the water."

Onnie growled and narrowed her eyes at him. "Just move him, please."

She pointed to a table in the center of the room and left Marco to the heavy lifting while she cleared off the long rectangular table for him to rest Elaric on. Once it was clear, she stood mostly out of the way.

"Give me a minute," she requested while he settled Elaric. She then closed her eyes to bring Kushima and Elaric's manifested forms into the room. When she looked at Elaric, he pointedly averted his gaze away from her.

"Just tell me they were closed, and I'll believe you." Elaric snorted in response, and Onnie rolled her eyes. "Great."

She walked over to Kushima and raised her hand for the First Keeper to mirror with her own as they said hello in their own unique way.

"He didn't close them, did he?"

This time, Kushima laughed, and Onnie glanced back to Elaric.

"I swear, you tell anyone I was naked dragging your corpse around my shop, and I will stick you back in that rock!" she pointed to the ceiling.

Marco's explosion of laughter caught her off guard, and Onnie groaned, her face flushing red.

"Shit, I forgot you were here." She covered her face and sighed. "Fine. Laugh, all of you." She stuck her tongue out at them, plopped into a chair, and crossed her arms defiantly.

Elaric smiled before kneeling in front of her. *For what it's worth, I tried to pay more attention to my own body than yours, but you've seen all my forms, so maybe now we're even.* He winked, and she couldn't disagree, considering that he was right.

"Ug, fine."

She scrutinized Marco, who forced a straight face and then quickly returned to examining Elaric's body when he struggled to keep the blank expression in place. A slow smile crept into his features, and she gave up.

"Fine, I'll admit. It was funny. Fucking freezing but entertaining, I'm sure."

Once again, I can say that you've shown me something I haven't seen in all my long years. Kushima grinned, *Between you and Dany, you ladies never cease to amaze me.*

"Oy!" Onnie said with a smile.

Elaric got to his feet and went to Marco's side the latter, who was still struggling not to laugh aloud. That said, if her embarrassment helped him laugh more, she'd do it again. Onnie could tell the two men were talking between themselves, and she felt herself smiling as she watched them.

Still envious, young one? Kushima asked as she sat in a chair beside Onnie's.

I am, but, she looked at Kushima, *I have you.*

Indeed you do. Don't forget what I said, though. You'll find your soul's mate.

Onnie looked back at the two men and was glad she could give this back to them.

"Oh," Onnie got to her feet. "Sorry, can I interrupt?"

Marco and Elaric turned to look at her, and Marco nodded. "Of course."

What's up? Elaric asked.

"Erm…would it be rude of me to ask if you could show me the blood link?"

"Oh," Marco looked at Elaric. "That's a question for you. I have zero issues with Onnie seeing my crest."

Sure, Marco can show you where it is.

"Was that a rude question?"

She walked to the opposite side of the table from the men, and Kushima followed along beside her.

"To us?" Marco shook his head. "No. Other sanguiste…depends. Just be careful. The subject is thought to be rather…."

"Personal?" she answered.

Intimate, Elaric clarified.

Onnie winced. "Shit, sorry. Thank you for the advice, Marco, and the permission, too."

"Of course." Marco pulled Elaric's clothing aside, and Onnie gasped.

"May I look closer?" she asked Elaric, who nodded. She bent nearer to Elaric's hip and squinted. "Wow, it really is a sort of tattoo. First Keeper, have you ever seen one before?"

Another first. Thank you, Kushima added to the pair, who beamed.

"One more thing about blood links, Onnie," Marco said.

She glanced up at him but stood up and gave him her full attention once she saw his expression. "What is it?"

Marco's eyes flicked to Elaric and then back to her. "Even the concept of a blood link is a highly guarded secret. It is protected and rarely discussed outside of sanguiste kind and those they link with. As far as I know, it's never been written down for fear of it ending up...well, here."

"Ah," Onnie nodded. "Keep my mouth shut. Got it."

Elaric laughed and shook his head, but Marco nodded more seriously. "I just ask you to be careful. I'll not have you at risk because of us."

She smiled and crossed her arms. "Marco, of all the things that put me at risk, do you honestly believe that knowing this information is anywhere near the top of that list?"

He didn't hesitate, and both he and Elaric snapped, *"Yes."*

Onnie swallowed and glanced at Kushima, who wore a similar expression to theirs and nodded. *Do not take this lightly, young one. Sanguiste are highly secretive creatures.*

Onnie sighed and then nodded. "Alright. I hear you. Thank you for the warning."

"Thank you for taking it seriously, Keeper," Marco said.

With their warning received, Onnie bent over to get closer to the mark again. "Let me see what I can find out about this then."

Marco and Elaric stayed quiet while she refocused on her examination.

"Hm," Onnie muttered, tilting her head to see the skin and ink in a different light. "Give me a sec."

She closed her eyes and saw what she'd hoped she would. The scarred wound that had been filled with Marco's blood swam with his Bond just beneath the skin's surface. It swirled and flickered, almost as if it were alive and trapped within Elaric.

"What is it?" Marco asked.

She opened her eyes but didn't look away from the mark, gently touching the surface of Elaric's skin with the tip of her finger.

"Marco, can you get me the athame from the shelf over there?" she pointed to her left and saw his aura shift colors from the corner of her eye. "Don't worry, I just need to make a pin-prick, and Elaric won't feel it. I promise it won't even bleed."

It's fine, Marco, Elaric reassured him.

When Marco left to do what she asked, Onnie closed her eyes again and refocused on the mark.

"It's brilliant. Marco, your crest is…saturated with your Bond. I wonder what it looked like prior to Elaric activating it?"

"No idea. I doubt there's ever been another person who could view or manipulate the Bond such as you can, let alone with the opportunity to examine one."

Onnie felt Marco slide the knife's handle into her awaiting palm.

"Thank you. Perhaps after all of this is over, you'd assist me with some research on the subject?" she asked while carefully using her left hand to pull the skin at the center of the mark taught.

"Perhaps," Marco replied, his voice growing more tense as the knife neared Elaric.

Onnie used the very tip of the extremely sharp blade to pierce the top few layers of skin, ensuring she only pierced to the same depth as the blood mark. When she removed the knife, she jumped back and opened her eyes but left her view of the Bond overlaying the world. Marco hissed and clutched his chest, and Elaric's form flickered like a candle flame in a breeze. Even Kushima looked at Onnie and raised one eyebrow.

"Sorry, I didn't expect it to be that…intense," she chuffed.

"And, what was *it?*" Marco asked, taking a deep breath.

Onnie looked back at the mark and saw that the Bond trapped under Elaric's skin had emerged from his body and split off into two directions—one towards Marco and the second towards the stone embedded in the ceiling above them.

"Simply put, I freed a piece of Marco's Bond from within the tattoo, which then reconnected to both of you—at a soul level."

Marco looked at Elaric and then back to Onnie. "I assume that's a good thing?"

"Honestly, not sure, but I think it may be temporary."

Elaric tilted his head, his brow creasing. *Why?*

"I think once the skin heals, it will block the Bond again. Part of why I asked to do some tests. Without much information or understanding of this whole blood link process, I'm frankly just guessing."

Keeper, Kushima said and pointed to the mark.

Onnie's eyes went wide. "Holy shit, well, that answered that question."

"What?" Marco asked, concerned.

"Everything's fine, but I was right, and thanks to Marco's sanguiste blood, look at the incision." She pointed to the mark, and Marco leaned over to examine it more closely.

"It's already healed." He looked up at Onnie, "Did the Bond disconnect again?"

"Yup. Apparently, it's not as jarring as when it reconnected since neither of you felt it."

Marco began to pace the room, and Onnie leaned in to take another look at the mark.

Kushima, what do you think about using their mark as a sort of entrance point for Elaric's soul?

Meaning?

I'm not quite sure, but I need somewhere to tether it from within the stone since I don't think I can physically replace his soul within his body.

Interesting. I think it would be possible.

"Hey, Marco," Onnie said, standing back up and interrupting his pacing. "Elaric, I want to do that one more time. I might know how to use it to our advantage. Marco, if I'm right, I'll need your help."

"Of course." Marco nodded and returned to the side of the table. "Just tell me what you need."

"Elaric, you fine with me doing it again?"

Do what you need. Then, he focused on Marco. *Was the pain a lot? Are you alright with it?*

Marco smiled and shook his head. "It wasn't painful," he inclined his head to Onnie. "Please, continue."

"Got it. I won't open my eyes until it's healed, so keep an eye out, alright?"

"Sure," Marco answered.

"Perfect." She knelt by the table to be at eye level with the mark again. "It doesn't look any different from before."

"That's good. I assume." Marco said.

She closed her eyes and inspected the trapped portion of the Bond. *I was wondering if there would be less of something after it healed,* Onnie said to only Kushima.

From what I can tell, that does not appear to be the case.

Agreed.

Onnie carefully reopened her eyes and made the small incision a second time, not yet removing the tip of the blade. "Ready?"

"Yes."

Yes.

She shut her eyes and lifted the athame, watching as the Bond within burst forth once again. This time, she continued to watch the wound and ignored everything else. After a few minutes, she observed the skin begin to knit itself back together.

"You're skin's healing," she said, watching as the Bond within the mark broke from the two souls and retracted back within the skin as it closed.

"Yes!" she cheered, opening her eyes and doing a little happy dance in place. "I was right!"

Kushima chuckled, and Marco smirked, one eyebrow raised in amusement.

"Sorry," she said, settling down. "When the wound heals, your skin doesn't sever the Bond thread. It detaches itself and then returns to within the mark."

Oh, I see where you're going with this. Elaric grinned.

"Exactly. If I can weave your soul into that portion of Bond...."

Marco snorted. "When it heals, it will do the work of connecting it to his body for you." He shook his head. "Honestly, Keeper. How is it that you still surprise me?"

"Pft, you? Shocked myself!" she laughed. "Alright." Onnie cleared her throat and tried to be more serious when she looked at Marco. "Can I ask you to make a thermos of tea again?"

"Sure."

"Thank you."

Next, Onnie wiggled her fingers at Elaric. "You. We need to talk about what happens if we manage to pull this off."

Elaric's eyes widened, and she laughed.

"I just want to talk about...." Onnie's eyes flicked to Marco briefly, but before she could continue, he gave a slight bow and left to brew her tea. "Sorry, I want to talk about Dany for a quick second."

Elaric's smile softened. *Understood, though for future reference, Marco doesn't feel awkward, so neither should you.*

"Shit, was that how it came across?" Onnie sighed. "I'll apologize. I just wanted to talk about your base form. I don't think you should use it until we've dealt with the rogue guardian. Since your body was in this form when I found it, I assume he also saw it."

A wise assumption, Kushima said at her side.

Will I have my other forms back?

"I'm unsure, but if you don't, I suggest you stay in Marco's apartment until I can take you out of town to find a different solution."

Agreed. What's the part about Dany?

"I've still not told her anything. She thinks I buried your body today. Can I please, as her friend and yours, ask you to wait until you have a safe form and we know you're stable to go see her?"

You needn't ask. Of course, I promise.

"Thank you, Elaric." Onnie shivered as the draft from the library door blew over her skin as Marco returned with her thermos.

"Ug, you're amazing. Thank you." She quickly poured a cup, which was drinkable in less than a minute due to the void's chill, and then knocked back the full cap in one shot.

"Have you decided how to do this?" Marco asked, settling into a nearby chair.

Onnie nodded and poured herself a second serving of tea. "Yeah,

I'd like it if you could help me, Marco. I need you to ensure the wound doesn't heal before I've completely connected his soul."

"How do you suggest I do that?"

"Honestly, I'm not sure. Everything I can think of is..." she grimaced, "a bit gross."

Elaric and Kushima tittered at her squeamishness.

"Hmm...."

Marco closed his eyes and tipped his head back, his dark hair falling behind him. From where she sat, Onnie could see his full neck, and something bothered her. She squinted and examined his aura, noticing it seemed duller than she remembered.

Elaric, is he alright?

Elaric looked at her and then quickly over at Marco, who didn't notice the silent movements or exchanges occurring around him.

What do you mean?

I don't know. His aura is just...less?

Elaric closed his eyes and mentally sighed. *Fuck. I bet he hasn't been eating.*

Anything I can do?

If I don't get my body back, I'll answer that. Fair?

More than. Thank you.

After that, Elaric seemed to watch Marco more carefully while the sanguiste spent time thinking, and she drank more of her tea. Once Onnie's fingers were less frozen and she felt more focused and less sleep-fogged, she set her cup down.

"Okay, you ready, Marco?"

"Yeah." He glanced at Elaric, "Let me run this idea past E. You're right. You don't need to know, especially since your eyes will be closed."

"Fine with me. As long as you keep it from healing, I don't need or want to know. Blegh."

While the two men spoke, Onnie swiveled to face Kushima. *What are you thinking?*

I think your plan is sound. Provided there's nothing unexpected.

Onnie rolled her eyes. *Hey, don't jinx it.*

Kushima smirked. *You'll be fine. You can do this, Keeper.*

Onnie held up her hand so Kushima could place their palms together. *I haven't gotten to talk to you about all of this very much. Are you sure you're okay with this? I mean, Elaric will be connected to you pretty much forever now.*

You're asking me this now?

Onnie winced.

None of that. I was teasing you. Yes, I would have spoken up long before now if I wasn't. Though Elaric has only recently met me, I have known him for many decades and Marco for millenniums. They are honorable beings, and I am glad to be of assistance.

Thank you, Kushima. Onnie lowered her palm as Marco cleared his throat.

"Ready?" he asked when she turned to look at him.

"Let's do it," she grinned.

Onnie wasn't sure how much time had passed, but she was absolutely running short on energy.

Deep breath, young one, Kushima consoled. *You're nearly finished.*

Onnie inwardly groaned but continued interweaving the fibers of Elaric's soul with the threads from the blood link. Each thread she picked through that was associated with a form Elaric had collected would shimmer as a projection of the individual and would appear in front of her within the void. After seeing the first few and realizing they would all be naked, Onnie had begun ignoring them entirely. Once the thread she was working with was integrated, the form would blink out of being, and she'd be alone once more.

She was nearly finished, with only a few left, when she felt her focus slip.

"Onnie," Marco said sharply.

Sorry, almost finished. Thank you. Keep me focused.

Marco didn't say anything else, or if he did, she didn't register it.

She held on to three fibers, the last of the bunch. It took her another fifteen minutes to mesh the fibers together into one, which was far longer than it had taken her at the beginning when she was full of energy. When the last piece was attached, she went back and checked over every single thread and connection point individually.

"I think…I think I'm finished," she said aloud without leaving the void.

"What do you need me to do?" Marco asked.

"Elaric, when Marco allows the wound to close, I think you'll have roughly three minutes before it heals. What I suspect will happen is you'll feel like you're being yanked and probably be a little disorientated, but my hope is you'll be where you belong after that."

Alright.

"I'm fairly confident this will work, but if you…need to say anything to Marco…do it now."

Marco's breath caught, but Onnie heard nothing from either of them for over a minute. Then Marco cleared his throat.

"Alright, we're ready, Keeper."

Kushima, ready?

I am. Proceed when you're comfortable.

"Marco. Let the wound close."

Onnie watched his Bond as he retreated from Elaric's body, and when he stepped back, his aura nearly blinded her with fear. It felt like time slowed to a crawl, and three minutes took days. Right before the time ran out, Elaric spoke only to her.

Either way that this ends, please know how grateful I am to you and the First Keeper.

Before Onnie could reply, she watched the new Bond connection shift, indicating that the wound was closing. As before, the blood link's Bond separated from Marco, but this time, instead of gradually receding from Elaric's, it snapped like a rubber band, pulling his now tethered Bond along with it. The result was similar to how she hid the souls of the roaches within her own Bond in the past.

Marco must have been watching the clock because although he shouldn't have felt a change, he became statuesque. Onnie examined the Bond within the mark and was relieved to find it was now a mix of the two men's Bonds, not solely Marco's. When she examined it, she saw a single Bond running from where they'd pierced the skin to Elaric's soul within the stone hidden among the flames.

Well done, young one.

Onnie opened her eyes, and when she saw Elaric's chest rise and fall, breath entering his lungs, she looked at Marco and nodded once.

"It...it worked?" he asked, unblinking—his eyes dilated and frightened.

"I believe so, but I'm sure it will take some time for his body to readjust."

Marco inhaled a shuttering breath and finally broke his eye contact with Elaric's body.

Onnie stood and stumbled, her knees buckling before she hit the edge of the table with her hip.

"Onnie!" Marco rushed to her side, catching her before she hit the floor.

"I'm sorry. Just...drained. We need to hurry. I'm not sure how much longer...."

Marco settled her back into her chair and ensured she was stable before hurrying to Elaric.

"Understood. Can you manage to get us and then yourself home? Or should I call Gabe?"

Kushima answered for Onnie. *I think she can make it, but she's right, you need to hurry. I'm keeping her conscious, but it won't work for long.*

Marco quickly picked up Elaric's body and carried him out of the room before returning to lift Onnie into his arms.

"Thank you, First Keeper." Before they reached the door, he asked, "May I come to visit with you again?"

Please do. For now, live well, Marco.

Marco carried Onnie through the door and pushed it closed with his foot. Then he set her on the couch next to Elaric.

"What do you need?"

Vocalizing, audibly or mentally, felt nearly impossible, so Onnie closed her eyes, hoping Marco understood that he should do the same. A handful of seconds later, she relocated them into his apartment. When she opened her eyes, she saw Elaric safely on their couch and Marco standing between them.

She managed a small, sleepy smile, and without saying goodbye, she relocated herself back to the bedroom hallway at home but didn't make it entirely to her door. Her legs gave way before she reached it, and she fell against the wall, the sound explosive in the silent hour before dawn.

As her eyes fluttered closed and she slid to the floor, she saw Gabe and Dany run from their rooms. Both were terrified, but she couldn't keep herself from smiling as she lost consciousness.

They'll forgive me....

Sleep, daughter of my blood. I'm so proud of you.

Chapter 11: Eye Opening

July 2022 - Alku | Elaric Rickson

Elaric blinked a few times.

His eyelids felt heavy, and the world around him was black. He tried to think back to the last thing he remembered, and when the image of his own body laid atop a table before him rose to the top, his heart rate sped up instantly, and he began to hyperventilate.

First Keeper!

Calm yourself, young one. You are safe.

Elaric took a deep breath, the scent of Marco's barely there cologne more potent than Elaric had ever smelled it before. He blinked again, this time realizing he could see shadows and shapes around him now that he knew what to look for. He was in their room.

Sorry, I thought...I thought I was still without my body.

Understandable. Take your time.

How's Onnie?

Safe.

Good.

As his heart continued to calm down, Elaric tried to sit up, but his body was unusually heavy, and he found it took him more effort than normal to move even his hand. When he couldn't move more than that, he tried harder, but instead of sitting up slowly, his body moved so quickly that he threw himself off of the bed and onto the floor with a thunderous thump.

"E!?" Marco exclaimed, suddenly beside him. His face was contorted with concern, and his aura was blindingly blue and drenched in sadness.

Over Marco's shoulder, even in the near dark, Elaric saw Stephan standing, silhouetted in the doorway, observing Marco. The elder sanguiste's aura was pink, and his unconditional love for Marco was unmistakable. After all the years and many conversations about Marco's aura reading ability, Elaric was thankful he'd paid enough attention to remember what the differing colors and patterns indicated.

"Are you alright?" Marco asked.

Now that his eyes and brain had adjusted to the situation, Elaric couldn't hold it in, and he exploded into laughter. When he felt how much it hurt to breathe that rapidly, he laughed even harder at his body's protests to being used again.

Stephan turned on a small light, and Elaric saw a look of slight amusement on his face, not fear or worry.

"What the hell?" Marco snapped.

"Sor...Sorry," Elaric choked out and took a few deep breaths. "I tried to sit up, and my body wasn't behaving. I tried harder, and...well, I apparently still have the blood link benefits at the moment."

Stephan sniggered, and Marco swiveled to look at him questioningly.

"I'll give you two a few minutes," Stephan said, a warm smile on his face when he looked at Marco. When he met Elaric's eyes instead, Elaric was surprised to see the man's smile brighten further. "It's good to see you, Elaric."

"You too."

He watched Stephan exit the room, pulling the door closed softly behind him. Marco twisted back to look at Elaric, and his panic receded slightly.

"Are you alright?"

"Yes, I'm sorry. I promise I was only trying to sit up. It never occurred to me that the link would still be active." Elaric grinned. "That said, I'm fine. So, stop worrying so brightly."

Marco's brows raised, and as laughter slowly began to bubble from him, the last remaining panic fled his aura. "Aura reading, too, I see."

"Yeah. Help me up? My legs still aren't quite listening, and I don't want to accidentally throw myself through our wall."

Marco smirked as he got to his feet and helped Elaric to his own. "What do you need?"

"Right this second? A shower."

Elaric winced. While it had lessened, he could still smell the foulness from below the well, and it was no surprise considering how long his corpse had been immersed in it. What he deemed worse was that even with Marco's elevated sense of smell, Elaric must have gone partly scent blind from it, as the smell was gross but still bearable.

"Alright. Do you need help?"

Marco carefully released Elaric's arm but quickly recaptured it when he teetered.

"Getting to it, yeah."

They took small steps together, but eventually, Elaric made it to the bathroom and in front of the shower.

"What else can I do?" Marco asked. "I don't want you falling over or slipping."

"You and me both. If you'll help me undress and then get back to the floor, I'd like to sit under the water for a bit."

"Sure."

Marco settled Elaric's palm on the edge of the sink so he could hold on to it while Marco went to warm up the water. Elaric examined himself in the mirror and had expected to see wounds, bruises, or scars from the trauma he'd endured, but all that stared back at him was his base form and unmarred skin. Yes, he'd seen his body when Onnie had retrieved it, and it was fine then, but his mind still expected the worst, apparently.

Marco returned to his side and helped Elaric strip out of his clothes and then get into the shower. As soon as he was sitting under the water and leaning against the wall, Elaric's stiff muscles began to relax, and he smiled.

"So much better. Thank you."

"Of course," Marco said.

"One more thing?" Elaric asked and smirked when Marco rolled his eyes.

"Better be more than one thing, but for now, what is it?"

"Burn my clothes."

Marco's eyes dilated slightly, and his aura flashed blood-red with fury, but he quickly recovered and returned to normal. His reaction made it clear to Elaric that Marco knew the implications of the odor and, as expected, wanted it gone as much as Elaric did.

"Understood. I'll come back to check on you in fifteen?"

"Yes, thank you."

Elaric watched as Marco gathered his discarded clothes and slipped from the room. Once he was gone, Elaric shivered, but not from the cold. The room still smelled of his clothing, and it had become stronger with the addition of steam. He reached over to the shower's corner for a bottle of shampoo. It only took a few seconds of washing his hair for the fragrance of the soap to overwhelm the putrid stench, and his lungs relaxed as his breathing was able to return to normal.

When he finished washing up, Elaric leaned his head against the tile and closed his eyes. Thankfully, the loud shower obscured whatever conversation Marco and Stephan were having in the other room. Elaric already had enough on his mind without accidentally eavesdropping with his borrowed super sanguiste powers.

Elaric had known how much Marco had been suffering—or at least he'd thought he'd known. But after being nearly blinded by the grief his best friend still carried, even now that Elaric was home, he realized how incredibly wrong he'd been. Even worse, it was extremely telling that when Stephan had seen him awake, he seemed happy to see him. No doubt the man probably would have some scolding words later that Elaric would deserve and take.

"E?" Marco said from outside the bathroom door. "Need

anything?"

A time machine to the night Dany was taken, Elaric thought to himself.

Everything happens for a reason, young one. Though I understand what you've all endured has been painful, trust that it was deemed necessary for whatever path the fates have placed before you all.

Elaric sighed but couldn't disagree, no matter how much he'd have liked to.

"I think I'm finished," Elaric called through the door and rested his head back again. "Help me?"

The bathroom door opened, and the draft made Elaric shiver, but Marco closed it quickly and squatted down in front of him, just outside the shower.

"Feeling a bit better?"

Elaric didn't answer right away while he tried to evaluate whether he actually felt any better. He must have taken too long to think about it because the next thing he knew, Marco had snatched his hand and pressed his fingers over Elaric's wrist. It only took a second for Elaric to realize his mistake, and he opened his eyes and smiled at the overwhelmingly terrified man who was now halfway into the shower himself and rapidly becoming soaked by the spray.

"Sorry, I didn't mean to scare you. I was trying to decide if I felt better or not so I could answer you honestly."

Marco groaned, reached up to turn the water off, and leaned forward to rest his forehead against Elaric's wet shoulder.

"It's alright, Marco," Elaric said, rubbing the back of Marco's neck using his free hand.

They stayed like that until chill bumps erupted on Elaric's skin, Marco snapping out of his fear when he saw them. He quickly grabbed both of them towels and then helped Elaric re-dress before changing his own wet clothes. He then led Elaric into the living room and over to the couch. When they'd passed through the bedroom, Elaric hadn't overlooked the missing sheets from the bed, and he'd wager they'd smelled of his clothes, and Marco had taken care of them, too.

Stephan was still in one of the armchairs, and his typical stoicism had returned to his features while he watched Marco fuss over him.

"Are you hungry?" Marco questioned, and Elaric's mouth watered.

"Yes, I am, actually."

Marco turned to Stephan. "Mind staying for a few more—"

"Go. He'll be here when you return." Stephan said, cutting him off, and a small smile crept into Marco's face before he left the apartment.

"He didn't need to do anything special." Elaric shook his head, "Toast would have sufficed."

"Leave him to it. It will do him good to step out for a few moments."

Elaric looked over at the closest thing Marco had to a father in his life and waited for Stephan's lecture.

"Don't be so concerned, Elaric," Stephan smirked. "I'm not angry with you."

"Aren't you?"

Genuine confusion spread through Stephan's aura. "Why would I be? Because Marco suffered?"

Elaric winced at the directness of his statement.

"He did, but that pain is not to be rested upon your shoulders."

"Isn't it?" Elaric stared out of the apartment's single window into the inky black night sky. "I'm the one who made that choice."

"Do you think it was the wrong one?"

"No," Elaric said without hesitation.

"Neither does he."

Elaric closed his eyes and rested his head back on the couch. After a few minutes, and when he was confident his voice wouldn't crack, he re-opened them and forced himself to look at Stephan.

"How bad was it? I only saw portions and only the last few days."

For the first time in their very long relationship, Stephan ran from Elaric. The sanguiste stared down at his hands in his lap and said nothing. He didn't need to.

Elaric nodded once. "Got it."

A few minutes later, Stephan finally spoke. "You know I consider Marco one of my own, and you, by extension, are also family. We all grieved for you, Elaric, but I won't lie to you. The night it happened, and Onnie came here to tell him..." Stephan paused and took a deep breath. "I feared I'd lose both of you that night."

Elaric leaned forward and dropped his head into his hands.

E, I assume you'd be alright with some pasta? Marco asked in Elaric's mind, along their newly strengthened Bond.

Perfect, thank you, Elaric answered and then looked back up at Stephan. "We don't deserve her. Our kind do not deserve her."

Stephan smiled, a fondness in his eyes that he seemed to reserve for family. "A debt I will never be able to repay, I assure you, but one I will spend eternity trying to."

"Did he tell you what she did?"

"He did. She's truly the Keeper of Prophecy, whether or not it has been triggered."

"Couldn't agree more." Elaric sighed. "I just hope at the end of it...."

He couldn't put into words his fear of how the prophecy would end, but he could feel it. Onnie was the *final* Keeper. That could mean many things—anything, but most of them were not outcomes he wanted for the precious woman and friend.

"You need to be ready, Elaric."

Stephan's sudden warning made Elaric look up, his brows furrowed. "Yes, but why?"

"I'm not sure how this will all play out, but Jakob is not to be underestimated. As I'm sure you know. However, there is something more at play here than a vengeful Guardian. We all need to be prepared for the worst because I have no doubt that is what is coming."

Elaric took a deep breath. "Yeah. I agree."

They were quiet for a few minutes, but he could feel Stephan still watching him.

"Elaric," Stephan finally said.

Elaric chuffed. "Yeah. I know. Aura's all over the place."

"Do I make you uncomfortable?"

Elaric sighed. "You? No. I...."

He hesitated and reached out to the First Keeper. *First Keeper, you said you think Stephan knows my true history, right?*

I believe so, but I think you needn't worry over it. You know Stephan.

Elaric risked a glance at Stephan but quickly did a double take when he saw that the man's aura was unquestionably guilt-ridden over upsetting him.

"Stephan, do you know about my past? The...true...one?"

"I assume you mean your race, not you specifically. Yes. I do."

Elaric lowered his head and stared at his hands in his lap.

"Elaric, I've known since before you were born. It matters not."

When he looked back at Stephan, his aura was calmer, and affection had replaced some of the despair and guilt.

"It doesn't bother you?"

Stephan's face was largely impassive, but a faint smile tugged at his lips. "Elaric, if parentage were a concern of mine, I would not have Marco, nor would I be able to look in a mirror. You are you, and you always have been. Since the day we met."

Elaric cleared his throat, his emotions suddenly gripping him tightly, but he forced out, "Thank you. Does Marco?"

"Not to my knowledge."

"Alright."

Stephan looked at the apartment door for a few seconds before getting up and opening it for Marco, who had his hands full with a tray of food, a bottle of wine, and two glasses.

"Thank you." Marco smiled and placed the tray in front of Elaric. "No wine for you," he teased. "No telling how your body will react."

Stephan chuckled, walked into the kitchen, retrieved a glass of water, and set it in front of Elaric.

"He's right." Stephan lingered with his hand on the glass for a few seconds extra and nodded slightly when their eyes met.

Marco took the wine into the kitchen and poured a glass for

himself and Stephan before returning to sit beside Elaric on the couch while he ate.

"Thank you. This is perfect."

Elaric took small bites and chewed slowly, having already bitten his tongue once in his impatience to devour the creamy pasta that his over-excited nose had never smelled in such a nuanced way before.

"Good. Eat and tell me if you want anything else." Marco sipped his wine and addressed Stephan. "Thank you."

"Unneeded," Stephan dismissed, cradling his wine.

Elaric drank half his water before clearing his throat. "Stephan, can you provide any insight on Jakob? You knew him, correct?"

"I did. As did Marco."

Elaric glanced at Marco, whose eyes had gone cold, but he was still entirely in control. Elaric, too, had known the traitor. They had never interacted much, though, as they'd only been briefly introduced early in Jakob's partnership with Abbot.

"Do you know anything that might help us? I only spoke with him a handful of times back then, and it was only small talk," Elaric asked Stephan.

"The man was an ass," Marco said without hesitation.

Stephan chuffed. "That is incredibly true."

"Really?" Elaric glanced from between the two of them. "He seemed superficial, but I assumed he didn't like me for whatever reason. Why would Abbot, hell, why would the shop choose him if he was a jerk?"

Stephan sighed and rubbed his eyes. "Because he wasn't always like that."

"It was only after his wife died that he began to show his true colors," Marco added.

"Gabe and Dany's mother, I presume?"

"Yes," Stephan confirmed. "She died when they were young. Gabe remembers her a little, but Dany does not. That said, I believe neither of them knows the reason for her death nor the true reason for Jakob's split from Abbot."

Elaric groaned, "I hesitate to ask. Abbot wouldn't have kept anything from those two without a *very* good reason. I'm surprised he kept it from me, honestly."

"Correct," Stephan said, and Elaric saw his aura shift to blue over their lost friend. "Her death was an accident, but it...broke Jakob."

"Completely," Marco added stiffly.

"Did he blame Abbot or something?" Elaric asked, but he suddenly became afraid of the answers he'd asked for.

"No," Stephan said. "Not for her death. Jakob blamed Abbot for not bringing her back."

"What!?" Elaric said a bit louder than he intended, and he made himself wince from the volume.

"When Abbot tried to explain to Jakob that it wasn't possible and even if it were, it wasn't something he, as Keeper, could or would do, Jakob snapped." Stephan sipped his wine before continuing. "They argued, and then Jakob walked out."

"On all five of them," Marco said, squeezing his eyes closed. "His kids, Abbot, Rebecca, and the shop. Without a backward glance, and we've never seen or heard from him since. Until now."

"Fuck me..." Elaric said quietly and twirled his fork in his pasta absentmindedly. "I see why Gabe and Dany don't know. There's no reason for them to bear that burden."

"Unfortunately, parents often burden their children with what they should not," Marco said quietly. Elaric glanced at Stephan, who was watching Marco intently. His expression pained for the man he considered a son, even if it were one-sided.

Elaric couldn't help but laugh softly at the true absurdity of the statement, considering the people in the room. "Well, if anyone would understand, I guess it would be us three."

A small smile flashed on Marco's face, but it was gone within seconds. "Can't disagree."

"So, what do we think his real aim is?" Elaric said, draining his glass of water, before adding, "I thought it was just to trigger the prophecy and watch the world burn, but...."

Stephan reached over to retrieve Elaric's empty glass and refilled it before retaking his chair without a word.

Marco frowned. "Stephan...."

"Yes?"

When Marco hesitated, Elaric shifted on the couch to look more directly at him. "What is it, Marco?"

"Their argument. Abbot's and Jakob's. Besides the moral portion, wasn't the reason Abbot had given for his refusal to raise her a lack of power or control over the Bond to accomplish what Jakob was asking him to do?"

"It was," Stephan replied somberly.

"Shit," Elaric hissed. "He doesn't want to watch the world burn. He wants to sacrifice it to regain his wife. Trigger the Prophecy and likely try to control the most powerful being we've ever seen so he can use her for his own purpose."

Stephan met Elaric's eyes, and they were sad and, somehow, empathetic. "I believe that is his intended outcome, yes."

"What do we do about Onnie?" Marco asked, barely above a whisper.

"I don't think it matters why he's doing what he is. The outcome from the Keeper and her companions will be the same. You must stop him." Stephan didn't mince words, and Elaric sat further back on the couch.

"We don't tell her," Elaric stated, and to his surprise, Marco glared at him angrily.

"You want to lie to her? After everything she's done for us?"

"No," Elaric said, suddenly weary. "I suggest we tell her *if* it becomes relevant, but right now, it's not. You saw how much it ate at her to lie to the others about me. Can you imagine what this would do to her if she had to keep it from Darcy and Gabe? Possibly forever."

Marco drained his nearly full wine glass before placing it on the table. "Alright. You're right."

"Stephan?" Elaric asked.

"I also hate to lie to her, but you're correct. I think the deception would do more harm than knowing the information would provide benefit to her."

First Keeper? Elaric asked, shifting on the couch again to rest his back on one of the arms.

Yes, young one?

Did you hear our conversation?

I did not. Our Bond is different than that of mine with Onnie's. Rest assured. You have privacy.

Thank you, though that wasn't what I was concerned with.

Oh?

I'd like to ask you something.

You're always welcome to, Elaric. What's on your mind?

I'm talking with Stephan and Marco, and we think we may know what Jakob's end goal is and the reasoning behind it. However, we've decided not to tell Onnie. The information would not make a difference in our confrontation, but it might break her as a person. I would like to offer you the choice. Would you prefer not to know as well?

The First Keeper was quiet for a while, and Elaric had nearly dozed on the couch before she finally replied.

I already know.

Chapter 12: Secrets Revealed

July 2022 - Alku | Onnie Moore

Onnie's eyelids felt heavy, but she forced herself to blink slowly a few times. When she yawned and finally fully opened her eyes, she was surprised to find herself in near-total darkness. Outside her bedroom window, it was utterly black, and she reached for Kushima.

Kushima, how long have I been sleeping? It's still dark outside.

"Cat?" Gabe said beside her, and she turned her head to find him watching her. His eyes were shining with worry, and he wore a deep frown.

"Ah...hi." She sat up in bed only to realize Mal wasn't at her feet, and Dany was missing, too. "Wait, where's Dany?"

Apparently, Gabe had been controlling his emotions until that point because as he sat up beside her, she found it challenging to breathe. He shifted and reached over her to click on the bedside lamp. Now that she could see his face clearly, Onnie knew something was absolutely wrong.

"Why?" she asked between gasps.

"You tell me," Gabe said as his eyes began to glow the blue of a Guardian losing control over their emotions.

"I don't—" Onnie's eyes widened as she started to cough from the pressure of his anger on their Bond. *Gabe. Stop. I can't— breathe—*

Mal appeared on the bed at that moment and sunk his claws into Gabe's thigh. "Dude, get a grip. We're all pissed, but you're suffocating her."

Gabe's eyes hesitated for just a second, but then the blue receded while Onnie coughed and hacked after she involuntarily inhaled a massive breath of air.

"I'll get you some water," Gabe said before getting up from the bed and leaving the room without looking back.

Mal turned to look at Onnie while she continued to cough. "You fucked up, girl."

Worth it. Trust me.

Mal's eyes narrowed before he hissed at her, his back arching and his hackles raised. "What did you say?"

Kushima, help? Onnie begged, but warmth and silence were her only answers. Evidently, she was on her own.

I'll explain, Onnie said as she rubbed her throat.

Gabe returned, and when he saw Mal's state, his eyes flickered blue once again.

"Please!" Onnie shouted. "I'm still too exhausted to block you out. Let me explain."

Gabe ground his teeth but handed her the glass of water before retaking his seat on the edge of the bed. When Mal sat down beside Gabe, neither reduced their angry glaring, but Gabe snapped, "Explain."

Onnie gulped down some of the water, coughed some of it up, and then nodded.

"One question, where's Dany?"

"My room. Asleep," Gabe answered, taking her glass and setting it on the nightstand. "Now, explain."

Onnie closed her eyes and took a deep breath. "Alright, but you must do one thing for me."

"You think you're in a position to ask for anything?" Gabe hissed and crossed his arms haughtily.

"It's not for me, it's for Dany. You cannot tell her any of this yet. I'll explain it all to her soon."

Onnie knew she was playing dirty by using Dany as leverage and justification against Gabe and Mal, but they needed to understand everything before Dany could know.

Mal agreed, and then Gabe rolled his eyes. "Fine. This is the last time I'm asking. Explain. Now."

"Elaric is alive."

What Onnie had been expecting, she had no idea, but what happened was definitely not it. She watched as the blood drained from Gabe's face, and his eyes were swiftly blue again. His reaction was so strong that Onnie reflexively erected walls between them and Dany, using nearly the last of her energy in the process.

Mal recoiled and then hissed a second time. Then he shook his head and hissed again. Onnie noticed Gabe's entire body was stiff, his tension so high that he had visibly begun to shake.

"We saw his body, Onnie," Mal stated.

"What. Did. You. Do?" Gabe growled between clenched teeth.

Onnie reached to place her hand on Gabe's forearm, but just as she touched him, he yanked himself away and to his feet a few feet from the bed. She closed her eyes, her heart breaking at how much worse their reactions had been than she'd been anticipating.

"It's a long story. It's taken weeks, but…."

"WEEKS!" Gabe bellowed, and Onnie's eyes snapped open.

Onnie's patience for his rage was running thin. While she understood his anger and fear, she needed him to be rational before she could speak with him again.

"Gabe."

"Don't!" he held up his hand, keeping her stuck to where she was and silenced.

"I can explain, but—"

"Keeper. Stop." Mal said, his own eyes glowing blue, making her flinch and snap her mouth shut.

All three of them sat in silent, seething anger for a minute until she'd had enough of it.

"Fine. When you're ready to hear me out, send Mal."

Then, she left her home and relocated to the hallway outside Marco's apartment. When he immediately opened the door, she had to bite the inside of her mouth to keep herself from saying anything.

"Onnie?" He scanned from her glowing eyes to her bare feet and legs and then to her oversized t-shirt. "What the fuck? Get in here." He gently placed his palm on her upper back and pushed her inside the door before he closed it behind her. "E, get Onnie something to wear."

All she could see was Marco's torso as he hugged her to himself as if her life depended on it, but she heard Elaric hurrying into the other room even if she couldn't see him.

"I'm sorry, I didn't know where else to go," she sniffled but refused to cry.

"Hush, you're welcome here whenever." Marco rubbed her back while she struggled to hold back her tears. A few minutes later, Elaric returned with a handful of clothes.

"I'm sorry. It took me a bit to find something small-ish," he smiled gently, and she laughed softly.

"Thank you."

"Go change, and I'll make you something warm to drink," Marco said, releasing her. "Bed and bathroom through there."

She nodded and scurried away from them, not wanting to overhear whatever they would say while she was out of the room.

Their warm bedroom smelled of Marco's light cologne mixed with Elaric's slightly stronger one. She slipped into their bathroom and quickly changed into draw-string pajamas that pooled on the floor at her feet when she let go of the pant legs. Between Gabe's shirt, which he had changed her into at some point, and what was most likely Marco's pants, which went down to her knees, she looked like someone playing dress up in their older brother's clothes. When Onnie realized she wasn't wearing a bra, she frowned. Her shirt was black, and she decided to ignore it the best she could, knowing neither Elaric nor Marco would care or judge her.

Onnie exited the bathroom and bedroom, being careful of her long pants, but she still managed to trip over them as she came around the short hall's corner. One minute, she was verticle, and the next, Elaric held her at a forty-five-degree angle while she lost herself in a fit of laughter.

"Sorry," Elaric said, grinning at the pant legs that entirely obscured her feet. "I tried."

She shook her head and wiped the tears from her eyes as he settled her back on her feet. "Naw, all good. I appreciate it." She gathered both pant legs into her arms and carefully scuffled over to the couch. "But I may refrain from walking if I can."

Marco carried over a steaming cup of something and passed it to her. "I wasn't sure what you'd like, but opted for warm cider."

Onnie grinned, the memory of Rebecca's cider on Thanksgiving coming back to her. "That's perfect, thank you." She bent over the cup and inhaled the sweet apple and spicy cinnamon steam.

Elaric sat on the couch beside her, and Marco took a chair across from them before quietly asking, "What happened, Onnie?"

She sipped her cider and then lowered it into her lap. "How many days has it been since I brought you two back here?"

Marco's eyes widened, and he blinked a few times. "Ah…three…. Why?"

"Shit. Well, I guess I understand why they're so mad then." She sighed. "I'm not sure what happened after I dropped you off. I made it home, but I don't remember anything after that. I woke up less than an hour ago."

"Oh, for fucks sake," Elaric groaned and leaned forward to settle his head in his palms.

Marco closed his eyes, and a pained expression crept into his features. "Oh, Keeper."

"Hey, don't start that shit!" she scolded them both. "Either of you.

That's not the point. Don't feel guilty, or I will tug on your Bonds every time you try to take a sip of coffee for the rest of your lives."

Elaric snorted, and the corner of Marco's mouth turned up slightly at her threat.

"Really. That's not the issue. When I woke up, Gabe and Mal were mad."

"Understandably. I assume you didn't tell them what happened before you passed out?" Marco asked.

Onnie shook her head. "No, not until I woke up. I made them promise not to tell Dany anything, but all I got to say after that was…" she glanced at Elaric, "that Elaric was alive."

"Oh, I'm sure that went well," Elaric frowned.

"Wasn't how I planned on telling them, but I've never seen Gabe like that." She lowered her gaze to her cup and watched the swirling steam patterns. "He physically flinched when I touched his arm, not to mention he nearly suffocated me, literally, with his anger." She reached up and rubbed her sore throat. "Even Mal's eyes were blue, and he was hissing at me."

Elaric groaned beside her. "I'm so sorry, Onnie. Do you want me to go talk to him or something?"

The agony on Elaric's face calmed her down a little. His response reassured her that she wasn't overreacting to their reactions, but she didn't want Elaric to own any of that guilt.

"Nope. He'll calm down, and then we'll talk. Mal will know where I am, so I don't think it will be long until we hear from them." She frowned at Marco. "Sorry in advance. I can go to the shop if you—"

Marco cut her off with a wave of his hand. "Nonsense. You'll stay here where you're safe and not alone. When he calms down, that will be a relief to him."

She nodded and sipped more of her cider. After a few minutes, she focused on Elaric. "You seem to be doing fine. What's with the super speed?"

Elaric snorted. "Yeah, I'm fine, back to normal, to be honest. You were right, though. I can't shift into any of my other forms."

"Damn. Okay."

"I think the speed's Marco's. I'm already slower than I was a few days ago, so I imagine it'll fade over time."

"Interesting," her brain immediately went into research mode, and Elaric smirked when he saw her do it and put his hand on her knee.

"Leave the research to tomorrow."

She paused and then giggled. "Got the aura reading, too, did ya?"

Marco snorted, and she looked over to find he was highly amused. "Yes, and the bastard has been on my case since he woke up."

"Hey! It's not my fault you were nearly starving!" Elaric snapped.

Onnie sipped her cider, sat, and listened to them playfully argue back and forth. She was so happy to see Elaric back to normal and Marco with life in his cheeks again. The two of them had been through so much, and Onnie knew this was only the beginning. She'd have to tell Dany about everything soon. Not to mention, they still had the Jakob situation to address. When she sighed, Elaric squeezed her knee.

"You good?"

"Sorry, yes. I'm fine. Am I keeping you up?" she looked at Elaric and then at Marco, "Or from work?"

Marco shook his head. "No, I took some time off, and E's been mostly on my schedule since he woke up."

"If you're sure."

"Completely." Elaric got to his feet and stretched. "More cider?"

"No, but thank you," she smiled as he headed into the kitchen.

You good? she asked Marco.

Never better. Other than seeing you upset.

Don't mind me. You're right. Gabe will come around, and my being here with you both will put him at ease.

Elaric's raised voice came from the kitchen behind Marco. "You haven't eaten in three days, right? What would you like?"

Onnie started to say she wasn't hungry but stopped herself before she opened her mouth. "Oh, yeah. I guess I should be hungry."

Elaric walked over and sat lightly on the back of Marco's chair. "I'd assume Xayn assisted with that. He did after the storm, didn't he?"

"Oh, yeah. You're right. Um, I'll eat whatever."

"Eggs, grilled cheese, a sandwich, or pasta? Or we can get something from downstairs."

She shook her head emphatically. "Oh, that's too much. Eggs?"

"Cheese?" Elaric asked, and she nodded. "You got it," he said, returning to the kitchen.

Kushima?

Yes?

Why didn't you...answer me?

You were not the only one overextended, young one. Do not worry, I was not angry, but I'm sorry if it felt like I abandoned you.

Do...do you think he'll forgive me?

I can promise you this. There was nothing to forgive. He was also not angry. You frightened him.

I know.

Then wait until he's ready to hear your explanation, and it will all be fine.

Alright.

Onnie carefully felt along her Bond with Mal and Gabe, and both were less hostile. Neither seemed in a place to talk to her yet, so she slipped away, hopefully unnoticed. When she checked on Dany, she was relieved to find her still sleeping peacefully.

"Would you like me to call Gabe?" Marco asked, and she glanced over to see him observing her over his steepled fingers resting against his lips.

"No, it's alright, but thank you."

"You know I can see your aura, Onnie. It hurts to see you like this."

His direct and authentic tone momentarily caught her off guard.

"Honestly, how did I get so lucky?" She grinned as Elaric returned to the room with a plate, fork, and napkin for her.

"Trust me, we all say that about you, too." Elaric smiled as he placed the plate on the table before her and retook his seat on the couch. "Now, eat."

When Onnie smelled the meal Elaric had prepared for her, her mouth began to water. She quickly dug into the fluffy eggs with ooey-gooey cheese running through them. It didn't take her long to clean the plate while she listened to Elaric tell her about everything that had happened after he'd awoken three nights prior.

"Thank you, that was perfect."

She pulled her feet onto the couch and squished more comfortably into it.

"Of course," Elaric said, his voice quiet and calming.

"Onnie," Marco said carefully, and the way his voice said her name so tenderly made her entire body tense. "How are you physically? You said his anger...."

She relaxed once she understood the intention of his unspoken words. "I'm fine. It was only a few seconds, and Mal snapped him out of it."

"You sure?" Elaric asked.

"Yes, thank you."

She focused on her hands in her lap, knowing the expression she'd see on the men's faces if she looked up. She'd seen it too often when she was younger. After someone would pretend to be her friend or care about her for a while, their true intentions would always come to light. Whichever brother that person was trying to get to through her would shut them down and then check on Onnie. Always with that face. That expression of pity and guilt.

Onnie, Marco said, along their Bond, *I will never be able to repay you for bringing him back to me, but I will spend the rest of your life trying to do so. So, if there is anything I can do, please tell me.*

She nodded and pressed the heels of her hands into her eyes but felt when Elaric pulled her into his side and said nothing.

Mal's...his eyes turned blue, Marco. The revulsion and...fear they both had.

Onnie heard movement from across the room, and then she felt him sit down on her other side and gently pull one of her hands from her face so he could hold it between his own.

"People fear what they don't understand, Onnie. Once you give them an explanation, they'll be fine." Marco squeezed her hand gently.

"And if they don't, we'll be there beside you until they do," Elaric said, taking her other hand.

She slowly peered up at them, holding her hands and smiling. Their eyes held no pity or guilt, only sincerity and determination.

They...they don't look at me the same way as the others do, Kushima.

They do not. I would assume that after seeing what you're capable of, they are a bit less frightened for you. They know you can handle yourself and your limits.

Why don't the others?

Kushima sighed. *I cannot tell you, though, if I were to hazard a guess, perhaps it's age. Those two have seen quite a lot in their lifetimes, and their perspectives are vastly different from young Gabe and Dany's.*

"Thank you."

Marco smiled and nodded, and Elaric hugged her a bit tighter.

"E, would you like tea? I'm going to make some for myself," Marco asked, giving her hand a final squeeze and getting to his feet. "I'm making rose," he looked down at her, "Would you like some?"

"Sure," Elaric answered.

"Um...I haven't had tea besides...." She shifted away from Elaric's hold and then nodded. "Yes. Please."

Marco smiled and gently squeezed her shoulder before heading for the kitchen.

"Here," Elaric reached behind her before handing her a throw blanket. "Your hands are cold."

She couldn't help but laugh. "Yeah, always." He draped it around her shoulders, and she thanked him but watched Marco's back as he moved around the kitchen.

He's going to be fine now, right? Onnie asked Elaric.

I think so.

Good.

Oh, um, Onnie....

She looked over at him and saw Elaric fidgeting slightly. *What is it?*

Sorry, not a bad thing. I spoke with the First Keeper before I got my body back. She's asked if I could help you...with the shop...because I can, um, still talk to her. Now.

Onnie let the words Elaric had said sink in, and then she grinned and nodded profusely. *Please! Oh my gods, would you?*

Elaric laughed softly. *Alright, I wasn't expecting you to be that excited.*

Sorry, Onnie said, grinning. *Yeah, few reasons. First, I'm happy to have the help. It's been less than a year, but I knew I would eventually run into issues. Not to mention, I'll have to visit my family at some point, and I'm sure I'll get sick like I did before.*

That's what she said, too.

Also, selfishly, it'll be nice not to always be alone. I mean, besides the First Keeper. Onnie felt her smile slip. *And...I'm happy she'll have someone else to talk to. She deserves more than just Mal and me.*

I agree. I promised her I wouldn't tell anyone she and I can speak, including Marco, though all three of us know he'll figure it out at some point.

I agree. Probably safer that way.

"Anything in your tea, Onnie?" Marco asked from the kitchen.

"No, thank you. Black is fine."

He carried over a white mug and handed it to her before returning for his and Elaric's.

Onnie bent over the steam, closed her eyes, and inhaled. She felt her shoulders loosen, her fingers begin to warm, and a similar comfort to calling her mom and talking over a pot of tea began to settle over her.

Marco's soft laugh made her open her eyes, and she saw him smiling at her.

"What?"

"Nothing. You simply look happy."

She glanced away. "I, uh, miss tea."

"Why are you ashamed of that?" Marco asked, and Elaric sniggered.

Onnie rolled her eyes but smiled. "Show off." Marco chuckled, but she continued, "I'm not ashamed, exactly. Or, at least, that's not what I thought it was. I guess I just feel bad about it. Like I'm misbehaving, and I should be drinking Keeper's Tea. Honestly, though, my Mom and I used to talk about things over a pot of tea. Jasmin green, normally. We haven't been able to lately with everything going on."

"Keeper," Elaric said, placing his palm over her forearm in her lap. "You need to make sure to take time to be Onnie, too."

"She's just as important," Marco added.

Onnie shrugged. "Maybe. But either way, it'll have to wait until after we deal with Jakob."

Marco frowned in reply, but she didn't elaborate further and just sipped her tea, making sure to enjoy it.

Elaric asked Marco a question related to the Day Night Cafe, and Onnie sat and listened to them talk about one topic after another. Once she'd finished her tea, she set the cup on the table, snuggled further into the blanket, and left them to their conversations.

Eventually, her eyelids grew heavy, and she felt herself drifting off. Someone shifted her on the couch, her head moving to a pillow, resting against their leg as they gently rubbed her back.

She felt safe, warm, and protected, so she let go of everything and slept.

Chapter 13: A Vow of Protection

July 2022 - Alku | Gabriel Vansand

Gabe's brain barely had a chance to comprehend the words Onnie had spoken before she vanished.

"Elaric is alive? What the actual fuck. How did she, how could she...." Gabe turned to Mal, his voice stiff, "Where is she?"

Mal was quiet momentarily, and then he sighed. "She's safe. She went to Marco's."

Gabe rolled his eyes and began pacing the small space in the center of their bedroom.

"Did she really just say what I think she did?"

"Yes."

"How? How is that possible?" Gabe rubbed the back of his neck roughly.

"Give me a sec."

While Mal spoke with the First Keeper or whatever he was doing, Gabe continued to pace. No one should be able to bring back the dead. Not even the Keeper of Prophecy. Whatever she'd done, it had to be—

"Okay, I don't have a ton of details, but yes, she did it, and she's going to be fine. It was just a lot for her and the shop. The First Keeper won't tell me any more past that, but...she said she was very proud of Onnie and the courage and strength it took to accomplish this."

Gabe groaned. "But why did she have to do it alone?"

Mal shook his head. "I'm sure she had her reasons. You know she always does, and more than that, if the First Keeper supported her decision, then I think we need to also."

Gabe sat heavily on the bed beside Mal. "She scared the crap out of me."

"Me too, my dude."

"She'll be fine?" he looked at Mal, who nodded. "She didn't do anything...against nature?"

Mal shook his head. "It doesn't sound like it. The First Keeper said that she put something back where it belonged."

Gabe leaned forward and set his head in his hands. He felt Mal walk over to his side and press his body against Gabe's flank.

"I understand why she asked us not to tell Dany," Gabe mumbled.

"Truth. While I'm not doubting either of them, if they actually did pull this off...."

"Yeah, Dany's going to...." he lifted his head, "Hell, I have no idea what she's going to do."

Mal snorted. "Well, whatever it is, let's hope it doesn't involve another round of ice skating."

"I can't imagine it will." Gabe stared at the floor. "Knowing Dany, she'll be happy and grateful, not to mention she'll know instinctively that whatever Onnie did wasn't forbidden."

"The trust between those two is...."

"More than ours," Gabe admitted.

Mal put his paw on Gabe's thigh. "It's just different, man."

No matter what Mal said, Gabe felt like an ass. His first instinct wasn't whether Onnie was alright. It wasn't even of relief over having Elaric back. No. He'd automatically assumed she'd done something wrong. Crossed a line. He'd proven to all three of them that he evidently didn't trust her. At least not as much as he should.

"Are you ready to hear her out?" Mal asked.

Gabe hesitated.

Was he? He was madder than hell at her.

No, he wasn't. He was angry at himself.

She'd been sleeping for three days, but she was okay, and she'd done nothing wrong. Xayn helped her stay hydrated and gave her nutrients, while Dany and Mal traded places with him as they kept watch over Onnie.

He felt Mal put a slight amount of pressure on his thigh, and Gabe sighed. "Yeah. Let's go get her."

Mal padded a ways down the bed, and Gabe quickly swapped his pajamas for jeans and a sweatshirt, slipped on his shoes, and grabbed his keys.

"Mal," he asked the feline, who was now on his shoulder, "if Dany wakes up, can you come back?"

"You don't even need to ask." Mal pushed Gabe's cheek with his paw. "Now, drive, man with thumbs."

Gabe snorted, "Says the manifestation who can teleport."

He softly closed the front door behind them and jogged down the front walk to his car. Mal appeared in the passenger seat before Gabe opened the driver's door, a broad grin on the feline's face.

Gabe backed out of the driveway, and the two of them drove in silence the few blocks to Marco's apartment. The streets of Alku were deserted in the middle of the night, as they usually were. Most sanguiste worked at the cafe, and few shops were open so late anyway. As they neared the Day Night Cafe, a few more people were wandering the sidewalks, and there was more hubbub in general, but Gabe quickly found a place to park in the small lot behind the building and headed around to the front entrance.

"Meet you there," Mal said before he disappeared.

Gabe entered the restaurant, and as soon as Stephan saw him from across the room, he beckoned him over.

"Be careful, Gabriel," Stephan said, agitated.

"You know?" Gabe asked, only slightly shocked.

"He's under my roof. I knew the instant he came home. That woman is incredible. Hear her out, but I warn you, all three of us will never be able to repay her, and there's nothing we won't do for her or protect her from."

Stephan squeezed his shoulder gently, and then he was gone, off to talk to a few patrons scattered throughout the restaurant.

Gabe wasn't sure what exactly Stephan knew, but he'd basically never used that tone of voice with him. Gabe took a deep breath before heading past a portly man with a ginger beard who stood beside the door into the kitchen. The man nodded at Gabe and let him pass, and he went straight through and into the hallway beyond it.

Stephan's serious demeanor still had him on edge, but he couldn't disagree. Their Keeper was incredible, and clearly, she'd gained a few more people devoted to her than she'd had a few weeks prior.

Gabe skipped every other step as he made his way to the second floor. Before he could knock, Marco opened the door, his finger pressed to his lips.

Shh, she's sleeping.

Marco's voice had spoken to him along the Bond, and Gabe's eyes widened as Mal reappeared on his shoulder. Marco laughed softly and stepped aside to let the two of them pass. Gabe made it two steps inside the apartment when he saw what he assumed was Elaric's base form sitting on the couch. He smiled kindly, and Gabe saw Onnie's head resting atop a pillow in the man's lap.

She's fine. Just fell asleep after some food, Elaric said.

Hearing his friend's voice snapped Gabe's mind and body out of the trance he'd been in for the last handful of seconds. He quickly crossed the room and sunk into an armchair before his legs gave out on him, and he ended up on his ass in Marco's entryway.

She seriously did it.

She did, Marco stated, taking the chair next to his.

How? Mal asked, jumping down to cross the room before jumping up to settle in at Onnie's side, where he curled up and began to purr.

It's a very long story, Elaric answered. *It's up to you if you'd like to hear it from us or her.*

Elaric looked down at the sleeping woman and smiled

affectionately at her. Gabe tensed at the wordless exchange and wondered what had happened between them the past few weeks.

Marco must have seen his aura because he immediately corrected Gabe's assumption. *You needn't worry about that, Gabe. His interests lie purely with your sister. His gratitude for Onnie, his Keeper, is all you're seeing.*

Indeed. Elaric returned his focus to Gabe. *Now, what's your answer? Would you like us to tell you what she's been up to, or wait and give her a second chance to explain?*

Gabe winced at the pointed jab and knew Onnie had told them about his and Mal's earlier reaction.

Yes, please explain.

Gabe couldn't wait any longer and needed to know what happened, what she'd put herself through, and, most importantly, how to approach her after he knew the whole story.

Marco began telling him and Mal what transpired, starting from the night Elaric fell into the well. He explained about the stone hidden among the flowers, Marco and Onnie's midnight trip to the cemetery, and the long nights the three of them spent in the First Keeper's library learning to communicate with Elaric's soul.

Elaric took over from that point and told them about his days within the library and the night three days prior when Onnie had tethered his soul back to his body.

Gabe's head was swimming, but at least he was less on edge than he had been. *That's everything?*

Elaric and Marco's eyes darted to each other, and Gabe already knew the answer before Marco spoke.

No, but you'll need to get the rest from her. It's not much, but there are a few details that we have no right to reveal to you or anyone else.

Makes sense, Mal stated before Gabe could argue.

Marco nodded at Mal before locking back to Gabe. *You have to understand, Gabe. If this woman told us to leave Alku and never come back, we would. We owe her everything, including her trust, which I will never break.*

Gabe sighed. *I get it. I guess I should be happy about that.*

Elaric chuffed. *I can't imagine being in your shoes right now, so don't worry. You've not offended us or anything. That said....* Elaric's words trailed off, and Marco picked them up.

While we will never interfere with her relationship with you or anyone else, we will also not allow anyone to harm her, including you. Do you understand? Marco's body was still, and Gabe saw his eyes dilate slightly.

He smiled and put his head in his hands once again. *Stephan just said something similar before I came up. Thank you.*

The tension slowly left the room, and Gabe knew his response had apparently appeased the angry sanguiste.

What's next? Mal asked.

Gabe glanced at Elaric, the man's expression sad and far away. *I have to....* He stopped and, a few seconds later, began again. *I no longer have my other forms. Per Onnie's request, I have not and won't leave the apartment until she can take me out of Alku to fix that. I can't have anyone see my base form. Present company excluded, of course.*

Was she planning on doing this alone, too? Gabe asked and instantly regretted his tone.

Marco replied before Elaric could, his mental voice equally clipped. *First, she will never be alone. She just may not be with you or Mal. Secondly, understand the trust E has given you by letting you see his base form. It is not something to be taken lightly. Not only does it put you at risk, but it also puts him at risk.*

Deservedly chastised, Gabe nodded. *Got it. Let me change my question. I want to go with you as well, please.*

I'm okay with it, but you'll need to talk to her. Elaric looked down at Onnie, *Though I don't think she'll argue with you about it. It was easy to see how difficult the lies and deception were on her.*

Do not mistake her necessity for desire, Marco said solemnly.

Mal lifted his head and met Gabe's stare. *I'm beginning to understand why she felt it necessary. Look how we reacted.*

How would we not? Gabe snapped.

She knows her limits. She knew she could do it. If she'd told us, can you really tell me you wouldn't have tried to stop her?

Gabe blinked at the feline a few times before leaning back in his chair and reaching up to run his fingers through his hair. *Fuck.*

Yup. Ditto, Mal said.

For what it's worth, Elaric added, *I'm sure we would have reacted similarly in your position.*

Gabe rolled his head side to side on the chair back. *Somehow, I doubt it. Just like I doubt Dany's first response will be anything but trust in Onnie and her morals.*

Gabe, Marco said, but didn't speak further until he lifted his head to look him in the eyes. *This situation is likely not written in the 'Guide to Being a Guardian,' so give yourself some grace.*

Gabe snorted. *Damn, do they have one of those? I should have asked sooner.*

Both men smiled softly, and Marco continued. *I promise you, I checked on her constantly.* He hesitated, and Gabe saw the man pale slightly. *Even though it was E, I would not have let her harm herself if that was the cost of getting him back.*

I know you wouldn't. Thank you for watching out for her…and doing what we couldn't do.

We won't make the same mistake twice, Mal said firmly.

Gabe felt like he'd been rung out like a sponge. His head had begun to throb, and his heart hurt from the emotional roller coaster of the last three days.

I assume Xayn came to see her? Elaric asked.

Yeah. We didn't know what was wrong, and Mal couldn't reach the First Keeper either, so Xayn did what he could.

I'm sorry about that, Elaric apologized. *We didn't know, or we would have said something.*

I know.

Gabe couldn't mistake their gratitude for Onnie, and he trusted them enough to admit they'd spoken genuinely. Had they known, one of them would have called. Cat probably had hidden her exhaustion from them, too.

Alright. I think it's time I took her home.

Elaric nodded as Gabe stood and crossed the room. He knelt before Onnie's torso and brushed her hair back from her cheek.

"Hey, Cat. Wake up."

Her eyes fluttered softly, and he held his breath, waiting for her reaction to seeing him after their earlier argument. He smiled softly, and she sat up quickly and launched herself into his arms, nearly knocking the wind from him.

Marco and Elaric chuckled, and Mal stood and stretched. "I'll see you at home. I'm gonna go check on Dany."

He disappeared, and Gabe shifted Onnie in his arms. "Ready to go home?"

She nodded into his neck, not releasing him, so he got to his feet, not releasing her either.

Elaric and Marco stood, and Gabe clasped Elaric's hand around Onnie's back. He felt his eyes glass over and quickly blinked away his guilt, sadness, and regret. *I can't tell you how happy I am to see you—all these complications aside. I'm glad you're safe and sound, man.*

Elaric squeezed his hand a little tighter. *Take care of them both. I'll see Dany after I have another form. I can't put her in danger before that.*

Gabe nodded in acknowledgment as Marco came to stand at Elaric's side. He softly brushed the back of Onnie's head and smiled at her. "If you're up for it, I'd suggest you go straight to the car, Onnie."

"Yup," she mumbled into Gabe's neck, not loosening her hold on him.

All three men chuckled, but Gabe smiled at each man in turn before holding her tighter. "Go for it."

The next thing he knew, they stood behind his car in the parking lot below. "Thanks, Cat. Come on. Let's go home."

She finally shifted in his arms and pulled away to look at him. Her cheeks were wet, and she still looked wary of him.

"I'm sorry, Cat."

All she managed was a nod, but he felt her press on their Bond, and he grinned and pushed back—with all the love he could.

She sniffled, and he carried her over, settled her in the car, and took them home. She was silent beside him. Her left hand held his right, almost as if the harder she held on, the less likely he would get upset again. Her head rested on the window, and he could see her watching the streets of Alku pass by in the reflection.

He carefully pulled into the driveway and went around to collect her and carry her into the house.

Mal, we're home. Going to bed.

G'night. I'll stay with Dany in your room.

Night, man, and thanks for tonight.

Gabe kicked off his shoes and carried Onnie into the bedroom without bothering to turn on any lights. He placed her on the bed, but she refused to let go of him when he tried to step away so he could change his clothes. He chuffed and decided she could have whatever she wanted. So Gabe slipped into bed beside her, jeans and all, and pulled her into his arms again.

"Get some sleep, Cat. We can talk again in the morning."

She snuggled in closer, but he could feel her muscles were still tense. He softly rubbed his palm over her back in small circles as he attempted to relax his own body. He kissed her temple and stared at the ceiling, content to hold her until the sun came up.

After a few minutes, she spoke, but it was scarcely above a whisper.

"Marco made me rose tea."

He smiled against the top of her head. "That's why you smell so strongly of roses." She said nothing further, and he wasn't sure why she'd mentioned it, but it was the first thing she'd spoken to him since she left earlier in the night.

"Xayn stopped by while you were sleeping," Gabe said softly, hoping maybe he could, truthfully, bore her to sleep. "He checked on you and worked his magic. We talked about Grandma Yvonne a little. She's...better, but she's struggling with some of her chores in the garden. Granted, her left wrist was the one that broke, but so much of what she does relies on using both hands. He's been going to Green Cottage nearly every day to help her. Elanor, too, apparently."

He checked Onnie's breathing. She was still awake, but her body had loosened significantly.

"He feels guilty. I think he's blaming himself for her fall because of their argument." Gabe frowned. "Well, they didn't argue, but his reaction wasn't the best. I'm not sure why he thought she'd disapprove or whatever he thought she would do. The Grandma Yvonne I know would never care about him any less just because he's gay."

"Fear," Onnie whispered.

Gabe sighed. "Yeah. I know. Even though, from my perspective, he's being an idiot, I know I don't fully understand what he's going through. I can't help him with this."

"Ask Marco and..." she trailed off. "They would probably be able to help you approach him differently."

For a few seconds, Gabe again felt that stab of jealousy at hearing Marco's name come from her mouth. He couldn't help but remember how peacefully she'd slept on Elaric's lap while both he and Marco wore their devotion to her on their sleeves. Luckily, Onnie hadn't noticed Gabe's irrational emotions, or she decided to ignore them.

"Yeah, good idea. I'll ask them."

He finally felt her drift back to sleep and rolled his eyes at himself.

Mal?

Yeah, man, what's up?

What did you think about earlier?

Which part?

All of it. Any of it.

Mal chuckled. *I think we're lucky to have them.*

Again, anger rose in Gabe's chest, and he quickly shoved it down.

Why does that make you angry?

Gabe inwardly groaned. *It doesn't.*

Pretty sure it does, dude.

I think I'm just...hurt that she let them help her. Stupid, isn't it?

Are you mad that it was Marco and Elaric or that it wasn't us?

That it wasn't us, I think.

Me too, man, but we can't change it. Next time, we just need to make sure she feels like she can rely on us, too. But that's on us, not her.

Can I ask you something?

Mal scoffed. *Gonna, even if I say no, but I wouldn't. Shoot.*

Other Keepers and their Guardians and Links...how did they interact? All I've got as examples are two outliers. Abbot's and ours.

Hmm, well. Mal went quiet for a minute, and then Gabe felt someone brush his Bond.

Hello, young Guardian, the First Keeper said.

Sorry, dude, but I didn't have an answer, and Master K said she'd help.

You're lucky they love you, feline, the First Keeper said with humor in her harsh words.

Gabe couldn't hide his amusement of the two of them, and he smiled up into the darkness around him before abruptly saying, *Thank you. For watching over her when we couldn't.*

No thanks are needed. I have waited a long time for Onnie; she is a gift I will always cherish. As with the rest of you—Dany, Elaric, Marco, you, all of you—it's been many millennia since I have felt so alive.

Hey, why wasn't I on that list? Mal whined.

Gabe listened to the two of them tease each other, and he realized he was still smiling.

Do you talk to her like this, too? he interrupted and then quickly apologized for doing so.

Yes. We speak quite frequently.

I'm glad.

Gabriel, do you remember what I told you a few months ago? About what we all were to her?

Yeah, I do.

Do not forget it, young one. As with any other being, we each have others we rely on and need for differing reasons. Onnie needs none of us any less than the other. We are all essential in our own way. Yourself included.

All three of them said nothing, and he tried to hold onto the First Keeper's words. He wasn't sure how long he lay there, but when Gabe felt his eyelids struggling, he shut them and gave in to sleep, the warmth of the woman he loved at his side.

Chapter 14: Escalation

July 2022 - Alku | Onnie Moore

A strange sense of deja vu settled over Onnie when she realized she was waking up back in her own bed. Gabe was beside her, one arm wrapped around her, holding her to him in a death grip. He was still wearing his jeans, and she blushed when she remembered not letting him change out of them the night before.

"Good morning, Cat," Gabe slurred in her ear.

"...Hi," she said tentatively.

When she woke up at Marco's and saw Gabe's face, with no anger visible, she checked his aura. When she found only relief and love filling it, she'd lost her mind for a moment.

"I'm so sorry, Cat."

It didn't make much of a difference, but Gabe attempted to pull her even closer to him, his nose in her hair behind her ear.

She struggled against his grip, but he gave her a little room, and she turned around to lie facing him. Or she tried to, but she mostly ended up getting tangled in Marco's long pant legs, which made her giggle, and Gabe raised one eyebrow.

"Nothing. From the moment I put these on, I think these pants were out to get me."

Gabe gently tugged the fabric free so she could get more

comfortable.

Once she was settled, she frowned. "Why are you sorry? I'm the one who…."

Before she'd finished her thought, Gabe leaned forward and kissed her quiet. When he finally pulled back to look at her, he shook his head.

"No. Elaric and Marco explained everything. You did…what you had to do. I'm just sorry you were made to feel that you had to do it alone."

She felt tears pooling in her eyes, and she stared down at the collar of his sweatshirt. "I…I wasn't alone, but I wish you could have been there, too."

Gabe kissed her forehead and pulled her against him again. Their bodies pressed together, one of his hands on her lower back and one tangled in her hair.

"Next time."

"How much did they tell you?"

"They told Mal and me what they could. They were both adamant about not sharing anything you'd asked them to keep private."

"Okay."

She was glad they'd stuck by her and kept their promises, not that she'd doubted they would. She still needed to keep some secrets, but if Gabe and Mal knew most of what had happened, she felt infinitely better.

Gabe's breath ruffled her hair as he laughed. "I'm not sure if I was more surprised to see Elaric on the couch with your head in his lap or when he and Marco spoke to us along the Bond."

She flinched, "Ah…."

He shook his head and kissed her temple. "Nope, you don't need to explain. Already understand."

She wiggled her arms around his waist and squeezed him.

"Elaric said you were—" Gabe started, but she pulled away from him and covered his mouth with her palm, having only just realized that they were speaking aloud.

"Shh, I don't want Dany to hear you."

Gabe's eyes widened for a second, but then he nodded, and she removed her hand.

"You're right. Sorry, habit, I guess."

"Trust me, I know." She looked away. *I had to mourn his death and bury him. All while suspecting he was out there somewhere. Every time I lied to you guys, I felt like I was being ripped apart.*

I can't imagine, Cat, and I'm sorry. Elaric said he needed to get a form besides his base before seeing Dany.

Yeah. I asked him to. It's safer that way.

We talked about it, and I agree with you both. I know I don't have a right to ask, but could you please let me go with you this time?

She nodded, and he leaned forward to press a kiss to her forehead.

"Alright, let's get you into some clothes that fit and me out of this torture device."

When he tried to shift his hips, she felt him constricted by his jeans, and she snorted, her ears beginning to flush. "Sorry about that."

She released him so he could roll out of bed, and then he re-situated himself with a wince and a groan. It didn't go much better for her when she tried to crawl to the edge of the bed but again got tangled in her pant legs. Instead, she fell on her back and laughed. Gabe stopped and watched her, one corner of his mouth raised, but his expression was light-hearted.

"I appreciate the assistance, but I will be washing and returning these as soon as possible."

Gabe's smile widened, and he leaned over her to kiss her lightly. "Come on, you. Put on something that fits, preferably something of mine, and meet me in the kitchen. You're probably hungry."

She tipped her head back, looking at an upside-down Gabe. His aura had a slight tint of jealousy, but it quickly faded among his more overwhelming emotions.

"I'll do what I can. Yes, please, about the breakfast, though."

He snorted and exited the room, pulling the door shut behind him when he left.

Onnie flopped her arms over her eyes and sighed. *That was way worse than I thought it would be, Kushima.*

Was it?

Onnie thought about it for a second before she groaned. *I guess you're right. Last night, I thought what I broke wouldn't be fixable.*

He loves you, young one. Everything is fixable. It just depends on the effort put into the repairs.

How are you...feeling? Onnie chuckled.

Kushima's voice was warm, and Onnie knew she'd amused her with her question. *Much better. Did you notice the shop as you left the other night?*

Onnie shot upright, her heart racing. *Oh no, tell me I didn't demolish it again!*

You most certainly did not. You've made significant progress controlling our power. Not a single book fell from the shelves.

Oh, thank goodness.

Onnie struggled with her pant legs again but managed to get to her feet and remove them before she changed into a pair of her own.

I still have a long way to go. I can't be out for three days every time something happens.

Remember that what you are accomplishing are feats that should not even be possible. Understandably, there are bumps and missteps along the way. Not to mention a cost.

Okay, fair point. Onnie stretched as she wandered out to the kitchen, the smell of coffee making her mouth water as it drifted down the hallway. *It doesn't mean I can't strive to be even more controlled.*

"Onnie!"

Dany jumped up from her seat at the kitchen bar. Mal fell from her lap before relocating to Gabe's shoulder as Dany rushed over. She searched her face and inspected her arms and hands, which made Onnie laugh, and Dany started tickling her.

"Dany! What's gotten into you?" Onnie wheezed.

"You stumble home from gods knows where half-conscious and are out for three days, and you ask *me* what's up?" Dany ceased her tickle onslaught and crossed her arms in a huff.

"Ah," Onnie wrapped her arms around Dany's neck and squeezed her into a hug. "You're right. I'm sorry. I'll explain what I can, but I need you to drop it for right now. Can you do that?"

Dany didn't answer, and when Onnie peeked at her friend's face, a wash of guilt rippled through her again.

"Please, Dany. I need you to trust me when I say I will explain everything. I just need a few more days."

Dany studied her for a minute, but then she looked over Onnie's shoulder and at her brother. "Gabe?"

Onnie's stomach dropped. Gabe was a horrible liar when it came to Dany, and there was no way he could keep something this big from her.

"Nope, I know nothing." He turned his torso away from them and made himself busy with his phone.

Dude, you're the worst liar, Mal said to Onnie and Gabe.

Yeah...there's no way she's going to drop it now, Onnie frowned.

"Oh, shit," Gabe snapped, the blood draining from his face.

"Don't try to get away from this, Gabriel," Dany scolded.

"Not now, Dany."

He turned his phone around and held it up for them to see, and Onnie walked over to read the news headline he had pulled up on the screen.

"*Family of four describes 'magical' city in the Pacific Northwest—* what the actual hell?" Onnie pivoted to Dany. "Isn't the memory manipulation ward supposed to stop stuff like this?"

Dany's eyes went wide, and she nodded, dashing over to snatch the phone from Gabe's hand. Her eyes shifted quickly through the text as she skimmed it.

Onnie closed her eyes and began inspecting the wards responsible for altering the memories of Outsiders once they left Alku, but from what she could see, everything looked as it should.

Kushima, everything looks normal to me. Do you notice anything?

I do not. It all looks stable and in place.

"The wards look fine. First Keeper double-checked for me, too."

Onnie exited the void and stuck her chin on Dany's shoulder so she could read the article over it. "Golden storm? This is talking about the night the rain was conjured, right?"

"Has to be," Dany said, ceasing her speed reading.

Onnie brushed against her Bond with Gabe. *We need to get Elaric sorted. Today.*

Agreed, the sooner, the better.

I'll be right back. Going to change and talk to him for a second.

Onnie groaned dramatically and gave Dany one more hug before she stepped away and headed into the other room. She called back over her shoulder, "Alright, so much for a quiet day. I'm gonna change. Gabe, can you make a thermos of tea?"

"On it." She heard the scrape of the stool legs on the floor as he got up to do what she asked.

Onnie dashed back into her bedroom and shut the door before leaning on it.

Elaric, are you awake?

Yeah, what's going on?

Gabe just found an article about Alku from outside of town. I need your help. Would you mind if we pushed our city trip up to today?

I'll be ready in an hour. Coming to get me here, I assume?

Yes, see you in an hour, and not by car.

Got it.

Onnie hurriedly tugged on a pair of jeans and a comfy long-sleeve t-shirt, sliding a few of her favorite rings onto her fingers on her way into the bathroom. After brushing her teeth and a quick check in the mirror, she was eighty percent ready to walk out the door, which was good since Gabe entered the bathroom as she was finishing up.

"I take it he said yes?"

"Yeah, one hour. No car. I'm gonna go talk to Dany." Onnie stepped up on her tiptoes to kiss his stubbly cheek, but he caught her around the waist and held her there. "What's up?"

He leaned over and kissed her softly, but when she pressed against him a bit harder, he lifted her off her feet, and she wrapped her legs around him. His hair was soft, and she ran her fingers through it. Gabe practically purred in response, and she smiled around his lips. After another minute, he pressed his forehead against hers, and she saw him smiling with his eyes closed.

"I love you, Cat. Again, I'm sorry about how I reacted last night."

Onnie placed both palms on his cheeks and forced him to look at her. "I love you, too. I won't say it's fine, but I do understand, and I'm sorry, also."

He nodded and kissed her again before settling her back on her feet. "Go and talk to Dany. It will only take me a few minutes."

As she hurried back to the kitchen, Onnie told Gabe how much she loved him with her emotions, ones he strongly returned, making her grin like a fool.

Dany had remained at the kitchen counter, talking to Mal while she warmed her hands on a cup of coffee.

"Hey," Dany said, pointing at Gabe's phone on the counter in front of her with her chin, "That article is insane. There's no way it was a coincidence. Too much of it was identical to what happened."

"Shit." Onnie dropped into a bar chair beside Dany and then scratched under Mal's chin. "Mal, any ideas?"

The cat shook his head. "Nope, I'm as stumped as you guys. Nothing *looks* wrong with the wards, but something sure as shit is broken if this sort of thing is happening."

"Yeah, that's the same conclusion I came to earlier when I looked at them."

Onnie snaked her arm over to Dany's coffee, which she stole, and took a big gulp of it. "Thanks," she grinned as she handed it back while Dany laughed at her.

"I'm going to head to the library today and see if I can find anything in the database about past articles or press coverage like this. Mind if I drop by the shop with what I find?"

Onnie shook her head. "No issues there. Call Mal if you need anything, but the First Keeper will let you in."

Dany tilted her head. "You're not going in today?"

"Oh, not in the morning. I'll go in this afternoon, but I'm going into the city with Gabe in a few minutes."

She tried to play her comment off like it was no big deal, but seeing as she hadn't left Alku since arriving nearly a year earlier, there was no way around her sudden trip seeming suspicious.

"Yeah...." Dany mumbled with apparent distrust, "Just another secret, huh?"

Onnie reached for Dany's cup a second time, but she pulled it out of her reach with a scowl.

"Look, I want to see if there's more talk about Alku outside the wards. We'll pick up local papers, magazines, and stuff. It's possible some of the smaller news outlets haven't put everything online yet, and we might get lucky."

Smooth lie, Mal's annoyed mental voice said.

What do you want me to do? Have a better idea?

No.

"Alright, that's not a bad plan."

Dany handed Onnie her mug, and after she'd taken another gulp, Dany downed the rest of it.

"I'm going to get dressed. Maybe you guys can give me a ride over to the library on your way out of town."

They weren't planning on taking Gabe's car, but Onnie nodded, accepting the need to change their plans.

"Sure, I'll give Gabe a heads up while you get dressed."

Dany led the way out of the kitchen, and Onnie ducked into her room and closed the door behind her. The sink was running in the other room, so she flopped onto the bed, her hair splayed out behind her as she stared at the ceiling.

I hate all this lying, Kushima.

It's almost over.

Yeah, but again, the question is, have I done irreparable damage?

With Dany? I think not. She'll come around.

But there are so many lies.

You know what they say about lies?

I'm not gonna like this, am I?

Lies may wound, but sincerity and good intentions are the best salves for healing.

Onnie snorted. *You made that up.*

Yup.

Onnie dissolved into a fit of laughter, Kushima's own ringing in her head.

Seattle - Onnie Moore

Onnie yawned, and Gabe slid her coffee cup closer to her with his pointer finger.

"Don't fade on me now, Cat. The hardest part is next."

She groaned and drank the last third of her coffee in one go before playfully glaring at him. "Don't remind me."

She and Gabe were sitting at a small table in the corner of a coffee chain in Seattle. They'd parted with Elaric a few hours ago and left him to do what he needed to do to acquire a few more shiftable forms. Onnie still couldn't rationalize that she was sitting around waiting for a man to find people he could use as blueprints for his body for the rest of his life. It felt like she was waiting for someone on a date that she might need to bail out if it seemed to be going badly. She tried to ignore it, but she'd now drank two cups of coffee and was starting to be both wired and emotionally exhausted.

Finished. I'm headed back to you, Elaric said.

Onnie sighed and flopped onto the table. "Oh, thank the gods," she whined, making Gabe chuckle.

"It's not that bad, Cat."

"You're right, though. Now's the hard part."

Onnie checked in with Mal and confirmed that he and Dany were at the shop in Abbot's study. *We'll return soon. I'll let you know Elaric's plan once he gets here.*

Same clothes, dark hair, sides shaved, Elaric informed.

Are you ready to talk to Dany, or do you want to wait?

Onnie peeked at Gabe, her eyes probably screaming, 'Please say yes!'

Gabe... Elaric asked, *thoughts?*

Gabe's mental chuckle made her smile.

We are way out of my league here, man. We'll support whatever you choose. Today or another day. It's your life, quite literally.

Elaric was quiet and finally said, *Be there in three.*

"I can't imagine how hard this is," Onnie said, picking at her cup's heat sleeve.

"Actually," Gabe said, and she looked up at the odd tone in his voice, "how are we going to do this? Last time we told Dany something like this in magnitude, she turned Abbot's into an ice rink."

Onnie grinned. "That was very entertaining now that it's over."

"Cat...." Gabe chided with a grin.

"Oh, I know. I already talked to the First Keeper about it. We're going to put them in her library."

Gabe tipped his head back and laughed so suddenly that he drew the gazes of most of the people around them.

"You're putting her in a soundproofed room."

Onnie held up one finger. "Correction...a *padded,* soundproof room. Yes."

A quiet bell jingled from the shop's front door, and she looked up as Elaric entered the coffee shop. His new form was an early thirty's caucasian male with hazel eyes and a chiseled face.

"How the hell does he find these people?" she murmured under her breath, and Gabe raised his eyebrow with a smirk. "Nothing," she said quickly. "That's him. He's flickering all over the place."

"Hey," Elaric said, coming up to their table. "Ready to head back?"

Onnie looked up at him and winced. "Honestly, you're going to give me a headache with all the flickering."

Elaric frowned and looked like he was about to say something, but she got to her feet and tossed her coffee cup in a nearby bin.

"It's fine. Just don't be offended if I don't look at you when you talk for a while."

Elaric and Gabe laughed as they followed her out of the cafe and onto the city's overly busy street. The day was warm and clear, so many people were exploring Pike Place Market, which is why they'd chosen it for Elaric. He'd struggle to find a place with a larger variety of people in such a confined space. It also helped that a large portion of people were tourists.

She led them down a less crowded street and headed for a darkened alleyway.

"Have you decided what you want to do?" Gabe asked Elaric from behind her.

"Yeah. Let's do it today. It's going to suck no matter what, so why put it off longer?" Elaric's voice hinted at his apprehension, but when Onnie studied his aura, he was filled with fear.

Onnie stopped, smiled at him, and tried not to wince. "It will be fine. Maybe not right away, but...you didn't see her. Trust me. She'll be happy and relieved in the end." She looked at Gabe. "Now, if she forgives me...that I'm not as sure of."

"Take your own advice, Cat."

She sighed and shrugged. "Let me tell Mal and the First Keeper the plan."

Both men nodded, and she spoke to Mal and Kushima directly. *We're coming back. Mal...take Dany into the First Keeper's library. Do NOT let her leave.*

Gotcha. Everything went okay?

Yeah, but we're all a bit anxious, so tell me when we're good to come back.

Hold, please.

Onnie caught Elaric up on how they were quarantining off Dany just in case, and by the time she was finished, Kushima informed them that they could return.

Onnie took a deep breath and looked at Elaric. "Are you ready? I'll drop us in Abbot's study, then go into the library and tell you when to join us."

Elaric squeezed his eyes shut, but when they opened again, they were clearer, and his aura flittered along with his form as some of his fear slipped away.

"Let's go."

"As you wish," Onnie said, returning them to Alku.

Chapter 15: As It Should Be

July 2022 - Alku | Elaric Rickson

The moment Elaric felt the floor at Abbot's beneath his feet, his heart raced, and his palms began to sweat. Onnie didn't look at him. She just crossed the room and quickly slipped through the familiar wooden door. When it closed behind her, he paced in circles and tried to remember to breathe.

"It'll be fine, man. Cat's right. Dany was wrecked and didn't talk to me for weeks. She'll be happy to see you. Onnie will hear the brunt of her annoyance if there even is any," Gabe said and leaned on Abbot's desk.

Elaric groaned. "That's also what I'm afraid of. I don't want to be the reason that they lose what they have."

Gabe shook his head. "Nope. There's nothing at this point that will break those two. Dany had no girlfriends growing up. Onnie is a treasure she'll never let go of."

Elaric, they're ready.

Thank you, First Keeper.

Have faith.

I'm doing my best.

Elaric swallowed roughly, walked over to the heavy door tucked into an out-of-the-way corner of the room, and closed his eyes. He counted to three, pulled the door open, and strode inside. Gabe was right behind him, taking the door from Elaric and closing it.

Onnie was standing off to one side of the room, and Mal was beside her on the floor. Dany was seated in a chair at the table where Elaric's soul-less body had rested less than a week prior, and he struggled not to laugh at the irony.

"What the hell, Onnie?" Dany said, crossing her arms in annoyance but keeping her eyes shut.

Want us to stay or leave now? Onnie asked him.

Stay until I know she'll be okay. If she…panics, I'll leave.

Onnie nodded, and Elaric took a tentative step toward Dany. Then a second, then a third. When he was only a few feet away, he quietly pulled a chair out and sat facing her, about five feet between them.

He knew he was stalling but couldn't help but admire the beautiful woman before him. Her hair was black, and she wore the sexiest pair of boots he'd ever seen—everything black. He winced at the significance behind it, and he couldn't bear to see her suffer even a moment longer.

"Ah…Dany…."

He knew his voice was different from the form he'd worn before, but there wasn't much he could do about it, and he just had to hope that she wouldn't freak.

Her eyes opened, and she immediately scanned his body, but she flinched when their eyes met. He hoped her moment of fear was because there was a strange man in front of her and not because she had already realized who he was and was revolted or angry—or anything else she had a right to be. Dany looked over his shoulder at Gabe, Onnie, and Mal, all nodding in turn. Her eyes were less confused and more suspicious when she focused on him once more.

Dany squinted at him. "Who are…"

"Hey," he said stupidly, internally rolling his eyes at himself.

Dany's gaze darted to Onnie again, and he saw the Keeper smile from the corner of his eye. When Dany looked back at him the second time, her eyes were brighter, but she shut them tight and took a deep breath.

She'll be fine. We'll leave you two for a bit, Onnie said. Elaric saw her and Gabe carefully head towards the door, Mal now in Onnie's arms.

Elaric lowered his voice so only Dany would hear him, and he leaned forward on his knees.

"I...I missed you. I'm so *so* sorry it took me this long to get back."

Dany's eyes were still closed, and tears leaked out the corners. It took every fiber of his being not to wipe them away.

First Keeper?

Do not worry, young one. All will be fine.

When Dany spoke, her voice broke. "I swear to the gods, if I...if I open my eyes and you're gone again, I will truly lose my mind this time."

Elaric took a gamble and reached out to carefully rest his palm over one of her hands in her lap. When she flipped over her hand and squeezed his back, it was hard enough to leave bruises. Relief spread through him until she sniffled, and he couldn't wait any longer. He put his free hand on her cheek, and when she leaned into it, he started pulling her towards him. They had only moved a few inches when she launched herself into his arms and kissed him like she was sure he would disappear again if she stopped.

While he didn't mind, and likely, neither would Dany, he was aware that they were not truly alone, so he pulled away. She finally opened her eyes and looked into his, and he took the chance to wipe her tears away with his thumbs.

"Hey, baby," he smiled. "I told you I'd be okay."

When she laughed, what little anxiety he had left was gone.

"You did. You're late, though. What took you so long?"

He pulled her to him, her nose rubbing his neck while she squeezed him back. "I'm sorry. It...wasn't...."

"It was Onnie. This is why she's been a cat thief recently."

Elaric frowned but nodded against her. "Yeah, please, don't be mad at her. She...she did it to protect you."

Dany was quiet for a few minutes, and he hoped he'd gotten through to her, but then she spoke, her voice barely a whisper, "And Marco…."

Be brave, the First Keeper encouraged.

"He…he's the reason I was able to come back. He knew."

Dany was quiet again, and when she didn't pull away from him, he hadn't realized he'd been holding his breath.

"So, she wasn't alone?"

"No," Elaric shook his head and shifted to see her face. "Not at all. Marco and the First Keeper were with her the whole time. I swear to you. I would *never* have let her do anything that would have—"

Dany silenced him with a kiss, and he didn't argue, but his confusion must have been evident when she stopped and smiled. Only a small amount of sadness still lingered in what little of her aura he could still make out now that Marco's blood link was nearly dormant again.

"Thank you."

She shifted in his lap to get more comfortable and rested her head on his shoulder. Elaric pressed his cheek against her hair and closed his eyes, breathing in the scent of her perfume mixed with old books. Dany was in his arms, and for now, that was enough. If she left him tomorrow or in five minutes, this would be enough.

"Elaric…" she said tentatively.

"Yes?"

"I missed you, too," she said quietly, and he felt his entire body relax with her words.

Everything was back to how it should be.

Finally.

"Are you sure you're good?" Elaric asked Marco, who responded by growling at him through the phone.

"E, you come home tonight, and I'll change the locks. I'll be fine. Go be with Dany. I had a head start and hope where she didn't. No matter what she tells you, she's not okay."

Elaric groaned but couldn't argue with him. "Fine. You're right, but don't call the locksmith when I stop by the cafe to pick up food."

Marco laughed softly. "I promise. Tell her I said hello, please."

"Will do, bye."

Elaric hung up his phone and slipped it into the pocket of his jeans before staring up at Alku's sky above him. It was bright blue, and only a few fluffy clouds drifted by. Even the delicate breeze was warm and carried with it the smell of flowers and earth from Elanor's shop across the street. He hadn't been outside in Alku yet, and he realized that he had missed the low hum of life the town had.

He'd stepped out of Abbot's to call Marco and give Dany some space for a few minutes, but now Elaric half dreaded going back inside. Sure, she'd been happy to see him, at least he was pretty sure, but what if she'd realized what it actually meant that he'd come back from being pretty much a corpse and was horrified?

Elaric rested heavily against Abbot's brick wall and leaned down to press his palms to his face. They still needed to figure out how to explain what had happened to him to the town, too. No one would believe Dany would jump to a new guy so quickly after his death, and they knew Dany had truly grieved, not simply put on an act.

Then there was Jakob to worry about. If he discovered that his turncoat lackey was still alive, he was crazy enough to find a way to hunt Elaric down and snip the loose end.

If Elaric left Alku again, maybe that would draw his attention elsewhere. Just for a little while, until everything was handled and Jakob was taken care of, and then Elaric could return. Except that would mean abandoning his friends, Dany, the First Keeper, and even Abbot. When Elaric thought about Marco and how he'd react if Elaric told him he was leaving again, pain shot through his chest, and he groaned, knowing he was staying right where he was.

"Elaric?" Dany said tentatively, and when she put her palm on his forearm, he jumped.

"Shit, sorry," he smiled weakly at her. "Was in my head."

"I know. I've been here for a few minutes." She frowned, and he felt even more guilty.

He glanced around the city street and then groaned again.

"We have to figure out how to deal with me being back and visually different. People are going to see you and—"

Before he'd finished, Dany wrapped her arms around his neck and kissed him. Hard. They were bordering on public indecency when she finally rested her forehead against his, and he could see her smile, but it was sad and weary.

"Elaric. I don't care. If people want to talk, they will. The people that matter will understand and figure it out. Forget everyone else."

"You're sure?"

He wanted nothing more than to shield her from drama, gossip, or negative assumptions, but she was right. The people who mattered would understand the situation. Those who didn't weren't important, or Alku's wards would take care of the perceived oddity.

"Granted, it's pretty tame right now, but do you think I could dress and change my hair the way I do if I cared how people viewed me?"

Elaric laughed. "Crazy chick that somehow looks brilliant in everything?"

She scowled at him. "I mean, the crazy chick part you've got right."

He pulled her lips back to his, and after getting enough of her to tide him over, he pulled her into his arms and held on tightly.

"I love you, Dany, and I missed you."

"I love you, too, and I'd appreciate it if you didn't do that again, okay? You only get one get-out-of-death-free card." She paused, and when she spoke again, her voice broke. "I can't do it again."

Elaric squeezed his eyes shut and focused on feeling her. "I know."

She nodded against him but eventually stepped back, wiped the tears from under her eyes, and held out her hand. "I'm starving. Food, then a movie at home?"

He took her hand and nodded. "Nowhere else I'd rather be. Do you want real food or coffee and sweets?"

Dany's hand tensed, and she pressed her other one to her forehead. "Um, has Onnie told you about Ana?"

"Who?"

"Well, that's a no then. Let's stick with real food and have coffee another day."

Dany led them to the street corner to cross and then started cutting them through City Center Park faster than before. It almost felt like she was running from someone, but also not quite. Then he figured it out.

She wasn't running. She was avoiding.

"Tell me who Ana is when we get back to your place?"

Dany nodded but didn't slow her pace until they were in front of the cafe.

When they walked through the cafe doors, Elaric glanced over to the counter and noticed when Sam saw Dany. The kid looked directly at her hand, joined with Elaric's, and then Vanessa turned around and saw them, too.

"Shit," Elaric mumbled.

Dany turned to look at him, and it only took her a second to understand. "Oh, crap. Who have you seen?"

"Only you and Marco. Well, and Stephan."

"Okay then." Dany skimmed the cafe, looked back at Sam, and pulled Elaric along behind her. "Better get it over with."

When they reached the front counter, she ignored it and led him past it to the doors that led into the kitchen.

"Can I borrow you two?" she asked over her shoulder at Sam and Vanessa. Both of their confused and frozen expressions highly amused Elaric, and he had to admit that Dany's way of ripping the band-aid off was probably the easiest.

Once they were in the kitchen, Dany smiled and waved to the two cooks and turned to wait for Sam and Vanessa to catch up to them.

"Dany, I don't think Stephan—' Elaric stopped when the door opened, and Sam came barreling in first. Elaric turned to the side, so

Sam came face to face with Elaric's bicep instead of his torso. Sure enough, the kid punched his arm with enough force to leave a bruise.

"I will fucking kill you myself if you ever pull that shit on us again!" Sam said, and then he jumped on Elaric, nearly knocking him on his ass from the force of his full-body hug.

Elaric let go of Dany's hand and hugged Sam back. "How the hell did you know?"

Vanessa laughed through her tears as she stopped beside Dany. "As if Dany would be with anyone but you?"

Elaric saw Dany blush, and he couldn't help but laugh as Sam finally jumped down so Elaric could hug Vanessa, too.

"I'm so glad to see you, Elaric. Please, please don't do that again." Vanessa sniffled, and he nodded.

"Not something I'd like to repeat, so yeah."

Vanessa released him and then hugged Dany. Sam indicated that Elaric should look over his shoulder and further into the kitchen. When he turned, both cooks shuffled closer, their heads down, and one sniffled.

"It's very nice to see you're alright, Elaric," a quiet young woman said.

The man beside her nodded and was the one who seemed to be sniffling.

Elaric knew both of them, but they'd not spoken much besides pleasantries. When he thought about it, the two cooks were surrounded by people who had grieved for him, and they were there to help pick up the pieces he'd left broken.

"I am. Thank you for caring for these two while I was gone," Elaric smiled.

The young woman blushed, and even the man's ears tinged pink. They both nodded and, after a few more words, returned to their stations. When Elaric saw Vanessa beaming at him, his chest warmed.

"I can't believe he kept this from us. How long have you been back?" Vanessa asked.

"Few days, but I lost my forms, so I was asked not to leave Marco's apartment until I could make sure you all would be safe, and I had a few new ones."

Sam snorted. "So that's why Stephan was being cagey. Made up some lie about Marco wanting to be left alone and no one was allowed to go up there."

Dany giggled. "I always figured Stephan would be better at lying. He's had long enough to practice."

Vanessa laughed. "Nope. He's horrible at it. Always has been."

"You gonna tell us what really happened?" Sam asked.

Elaric glanced at Dany, and then he shook his head. "Honestly, it's not important, but I will say this: I will be repaying Onnie for the rest of my very long life."

Sam rolled his eyes and smirked. "Course she did. Fine." He clasped Dany's arm and tugged her toward the dining room. "Come on, you obviously came for food. Let's get you hooked up before someone else comes in, and you have to explain this all over again."

Elaric nodded at Sam as they exited the kitchen. Vanessa sniffled a second time, and Elaric saw she was trying not to cry again, so he pulled her over for another hug. Vanessa was the closest thing he had to a mother figure in his life, and just like Marco, Sam, and Stephan, Elaric considered them family to him.

"I'm fine, Vanessa. Truly."

"I believe you. It's just...."

Elaric sighed. "I know. Stephan told me. I'm so sorry Marco suffered because of my choices, and you all had to carry them for me."

"Nope," she stepped back, placing her palm on his cheek. "Don't carry that guilt with you. Start off light and with a clean slate."

"I'll try," he smiled at her.

"Alright, now let's go get you two something to eat so you can spend some time spoiling that young woman with your time."

Elaric chuffed, "Yeah, I've fallen quite behind."

He said goodbye to the two cooks and followed Vanessa to the dining floor, where Dany had a to-go bag ready, and Sam passed her a cup. She smiled when she saw Elaric, and his stomach flittered like it had the first morning she'd joined him for coffee.

"I got us some of Vanessa's chai. I know it's the middle of summer, but I felt like the comfort."

Sam handed him a cup, and Elaric smiled. "Perfect. Oh," Elaric looked back at Vanessa, "I now understand what Marco means when he says it's hell on Earth to wake up at two in the afternoon, stuck in that apartment and forced to smell the things you're baking down here. Won't lie. I struggled."

Vanessa laughed and blushed slightly.

Sam grinned, "Alright, I'll consider us even then. That is a special level of punishment."

Dany turned to look at Elaric, her eyes wide and expression serious. "I am truly sorry you had to suffer through that. I know what it's like to wake up to Onnie baking cookies, and I can't even imagine doing that with Vanessa's food."

Elaric laughed at how solemn everyone had gotten, but it was a testament to Vanessa's passion and skills.

"Alright, enough, you two. Go enjoy your lunch." Vanessa smirked, "I think I may need to head home early and bake a few loaves of bread while my husband sleeps."

Sam winced, "Ooo, cold," then he grinned, "Can I help?"

"Of course," Vanessa fist-bumped him, and they both giggled.

Dany shook her head at the two of them and then laughed at Elaric when he'd been stupid enough to take a sip of his chai as they started their revenge planning and inhaled it instead of swallowing. He glared at Sam but waved goodbye to him and Vanessa and followed Dany out and back to the street. He took their bag from her while mentally checking to see if he could somehow shift into a form with three arms so he could carry the food and his drink and still hold her hand.

"I'm sorry about that. I didn't realize you hadn't seen them yet," Dany said, rubbing her forehead.

"It's fine. How were you supposed to know? Besides Marco, Stephan, and Onnie, only Gabe and Mal knew, but only because...."

"What?"

"Three nights ago, when she came home basically at dawn."

"Yeah, what about it? Scared the crap out of us, and then she slept for...oh." Dany stopped and sighed. "That was you."

He nodded. "Yeah. To be honest, after she dropped Marco and me at his apartment, he said she made it home, but we didn't hear from her after that. Then, last night, she showed up on our doorstep in only her pajamas, shaking and terrified. Well, not outwardly, but yeah."

"I had no idea. What happened? Why didn't they wake me up?"

"She told your brother and Mal what we'd done when they demanded answers, and, well, they didn't take it the same way you did."

"Can I.... Should I not ask?" Dany said tentatively.

"Well, she said Gabe flinched and recoiled from her."

Dany's step faltered for a second, and then she nodded, "Yeah. I see why she left then. There's no talking to him when he's like that. It's rare, but...."

Elaric cleared his throat. "I'm aware. I've seen it."

She glanced sidelong at him curiously and then shook her head. "Nope, never mind. Got it. Yeah, I imagine he was. What got through to him?"

"I'm not quite sure what got him chilled out enough to come to pick her up, but," Elaric couldn't help but grin. "Mine and Marco's Bond with Onnie is a bit more complicated now, so when he got there, and we both told him to be quiet and not wake her up...along the Bond, I think he snapped out of whatever was left."

Dany snorted. "Damn. Sorry, I missed that part."

"Yeah, once we explained more, he and Mal realized why she made her choices, and they took her home."

"Good. I get why someone could jump to assumptions over a situation like that, but...it's Onnie. My first and only worry was if she was alright, not if what she did was wrong."

Elaric smiled. "Yeah, she may look at rules and bend them a bit, but she's not one to recklessly break them."

"Nope, and those two should have known better."

"Trust me, they know that. I think that part is what annoyed them the most."

"What?"

"Gabe commented on how he and Mal jumped to negative conclusions. They both admitted you wouldn't react that way and that you trust Onnie in a way they now acknowledge they don't."

"Hmm, yeah. I can see that."

Elaric stopped when Dany fished out her key and let them into the stand-alone cottage apartment that used to be Gabe's. When he'd moved in with Onnie, Dany had taken her brother's lease and most of his furniture. They walked into the space, and Elaric couldn't help but smile at the eclectic decor that fit her perfectly. More than that, it smelled like her, making him feel welcome and lucky to be a part of it.

Dany put her things down on a small table, took the bag and cup from him, and did the same with them too. Then she led him to the couch and made him sit so she could climb into his lap.

He laughed softly, but truthfully, he didn't mind. He'd be happy sitting and holding her for the remainder of the day if that's what she wanted. He rested his cheek against the top of her head and wrapped his arms around her.

"I missed you, Dany."

It mentally hadn't felt like nearly two months had passed, but it was as if his body knew it had been that long.

"Elaric?" Dany said timidly.

"Yeah?"

"This...isn't temporary or anything...right?"

He blanched and shifted so he could see her face, and he placed one of his palms on her cheek and rubbed his thumb lightly over it. "As far as we know, it's permanent. Extremely."

"Meaning?" Dany's forehead creased in unease and confusion.

"Ah, so my race was already longer lived, but what Onnie did pretty much made that irrelevant. My soul was separated from my body, and she tied me to the shop. I'm part of it now."

Dany's eyes went wide. "What does that mean?"

"Truthfully, not exactly sure. I'd suggest you ask Onnie. However," Elaric caught her gaze and wouldn't let her look away, "I need you to understand that there are portions she does not want to share, and I won't betray that trust to anyone. Even you, so if she tells you no, please, leave it."

"Of course. You said she was fine, though, right?"

Elaric smiled and relaxed his grip. "She is. If she isn't, she's hiding it from Marco and me, too, but I truly don't think that's the case."

Dany's lips turned up in a small smile, "How the hell will I ever repay her for this."

He chuffed, "You figure that out. Let me know. I'll do it twice."

Dany leaned into his palm, and a full smile finally spread across her features. "She's truly amazing, isn't she?"

"Incomprehensible."

"You said you had to get new forms. Can I ask what happened?"

Elaric's chest tightened, and he tried to force a smile but gave up when he knew it wouldn't fool Dany anyway. "I don't know. Not even sure if Onnie does, but when I woke up, we knew there'd be a chance they were gone, and they were."

"She said she..." Dany swallowed roughly and looked away, "Buried your body."

He sighed. "I'm sorry, she lied—to all of you. She went to get it and see what...um...state it was in. She relocated it to the shop, not my grave."

Dany nodded, but Elaric could see her jaw was clenched.

"None of us wanted to give you false hope. I'm sorry."

"I get it. I'm not mad, just...processing."

He kissed her cheek and rubbed his nose along her smooth skin. "Thank you for the flowers," he said.

She nodded and sniffled. "I—will you tell me more about what happened...later? I don't think I can—"

"Yes, of course." Elaric turned her cheek towards him and kissed her gently.

When she pulled away, he saw Dany suddenly blush and look across the room.

He smirked, "Dany...?"

"Yes?"

"Why are you blushing?"

She shook her head, "I'm not."

He laughed. "You are, baby," he said, brushing her ear with his thumb. "What's up?"

"I was just wondering, um...about your...body..." she groaned. "Gods, I feel like such a perv."

Elaric snorted. "If you're asking if everything functions as it should...then I assume so? Has so far." He laughed involuntarily. "Well, except when I first woke up. Legs were highly confused, and I ended up on my ass."

Dany giggled and looked at him again. "Really?"

"Completly. Scared the crap out of Marco and Stephan. I'm not a light dude, and I'd been sleeping."

"I'd bet, and with their hearing, it probably sounded even worse."

Elaric nodded with a grin. "Pretty much."

He made it a point to distract Dany enough from her embarrassment over her question and pulled her closer to kiss her again and wipe away the last of her worry. She shifted in his lap and wrapped her arms around his neck. Their new position allowed him to press his palms against her back and hold her even closer. Even though he'd intended to distract her, he lost himself in the feeling of her lips and faint perfume. She gently pushed away, and her eyes stared at him as a thousand thoughts and emotions flickered through them.

"Dany," Elaric cleared his throat, and it was his turn to look away and flush. "Can I ask you for something?"

"Course. What is it?"

Elaric groaned and then laughed at himself. "Sorry, I'm not sure why this is so difficult."

Dany chuckled. "Well, now I'm really curious."

"I guess I should preface this with the warning that you could be at risk if people found out you knew."

She stiffened. "Now you're worrying me."

He shook his head. "Sorry, that wasn't my intention." With a deep breath, he looked back at her. "I want you to see my base form—the *real* me."

After a second of comprehension, she smirked. "Why was that a difficult question?"

"As I said, if people found out you know what I truly look like, it could put you in danger."

"Okay, I understand. Can I ask who else knows?"

"Onnie, Marco, and Stephan have seen it, and Gabe and Mal saw it last night when they came to get Onnie. Far as I know, there is no one else in Alku. Though Sam and Vanessa may have, but they probably wouldn't have known it was my base form and assumed it was just another alternate one."

"The expected list. Alright, then, yes."

Elaric nodded but was still incredibly anxious. He realized it was because he was scared, but not just for her safety. All the forms he'd taken when they were together were similar to his base form, but what if she was expecting something radically different?

Dany's quick movement pulled him from his self-doubt as she got to her feet so she could sit back down but with her thighs straddling his lap. Before he could say anything, she pressed her body to his and kissed him like she had in front of the bookshop.

"Elaric," she said between kisses, "if it's difficult, then don't."

He tangled his fingers in her hair. "Truthfully, I'm scared."

"Why?" She pressed her forehead to his and smiled, "Do you honestly think there's a chance I won't love the real you, too?"

He closed his eyes and smiled. "Damn, smart woman."

"Keep your eyes closed."

He felt her sit back from his torso, but she didn't leave his lap. "Alright."

She gently pressed her palms on his chest. "Now, do it."

"Wha—"

"Nope. Keep your eyes closed and do it. Not a single part of me thinks this will be an issue, but if you're not worried about my first reaction, maybe it'll be easier if you don't see it."

Elaric swallowed roughly and nodded slowly. Then, he gradually shifted back to his base form and held his breath.

"Oh, you're fucking kidding me," Dany exclaimed.

He winced and opened his eyes, and when she saw them, she burst into laughter. When he tried to look away, she grasped his face and turned it back to her.

"Stop. I'm laughing because you're an idiot, not because I find you repulsive or anything. So stop thinking that shit." Dany shook her head and recomposed herself. "I'm sorry. As I said, you're an idiot. My idiot, and I love you. *All* of you. You surprised me, that's all."

"How so?"

"Because my first thought after, "you've got to be fucking kidding me," was "as if he wasn't your type already," and then you opened your eyes, and I swear I had to physically refrain from jumping you."

"Ah, yeah. I see your point." He raised his hand. "Idiot."

She smiled. "Maybe, but," Dany leaned over to whisper in his ear, "you're my incredibly hot idiot."

Elaric groaned as his body instantly reacted to her teasing. He pulled her neck the last inch to his mouth and gently kissed and nipped it. When Dany hissed, he smiled against her skin.

"Oh gods, Elaric, honestly," she whined.

"Yeah, baby?" he trailed a line of soft kisses to her collarbone.

She put her hands on his shoulders and squeezed. He used the opportunity to slip one of his palms under the back of her shirt and against her skin. The other he used to pull her lips back to his.

They kissed and teased each other relentlessly until he pulled away and groaned. Dany dropped her head to his sternum, and he laid his own back on the couch as they both caught their breath. When he saw her blue-black hair against his white t-shirt, he frowned and ran his fingers through it again, careful not to tug on any knots he'd likely caused.

"I hope I never have to see you with this color ever again, Dany. It's not vibrant enough for you."

Dany nodded against him, but then he heard her faint sniffle and rolled his eyes at his stupid mouth.

"Baby, look at me?"

He spoke softly, but Dany didn't look up. He shifted to sit up straighter and wrapped his arms around her instead.

"I will spend my life making this up to you, Dany, but I also need you to know that if I had to go back and do it again, I would make the same choice. Even if it meant I couldn't come back a second time."

"I was so angry at you for weeks. I switched between hiding the agony and hiding the rage."

"Justified."

Dany unburied her face, and he brushed the tears from her cheeks.

"Make it go away," she begged, unblinking. "Erase it and make my heart and body understand what my brain...mostly believes. I don't want to be sad and angry anymore."

Elaric clenched his jaw at the damage his choice had done to those he cared about. He hadn't been lying, though. He'd do it all over if it meant keeping her safe.

"Anything. Tell me what you need."

Another tear rolled down her cheek. "Just you. I just...need you."

He pressed his forehead to hers. "Dany, I've been yours since that first morning we had coffee."

When he felt her struggling to hold back more tears, he whispered in her ear, "Hold on."

Then he got to his feet. When she buried her face in his neck and held on to him, he carried her into her bedroom and pushed the door slightly closed with his foot. When he rotated and saw that even most of the things strewn about were black, he walked over to the bed and carefully lowered her to the edge of it.

He slipped her arms from around his neck and began taking off her boots. The damn things were amazing, and they matched the woman who wore them, but the color made his stomach turn.

When he'd freed her feet and calves, he rested his head in her lap and rubbed her muscles. She ran her fingers through his hair and dragged her nails over his scalp.

Elaric laughed softly. "At this rate, we may race to see who passes out first."

To his relief, Dany laughed and didn't sniffle.

When he felt her muscles loosen, he sat up and quickly removed his boots. Dany looked a bit more settled than she'd been in the other room, and while she was still too quiet and lifeless, her eyes followed him as he did things and finally had a bit of sparkle again.

He went to the side of the bed he always slept on when he'd stayed with her and sat atop the blankets before he beckoned her to move up further. She moved to lie beside him, and he pulled her closer, wrapped one of his legs over hers, and was rewarded when she chuckled softly. Then she wiggled herself closer to him, and he smiled and closed his eyes at the feeling of her. Her fingertips brushed the bar in his eyebrow, and he opened his eyes to see her examining it and smiling.

"Suits you," she said softly.

Elaric smirked, "I'm glad. Thing was a pain in the ass to do."

"Why? Wait, how did you get it done."

"I didn't. Told you, people can't see my base form, if possible."

"Are you saying you did it?"

He nodded. "That one, yeah. Not my ear. I can shift partly, and my ear won't give anything away. My eyes would have."

"Good gods, Elaric. Why would you put yourself through that?"

He looked away. "Ah. Long story. The short version is it pissed off my family."

She giggled into her palm, "Really?"

He nodded.

It had. So much so that his mother disowned and banished him from the family. They'd all assumed he'd broken their code and shown his face to someone. Not to mention, he'd marred his base form, which was a direct violation of orders and should have been kept pristine since no one would ever see it anyway. Their reaction was what he'd expected and hoped would happen, so when it had, he'd quietly packed a small bag and left and never looked back.

"Elaric?"

"Hm?" he looked back at her but quickly closed his eyes when she pressed her lips to his.

When their kiss deepened, he drew her closer. His breath caught when he felt her hands press against the skin on his lower back. She chuckled around his lips, and he smiled.

"Laughing... at... me?" he asked, broken up by her kiss.

"Yup," Dany said, biting his lower lip with near to no pressure.

His fingers flexed on her back, and he moved his leg from atop hers to between them. When he pressed his thigh against her, she made a contented noise, and he buried one hand and then his face in her hair.

Dany arched her back, making him groan, and then he rolled her onto her back. She smiled sweetly up at him, and he was torn between wanting to tear her clothes off or snuggling and sleeping.

He leaned on one forearm and then ran his other palm up her toned stomach beneath her shirt. She squirmed when he tickled her slightly, and he ground his teeth and rolled his eyes at the consequences of her movement. He leaned forward to kiss her neck while his fingers explored her sternum, ribs, and eventually lower back.

She wrapped her arms around his neck, and when he pulled her up to a sitting position, she didn't hesitate to lift the hem of his shirt, and he pulled it over his head. He kissed her again as their hands clumsily rid her of her shirt. When he could, he pressed her back into the blankets, and he couldn't tear his eyes from the gorgeous woman beneath him.

He'd missed her so much, and because Onnie had kept her from entering the First Keeper's library, he'd not gotten to see with his own...soul that she'd healed. From the looks of it, Xayn had worked his magic, and there didn't seem to be any scars marking her skin—well, nothing visual.

"Elaric," Dany said, running her palm to the back of his neck.

He blinked a few times and shook his thoughts from his head. "Sorry. Ah, distracted."

She smiled, but he was pretty sure she'd known where his mind had gone.

"Only the invisible ones left."

Shit, he thought, kicking himself. Yeah, the woman was brilliant. "Sorry, I uh...."

"Tomorrow?"

"Hm?"

She smiled. "We can deal with all the hard stuff tomorrow. For today...."

"Good plan."

"Good. Then get back over here and finish what you started," she teased.

She giggled and squirmed beneath him, and her laughter was enough to stop his breathing. It sounded beautiful, authentic, and like the Dany she'd been two months prior.

Chapter 16: Sunshine and Sleepovers

August 2022 - Alku | Onnie Moore

Onnie blinked at the sun, high in the clear sky above her. It was warm, and she was stretched out on a towel on her back deck, soaking it up as if she were a lizard. She'd evidently gone rather pale in the winter months in Alku, and her skin practically glowed in stark contrast to her dark hair, jean shorts, and black tank top.

Beside her, Dany's hair was cotton candy blue, and it brushed the straps of her light pink flowy top. Unlike Onnie, who had spent most of the summer indoors, Dany had swapped between research and helping Gabe at the school, making her best friend look less ghost-like and more like a healthy human being.

"You're gonna go blind if you keep looking into the sun," Dany teased from behind her dark sunglasses.

Onnie chuckled and reached over to poke her in the side. "I can't help it. I still find it hard to believe that that," she pointed to the sun, "is actually shining, and on top of that, it's *warm.*"

Dany snorted. "You were here last summer. You know it gets warm here. It doesn't only rain."

Onnie closed her eyes behind her sunglasses. She hadn't been in Alku the previous summer. It hadn't even been a year since she'd moved to Alku and discovered she was a Keeper. It was only a few months ago that she discovered she wasn't just a Keeper but the Keeper of Prophecy and would either save or sacrifice the world. So much had happened in such a short time, and when she thought about all of it, Onnie understood why it felt like she'd been in Alku longer than she realistically had been. That wasn't even taking into account the relationships she'd formed. There wasn't a single person she'd met since moving that didn't feel like a family she'd not known she'd been missing.

"Dany, Onnie, tea?" Elaric shouted from the back door of the house.

"Yes, please!" They both called back in unison and broke into a fit of giggles.

It had been nearly a month since Onnie had gotten Elaric's soul back into his body. Her best friend had life in her again, and their group was together, but it had also grown.

Marco would join them on occasion, and slowly, he'd become more and more relaxed around the others, as well. Though nothing like what he was when alone with just Elaric or her. When she'd asked Elaric what she could do to make Marco more comfortable, he'd shrugged and told her to give him time. Onnie had frowned and thought about it for a few days before asking Elaric again, and he'd explained that the more people Marco had around him, the more of them he had to lose, at least in his mind. While she disagreed, she'd let it go after that and focused on being as supportive of him as possible.

They'd spent weeks playing whack-a-mole with the rogue guardian's efforts to break the town's warding, and any spare time was spent with their noses in books. Elaric didn't seem to mind and seemed happy as long as he was with them—specifically Dany. Gabe and Mal, on the other hand, already wished for the fall semester to start, the man's eyes burning with too many books with tiny writing and the feline, more often than not, covered in dust.

Onnie heard the two sets of footsteps approaching them from the house, and she grinned and sat up, Dany mimicking her. Elaric got to them first and handed them tall tumblers filled with iced tea.

"Black for you," he said as he handed Dany one, "and Keeper's for you," Elaric said, giving Onnie the other.

"Okay, someone please explain why it took me nearly a year to try this stuff cold? Not just cooled but actually over ice?"

Dany laughed and took a big sip from her cup. Elaric sat down behind her, and she leaned into his embrace.

"You'd think any tea is good tea, Cat," Gabe said, setting two plates on the towels between them—one with fresh fruit and another with salty snacks. He sat down beside her and pulled her into his lap.

"How did your trip into the city go?" Onnie asked Elaric.

For the last few weeks, he and Dany had been following information about Alku after it left the town, something that shouldn't be able to happen considering the warding, but it was happening all the same.

"Yeah, about that," Elaric answered while Dany nibbled on snacks, "actually, I think we may have figured out how the information is getting past the wards."

"Oh?" Gabe said, reaching around Onnie for a slice of orange.

"It's not," Elaric sighed. "I don't think it's getting out. I think it's being spoken of outside the wards itself."

"Wait, you're saying someone in the magical world is actively spreading information...." Onnie's eyes went wide. "Oh shit."

Dany nodded. "He's doing it intentionally."

"Okay, so how has this been handled in the past? At some point in history, there had to have been someone vindictive enough to try this." Onnie said, then called Mal, who appeared on her lap and draped himself across it to sunbathe.

Dany leaned forward and scratched under his chin. "We police our own has always been the model of the magical races."

Gabe leaned back on both his wrists. "We're getting close. He's being too brazen. He's waiting to get caught."

Elaric nodded. "I think so too. Marco also agrees. I asked his opinion last night, considering he's outlived us all by multiples."

Dany chuckled. "Be nice." She elbowed Elaric in the gut, and he poked her side.

"It's not like it's not true. Besides, I had the same question as Onnie, and considering my kind tends to lay low, I've not seen this situation either."

"He had nothing helpful on that front, I take it?" Onnie asked, and Elaric shook his head. "Damn." Onnie chewed on her thumbnail and scratched one of Mal's ears.

"Okay, question…." Dany said unexpectedly.

"Okay, answer," Gabe teased, and Dany stuck her tongue out at him.

"Why do we think he's doing this? The micro reason. We know the macro reason."

"Why do we think he's blabbing to the whole world?" Gabe asked, and Dany nodded. "Um…to piss us off?"

Dany rolled her eyes. "Well, yeah, but he has much easier options for that. He's not threatening the Keeper or Alku with this stunt. He's risking the entire magical world's exposure."

"Attention," Mal said with his eyes still closed.

"Exactly!" Dany exclaimed. "And how do you deal with a spoiled brat who wants attention?"

"Beat them up?" Gabe answered.

"Make them feed the ducks for a week," Onnie added.

"Be thankful they're not yours?" Elaric said with a grin.

Dany's eyes popped open, and she shoved her fists on her hips. "No! You ignore them!" She took turns glaring at each of them. "Damn, it's probably a good thing none of you have children."

Onnie snorted. "We were kidding. Obviously."

"Speak for yourself," Elaric said with a wink, earning himself another pinch from Dany.

"You're saying you want us to ignore him? You want to let him tell the world about Alku and magic?" Gabe asked, mystified.

"Kind of. If *we* ignore him, he'll be forced to escalate, and then others will take notice. He'll either be dealt with by someone else or give up that tactic and return to targeting us directly. Hopefully, he'll be backed into a corner and make a mistake by then."

"That's a lot of gambling, Dany," Mal said with a yawn.

"I know, but what else do we have right now?"

Onnie grabbed a hand full of pretzels. "Well, I think for the immediate future, she's right. We have no idea where he is or what he's planning right now. We need him to slip up."

"I hate to admit it, but I think I also agree," Gabe sighed. "Damn it."

Onnie's phone began vibrating on the deck next to them, and she and Mal jumped, causing the entire group to laugh. She saw the caller ID and got to her feet.

"It's Miranda's mom, be right back."

She took the phone to the deck railing, far enough away from the others that they wouldn't distract her, and she answered.

"Hey, Erika! What's up?"

"Hi, Onnie! I'm sorry to bother you," Erika said apologetically.

"Not a bother at all. Everything okay?"

"Yeah, actually, I was calling to ask you for a favor...."

Onnie grinned. "Ask away. How can I help?"

Erika sighed heavily. "I just found out a friend from college is having surgery, and she needs someone to help her for the night she returns from the hospital. She's only in the city, but I don't want to take Miranda to the hospital if I don't have to."

"Sounds like the perfect opportunity for a sleepover," Onnie said with a grin she couldn't suppress.

"Ah, do you really mean it? If she's with you, I know she'll be fine, and I can focus on my friend."

"Absolutely. What day?"

"Next Thursday."

"Sounds perfect. Do you want me to come pick her up from home? Actually, would you prefer I stay there? She's welcome here, but it's up to you."

Erika chuckled. "If Miranda found out that she'd had the

opportunity to spend the night at your house and I made you stay at ours, she'd be mad at me for a month."

Onnie giggled. "Actually, you're probably right."

"The surgery is scheduled for noon. Would ten be too early? You tell me, I can bring her to you or the shop."

"Ten is fine. Why don't you drop her here? Then we can go out and have some fun, maybe after lunch."

"You're honestly my hero, Onnie."

"Naw, she's a sweetie, and I'm honored you asked and that she'll actually find it fun, not just me babysitting her."

"Oh, I'm sure she will." Erika let out a deep breath, "Alright, I'll let you go."

"Looking forward to it."

"Thanks again. Bye!" Erika said and hung up.

Onnie looked down at her phone and smiled. Her back was to the group, and even though she knew Gabe was walking up behind her, she ignored him. He put his hands on the railing on either side of her and kissed the spot behind her ear.

"What's up?"

"Miranda's going to stay with us on Thursday. Erika's going to take care of an old friend after surgery in the city and doesn't want to subject Miranda to the chaos or hospital."

That was obviously the last thing Gabe had expected her to say, and he chuckled, blowing her hair against her neck. "Oh, sure. Sounds like something she'll be okay with."

Onnie snorted. "Erika had it right. If Miranda knew she could have had a sleepover here and then weren't allowed to, she'd talk to none of us for months—more than she already doesn't."

"Very true." Gabe kissed her again and released her from his arm's cage. "Alright, that sounds like fun. Do you want me out of the house? Dany can stay?"

"Not sure. Let me ask." Onnie squeezed his forearm as she returned to the towels, snacks, and the others and then plopped down in her original spot. She shoved a grape in her mouth and waited for

Dany and Elaric to finish their conversation on how to blend into a room properly.

"Baby, there's nowhere you'd *ever* blend into the room," Elaric said with a grin.

"What does that mean?" Dany shrieked, and Onnie nearly choked on her grape, drawing Dany's attention. "Do you have something to add?"

Onnie coughed and sputtered. "He's right, but it's not because you're bad at it."

Elaric leaned in to whisper in Dany's ear, and Onnie barely caught him saying, "It's because you're gorgeous."

Dany's cheeks went red, and Onnie just shrugged at her. "He's not wrong."

"Ug, so what was that about?" Dany asked quickly to distract from her embarrassment.

"Miranda's going to sleep over on Thursday. Erika needs to help a friend for a night."

"Cool! Can I stay, too?"

Gabe wandered back over and pulled a chair over to sit beside them, "As if you don't do that whenever you want anyway."

"Also true," Dany said with a grin. "So, is it fine?"

Onnie giggled. "Completely. How about we have a barbecue?"

"Sounds good to me," Gabe said. "Elaric and I can make ourselves scarce after that."

"For sure," Elaric grinned.

Any objection to inviting Marco, too? Onnie asked Dany separately.

Nope, never. Dany replied quickly.

"Invite Marco, too, would you?" Onnie said to Elaric.

He glanced at Dany, who was grinning and nodded in agreement.

"He said something about Miranda once, and I'd like to know more," Onnie added

"I'll see if he has to work or not."

"Thanks. If you'd rather I ask him, that's fine, too." Onnie offered but already knew the answer.

"Naw, it's fine. I'm headed back there tonight, so I'll ask him when he gets up."

"Gabe," Onnie turned to look at him over her shoulder, "can you do the whole food thing?"

He grunted and crossed his arms. "Yeah, but I'm dragging him into it, too," he said, implying Elaric.

"Fine with me," Elaric agreed.

"Perfect! She's going to be so excited."

Onnie smiled and tipped her head back to enjoy the warmth of the summer sun a bit more.

Elaric Rickson

Dany's fingers were entwined with his as they walked along the sidewalk toward the Day Night Cafe.

Summer days in Alku were extremely long, meaning that Marco and the other sanguiste were confined to their homes for far more hours than during the winter. That didn't mean that they were sleeping, though, and when Dany had asked if she could come back with Elaric to Marco's apartment after their day spent on Onnie's back deck, he'd agreed.

Dany had insisted they stop past A Shot in the Dark before asking what Marco's favorite was and ordering it along with Elaric's and her own. He'd offered to pay for them, but she'd shook him off and said she'd needed to do it. Elaric could tell something was upsetting his usually vibrant and outgoing girlfriend, but whatever it was, she didn't want to talk about it.

As they approached the cafe, one of the high school-aged kids who helped switch the restaurant's daytime and nighttime decor opened the double doors and locked them in place.

"Hey dude," the kid said and waved. "Coming in?"

"Yeah, just passing through to head upstairs, though," Elaric answered, releasing Dany's hand to fist-bump the teenager. "How've you been?"

"Good. Hard to believe summer is almost over."

The kid pouted slightly, and Elaric glanced at Dany, expecting her to be amused by him. Instead, she was looking at the floor and hadn't even been listening. When Elaric looked back at the boy, even he seemed to notice Dany's funk and frowned at her.

"Catch you later, man," Elaric said. The kid nodded and let them pass by him, his concern still evident in his expression.

Elaric retook Dany's free hand and led them around the chaotic placement of tables and chairs as various other day staff and high school kids were working. In each corner of the central area, someone was lowering the dark fabric coverings from where they were hidden in the ceiling during the day while someone stood in the center of the room helping to adjust each person's progress to ensure they all lowered simultaneously.

When Elaric entered the kitchen, the door to which was also propped open as a flurry of people constantly went in and out of it, he saw a petite man on a small stool in one out-of-the-way corner, tuning his violin. A few of the staff nodded to Elaric as he passed, but they all visibly started when they saw Dany's body language.

Hey, Marco. You awake?

Yeah. Is everything alright?

I'm not sure, Elaric said. *Dany's with me. We are headed up. She wanted to see you, but she's extremely...quiet.*

Interesting. Okay, well, I was just reading on the couch.

Be there in one.

Dany trailed behind Elaric as he led the way out of the kitchen and up the staircase to the second-floor apartments. She didn't release his hand, but she didn't make an effort to walk at his side either.

Since he'd already warned Marco, Elaric let them into the apartment, and his eyes met Marco's, who switched to Dany immediately, and then his pupils dilated slightly.

"Morning," Elaric said as evenly as he could.

Marco nodded but didn't take his eyes off Dany, who was staring at the floor in front of her.

Give us a minute, E.

What's wrong?

She'll be fine. Just go get changed, and I'll talk to her. It's about me anyway.

As much as Elaric wanted to argue, he turned and kissed Dany's temple. "I'm going to change clothes. I'll be back in a few minutes."

He placed their drink carrier on the coffee table and then went into the bedroom, pushing the door only part-way closed. Whatever was up with Dany had him worried, but what worried him more was Marco's reaction. Even the slight slip of his instincts had Elaric confused, anxious, and trying not to panic. He did his best not to eavesdrop, and he busied himself by pulling off his shoes and socks, swapping his jeans to something softer, and then splashing cool water on his face.

Unfortunately, all of that took him less than five minutes, and he didn't feel he should return to the other room yet. With how little he'd closed the bedroom door, he could slip through it and listen into the other room to check on them. It was remarkably quiet, and he took one step to go back out when he heard Dany's sob. He yanked his foot back, leaned against the hallway wall just outside the bedroom door, and listened.

"You have nothing to be sorry for, Dany."

He heard Dany's crying increase and then Marco's sigh.

"I'm fine, Dany. He's back, you're safe, and that's all that matters."

"But I—"

"You did nothing, Dany."

"Exactly!" Dany said, her voice raising through her tears. "I should have been here. I shouldn't have left you to deal with this alone."

Elaric's chest constricted, and he pressed his palm over his sternum as he tried to rub the horrible ache away.

"And what would you have done, Dany? I wasn't grieving the same way you were, but it would have been nearly impossible for me to keep that from you."

"It doesn't matter. Elaric told me it wasn't a sure thing that Onnie could bring him back. Don't tell me you weren't still worried she'd fail."

"No," Marco said abruptly. "I can't lie and tell you I wasn't. Every minute of every day, I worried she'd finally hit a problem she couldn't solve. That..." Marco's voice broke, and he cleared his throat. "That whatever I said to him last was all I'd ever get to say. But my grief was different, and I wasn't alone. I promise."

Dany sniffled, and then she said so softly, Elaric barely heard it, "I'm sorry you nearly lost him because of me."

Elaric stiffened, and then he felt Marco's intimidation press on him slightly. Before Elaric had a chance to run into the other room, Marco stopped him.

Don't. She's fine.

I'm not worried about her, Marco. You'd never hurt her.

Immediately, Marco's intimidation receded.

"Dany," Marco said, but there wasn't a response. "Dany," he said more sternly. "He did the right thing. I don't hold you, or anyone, except Jakob, responsible for what happened. Would it have been me in his place, I would have done the same. While Elaric means everything to me, and I would give my life for his...I would *never* give your life up in exchange for his friendship."

Elaric squeezed his eyes shut and wasn't surprised when moisture rolled down his cheeks. Marco had said that Elaric had made the right choice many times, but now he truly believed him. That man was his family, he had been since the day they'd met, and even though there was much about Marco that Elaric didn't know or understand, there was one thing he knew, without a doubt.

Elaric was no longer enough for him.

Chapter 17: Night Owl, Early Bird

August 2022 - Alku | Elaric Rickson

Elaric was mostly still asleep when he felt the other side of the bed dip. Marco must be headed to bed for the night, and even though Elaric knew he needed to get his own ass out of bed, he was tempted to roll over and sleep for a few more hours.

"E?" Marco asked softly.

"Hmm..." was all Elaric managed in reply.

"Sorry, didn't mean to wake you. That said, I can see your phone blinking on the side table."

Elaric groaned, reached over to the table, and groped around for a few seconds before Marco chuckled and said, "Left."

Elaric moved his hand to the left and felt it settle over top of his phone. He dragged it over to his face and winced when the screen turned on and blinded him. After seeing the time, he groaned again. No wonder he was still tired. It wasn't even seven yet. Marco's side of the bed shook just a little, and Elaric knew he was being laughed at.

"You never were a morning person. Want me to look?"

Elaric bent his arm at an odd angle over his shoulder, handed Marco the phone, and then stuck his head back under a pillow.

"Ah, Dany texted. She wants to bring us breakfast. Well, you really." Marco said.

Elaric pulled up one corner of the pillow to look at him. The light was bright, and he hissed and hid his face once again.

"You really are something else," Marco said before tapping on the phone's glass screen. "I'm telling her yes, but mostly for her sake, I'll tell her to wait until nine."

Elaric growled.

"Fine, fine. Ten, but no later than that, you'll ruin your sleep schedule again."

All Elaric could manage was some incoherent sound of agreement mixed with complete disregard for future consequences. At some point, he must have dozed because he felt Marco lean over him on the bed and press his chest to Elaric's shoulder blade as he reached for the table.

"There. She'll be here at ten. I've set you an alarm for nine-thirty. Phone's on your table again."

Marco's body warmth faded, and Elaric felt him settle into his spot on the bed and begin to relax.

"Thanks," Elaric mumbled through the pillow.

"Not necessary. That said, you should definitely warn that poor woman of your sleeping…quirks."

Marco's voice was obviously smiling, and Elaric sacrificed his darkness for a moment of slightly brighter darkness. He smacked his pillow over Marco's face and then immediately put it back over his head again. Marco didn't hold his laughter back this time, and the bed shook because of it.

"Go back to sleep, E. See you tonight."

Elaric shifted so his elbow pressed against Marco's back, and then he was quickly asleep again.

"Ah…he did say ten…" Dany said cautiously when Elaric opened the door for her.

Elaric covered his mouth before yawning. "He did. It's perfect. Come on in."

Dany quietly entered the apartment and handed him a carryout bag and drink caddy from A Shot in the Dark. She slipped off her thin green coat and hung it on the rack next to Marco's. When she turned back to Elaric, she smiled and retook their breakfast.

"Come on. I brought the strong stuff."

Elaric snorted but closed the door softly behind her and watched as she walked toward the kitchen. The alarm Marco had set for him had given him enough time for a quick shower and change of clothes, but not even hot water was enough to rouse him this morning. He ran his hand through the hair of his chosen form, and water flicked everywhere.

"Be right there," he whispered.

Dany nodded, and Elaric wandered back into the bathroom only to retrieve a dry towel for his hair and take it into the other room with him. As he rubbed the water from it, he watched Dany as she puttered around Marco's kitchen, looking for plates and utensils. She wore lightly distressed jeans and a pair of chunky black heels topped with a burgundy tank top with more straps around her waist than over her shoulders. Her hair was a deep red today, and as he'd requested, she'd not gone back to any color close to the blue-black she'd had when mourning him.

It never occurred to him before then, but Dany changed her style and hair color almost as much as he changed forms. The similarity made him laugh audibly, and Dany jumped at the sound of it.

"Yipes! Why are you sneaking up on me?" she clutched her chest, and her cheeks began to flush.

"Sorry, I hadn't meant to. What are you looking for?"

"Cinamon, I forgot to add it at the coffee shop."

"Third cabinet on the left. Closest to the stove."

Dany turned around, opened the cabinet, and groaned. "The only one I hadn't checked."

She grabbed the shaker, popped the lid off of one of the coffees, and dusted some brown powder on top before looking over at him. "Want some?"

"Sure, but just a little, please. It'll make me sneeze."

Dany scoffed but added the small amount he asked for and returned the spice to where it belonged.

"Here," she said, handing him his cup with the lid firmly replaced. "I also brought a few different pastries that Rosalie made. I wasn't sure what Marco liked, though."

Elaric kissed her cheek and picked up the two plates she'd pulled out for them. "Thank you. He'll enjoy that when he wakes up. Oh, and he likes anything with chocolate, but he'll tell you otherwise."

Dany carried the bag of pastries and her coffee as she followed Elaric to the coffee table and couch.

"Who would hide a love for chocolate?"

"He doesn't hide it. He'll make sure he's the last to take his pick, and by then, there's not normally any with chocolate left." Elaric took a massive gulp of his coffee and sighed in happiness. The cinnamon Dany had added was perfect, and he enjoyed the added warmth it brought to the drink.

"Yeah, that sounds like Marco. He's a lot like Onnie in that respect."

Elaric nodded, and they said in unison, "Everyone else always comes first." They paused and looked at each other before laughing.

Dany opened the bag and held it out to Elaric. "Well, let's give him first pick. What should I set aside for him?"

Elaric peered in and scanned the options. Croissants, scones, bagels, and even a few muffins. "Is that a chocolate croissant?"

"Sure is!"

Elaric looked up, "That one."

"You got it." Dany carefully pulled out the croissant and took it back to the kitchen, where she placed it on a plate and flipped a bowl over the top of it. "There. Now, when he gets up, he's got breakfast, too." She grinned and moved back over to the couch, and they began making their selections from the remaining options.

After a few minutes of silent nibbling and much coffee, Dany looked at him sideways and smirked. "You look much more awake now."

Elaric groaned, "Yeah. Coffee helped. Thanks for that."

"Don't thank me. I cheated. I was given a hint." Dany smiled warmly and went back to eating her blueberry bagel.

"Of course he did." Elaric rubbed his forehead, "Come to think of it, I didn't check my phone this morning. What did he tell you? I assume he told you it was him, not me, you were talking to."

"Of course. He merely recommended I get you a double shot. Said it would ensure I got to eat with my boyfriend and not a brick wall." She chuckled, and he couldn't help but join her.

"Yeah…I'm not a morning person." He rolled his eyes and sat back against the soft couch. "Soooo, not a morning person."

"Who is? Those people are honestly from another planet," Dany said, slipping her feet out of her heels and pulling her legs underneath herself on the couch.

Elaric narrowed his gaze at her, "Says the woman who texted me before seven."

Dany clicked her tongue, "Oh no, that wasn't my preference. I stayed at Onnie's last night, and as much as you and I are night owls, those two are early birds."

Elaric laughed, "I'd imagine so. Gabe gets up pretty early to get to school, right?"

"Yeah, but he does it on the weekends, too. Who goes for a run at six in the morning?"

"I'm guessing Onnie goes with him?"

Dany rolled her eyes but grinned. "Of course! Most of the time, I end up sleeping in with Mal."

"What's Mal?"

Dany cocked her head to the side, "Huh?"

"Night owl or early bird?"

Dany snorted. "Asleep. Always."

Elaric laughed, "Well, I guess he is a cat. Though I do admit, I often forget that detail."

"You and me both." Dany's face paled a bit, and then her smile faltered.

"What's up?"

Dany instantly had her smile back in place, but it was a polite one, not a genuine one. "Nothing, don't worry about it."

Elaric shifted, tucked himself into the side of the couch, and gently tugged Dany until she'd moved to rest against him so he could wrap his arm around her. "Come on, talk to me, please?"

Dany sighed but spoke. "Mal has been coming to sleep with me before dawn every day."

"Oh, why?"

"Well, first off, he doesn't realize I know. None of them do."

"Why are you keeping that hidden? No judgment, just curious." Elaric rested his head on the back of the couch.

"At some point after my...recovery, I started to have nightmares every morning. I think by chance, Mal figured it out and noticed that I had them less when he was beside me."

"Ah," Elaric said with a smile, "I see. Is there something wrong with him caring enough to do that?"

"No," Dany shook her head and sipped her coffee. After a minute, she continued. "Before you came back, everyone walked on eggshells around me. Treated me like a sandcastle at high tide."

Elaric brushed a few strands of Dany's hair away from her cheek. "I know that probably felt like they thought you couldn't handle what was happening, but you are a smart woman. You know they were letting you heal."

Dany groaned. "You're right. I do. Wounds won't heal if constantly re-opened."

Elaric smiled and closed his eyes, his head back and a piece of Dany's hair between his fingers. After a few minutes, Dany started to fidget, and he moved his arms so she could get up. She moved to sit on the other side of the couch and looked at him with determination.

"What's on your mind?" Elaric asked and sat up straighter.

Dany glanced quickly at the bedroom door and then back at him. Her cheeks were slightly pink, and Elaric couldn't tell if she was embarrassed or uncomfortable.

"Why only me? Why didn't she keep it from Marco, too?" Dany flinched. "Gods, that makes me sound like such a bitch." She looked away quickly.

Elaric pinched the bridge of his nose. "How much did Onnie tell you of *how* she was able to bring me back?"

"Not… Well, basically nothing, actually. Said it was better I didn't know. She did say it was my choice, but I trust her, so if she says I don't need to know…then I'll respect that."

Elaric looked up and smiled. "Ah, okay. Give me your hand." He held out his own, and she did as he asked. "Marco knew because he *had* to know. Our Bonds are connected, and Onnie found me by following his. Then, once I made it back, Marco made decisions when I couldn't or offered himself if something was needed."

Dany looked away again, and Elaric gently held her hand until she turned back. "Okay."

Elaric smirked, "Just okay?"

Dany nodded.

"All that stress and your response is okay?"

She nodded again. "Yes. I understand now. Marco was suffering more than I was, not because he thought you were gone, but that you weren't, and he didn't know if they could get you back."

Elaric was never ready for the intelligence that the woman before him had. Not to mention her emotional understanding.

"Exactly." It was his turn to look away, and he tried to keep his voice steady.

Dany leaned over and kissed his cheek, startling him. When he turned to look at her, she smiled, "Sorry. I didn't mean to bring down the room."

"It's fine." He brushed her hair behind her ears and leaned in to kiss her softly. "Actually, I think it's my turn."

"Hrm?"

"I know you said you were okay with my past with Marco, but are you okay with me staying here?"

"Like in the apartment? With him?" Dany asked, seemingly

confused.

"Yes. Even knowing that our relationship isn't like that, at the end of it, we are sharing a home and a bed."

Dany pulled her hand away and put down her coffee before she crossed her arms. "Elaric, are you okay when I spend the night at Onnie's? When we share a bed?"

"Of course. What does that have to do with it?"

Dany grinned but narrowed her eyes at him. "Tell me what the difference is?"

Elaric snorted, seeing the path of her thoughts. "Ah, you never dated her?"

Thankfully, Dany chuckled. "Alright, you've got me there, but you're not with him now, and that was so one hundred years ago." She rolled her eyes playfully. "That said, she's my best friend, and I would do absolutely *anything* for her. Can you tell me that you and Marco are any different? Are you not just two people, *family*, taking comfort in someone being by your side when you need it?"

Elaric searched her face for any iota of false acceptance or deception, but she genuinely seemed okay with it. He raised both his hands in surrender, "Alright, you win. I'll drop it."

She reached for her coffee. "Good. I do wanna know if you two like clap hands and tag out as you swap shifts? Are the blankets like perpetually warm? Wait, do you even have to make the bed?"

Elaric stared at her for three seconds, then burst into laughter so hard he was worried he'd wake Marco. When his sides ached, and he could breathe again, he nodded.

"Actually, pretty close."

Gabriel Vansand

His muscles burned as sweat dripped into his eyes, but all Gabe could focus on was the feel of the gloves on his hands as they impacted the bag he stood in front of. He bounced on the balls of his feet and hit the leather a few more times, his hits synchronizing to the music playing from his phone over the school gym's AV system.

Cat was off with Dany and Mal somewhere, noses still in books and cookies surrounding them, but it was apparent very quickly that Gabe was not helping in their research. He'd refilled tea, lit a fire for them in the living room, and he and Mal had eaten dinner together, but as soon as the two women lost themselves in their books, Gabe slipped away. Even if he couldn't help them research, he could help by protecting them, which is how he'd ended up at the gym, beating the crap out of a stuffed foe.

The song that had been playing ended abruptly, and Gabe bent over and rested his fists on his knees as he took deep breaths. He knew his playlist well enough that he pulled off his gloves before the next song began to play. The switch from a metal band and their screaming paired with searing vocals and expert instruments was jarring as the next song filled the large, echoing space with a soothing female voice whispering in a foreign language. The switch signified the end of his session, and he was about to lower himself to the mat to stretch out when the gym's door squeaked open, and a shaft of light flooded the dimmed space.

Gabe's body dropped into an immediate defensive stance in response to the stranger's appearance, but when Xayn stepped through the doors and saw him, he froze with wide eyes.

"Shit, sorry."

Gabe shook his head and relaxed, finishing his movement to the mat beneath him.

"No big, man. What's up?"

Xayn shut the heavy gym door behind him, wandered over to the far edge of the mat Gabe was sitting on, and sat down.

"Onnie said you were here."

Gabe snorted. "She noticed I left? That's surprising. She and Dany were so far into their books I wouldn't be surprised to see text on their foreheads tomorrow morning."

Xayn laughed quietly, but his smile was wide and genuine. "Nope. Mal told me, but she overheard him."

"Figures." Gabe began stretching his tired muscles but kept his gaze on Xayn. "You okay?"

"Yeah, fine."

Gabe dropped his arms from where he'd been stretching them over his shoulders and glared at his best friend.

"Wanna try that again?"

This time, Xayn swiveled so his back was to Gabe. "I just haven't been in town for a few days and wanted to see how things were going," he said.

Gabe felt his jaw tense as his fists clenched on his thighs. He didn't need to be connected to Xayn's emotions to know what his chosen brother was feeling but tried to hide. Whatever guilt Xayn carried over his grandmother's fall was misplaced, but it seemed like no matter who told him that, including the woman herself, he couldn't get past not being there when she'd needed him to be.

"I haven't eaten yet. Mind if I grab a quick shower, and then we can grab something?" Gabe asked while climbing to his feet.

"Sure."

Xayn stood up and followed behind Gabe as he made his way to a small communal bathroom located on the opposite side of the gym to his office. It only had a unisex bathroom, a few sinks, and five shower stalls, but it did the job. It was rare that the students used the showers at all, and more often than not, it was because of a mud fight or a tiny, messy painter, not an entire sports team.

The lights flickered on as Gabe entered the room. He made his way to the farthest shower before turning it on and then glancing back at Xayn. As Gabe had expected, he'd followed him into the room and leaned on one of the sinks on the far wall by the doorway. His arms were crossed in front of him, and he was staring at his feet, deeply in his head.

Gabe didn't hesitate and began peeling off his sweaty clothes and draping them over a nearby bench before he stepped under the warm water. A tiled wall obscured him and Xayn from each other's view, but Gabe called out over the water's din.

"Food preference?"

"Uh...not really. I have stuff for burgers at home if you want."

Gabe's mouth watered. Xayn was an excellent cook, and considering Vanessa had taught him most of it, there was no misunderstanding as to why.

"Works for me. Do we need to grab anything before heading over?"

They made small talk about dinner as Gabe rinsed off the grime from his workout, and it didn't take him long to finish and dry off. A small cabinet held fresh towels and supplies, and he always stashed a few sets of clothes inside of it as well. He pulled on the clean clothes, gathered up his dirty ones, and chucked everything into a gym bag to bring home to wash.

When he approached Xayn, who was still at the sink, his friend's eyes glowed softly in the dim room, but they seemed brighter than when he'd first arrived.

"Come on, I'll drive. Just let me grab my phone and turn everything off."

"Okay."

Gabe did as he'd said but stopped to look at his phone and saw a text from Elaric.

You around? Marco's working tonight, and Dany and Onnie seem...focused.

When he started laughing at his phone, Xayn came over and peered over his shoulder to read the message.

"Oh, you can go see him if you want. I can just—"

"Mind having a third for dinner?" Gabe gazed at Xayn's profile over his shoulder and saw obvious shock at the question.

"Um...no, but wouldn't you—"

"Xayn Ellwood, don't make me call Dany," Gabe growled.

His threat worked, though, and Xayn snorted before smiling and nodding. "Sure. I have enough."

Gabe quickly texted Elaric back and told him that he and Xayn would pick him up in ten minutes. Then, he and Xayn cleaned up the gym equipment and locked up the building before heading over to get Elaric.

They had eaten and talked about sports and town drama, and Elaric had even shared some of his stories from when he traveled the world. Neither Gabe nor Xayn had ever really left Alku, so both peppered the man with questions, but he didn't seem to mind. Now that they were all full, slightly warm from their ciders, and it was just after midnight, Gabe didn't bother holding back his yawn.

As the night went on, a little of the tension Xayn had been holding in his shoulders seemed to loosen, but when Xayn spoke so abruptly, Gabe saw some of it had returned.

"What about your family?"

Xayn's question was directed at Elaric, who stilled but glanced at Gabe and then back to Xayn. He must have seen the tormented expression he wore.

"What do you mean?"

"When you travel. Don't you miss them?"

Gabe saw Elaric's eyes darken, but he took a sip of his cider before putting it on the table.

"I don't have a family. Well, not in the way I think you're implying."

Xayn looked up and cocked his head but said nothing, and Gabe kept his mouth shut and decided to stay a spectator to their conversation.

Elaric sighed and leaned forward to lace his fingers across his knees. "I was banished, exiled, thrown out, whatever you want to call it. A long time ago."

"Oh, I'm sorry," Xayn said, but Elaric smiled and shook his head.

"It's fine. I forced their hand intentionally. I hated their ways and wanted out, so I made it so they had no choice. Then I left."

Gabe hadn't known about Elaric's relationship with his family, but considering no one had come to his funeral, he'd assumed. Marco may have been grieving, but if Elaric had people in his life who should have been there, Marco would have ensured they were.

"What about Marco?" Xayn asked.

Elaric's face lit up as he smiled, but even Gabe could see the difference between when he looked at Dany and Marco now. There was no comparison.

"Yeah, well, you got me there."

Xayn smiled and then downed his remaining cider. "Sorry, I didn't mean to pry." Then he went into the kitchen, leaving Gabe and Elaric to stare after him.

Anything I can do? Elaric asked.

Dany told you about Grandma Yvonne falling, I assume.

He thinks that's his fault?

Gabe nodded.

Elaric looked over his shoulder and called out, "Hey, Xayn, need help?"

"Um, no. I'm fine."

Elaric glanced at Gabe before getting to his feet and going to Xayn. Gabe ran his fingers through his hair and then reached along the Bond to Cat.

Gabe?

Sorry, just needed to feel you. As requested, his body flooded with the feelings of love and safety she passed to him, and he couldn't help but smile.

What's wrong?

Nothing. I'm with Elaric at Xayn's. He's still punishing himself for Grandma Yvonne's fall.

Onnie sighed, and he knew she had likely frowned when she'd done it.

Let me know if I can help. Or Dany. Hell, I'll send Mal if you think it would help him.

Gabe's smile widened as he was overwhelmed with the love and compassion his amazingly wonderful girlfriend had.

I will, thank you.

Love you.

Love you, too, Cat.

Xayn and Elaric returned, each holding a fresh cider, and Xayn handed Gabe one on his way back to his seat on the couch.

"Have um," Xayn hesitated and glanced at Elaric but apparently decided to continue, "you heard anything from him recently?"

It took Gabe a second to realize who Xayn was talking about, but his look at Elaric made sense.

"Oh, no, we haven't," Gabe replied. "Other than the shit he's pulling with the media, he's only been testing the wards, but Jakob himself hasn't shown himself."

"It's a good thing there are so many press from our world in Seattle," Elaric added.

"Not to mention that he hasn't gone national," Gabe said.

"Yet," Xayn stated.

"True," Gabe agreed before finishing his cider and switching to the cold one. "I can't see what he thinks he can gain from that. Right now, it's only us after him. What can he possibly want the whole magical world after him for?"

Elaric shook his head and stared in front of himself, and Xayn merely shrugged.

"Either way, I'm ready for this shit to be done. I just wish I knew where he was." Gabe growled.

"I'm glad you don't," Xayn whispered, "You'd do something stupid or alone."

Gabe snorted, but he couldn't argue with him. Instead, he wrapped his arm around Xayn's shoulder and pulled him against his side.

"Can't say you're wrong, but I'll behave. Swear."

Elaric finally looked up again, and he smiled at them. "Don't worry, Xayn. We won't let him get into trouble. Dany would kick his ass if he even thought about it."

Xayn nearly inhaled his cider, and Gabe shoved him back upright so he could pat his back. Once he'd coughed up the fluid in his lungs, Xayn nodded.

"She would—and she'd win."

Gabe laughed loudly but nodded along with Elaric.

"That she would," Gabe admitted.

"Did she ever tell you about the time when Gabe spoiled my Christmas gift?" Xayn asked Elaric.

Gabe groaned, "Oh, no. Not this story."

Elaric leaned forward to set down his bottle and then focused on Xayn. "Oh, this I have to hear."

Xayn grinned, and Gabe just rolled his eyes. Whatever brought Xayn's smile out, even if it meant telling Elaric embarrassing stories from their childhood.

Gabe would let Xayn tell them all if it brought life back to his best friend's cheeks.

Chapter 18: Friendship and Fortunes

August 2022 - Alku | Onnie Moore

"What's your plan for the day, Cat?" Gabe asked from beside her on the couch, where he was rubbing the bottom of one of her feet.

"Miranda should be here close to ten, so after my tea, I'll probably read that book about the town's wards that Dany found until Erika drops Miranda off. What about you?"

"Elaric asked to train with me. He isn't as coordinated with his main form as he'd like to be. We'll probably be at the school until we need to pick up the food for dinner."

Onnie sipped her tea and laid her head back on the sofa arm. "Okay."

"When's Dany crashing the party?"

"Not until this afternoon. There's a group meeting at the library, and she promised she'd be there to run it."

"What is it this time?"

"The Alku Demonological Society." Onnie couldn't keep a grin off her face, and when Gabe's hands stopped their movement, she chuckled. "Yeah. Apparently, that's a thing."

"I'm still shocked that this town can surprise me."

"Me too, honestly. I hope it never stops."

Mal's tail whacked Onnie in the side of the head. It startled her, and she jumped, knocking him off the back of the couch. He disappeared before he hit the floor and reappeared next to Gabe instead.

"Mal! You scared the crap out of me."

"You said you like surprises," he grinned.

Onnie glared at the feline while Gabe shook his head at their antics.

"While I'd love to continue with this," Gabe said, shifting Onnie's feet off his lap and getting up, "I've gotta go before I'm late." He kissed Onnie quickly and then headed for the front door.

"Bye! Go easy on him!" she shouted at his back.

Gabe replied with a muttered, "Yeah, right," under his breath as he left.

"Ready for the tiny human?" Mal asked as he stole Gabe's previous place on the couch.

"Yup," Onnie said, tucking her legs underneath herself and giving Mal more room to curl up.

"Wake me when she gets here," the feline said with a yawn before he closed his eyes.

"Didn't you just wake up?" Onnie teased as she reached for her book on the side table.

"Shut it. Don't judge me." Mal sassed before relocating off somewhere.

Onnie grinned, setting her tea aside, and then flipped her book open on her lap.

Who designed all these wards, Kushima?

Generation after generation of Keeper. Each has added on to what existed with what was needed during their reign.

Did you create one?

Kushima chuckled. *In a way.*

Onnie flipped a few sections forward, skipping the generalized description of wards and their various types. She'd learned that from Dany already, so she went straight to the third section, which explained how to create wards and then tie them to the existing ones.

These wards aren't the same as the warding Xayn does, right?

Correct. A hedge witch's wards are created via sigils, physical elements, and energy from the forest. They tend to be very specific and can be altered or destroyed easily since they exist in the real world, not the Bond plane.

Interesting. Onnie read a few sections but then paused. *Wait, how did past Keepers create wards if they couldn't see the Bond the way I can? Were they doing it blind?*

Kushima must have been amused because the warmth from Onnie's Bond bloomed from within her chest.

In a way. Do you remember what Dany taught you about creating wards? How Keepers would utilize rituals to aid in their creation?

Yeah, sure.

That's all pointless.

Onnie snorted. *Why?*

Because you are correct, none of the past Keepers were making or altering the wards. They could not have done so without the capability to see and manipulate the Bonds in the world around them.

Onnie rested her head back with a smile and closed her eyes. *You did it.*

I did.

So, what's all this stuff in these books about ward-making?

Useless nonsense.

Onnie laughed abruptly, and Mal brushed her Bond from the other room.

Sorry, Mal. All good.

She felt him return to his nap as she wiped tears of laughter from the corners of her eyes.

I guess that's not an entirely fair statement. Those rituals did show me what they wanted to create. That aside, they were essentially pointless, and beyond that, they could have told the ceiling what they wanted instead.

So, why are there books about making them, and why am I studying them if they are bogus?

It was Kushima's turn to laugh. *In general, there's something to be learned from ritual work. It's just not about creating wards. Besides, we are*

Keepers and do not exclude knowledge that is not based on fact. We have entire sections dedicated to fiction.

Yeah, but they are labeled as fiction!

Are they? Kushima said with a sly tone. *Can you tell me, without a doubt, that the religious texts we have are based on true events?*

Are you trying to say the Bible is a fantasy? Onnie sniggered.

I said no such thing.

Onnie didn't respond, and Kushima said no more on the subject. When the doorbell rang, Onnie put her book on the couch and went to receive Miranda and her mother.

Right before she pulled the door open, Onnie said, *It's totally fiction, isn't it?*

Oh, one hundred percent, Kushima added with a laugh as Onnie opened the door.

"Onnie!" Miranda shouted and rushed up to hug Onnie's waist.

"Hey, girly! Ready for our sleepover?" Onnie asked, squeezing the little girl in return.

"Yup! Mommy said I get to stay here. She even packed my favorite jammies," Miranda looked up and grinned.

"She did!" Onnie said with exaggerated awe. "That's wonderful. I can wear my favorite pajamas, too!" Onnie looked up at Erika and smiled. "Are you all ready for what you need to do? Do you need anything?"

Erika shook her head. "You're doing plenty already. Thank you again."

"No trouble, really." Onnie looked down at Miranda. "Hey, Miranda, can you run into the library and get Mal for me? It's the first door on your right in the hallway."

"Sure!"

The little girl grinned, overjoyed at being asked to do something for Onnie. She and Erika watched her disappear around the corner, and then Onnie reached for the small purple duffle bag Erika was holding.

"Here, let me take that."

"Thank you. Change of clothes, toiletries, her stuffed squirrel, and a small blanket she loves."

"Wonderful. Any medications she takes, allergies, stuff like that?" Onnie asked as she set the bag on the small bench by the door.

"No medications, standard stuff if she has a headache or something like that. No allergies, either. She really is a pretty normal kid...." Erika's eyes darkened, and she looked away. "Except for the talking thing."

Onnie squeezed the woman's hand. "She's a normal kid even with that. Give her time. You never know."

Erika nodded. "Yeah, I know. You're right."

She and Onnie looked toward the hallway when Miranda came around the corner, Mal trotting along at her side.

"Found him!" she said and patted his head gently.

"You rock! Thank you. Why don't you come and say bye to Mom? We don't want her to be late," Onnie said, stepping aside so the little girl could get to Erika.

"Bye, Mommy!" Miranda said as she dashed over and nearly knocked Erika over with her hug around her legs. "I love you!"

Erika squeezed her eyes shut but knelt down to her daughter's level and gave her another hug. Then, looking up at Onnie with tears in her eyes, she said, "I love you, too, baby. Be a good girl for Onnie, okay?"

"I will. You be good, too, okay? Tell Auntie to get better soon."

Onnie covered her mouth with her hand to hold in the laugh she made at the little girl's very adult-like statements.

"I'll be good, I promise, and I'll tell her. That will make her happy." Erika smiled and kissed Miranda's cheek before standing back up and ushering her little one back inside the house. "Alright, have fun, you three."

"Drive safe."

The three of them watched as Erika returned to her car and waved. Once she was gone from view, Onnie closed the door and locked it behind them.

She turned around and knelt in front of Miranda. "So, do you have anything *you* want to do today?"

Miranda put her finger on her chin and tilted her head to the left, her 'I'm thinking' face exaggerated and extremely cute.

"Hmm…" she shrugged, her little shoulders traveling up multiple inches before quickly dropping back down again. "I don't know."

Onnie giggled. "Okay, how about this? You and I go do something fun this morning, and then later, Dany, Gabe, and a few of our other friends wanted to come to have dinner with you and me. Does that sound alright?"

"Yeah," Miranda said, nodding.

"Okay! Then what should we do this morning? Have you had breakfast?"

"I did. It was yummy. Mommy made eggs." The little girl stuck out her tongue and grinned.

Mal, on the other side of the room, chuckled at that, and Onnie gave him a dirty look for it.

Careful!

Sorry, she's just too much.

"Do you wanna be inside or outside today?" Onnie asked, desperately trying to narrow down something for them to do.

"Outside!" Miranda cheered with a slight hop in place.

"Would you like to go for a walk or to the park, or maybe we could play in the backyard?"

The little girl's face lit up instantly. "I wanna see your backyard!"

"Alright! That's a plan. Oh, maybe you could help me with something…" Onnie was fully aware she was manipulating the little girl's excitement, but if it made her happy, Onnie didn't care.

"Yeah, I'll help!"

"Will you help me make some art from my walls? Do you like painting?"

Miranda jumped up and down in place again. "I do! I do!"

Onnie stood up and grabbed the purple bag from the bench. "Yay! I'm so excited!" She held out her free hand for Miranda to take and led her into her bedroom. "We need to change into different clothes, though. I'm a messy painter. Would you like to wear one of my T-shirts?"

Onnie was pretty sure she was undeserving of the hero worship she was receiving, but Miranda's happy smile and rosy cheeks made it something she could ignore.

"Yes, please!"

Onnie led her to the bed and counted to three before hoisting her onto it and setting her bag beside her on the quilt.

"I'll be right back. Let me go get a shirt for you."

"Okay!"

Onnie headed over to the closet and grinned as Miranda's eyes seemed to examine everything in the room, one at a time.

"You have a lot of books, Onnie."

"I do! I love books," Onnie called over her shoulder. "Do you like books, too?"

"I love them."

"What's your favorite book?" Onnie dug through her older shirts and found two she no longer cared about, quickly changing into one of them.

"I really like the one you gave me last time."

Onnie froze for a fraction of a second before regaining her composure. "The one about the prince who liked the color blue?"

"Yup, it had a really happy ending."

Miranda flopped back on the bed and stared at the ceiling, her little legs swinging back and forth.

"It...did?" Onnie asked cautiously and truthfully, optimistic. Sure, the book was supposed to be a fairytale way of explaining the prophecy to children, but maybe the book's ending was accurate without knowing it. Stranger things had happened.

"Uh-huh! He saved everyone. His friends helped him, though. He couldn't do it all by himself."

Miranda sat back up and tried to pull her t-shirt over her head once she saw Onnie had the other one ready. She only made it halfway over her head before Onnie bit her lip to hide her laugh at the cute girl's struggle.

"I see. It's good to rely on others sometimes."

She put down the larger shirt and helped Miranda out of her pretty little one before Onnie slipped the bigger one over the girl's head and the tank top she still had on.

"Do you, Onnie?" Miranda asked as her head popped through the neckline of the t-shirt. She looked up, and Onnie couldn't help but think that the age in her eyes was not that of a six-year-old.

"Ah, I try. Gabe, Dany, Mal…Yeah. I think I do." Onnie blushed as she tried to answer honestly, and she felt Kushima's amusement over the entire exchange.

Hey, you try having a six-year-old look through you like a pane of glass.

Kushima laughed but said nothing.

Miranda smiled at Onnie's answer as she poked her arms through the t-shirt's holes. Then she looked down at the baggy cotton shirt and tried to see what was on the front.

Onnie had given her an old Knott's Berry Farm t-shirt from one of Halloween's Knott's Scary Farm events. Snoopy was on the front of it with Charlie Brown under his sheet ghost costume. When Onnie realized Miranda probably had no idea who the Peanuts were, she suddenly felt ancient.

"Ready?" Onnie asked, and when Miranda nodded, Onnie helped her down from the taller-than-average bed. When her feet hit the floor, the shirt fell to its full length, and Miranda giggled as she swished her hips side to side. Considering the shirt had been Onnie's brother Jace's and was big on her, it went to Miranda's ankles and made more of a dress than a smock.

Miranda looked up with a goofy grin. "It's a dress!"

Onnie giggled with the little one before leading her into the kitchen.

"It is. It's adorable on you, but try to make sure you don't get paint on your shoes, okay? Or we can take them off."

When Onnie unlocked and opened the back door, Miranda's eyes went wide. She immediately grabbed her shirt's hem, hiked it up, and dashed down the deck to the dock.

"Can you swim?" Onnie called out after her and followed behind her at a jog.

"I can, but I won't go in. Promise!" Miranda giggled, and Onnie sighed with relief and slowed to a walk.

It's going to be a long afternoon, Onnie said to Kushima, who didn't bother to hide her laughter.

A few hours later, Onnie and Miranda sat on opposite sides of a drop cloth spread out over the wooden deck. They each had a canvas in front of them, and a few plates and bowls had various paint colors lined up between them. They'd been painting for a few hours now, often getting sidetracked by either conversation or the occasional animal wandering onto the deck that Miranda stopped to sit and watch.

Onnie's canvas was a mess, art not being her forte. It was a splotchy mix of colors, and she hoped that if someone squinted *really* hard, they'd see a butterfly. She highly doubted it, though.

Realistically, she'd gotten lucky with her painting suggestion. She hadn't been sure if Miranda would be interested in it, but Onnie had hoped the little girl would be willing to humor her.

She hadn't been making up the need for art, though. So far, Abbot's house was still that—Abbot's. She and Gabe had done their best to make their new house feel like their home, but Abbot was still everywhere. They'd likely never get away from that, and they didn't want to, at least not entirely. But it was their home now, and they needed it to feel like it was. Art for the walls had been one of the first things on her list. She hadn't planned on being the painter, though.

"Do you like it?" Miranda asked, pointing to the canvas at her feet.

Onnie got up to see Miranda's canvas and gasped. It showed a tiny figure surrounded by golden light on a background of beautiful swirling blues that were so dark that they were almost black.

"I love it!"

"Yay! I…" Miranda looked down and bashfully twirled her big toe. "I see her when I have nightmares. She chases them away."

Onnie swallowed roughly. "I see. Well, I'm glad she's there then."

Miranda smiled again and nodded. "Me too!"

Kushima, look at this. Onnie projected her view of the painting for the First Keeper to see. *What do you think? This has to be the night of the storm, right?*

Very interesting. I would not worry overmuch about it.

Are you sure—

"Where my sleepover girls at?" Dany's voice called from the back door.

"Dany!" Miranda said and jumped up and down.

Onnie grinned at her best friend, whose excitement was contagious.

Dany rushed over exaggeratedly to Miranda and bent for a high-five. "Hey, girly!"

Miranda looked at her palm, wiped the paint onto her shirt, and gave Dany a high-five. "Hi Dany, look! I painted the girl who makes the bad guys go away in my dreams."

The little girl grinned so proudly that her eyes shut. Onnie watched as Dany glanced at the canvas and immediately did a double-take.

Yup. That is exactly what I did, Onnie said to Dany along the Bond.

Dany was more used to working with kids, and she quickly controlled her emotions and made 'Ooo' and 'Ahh' sounds while Miranda pointed out details in the picture.

"I think it's beautiful. What're you going to do with it once it's dry?" Dany asked as she sat on the deck beside them both.

"It's for Onnie! She wanted to make art for her house, so I made her this. Maybe she can chase away the bad guys in your dreams, too."

Miranda had spoken to Dany, not Onnie, and it seemed to rattle the woman where few things ever did. For the second time, though, Dany shifted back into teacher mode and past the child's all too perceptive comment.

O-M-G, this girl! Dany said to Onnie.

I know. She's been like this all morning.

Onnie leaned forward, tapping one of her clean fingers on Miranda's nose. "It's perfect. I'll make sure to put it in my room. Thank you."

Miranda giggled and carefully inspected the painting, suddenly lost in her own world again.

"How was your...gathering?" Onnie asked with a smirk.

Dany rolled her eyes. "Oh, I'll tell you later, but entertaining, to say the least."

"Have you eaten?"

"Nope," Dany shook her head. "What time are the guys headed over?"

"A bit later than normal. Marco will be here after dinner, obviously."

Dany groaned. "Yeah, summer is rough on him."

Onnie shrugged. "He gets more in the winter. It balances out, I guess. For Sam, too. From what I understand, they're just used to it."

"I guess they could move to a place where day and night were more even all year round." Dany picked up a clean paintbrush and fiddled with it.

"Who knows, maybe something will change one day," Onnie shrugged. "So yeah, we'll eat around seven, and then afterward," Onnie looked at Miranda, who was still profoundly analyzing her painting. *I'm not sure how late she'll stay up, so maybe after Marco gets here, we'll have cookies and then bedtime or something.*

Dany nodded. "So, what you're saying is it's snack time now!"

Miranda's focus broke from her painting at the mention of snacks, and Onnie and Dany heard, *Snacks?* along their Bond with Mal.

Onnie couldn't hold it in, and her whole body shook with laughter.

Get in the kitchen then, you brat, she said to Mal. "Yeah, I think I'm hungry. Are you hungry?" Onnie asked Miranda, very aware of the answer already.

Miranda nodded. "Yup! Yes, please!"

Dany got to her feet. "Why don't you two go in and get changed out of your painted clothes? I'll clean this up and meet you in the kitchen."

"You don't mind?" Onnie asked, but Dany waved her off, so Onnie got to her feet.

Miranda dashed over to Onnie's side and grabbed her hand. "Thank you!" she smiled at Dany and let Onnie lead her back to the house.

"Okay, check your shoes for paint!" Onnie said when they'd made it to the door, where she made a big show of checking her own.

"All clean!" Miranda said before holding out the front of her shirt. "Shirt got messy."

"Yup, mine, too. That's okay. You've still got your tank top on under. Do you wanna take off the shirt out here, and I can put it in the wash?"

"Sure!" Miranda's ears turned pink a few seconds later. "Um... could you help?"

"Of course."

Onnie carefully held Miranda's shirt away from her body so she could wiggle out of it without getting paint all over herself.

"My turn," Onnie said, taking off her own messy shirt, and they both entered the house. "Do you want to get your other shirt from your bag? I'll be right there after I put these away."

Miranda skipped off down the hall to Onnie's bedroom while she went to put their messy clothes in the laundry and give her hands a quick rinse. When she returned to her room, Miranda had put her clean shirt back on and was looking up at the books on a shelf, her head nearly ninety degrees sideways as she read the spines on one of the lowest rows.

"You have lots of really neat books." Miranda was smiling, but she continued perusing them while Onnie changed.

In the last few months, Onnie had moved some books between rooms in the house and the shop. More of her favorites were now in her bedroom, and Abbot's were in his study at the shop. It helped make the space feel like it was hers while still keeping the comfort of her Grandfather's warmth around her.

"I'm glad you like them. Would you like to read something while I get some snacks ready?"

"Can I read this one?" Miranda pointed to one, and Onnie crossed the room to see what it was. "Mythology by Hamilton?"

"Yeah," Miranda smiled expectantly.

Kushima, anything in that book that she shouldn't read at her age? I haven't read it in forever.

I...don't think it will hurt her...but it is a bit...

Mature.

Exactly.

Onnie nodded and pulled the book out to hand to her. "Sure, you can read that. Maybe Dany will sit with you while I get tasty goodies together."

"Okay!" Miranda said with a cheer and then dashed out of the room, book clutched in her tiny fingers as she excitedly called out to Dany.

Everyone but Marco, who had yet to arrive, sat on the back deck around a portable fire pit. Miranda was sitting on Dany's lap in an outdoor armchair, and they were still looking through the book about mythology from earlier in the day. Onnie was seated in another armchair nearby, simply listening to the two of them and petting Mal. It was wonderful to hear the little girl's sweet voice as she pointed sections out to Dany, who would then explain them while Miranda listened and nodded intently.

The sun was nearly set, and Gabe and Elaric were cleaning up the remnants of dinner and setting aside a serving for Marco. The two men talked about their earlier training session as they went back and forth from the barbeque, outdoor table, and kitchen, carrying things away.

When they were just about finished, Onnie heard Marco along their Bond, *Nearly there.*

Come in when you get here. The front's open. Just lock up behind you, please.

Absolutely.

She relayed his imminent arrival to the others, and Gabe stayed inside to greet him and get him some food while Elaric joined her and the others on the outdoor sofa. Dany looked up and smiled at him but continued reading a passage from the book to Miranda.

Onnie pulled her knees up to her chest, rested her head on her arms, and closed her eyes. The Bonds around her became visible, more by habit than a need to actually look at them. Since they were visible, she checked Miranda's aura because she could and was relieved to find the young girl happy and comfortable in her surroundings.

Gabe and Marco's voices carried from the house along the quiet night air, and Miranda looked up and grinned at them. Then she wiggled out of Dany's lap and ran over to wrap her arms around Marco's waist to hug him.

"Hello, Miranda," Marco said, ruffling her hair and smiling down at her fondly.

She looked up and giggled at him before returning to Dany, where she crawled back into her lap and picked up the book again.

"Hey, Marco," Onnie said, and she squeezed his hand when he placed it on her shoulder.

"Nice to see you, Onnie. Thank you for having me."

His smile was genuine, and his dark eyes flickered in the firelight, contrasting with his pale skin and white teeth. The image helped Onnie better understand why a sanguiste on the wrong side of morality could be so fearsome even without using intimidation.

"You're welcome anytime. Sit. Did Gabe get you something to eat?"

Marco shook his head and took the spot next to Elaric on the couch. "I'm satisfied at the moment, but I appreciate the thought."

Onnie giggled at his roundabout way of implying that his dinner was currently occurring around him but said nothing more about it, trusting him to ask or just get whatever he needed.

"Cat, share?" Gabe said from where he stood behind her.

She tilted her head back to look at him, Mal opening his eyes to do the same.

You kicking me out? Mal said, along the entire group's Bond.

Go sit with Dany, Gabe said, giving him a scratch under the chin.

You've convinced me, Mal said and stretched before making his way to Dany, the old-fashioned way—by walking. He jumped up to sit beside her and Miranda, the three of them making it a tight fit.

Onnie stood up, let Gabe take the chair, and settled herself into his lap. They were one chair short for the group, and Onnie was the smallest besides Miranda, but she wasn't complaining anyway.

As she shifted to get comfortable, Miranda wiggled down again, took her book from Dany, and climbed onto the couch between Elaric and Marco. Mal quickly took over Dany's lap, and she began petting him while she watched the little girl.

"Here," Elaric helped Miranda get comfortable, and she looked up at him with a smile.

"Thank you." Before she looked away from him, she nodded once and then looked back down at her book. "Thank you for saving me from the scary monster when it was raining, too."

Miranda started humming a little song as she flipped through the book while all the adult and feline eyes around the fire widened.

"Ah..." Onnie cleared her throat. "Miranda, what do you mean when he saved you?"

Miranda looked over at her, her little head cocked in confusion. "When there was that big rain, we all had a sleepover in the school. Mr. E saved me from the bad men."

Marco chuckled at her response, and everyone else remained silent. Once again, Miranda returned to her reading, and the only sound was the crackling fire and her turning old book pages as she hummed.

"Um... Onnie," Dany asked along the Bond, *"did you tell her who—"* Before she finished her statement, Onnie was already shaking her head.

"I think I might be able to help clear a few things up," Marco said, instantly drawing six pairs of eyes to his.

"Clear what things?" Miranda asked, clearly confused with only hearing half of their conversation.

Marco smiled at the little girl, pushing an unruly curl behind her ear.

"How did you know that was Mr. E? Doesn't he look different from the night of the storm?"

Miranda's little forehead wrinkled, and she looked over at Elaric and squinted. She tilted her head back and forth and then climbed to her knees and put her little hands on both of his cheeks so she could look closer. After another few seconds, she made a huffing sound and plopped back down on her butt.

"A little, I guess. But not really."

Dany's mouth opened and closed like a guppy, and even Mal looked confused.

Marco stared fondly at the sweet girl. "Miranda, do you remember what I told you when you were little?"

She looked back up at him and nodded. "Yup!"

"Would you be okay with me telling Onnie and your other friends that are here right now? We both know that you can trust them."

Miranda scowled at him and crossed her arms. "But you told me not to tell anyone but Mommy."

"You're right. I did. I think you'll be okay telling these friends, though. You know Onnie is the Keeper, right?"

Onnie was aware that most people knew what her title was. Even the ordinary humans in Alku knew it, so she wasn't surprised when Miranda said yes. But when she giggled and pointed at Mal and said, "Yeah, and Mal is her Link kitten, right?" Onnie nearly had a heart attack.

"That's right," Marco praised.

Miranda then said, in her usual, everyday little girl tone of voice, "Is that why he can talk?" She didn't blink even though she'd just shocked four full-grown adults enough for them to stop breathing.

What. The actual. Fuck. Dany stated, and Onnie and Gabe could only nod in agreement.

"You're right. That is why he can talk. See, so they have a secret, too. That's why I think you'll be safe telling them yours." Marco ruffled her hair again, and she grinned and bounced in place a few times.

"Okay! You can tell them if you want!" She beamed at the rest of the group and then returned to her book.

"Marco…?" Elaric said, verbalizing what everyone was feeling with his tone.

Marco smiled, and for a second, Onnie wasn't sure he would say anything, but then he smiled at her again and said, "Miranda is a truth seer."

Dany gasped and covered her mouth. "You're kidding!"

"A what?" Onnie asked and looked at Gabe, who had put his head in his hand to cover his eyes.

"Well, that explains it," Elaric said, draping his arm over the back of the sofa, now fully relaxed as if those five words solved everything.

"Hello?" Onnie said, prodding the group to answer her for a second time.

"Sorry," Marco smirked. "She's a truth seer, and to be frank, it's pretty much exactly as it sounds like."

Thankfully, Elaric expanded on Marco's explanation after seeing that Onnie was still confused.

"Think prophet or fortune teller mixed with a lie detector. Kind of?"

Marco gently tapped Miranda's shoulder. "Miranda, when you look at Mr. E, does he have a sparkly thing right here?" Marco asked, pointing to his own eyebrow.

Miranda didn't look up from her book but nodded in response. Onnie knew Elaric's base form had an eyebrow piercing, and she suddenly began to understand.

Then, it was Dany's turn to try and clear up the compounding confusion. "Is that why you don't like talking, Miranda?"

The young girl nodded again. "Yes. It makes people feel bad, and I scared Mommy."

"Oh, I see." Onnie's heart ached for the mother and child and the difficulties they must face every day. "Well, Miranda, Marco was right. We both have a secret, and we promise not to tell yours to anyone. Okay?"

Miranda slowly tilted her head up, and Onnie could see her eyes glitter in the firelight, unshed tears barely held within them.

Onnie quickly closed her eyes and rechecked Miranda's aura. She was surprised to find the little one so frightened.

She's scared, Onnie informed Mal.

He took the opportunity to jump off Dany's lap and get into Miranda's, then stuck his cold little nose on hers.

"Don't be scared, okay, little one? We're going to keep you safe, and you can say whatever you want with us, alright? You won't scare us."

Miranda's tightly held tears burst, and she snuggled Mal, who purred in her arms.

Onnie felt like she already knew the answer that was coming but asked it anyway.

Marco, Truth Seers…they're….

Hunted. Thought to be extinct.

Onnie squeezed her eyes closed and swallowed hard. *Understood. Thank you.*

When she reopened her eyes, Marco nodded subtly, and Elaric softly rubbed circles on the girl's back.

Miranda sniffled and then looked over at Onnie as she wiped her eyes with her arm. "Onnie…."

"What's up?" Onnie asked far more cheerily than she felt.

"Why are you going to break the tunnel?"

With Mal's promise to the girl fresh in her mind, Onnie forced a smile to her face and replied, "What do you mean?"

Miranda hesitated, and Onnie went over to kneel before her. "If you don't want to tell me, you don't have to, but it looks like what I'm going to do is bothering you. So, help me answer your question so you'll feel better?"

"I—I don't know. I just know that you're going to break it sometime soon, and," she looked at the rest of the people around them, "they will be there, too. Lots more other people, too, but I don't think they're very nice."

I think we just found where we meet the rogue. Onnie smiled at the miracle little girl in front of her and the gift she'd just given them all.

"Thank you for telling me more. I think I'll probably have to do it to protect Alku."

Miranda's brows crinkled again before she looked down into her lap. Onnie ducked her head to get back into Miranda's line of sight. "Is that an okay answer?"

The little girl nodded and buried her nose in Mal's fur again.

Dany cleared her throat from the other side of the fire. "Well…I think this calls for cookies. What do you think, Miranda?" The little girl's cheeks were rosy from crying, but she nodded. "Gabe, mind starting the oven?" Dany asked.

"Ah, sure," Gabe got to his feet and left the group to head back inside.

Dany held her hand out to Miranda. "Wanna come help me make them?"

"Okay," she said, giving Mal a few pets, which gave Onnie time to go back to her chair and get out of the kid's way.

Mal jumped down and padded into the house after Gabe, but Miranda stopped and tapped Marco's arm. He looked down at her, and she gestured for him to lean over so she could whisper into his ear. When she finished, she hugged him around the neck and kissed his cheek, then slid off the couch and ran after Dany.

Onnie stared at Marco, who hadn't blinked yet.

"Ah, Marco?" Elaric said with a raised eyebrow. "Everything okay?"

When Marco didn't react, Onnie gently brushed their Bond. "Marco?"

He jumped and then shook his head. "Sorry. Ah, what did you say?"

"Are you alright?" Elaric asked, and Onnie nodded in agreement with the question.

"Yeah, fine." He smiled, but both Onnie and Elaric pursed their lips at him, neither believing his off-the-cuff lie nor willing to call him out on it. "Ah, sorry. Habit." Marco shrugged and ran his fingers through his hair. "Ah, she said I shouldn't be sad and that if I waited for the man who likes feathers, I would be happy."

Elaric tsked. "Now you're getting dating advice from a six-year-old," he teased, and Marco's smile was genuine this time and not without an eye roll.

"How do you know that that was…real?" Onnie scrunched up her face, the word feeling incorrect. "Versus just the words of a child."

Marco returned to his internal brooding, and Elaric answered Onnie. "Though she's a six-year-old girl, nothing she says isn't *real*. That's why she chooses not to speak. She can easily say something that she thinks is unimportant, but to whomever she's speaking with…."

"Ah, I get it. So, why does she talk to me?" Onnie asked as she tried to piece together everything that she'd learned.

"Easy," Marco smirked, "she knew who you were the moment she met you."

Onnie nodded and spaced out into the fire. When she heard Kushima's voice, the corners of her lips curled up happily.

Don't think too hard about it now, young one. We can discuss it more another day. For now, know that the little one in your care is in a rare situation where she can be free to be herself. Help her make the most of it.

Right, as usual.

Onnie got to her feet. "Alright, I'm going to go check on the cookie monsters. Mal's probably ear-deep in a frosting tub by now."

Elaric snorted. "I could see it."

"You two, feel free to stay out here. I'll send Gabe out with cookies. I think Miranda's had a busy day. She'll probably eat and pass out."

"Highly likely," Marco said, his voice thick with affection.

"If you two don't mind sticking around, I'd like to talk more about everything after she's asleep."

"Of course," Marco said, and Elaric agreed.

Onnie left the two of them by the fire pit and went into the house to see how bad the sugar infection would be.

Chapter 19: Digestion

August 2022 - Alku | Elaric Rickson

Elaric lay his head back on the outdoor couch. His whole body hurt thanks to the earlier beating that Gabe disguised as training. Surprisingly, the form Elaric had taken to be his everyday one responded better than he'd expected to the workout regimen and he already felt more comfortable in it.

Only moving his eyes, Elaric glanced at Marco, who was immensely in his head and likely thinking of what Miranda had foretold. If Elaric was being honest, he was, too.

"What're you thinking?"

Marco didn't answer immediately, but eventually, he sat forward, resting his elbows on his knees, and held his hands up to the fire. "Whatever you're thinking is probably correct."

"Dread mixed with guilt and a touch of excitement that you're trying to suppress?" Elaric said with a laugh.

Marco glanced at him sidelong and smirked. "Still have the aura reading ability, I see."

Elaric snorted. "Yeah, no. That faded a long time ago." Marco's eyes went a touch wide, and Elaric grinned, knowing he'd shocked the man.

"Oh, I see." Marco returned to watching the flames but eventually added, "You're correct, though."

"I know." Elaric stared up at the stars above them. "Do you remember the time we stole Stephan's lunch and had a picnic out by the lake?"

"Of course, he still brings it up when frustrated with me." Marco chuffed. "Actually, he will scold Sam and use our theft as an example. 'At least you're not as bad as those two scoundrels.'"

"That somehow doesn't surprise me at all."

Elaric began naming constellations in his head as he located them in the sky. Even after modern hotels and lodgings became easily accessible, Elaric spent most of his nights under the stars while traveling. Crowds could be overwhelming, and he found that sleeping in the fresh air and on the hard ground actually gave him a better night's rest than a mattress in a busy city would.

"Why do you bring it up?" Marco asked.

Elaric sighed. "Marco, you've been alone for too long. You've gone cold. While I don't blame you, and I know the reasons why...."

Marco sighed and put his head in his hands.

"I just want to see you happy. *Real* happy."

Marco didn't respond, so Elaric kept quiet and resumed his constellation identification. A few minutes later, he heard someone exit the house, and it was easy to recognize the individual's gait as Gabe's.

"Mind if I join? I brought bribes."

Elaric raised his head and took the glass bottle Gabe was holding out to him.

"Thanks, and sure."

Gabe handed Marco a glass of red wine as Elaric popped off the cap to the beer he'd been given. Elaric took a sip, and the cool liquid relaxed his body very quickly, making him laugh.

"Apparently, this kid's a lightweight."

Marco raised his eyebrows over his wine glass as he sat back against the couch but didn't comment.

"That's gotta be rough," Gabe said as he opened his own bottle.

"Meh, I have other forms who could drink any sailor under the table. Well…" he paused, "I did. Not sure anymore. I'm going to have to test that at some point."

"I've said it before, and I'll say it again. What a life you live, Elaric." Gabe smiled, but when he glanced at Marco, he quickly looked back at Elaric.

Elaric barely shook his head, but Gabe got the point and didn't ask about Marco's suddenly solemn behavior change.

"So, what do you two think about the tunnel comment from Miranda earlier?"

That got Marco's attention, and he was instantly more animated than he'd been since the girls left. "If Miranda said it, it's true."

"So, how can we use that?" Gabe asked.

"I think it gives us an advantage, actually. If there was that kind of damage or will be, then chances are, that's where we'll end things. One way or another."

"Agreed," Marco said, "and she said multiple people were in attendance. All of us, including me, so we can assume it was at night."

"Ah, good catch," Gabe agreed. "She also mentioned multiple bad guys, though, right?"

"Yeah," Elaric recalled the little girl's commentary on the future they had yet to live. "What do you two think are the chances it's also when the prophecy triggers?"

Gabe groaned and roughly ran his fingers through his hair before yanking on the ends of it. "Yeah, I'd rather it not, but I can't disagree with you."

"I'm also afraid to say it, but I think that's a very solid assumption," Marco said, swirling his wine in its glass.

"How the hell am I supposed to protect her from this?" Gabe's quiet, small voice immediately drew Elaric's attention.

"Hey," he said, waiting until Gabe's eyes met his own. "I know she didn't say it directly, but I'm pretty sure Miranda implied that Onnie would be fine."

Gabe took a long pull from his beer and sighed. "Gods, I hope so."

"We'll make sure of it. Don't worry, Gabe. You're not alone in this fight," Marco said gently. "Or in protecting Onnie. Guardians or not, we'll be by her side, too."

Gabe nodded, his lips still pulled down in a frown.

Mal appeared on Gabe's lap and poked the man's cheek with his paw. "Stop it, dude. I can feel you brooding from the house."

Elaric chuckled. "That's got to be one handy trick."

Mal laughed loudly. "Yeah, one out of ten times. The other nine are one of these two turning the volume up past max." Mal was obviously teasing, and Gabe poked his belly.

"Quiet furball, you're no better."

Mal stuck his tongue out at Gabe and then relocated to the free chair.

Elaric only had Marco's aura ability for a short time, and though Elaric didn't need it to survive, he found it overwhelming and was glad when it faded. His own emotions were complicated enough. Being able to see others' emotions and trying to decode them, or even ignore them, wasn't easy.

"I have no idea how you all do it."

"Do what?" Gabe asked.

"Between his," Elaric gestured to Marco, "aura ability and you guys having your emotions on display for each other all the time, I don't know how you do it. Doesn't it…get overwhelming?"

Elaric expected one of them to agree or contradict him, but no one said anything, almost to the point that he wondered if he'd not spoken aloud.

But then Gabe spoke first. "When you and Cat were…fixing things, did she ever show you what the Bond looks like?"

Elaric nodded. "When she bound my powers."

"Yes, I've seen it as well," Marco added.

"You probably saw a dark space, the void, and a few strands of light, right?"

"For the most part," Elaric answered.

"Imagine that in reverse. A few hints of void and the entire world around you in the glowing strands. Some bright, some faint. Some are strong and rope-like, but others are whispy, barely there. They touch everything. Living beings, inanimate objects like cups and books, trees and rocks, and, as you're both aware, souls. That's what Onnie sees."

Mal added, "That's her default. She only saw the Bond in the simplicity that we do for a short while. There was an incident at Abbot's funeral. After that...."

Gabe continued. "Her powers grew, and so did her control. Hell, now she can even see the Bonds around her without going into the void. She explains it as an 'overlay' on the world before her eyes."

Elaric's head hurt just thinking about it. "So, you're saying I should shut up about my trivial and temporary situation." He chuckled, and so did Gabe.

"Not at all," Gabe said, shaking his head. "First off, everyone's threshold is different, and there's nothing wrong with that. I only mentioned it because the way I chose to think about the entire thing is that I have it easy with my limited exposure. I try to control what I can and apologize when I fuck up."

"Which is a lot," Mal interjected.

Gabe snorted. "Which is a lot."

Elaric smirked and sipped his beer. He'd learned so many things about Onnie since he'd met her. Dany and Gabe, too, but Onnie was... complicated. When she bound his powers, she saw all of his forms. Then, when he'd died, she literally gave him back his life by caring for his soul. He'd spent a lot of time in the First Keeper's library and learned a lot when he could do nothing other than sit back and watch. Onnie had some secrets, and at first, he was confused and concerned that she'd keep things from her Guardian and her Link. But he no longer worried after seeing her interactions with the First Keeper and hearing *why* she kept her secrets.

Onnie wasn't acting alone. She *had* someone to rely on—the First Keeper. She knew everything that was happening, which had calmed Elaric's fears, both for Onnie and the magical world.

Hey, Onnie?

Yeah? You okay?

Elaric warmed, hearing her concern over him with only two words. *Yeah, I just wanted to talk to you about something, but…I'd like to do it privately, if you don't mind.*

Onnie didn't answer immediately but apologized for being distracted by Miranda for a moment. *Would tomorrow be alright? We could meet at the shop and use the First Keeper's library if you want that level of privacy.*

That's perfect. Thanks.

Duh, she said, and he heard her small mental chuckle.

Elaric looked up when he saw movement in his periphery, and Dany was coming over, a platter of freshly baked cookies in her hand.

"I brought sweets." She smiled and handed the plate to Gabe to take one and then pass around. Then Elaric heard her ask, "Can I?"

He saw that she had pointed to the space between him and Marco. He was about to answer when he realized she wasn't asking him.

"You needn't ask, Dany."

Marco shifted so she could get past him and join them on the sofa. When she tucked her feet under herself and leaned into Elaric's side, Marco smiled at her, and Elaric didn't miss his subtle nod to her.

Gabe held the plate back to her, and she grabbed a cookie before handing it to Marco.

"Onnie's laying with Miranda. That girl is a chatterbox with Onnie, and we'll be lucky if she sleeps at all tonight."

Marco selected a cookie and rested the plate on a small nearby table. "I'm delighted to see her comfortable. It's been a long time since I've seen her so animated." He had a soft smile when he spoke of the little one, and Elaric wondered what had happened for Marco to have that much affection for her.

"Me too," Gabe said. "I hate watching her by herself at school. Kids are cruel, and even the ones who don't mean to be can cause lasting scars."

Dany snorted. "Honestly, that girl is stronger than I am, and at her age, it makes me excited to see who she'll grow up to be. Granted, I love both sides of her—her quiet side and her giggle machine—they're both wonderful."

Elaric glanced at Marco, who was trying to keep his face blank and use his wine glass to hide what he couldn't. Even from the other end of the sofa, Elaric could tell Marco was thinking of the parallels between him and the little girl.

"I'll be honest," Mal said, "when she called me out as a talking cat, I thought I'd eaten too much catnip."

Gabe laughed. "Yeah, I do have to admit, it was entertaining watching you all react."

"Oh, shut up," Dany teased, "you were just as shocked."

"Never said I wasn't. I guess after all the years working at the school, the things kids say no longer throw me. It doesn't matter if they are true or a fairytale."

Elaric lost track of the conversation as his mind wandered. His thoughts drifted back to the comment she'd made to Marco. Elaric knew that whatever came of it, Marco would likely fight it. Abbot was only the most recent of the people Marco cared about and then lost. There was no way the tortured sanguiste would let someone else in willingly. Elaric was still shocked that Marco had joined their group on rare occasions. In the past, he'd often stuck to the occasional meal with Stephan and his family. Now, Onnie had pulled him from his lonely apartment, and even though Marco was still hiding behind his mask more often than not, more recently, Elaric would see the real man he cared about so much shine through—before he was quickly hidden away again.

Elaric must have been quiet for too long because he felt Dany poke him in the side, and he flinched.

"Yipes, what?"

Everyone was staring at him, and he felt the tips of his ears heat up, but thankfully, the flickering firelight hid it.

"Where'd you go?" Dany asked. "You've been quiet for like ten minutes."

"Shit, really? Sorry, I was just thinking. Guess I zoned out."

He sipped his beer, and sure enough, it was warm, and he grimaced.

Onnie suddenly appeared behind Gabe and groaned. "Ug, I swear, if we could harness that child's energy, we'd be set for eternity."

She walked around Gabe's chair and slumped onto his lap, making him grunt. Elaric saw him wrap his arm around her waist and pull her closer to him. His love for Onnie was in every move he made, and Elaric was beginning to understand why Gabe often made the choices he did.

"Why didn't you just walk?" Gabe asked and stuck his nose into her hair.

"I was afraid if I moved, even an inch, she'd wake back up." Onnie rubbed her temples, but her eyes still sparkled with joy. She glanced at Marco and did a quick double-take before Elaric heard her say only to him, *What she said genuinely shook him, huh?*

Yeah. I can tell you more tomorrow, but I think so.

I don't need to know unless you think I should. He deserves secrets, too. That said, if I can help, please tell me.

Will do.

"So, I guess I get to destroy the tunnel," Onnie said matter of factly, and Elaric was pretty sure he heard excitement in her voice.

Evidently, he wasn't the only one because Dany laughed and said, "Why do you sound excited about that?"

"I'm not...much." Onnie giggled. "I just think it's entertaining. I have no idea how I'd even do that, let alone why. So, obviously, we'll learn something new before then."

"True, but Cat, you need to take this seriously. If what Miranda said was true—"

"It always is," Marco interjected quietly.

Gabe started over. "Since what Miranda said will be true, we can't rule out the possibility of the prophecy being connected to it."

"I'm aware," Onnie said sharply, but then she sighed. "Sorry. I know, and you're right, but please, let me have a few days to digest all of this. It sounds like this isn't going to happen tomorrow, so can I just have a little time?"

Gabe squeezed her for a second and then kissed her temple. "Yes, I'm sorry. You're right."

"Take the time you need, Keeper," Marco said without looking away from the flames he'd been watching for quite a while.

Elaric knew that when Marco called her by her title, he was doing it for the same reason Elaric did—to distinguish between Onnie, the person, and Keeper, the role. Both were important, and neither should be neglected.

"Thanks," Onnie said and shifted in Gabe's lap, resting her head on his shoulder.

Elaric looked at Dany, and at some point, she'd shifted, too. She was leaning on him, and he'd put his arm around her. Even more surprising was that her legs were draped over Marco's, and he gently rubbed one of her calves absentmindedly. He looked relaxed and engaged with those around him, and a portion of his mask had fallen, probably without him realizing it.

It was a good step. One Elaric would gladly take.

Gabriel Vansand

"Dany, you sleeping in my room tonight?" Gabe asked as he checked the time on his phone.

"You mind? You can stay at my place if you want."

Gabe kissed the top of Onnie's head. "All good. I think I'm gonna go see Xayn. Probably crash with him."

"He doing alright?" Elaric asked with hesitancy.

"For the most part. I think he's finally gotten over the shock from meeting you." Gabe chuckled but saw Elaric wince. "The other night helped, too. Thanks for that."

"Damn, that honestly hadn't been my intention, but I'm glad he's not as upset."

"What did you do?" Marco said, his eyes narrowed at Elaric.

"Nothing," Gabe added quickly. "He told Dany's other brother they were dating and warned him of your past so he wouldn't overreact if he heard rumors."

Elaric groaned and rubbed his eyes. "Honestly, I didn't mean to make him uncomfortable."

Marco was quiet, and after he glared a bit longer at Elaric, he looked away. There was a subtle smile on his face, so they'd clearly worked it out along the Bond.

"Xayn's fine. I think he's still getting used to the fact that he doesn't need to hide anymore." Dany frowned, "Not that he ever had to in the first place."

Marco cleared his throat softly. "While I love you, Dany, and I know you're a brilliant woman, trust me when I say this...you wouldn't understand."

Gabe watched his sister more closely, half expecting her to be angry at being excluded. As he should have predicted, she chose the other response and shifted on the couch to tuck herself into Marco's side for one of her cuddle hugs.

"I know, and I'm sorry. I didn't mean to imply that I did. No one should have to, but I get that's not how the world works or even parts of Alku."

Marco put his arm around her and squeezed her gently but said nothing else.

Sometimes, I wonder if we raised her too well, Gabe said to Marco and Elaric. *She and Onnie are similar in that way. They expect the best of people.*

She's perfect the way she is, Gabe, Marco said fondly. *I only said what I did so she wouldn't get herself into trouble in another situation—one where the other person might see it as minimization, not empathy.*

Agreed, Elaric added. *Though, in my opinion, I don't see Onnie that same way.*

Meaning? Gabe asked curiously.

There's a...fear...that Onnie carries that Dany doesn't. While she may expect the best of people, she's always preparing for the worst.

I agree, Marco added.

Gabe kissed Onnie's temple and gave her a slight squeeze.

"You okay?" she whispered.

"I am, but I should head out."

Onnie nodded and climbed out of his lap. "Tell him I said hi?"

"Course." Gabe kissed her briefly and then looked at Marco and Elaric. "You two heading out or staying a bit longer?"

Elaric briefly tickled one of Dany's feet with a grin. "We'll head out, too. I'm exhausted and think Onnie's Guardian may have bruised this form permanently."

Gabe snorted and grinned. "Sounds like you need more practice."

Elaric groaned and got to his feet. "Relentless."

Their session had gone perfectly earlier that day. Gabe had helped Elaric test a few of his form's capabilities, and then they'd settled on the one he used as Elaric in town and started pushing it a bit more. He'd kept up, and they found he was more nimble than his Andrew form had been once he'd acclimated to it. They agreed they could work with that and began outlining a fitness plan. Apparently, Elaric wasn't only looking for help to increase his familiarity with his form but also to expand his weapon skills.

When Marco got to his feet, Onnie took his wine glass and Elaric's bottle from them. Gabe grabbed the plate of cookies and his own bottle but caught Elaric's eyes.

"I'll grab my stuff and meet you out front. I'm planning on walking."

"We'll meet you there shortly," Marco said around Dany's energetic hug of both apology and goodbye.

Gabe left them all on the back deck and set their dishes on the kitchen counter before he slipped into his room. He pulled an overnight bag from under his bed and shoved a change of clothes into it. Then he carefully poked his head into Onnie's room and saw Miranda sleeping peacefully under Onnie's quilt. He shut the door quietly and went to say goodbye to Onnie, whom he heard talking to Mal in the kitchen.

When she saw him, she put the stuff in her hands on the counter and stood on her toes to kiss him. "Be good," she murmured against his lips, and then she kissed him again, this time in a way that made it extremely hard for him to want to leave.

He forced himself away from her and placed a light kiss on her lips. "Sleep well, Cat."

She nodded, and he turned toward the front door after waving over Onnie's shoulder to Dany as she entered the kitchen.

"Night, Mal."

"Night, man. Tell Xayn hi."

Gabe left the house and found Marco and Elaric talking in whispers on the sidewalk. They turned to look at him when he approached and stopped their conversation.

"All good to go?" Elaric asked with a smile.

"Yeah, most of my stuff is already there." Gabe grinned. "For a while, I'm not sure why we had separate apartments."

"Preaching to the choir," Elaric said with a glance at Marco, who had a contemplative smile and far-away eyes.

He good? Gabe asked Elaric.

Processing.

"We'll walk with you for a bit then." Elaric rolled one of his shoulders, and Marco snickered.

"Get your ass kicked?" he said to Elaric, who replied with a groan.

"He did fine," Gabe answered. "He's just complaining."

"Sure as shit I am," Elaric laughed. "I may be asleep until dinner."

"Nope, not allowed," Marco teased. "As your girlfriend so eloquently said, we wouldn't want to miss our high-five at shift change."

Gabe stopped and looked at Marco to see if he was joking. When he saw a rare, genuine smile on his face, it was clear he wasn't. Gabe groaned and brushed his hair back from his forehead. "Sounds like my sister."

Elaric lightly elbowed him in the side. "Don't worry. It was cute, and we laughed about it. As you can see, neither of us is offended."

"Not to mention, she's not wrong," Marco smirked. "Considering the situation, the fact that she can joke about it just adds to how special she is."

Elaric chuffed. "She gave me a lecture about it, actually. She asked if I was uncomfortable when she slept beside Onnie and said it was the same thing—friends and family taking comfort in the presence of another when they need it."

Gabe couldn't help but smile at his compassionate sister, but he scoffed and mentally kicked himself. "Damn."

"What?" Elaric asked, and Marco glanced over at him, too.

Gabe shook his head. "Just a moment of self-reflection. I was about to praise her for being so accepting when I should really be scolding myself for being so closed-minded."

"Not that I agree, but may I ask why?" Marco said, confused.

"I'm walking to my best friend's house, a dude, gay, and will share a bed with him when we crash out later. No different than you two or Dany and Onnie." Gabe explained.

"Ah," Marco said before smiling ahead of him again.

"Yeah. Dany's not accepting of it. She's normalized it. In her mind, there's nothing odd about the situation." Gabe quickly added, "Not that there is anything odd." He rolled his eyes, "But like it or not, most of the world doesn't agree with her."

"They do not," Marco said quietly.

"But they are getting better," Elaric added solemnly.

"Xayn?"

The man sitting beside Gabe on an outdoor couch turned his head to look at him. "Yeah?"

Gabe stared down at the bottle of cider in his hands, long since empty and the glass warm. "Do you think she's happy here?"

"Onnie?"

"Yeah."

Xayn returned his gaze to the tree line in front of them. "I do."

"But is it what's best for her or best for us?"

Gabe remembered his conversation with Dany and Mal when Onnie was sick and after she'd gotten hurt because of their plan. All of them had been worried, but more than that, they were all cut off from their Bonds with each other. Gabe was shocked when he realized how lonely he felt without her and his friends and family connected to him. Onnie was the center of that connection.

The Bond that joined them all.

"I think today, it's both. Tomorrow might be different, but then so will the next day."

"What?" Gabe asked.

"Sorry. Yes, I think it's best for her *and* us, but there are days when it might not be, but that's just how it is."

Gabe rested his head back on the couch cushion and closed his eyes. He'd told Xayn what they'd learned earlier that night, minus the part about Miranda, and as expected, his best friend had listened and let him spill out everything he'd been thinking.

A soft fluttering of wings brushed Gabe's cheek, and he smiled.

"Hey, Zamio."

A small raven head bonked his cheek, then hopped back to Xayn's shoulder. When Gabe looked over, the bird had his eyes closed and his head pressed to Xayn's temple. Gabe smiled at the pair's affection and then looked back at the bottle in his hands.

"I'm terrified."

"I know," Xayn said quietly.

"What happens if we don't win this?"

Xayn sighed, and when he shifted, Zamio hopped down to sit between them, tucked against both of their thighs.

"I believe you'll all make it out of this. We've seen Onnie do some..." he laughed softly, "impossible things. She won't let him win."

"But what if it's at the cost of herself?" Gabe said, his voice thick with emotion.

"I honestly don't think that will be the case, but if it is...you'll need to keep going."

Gabe? Mal asked.

Shit, screwed up again, didn't I? Gabe tried to laugh, but he knew the feline was more intelligent than to buy his cover-up.

Onnie's asleep, so you're fine. What's on your mind?

Talking to Xayn.

About?

Gabe couldn't even force his mental voice to say the words for a few minutes, but eventually, he said verbally to Xayn and to Mal mentally, along the Bond, *"I can't lose her."*

"Then make sure you win."

We won't.

Gabe squeezed his eyes closed and tried to hold on to the words they'd both said.

Chapter 20: The More the Merrier

August 2022 - Alku | Onnie Moore

"Mommy!" Miranda hollered in the quiet bookshop as she ran down the center aisle and jumped into her mom's open arms.

Onnie stood behind the counter in Abbot's, Elaric leaning on the front side of it. They watched the very excited young girl start rattling off all the fun she had, and Onnie could see Erika's expression shift as she began to get overwhelmed. Onnie took pity on her and walked around the counter to bring Erika Miranda's bag.

"Miranda, don't forget your bag."

When she set it down beside her, it broke Miranda's endless stream of commentary.

Erika stood up and hugged Onnie. "Thanks again, Onnie."

"Anytime. She was wonderful to have." Onnie played with one of Miranda's curls. "Oh, Miranda, why don't you go say goodbye to Mr. E, too."

Elaric, can you stall a second? I want to tell Erika that we know.
Got it.

Miranda nodded excitedly and skipped over to Elaric, but Onnie quickly turned to Erika.

"Marco was with us last night, also. I wanted to let you know that

he and Miranda talked, and they decided to tell us about Miranda's...
unique capability."

As expected, Erika's already weary face paled. "What?"

Onnie quickly grabbed one of Erika's hands and squeezed it
reassuringly. "Please, don't be anxious about us knowing. We would
never do anything except protect her, and now that we know, I can be
even more vigilant. We all can."

"I," Erika looked away to hide unshed tears. "Please, don't tell
anyone. I can't lose her."

"Oh, Erika, why would you think we would do anything to put
her, or you, in jeopardy?"

"I'm aware of what happens to...people like her if others find out."

Onnie shook her head and smiled. "I swear to you, as both Keeper
and Onnie, all of us, will *never* harm your child. We will protect her as
our own. Always."

Erika sniffled and nodded before Onnie pulled her into a hug and
rubbed her back gently.

"Were you aware she knew of my Link and *his* situation?"

"What?" Erika said, slightly shocked, though it quickly changed to
understanding. "Actually, I shouldn't be surprised."

Onnie stifled a laugh behind her palm. "She sure as hell surprised
all of us last night when she told me my cat could talk like it was as
normal as the sky being blue."

"I imagine so." Erika looked over at Miranda, who was playing a
hand-clapping game with Elaric and giggling freely.

"Alright," Onnie said, giving Erika one more quick hug. "I'm sure
you're exhausted, and you miss her like crazy. Why don't you two head
home and spend some time together? I didn't mean to add to your
exhaustion, but I also didn't want to keep from you that we knew."

"Thank you. I appreciate it, and now that I've gotten over the
shock of finding out, I'm glad you know. If it means more people to
protect her, then I am honored it is you." Erika said, then called
Miranda over to leave.

"Are we going home now?" Miranda asked, and Onnie squatted closer to the little girl's eye level.

"You are. Mommy needs some love and snuggles. So, make sure you take her home and curl up together with a book or a movie, okay?" Miranda nodded with a huge grin, and Onnie tapped the tip of her nose with her finger. "Good girl. Give me a hug before you go." She stood up, and Miranda squeezed her waist.

"Thank you, Onnie. I can't wait to come over and play again."

"Anytime you want. You're always welcome wherever I am."

She looked down at Miranda and held her gaze until the little girl's eyes registered her larger meaning. Then she nodded and ran over to grab her mom's hand.

"Thanks again, Onnie."

Erika smiled and waved to Elaric at the counter before the pair left the shop hand in hand.

Elaric walked over to Onnie, draping his arm around her shoulders. "She's a good kid."

"She is," Onnie said, patting Elaric's wrist. "I wish there were more I could do for her."

Elaric chuckled. "Give yourself time. You'll figure something out to help her. I have no doubts."

Kushima laughed, too, and Onnie knew she agreed with Elaric.

Are you two teaming up against me? she teased them both.

Never against, always beside, Kushima replied.

"What she said," Elaric added.

"Oh, you two are gonna cause all sorts of trouble, aren't you?" Onnie teased again and slipped from under Elaric's arm as his and Kushima's laughter followed her into the shop's back room. "Tea?"

"Sure, thanks." Elaric leaned on the doorframe and crossed his arms. "How'er you feeling about last night?"

Onnie stopped briefly and sighed. "I'm sure you can guess."

"Yup, probably can, but why don't you tell me anyway."

Onnie brought water to a boil and prepared two travel mugs with tea. She opted to use something less delicate and small for Elaric, considering he'd drain a tea cup in two gulps.

"Terrified. Exhausted. Anxious," she paused, and when he said nothing, she took a deep breath, "and relieved, determined, and thankful."

She saw Elaric's smirk from the corner of her eye.

"Good. I'd be a bit concerned if you weren't feeling those things."

He's correct, young one. You needn't worry. We're all here with you.

"I know," Onnie nodded and fiddled with a tea bag string. "I just wish we knew how much time we have."

"Would be nice, but we don't," Elaric stated matter of factly, and she couldn't help but smile at his directness.

"I need to get started on new powers and research. I also want to know more about the prophecy. Not to mention, oh," Onnie turned to Elaric, "I'm sorry. Miranda took up all my brain. You wanted to talk about something."

Elaric nodded. "I do, but let me ask you this first. Are you comfortable discussing what you're storing in the library fires out here?"

Onnie's eyes widened. "Um...yeah...let's not...do that here."

Gabe, Elaric, and I are going into the First Keeper's library for a few minutes—the shop's locked. I'll let you know when we're out.

Alright. Thanks for the heads up.

"Fine with me. I figured that would be your answer, and to clarify, please relax. I have a proposition for you, not an ultimatum."

Onnie did relax a little, and she tried to focus on calming her jittering nerves while the water came to a boil. At some point, Elaric had walked into the other room, and Onnie flopped onto the couch.

Calm yourself, young one. You know Elaric, assume best intentions.

I know. Onnie looked at the kettle on the hot plate and growled. *Why does it take so long to boil water?*

Kushima chuckled, and Onnie took some deep breaths until the water was ready, and she made them both tea. She brought Elaric's to him where he'd been flipping through a book on magical species.

"Here."

"Oh, thanks," he smiled and shelved the book before taking the drink and following behind her to the door in Abbot's study. She heard him laugh behind her.

"Onnie, I'm not sure why you're so nervous, but please, you know I'm not going to do any of the things you're thinking."

Onnie didn't turn around but mumbled, "I know," and then yanked the heavy door open. She shivered instantly, her summer clothes not fitting for the void-chilled room.

"Wait," Elaric said, and she turned around to where he held out the sweatshirt that had been on the couch.

He took her cup while she put it on, and she blushed when she took the tea back. She was being stupid. He and Kushima were right.

Elaric shut the door behind them, and she went over to her blanket and didn't waste a moment before wrapping herself up in it and sitting down. Elaric grabbed a chair, sat in it backward, and then looked at the ceiling.

"She joining us?"

Onnie smirked and closed her eyes, calling Kushima's astral form into the room to join them.

Hello again, Elaric. It makes me sincerely happy to see you whole and recovered.

"Thank you. It's nice to see you as well. I do miss our conversations."

You may speak with me anytime, though I continue to think it wise not to tell the others about that.

Onnie coughed as she tried to laugh and drink her tea simultaneously. Kushima and Elaric looked at her in confusion, and she waved them off. She took one more sip and then took a deep breath.

"Alright. What would you like to know about the souls?"

Onnie focused for a few seconds, pulled her view of the Bonds and auras into her field of view, and left them to overlay the real world. Thankfully, Elaric was amused and not angry. He leaned on the chair's back and narrowed his eyes at her.

"I told you, I'm not going to scold you or anything. I actually want to ask you for a favor."

Onnie's eyes went wide. "Ah, what?"

We told you to calm down, Kushima said with a soft smile.

"Yeah, I'd like to ask you to borrow the souls you have been keeping safe."

It only took Onnie three seconds to smack her forehead and curse. "I'm an idiot."

"Far from it," Elaric assured her. He then sipped his tea, his aura becoming more relaxed as he sighed in contentment. Considering she'd made some of Xayn's anxiety-reducing tea, it made sense.

"You want to use them to add to your shiftable forms."

"Sure do."

"Why didn't I think of that sooner? That's brilliant. Wait, one problem," Onnie frowned. "You can't use any of these forms in front of the others or in Alku. At least not until this is all over."

"Makes sense. The last thing I want to do is put you in a position to explain your motives or scare the shit out of the others when a tormenter's face suddenly reappears."

"Glad you understand." Onnie shook her head and then dropped it into one of her palms. "Can I ask a favor in return?"

"You don't need to ask, but yes."

Onnie looked up at Elaric, and she knew her face must be betraying her emotions because Elaric's aura shifted to concern instantly.

"After this ends, can you help me get them to where they belong?"

"Of course, but why do you seem…." Elaric hesitated.

"Guilty?"

Because she takes too much on herself, Kushima said with a slight frown.

"Yeah, I'm beginning to learn that."

"Oy, stop it, you two." Onnie pouted and curled further into her blanket cocoon.

"Yes," Elaric said. "I'll help you however you need. Unless

something's changed, you have to notify the angels of death in sanctuary cities, right?"

Correct. That is partly why we've been able to keep them safe for so long.

"Sounds good. Just tell me what you need and when you need it."

"Thanks," Onnie mumbled.

Onnie, you'd better head back out. You've got company. I let them in.

"Shit!" Onnie jumped up and dashed over to the door, using her body weight to shove it open and subsequently close it behind her. *Fine with Elaric staying?*

Of course.

Onnie could hear voices as she walked to the front of the shop and recognized them after only a few words. When she turned the last corner into the main room, she smiled when her recognition had been correct.

Ana and Rosalie were walking up the center aisle, chatting and laughing. Ana, who used to be called Gemini, was one of Jakob's past pawns. She'd tortured Dany and had been there when Elaric fell. After heads had cleared, Gemini had asked Onnie to remove the pain, influence, and memories of her time as Gemini. So, Onnie erased Gemini and brought Ana back into the world.

The young seventeen-year-old was bouncy and bubbly. Her heart was huge, and her passion for baking even more so. Onnie had contacted Rosalie, Alku's pastry chef from A Shot in the Dark. She was a single woman and lived alone in a rather large house, and Rosalie had agreed to take Ana in as a live-in apprentice. Judging by their interactions, it had been the right choice for both of them.

Ana's blonde hair was shining. She wore jean shorts, a T-shirt, and sneakers. She'd regained some of the weight she'd lost due to drugs and abuse, and she looked healthy again.

Even Rosalie was glowing. Her late thirties seemed to have reversed after Ana moved in, and Onnie was positive she appeared younger.

"Onnie!" Ana ran over and squeezed Onnie in a hug.

"Opfh." Onnie couldn't help but grin at the young woman's enthusiasm. "Hey, you! How've you been?"

Kushima, warn Elaric, please.

No problem.

"I'm good!" Ana stepped back and let go of Onnie, only to tilt her head and frown. "Onnie, are you eating right? You've lost weight."

"Anastasia!" Rosalie scolded from behind her. "Don't be rude!"

"I wasn't. I only asked because I'm worried," Ana looked at the floor.

Onnie ruffled the young woman's hair. "No, she's fine, and she's right. I have. I...had some trouble sleeping for a while. I'm doing better now."

Onnie was relieved when Ana looked back up at her, her eyes shining again.

"Then I guess it's a good thing we brought presents!" Ana said with a smile ear to ear. She ran over to Rosalie and took one of the bags from her. "Look!"

Onnie glanced at Rosalie, who simply smiled and shrugged before putting the second bag filled with presents onto the front counter.

"Ooo, what is it?" Onnie asked and went to stand on the other side as Ana began unloading multiple takeaway boxes and even a few to-go cups.

"They're desserts I made. Rosalie taught me!"

Ana's voice was bursting with excitement, and judging by the spread, Onnie thought the girl earned it.

"Wait, you made all of this?" Onnie glanced at Rosalie, who nodded.

"She did. She'll out-bake me soon. Girl's got a gift." Rosalie said as she watched Ana with pride.

"That's incredible!"

Onnie listened as Ana opened each container to show her what was in it and explain the treats.

"We brought you a few coffees, too. I wasn't sure if you were here alone today, but I figured you may need it. Especially with all this sugar," Rosalie said with a smirk.

Onnie walked over and hugged each of them in turn. "You both are amazing. Thank you for thinking of me and then sharing. I'm so excited to try what you made."

"I hope you like them," Ana said as her cheeks turned pink.

"I'm sure I'll love them," Onnie grinned. "Do you two want to stay to help me eat some and have some tea, maybe?"

Ana pouted, and Rosalie shook her head. "We'd love to, but we've got a few more errands today." Rosalie gently nudged Ana with her elbow, "Right?"

"Yeah...." Ana said dejectedly.

Onnie raised one eyebrow, and Rosalie chuckled. "Ana here has asked if we can get a cat."

"Oh! That's wonderful. Why are you upset about it?" Onnie asked, confused by the shift in Ana's aura.

Rosalie continued, "We're going to get a foster...for now."

"Ah," Onnie rested her hand on Ana's shoulder, and the young woman looked up. "Are you worried you'll have to return it?"

"Yeah."

"That's not always the case. Besides, think about it this way, if you help one foster and then have to send them to a different home, maybe you can help another. Two cats can experience your love then, not just one."

"I guess that's true," Ana nodded, her brain processing what Onnie had said.

"Well, then, I won't keep you from your new friend. Thank you," Onnie pulled Ana into a big hug, "again, for thinking of me. I'll call Dany and make her come split them with me."

Ana squeezed her back. "Alright. Don't forget Mal. He was always stealing my whipped cream."

Onnie laughed. "Couldn't if I tried. Honestly, that cat will eat anything sweet."

Rosalie laughed softly and waved as she and Ana returned to the front door. "Enjoy, Onnie."

"I will. Thank you again. See you soon!"

Ana left with a goodbye smile, and Onnie cracked into laughter the minute the door shut.

Dany, come to the shop. I need help. Onnie was laughing, and she knew her amusement would reach her best friend and that her words wouldn't worry her.

Um…why do I feel like I should decline?

Only if you want to miss out on the counter covered in treats that Ana and Rosalie just brought me.

Rosalie!? Mal said, appearing on top of the register.

Is he already there? Dany asked, panicked.

Onnie chuckled. *Yes, I was talking to both of you.*

Shit! Save some for me! Dany said, and then Onnie felt her pull away from their conversation.

"Mal, you wait until Dany's here, understood?" Onnie scolded as Mal's paw approached an opened container with a small cake covered in whipped cream.

"Why do I have to wait? It's not my fault she can't relocate."

Onnie gently poked the cat's middle. "Maldwyn, you behave, or I'll let you have nothing."

"Woah!" Elaric said as he walked into the room and caught sight of the counter. "Did you rob a bakery?"

Onnie chuckled and handed him one of the four cups. "Nope. Ana and Rosalie brought them over. Apparently, Ana made all of this."

Elaric hesitated to take the cup Onnie offered, but before she could say anything, he took it and drank some.

"That's sweet of her."

"I see what you did there," Mal said with whipped cream on his nose.

"Mal!" Onnie scolded and picked him up. "Don't make me lock you in the First Keeper's library until Dany gets here."

Mal hissed. "You wouldn't dare!"

Onnie narrowed her eyes and glared at him. "Try me."

They had a staring contest for a few minutes, but eventually, Mal gave up. "Fine."

He disappeared from her arms in a huff.

Where did you go? Onnie asked the petulant cat.

Study couch.

Elaric snorted into his cup. "And Gabe thinks *my* life is interesting."

Onnie grinned. "Never bored. That's for sure."

She looked through the cups and saw that Rosalie hadn't forgotten Mal, and there was a small cup of hot cocoa. Ana was still an Outsider, so to her, Mal was just a normal cat, but Rosalie knew the fur ball for what he was—a sugar fiend.

"This should make him happy." Onnie took the cup into the study and popped off the lid. "Peace offering?" she said as she entered the room, and Mal raised one eyelid.

"Is that...."

"Yes, come get your cocoa. Thank Rosalie when you see her."

Mal appeared on Abbot's desk, and Onnie carefully poured some of the cocoa into a clean tea cup. "Try not to spill."

"Thanks, Onnie," Mal said, lapping up the drink while he watched her leave the room again.

When Onnie re-entered the shop's front room, Elaric was over by the antique section. Again.

"You've been over there a lot today. Can I help?"

He must have been focused because he jumped at her question. "Wow, sorry. Ah, no...it's okay." He closed the book and replaced it on the shelf as he did every time she caught him reading it.

Onnie crossed her arms and glared at him. "I'll only ask one more time, and if you tell me to drop it. I will. Are you *sure* I can't help you? Even if it's just finding a piece of information?"

Elaric sighed, but she saw his stubbornness crack. "I'm being stupid."

Onnie snorted. "As if that's even possible. Talk to me." She grabbed a coffee for herself and took a sip, the tension in her shoulders falling away with the warm, rich goodness.

Elaric rubbed the back of his neck. "I've been thinking about what Miranda said to Marco."

"Ah," Onnie smiled. "I get it. Alright, so what are you looking for exactly?"

Elaric shrugged. "Not much to go off of, so I was looking for races or peoples associated with feathers."

"Okay, well, I'm still playing catch up, but I can think of a few. Paranams, maybe hedge witches, nymphs maybe…."

Elaric sipped his coffee and listened to her rattling off whatever she could pull out of her over-stuffed brain.

"I'm sure there's probably a demon or something out there that has a feather fetish."

Elaric snorted and coughed up his coffee, but she grinned and continued.

"Oh, I guess we can't rule out an angel of death. They've got wings if I remember correctly."

Elaric sighed, and Onnie stopped and tipped her head to the side. "Uh oh, have I touched a nerve?"

"Not exactly. I don't know. It's just a gut feeling. Have you met an angel yet?"

"Maybe? Can't they hide their wings and pass as humans? Would I have even noticed?"

"Yes, they can hide their wings. Though, I wonder if you'd see them similar to my flickering? But that's beside the point. You'd know. They have some distinct features and *very* consistent personalities."

Do you know if I've met any First Keeper?

You have not, as far as I'm aware. They don't come to Alku often. As Elaric implied earlier, they only come when informed of a soul needing retrieval.

"I've only met a handful in my life. They leave a lasting impression," Elaric smirked.

"Well, let's hope those aren't the ones we're waiting for. Can I ask you something, though?"

"What's up?"

"Besides the obvious answer, why do you care so much? Wouldn't this be a good thing for Marco?"

Elaric sighed. "Yes and no. I want to say that judging by Miranda's phrasing, it will be a positive encounter, but you know Marco. It takes so much for him to open up to people. I'm worried he'll let whoever it is pass him by or shut them out for fear of adding another person to his list of people who will eventually leave him."

"Hmm, you're right."

Onnie sipped her coffee and went into the back room to fetch the tea tray. She pulled the tea set off of it and used the tray to load the desserts and drinks on.

"Let's take this to the sitting area and wait for Dany. I'm sure she'll be here soon."

Elaric grabbed a stack of dessert boxes and followed Onnie over to the sitting room on the antique side of the shop. They set everything down on the ottoman and sunk into cushy wingbacked chairs.

"Elaric, how did you meet my grandfather?" Onnie asked, slipping off her flats and pulling her legs underneath her.

Her question must have shocked him because it took Elaric a few wide-eyed seconds to reply.

"Ah, I met him when he was young, maybe…ten?"

"Did he live here as a kid?" Onnie knew little about his life before being a Keeper, and since he and her mother had been estranged, there was no one left to ask.

"Yeah. I think he moved here not long before I met him, though."

"Wait, so how old were you? In human age."

"Late twenties, I think."

"Huh, okay. I'm sorry. Continue. I'll shut up." She stuck her coffee cup in her mouth.

Elaric smirked. "You're fine, but yeah. He was following Sam around, playing with the older cool kid."

Onnie snorted but said nothing.

"I can't remember if we already knew he was the next Keeper. I don't think we did, but either way. It was clear he wasn't an Outsider, so Sam and I taught him about the different magical races."

"I bet for a ten-year-old that was like stepping into a fantasy book."

Elaric's eyes went far away, but he still smiled. "It was. For some reason, mine was the hardest for him to believe. That's why I have his form from a few different ages."

Elaric paused, and Onnie hadn't been paying explicit attention to his aura, but his shift from mournful to heart-wrenching despair was so abrupt she couldn't have missed it.

"Hey," she leaned forward and touched his knee to bring his focus back to her. "What's up? If this is too hard, you don't have to—"

"Had," Elaric said firmly. "Had his forms."

Onnie's eyes went wide. "Ah, I see."

Now that Elaric had lost his previous forms, he'd also lost Abbot's. *Kushima,...would I be able to talk with my grandfather again? Or, if not me, maybe just Elaric?*

Kushima was silent for a moment, and Onnie thought maybe she'd ignored her, but then she spoke, *Let me think about it.*

Alright. Thank you for even considering it.

Onnie felt the shop's gentle nudge when someone entered, but before she could get up to see who it was, Dany shouted to see where they were.

"Sitting area," Onnie shouted back and then looked back at Elaric.

"I'm sorry I brought it up. I didn't think it through."

Elaric patted her hand and sipped his coffee, so Onnie sat back in her chair. Mal appeared on her lap as Dany came around the corner.

"Now, can we eat?" Mal complained, and Dany lightly bopped his head with her finger as she went by.

"Oh, keep your pants on, you glutton." Dany smiled at Onnie, but her smile faded when she looked at Elaric. "Elaric? What's wrong?"

My bad, Onnie said to Dany, but Elaric clarified further.

"Nothing. Sorry," he smiled, and Onnie knew it was forced since his aura didn't shift away from sadness. "We talked about Abbot, and I got a little carried away. I'm fine." He stood, kissed her cheek, and handed her the last cup of coffee.

That's all? Dany asked as she sipped her drink.

Um, he hadn't registered that when he lost all his past forms, he also lost Abbot's.

Oh, shit. I see why he's upset.

Yeah.

"Oh, stop it, you two," Elaric said with a genuine laugh. "You two are only ever that quiet if you're side-chatting. I'm fine. It'll just…take a bit of time."

Onnie giggled but began opening to-go boxes while Dany consoled him.

Hey, Gabe?

What's up, Cat?

Would you be up for a drive later tonight?

Sure, but tell me what's wrong.

Nothing is wrong. I just..need a bit of space from Alku for a night. I can always bring us back if we need to.

Alright. I'll pick you up at six. We can go for dinner if you're up for it.

Sure. Thank you.

You don't need to thank me, Cat.

"I can't believe she made all of this!" Dany squealed, and her enthusiasm for Ana's treats brought Onnie back to the present company.

"Yeah, Rosalie said it was her. It looks like she truly did get a second chance at life. I'm glad she's not wasting it either."

"Ain't that the truth, and we get to reap the rewards," Dany said, snagging a gooey brownie from one of the boxes.

Some aren't so lucky, but those of us who are, thank you for it, Elaric said along their Bond, and Onnie smiled into her lap.

Don't thank me. Just don't waste it.

Elaric's aura shifted to a happier state, and Onnie relaxed.

She pulled a small cupcake from a nearby box and dug in, unable to hold off any longer.

Chapter 21: A Night for Driving

**August 2022 - Forest outside Alku |
Gabriel Vansand**

Gabe knew something was up the moment Onnie had asked to go for a drive earlier in the day. He didn't need to be her Guardian to see she was tied up in knots. Anyone would have been able to.

He carefully pushed against their Bond and could tell that she hadn't blocked him out. Unfortunately, it also told him that she was pretty miserable.

They'd driven on the only street out of Alku and through the tunnel under the mountain. Then, they were winding through loose turns and curves among the trees with nothing but the stars above them. He'd opened the sunroof, and the roar of the wind and the chill it flooded the car with helped him feel connected to the world around him, and he hoped it would do the same for Onnie.

Gabe reached his free hand over and took hers, their fingers lacing together. She didn't turn to look at him, instead concentrating on watching the trees rush by, but she did squeeze him back so she was at least aware of her surroundings. Her body was leaning on the car door, as far away from him as she could possibly be. He couldn't shake the feeling that she wanted out of the car, and while he couldn't be sure, he didn't think she wanted away from him specifically.

"Do you wanna talk about it?" He already knew the answer would be no, or she would have already talked to him about it, but he asked anyway.

"Uh, sure," Onnie said, shifting away from the window and sitting up straighter in her seat.

Gabe's eyes widened, but he quickly pushed away his shock. "Can you give me a hint, or should I start a game of twenty questions?"

She laughed softly, and his chest tightened. The more he saw of her tonight, the more worried he became. Onnie's laugh was guarded, and he'd not heard it since she'd first come to Alku and had still been hiding behind her walls.

"It's a few things. I think the easiest one would be my conversation with Elaric today."

Gabe raised one eyebrow. "Okay...."

"I was asking him about Abbot, and when we were talking, he realized that because of all this, when he lost his forms, he also lost Abbot's."

"Wait, he had Abbot as a form?"

He'd known the two men were close, but Elaric having his form opened up many stories that Gabe really wanted to ask more about.

"Yeah, from when he was around ten. I guess they played pranks on people together." Onnie smiled as she stared at her hands, holding his in her lap.

"Well, sounds like Abbot. He was a silly, jovial man, so I'd expect he was a handful and happy kid." Gabe missed the old man. They all did. "Why are you upset, though, just because Elaric is?"

"I...I just wish I had been able to save *all* of him. It feels like his forms were such a part of him, and I couldn't get those back."

"Cat, listen to me. You did plenty. I'm willing to bet that Elaric is upset that they are gone, not that he didn't get them back."

Gabe squeezed her hand once, took his back, and carefully pulled into a turn-off at the edge of the cliffside.

"I know, you're right, and I'll get over the guilt. I'm just not...there yet."

He put the car in park, switched off his headlights, and shifted in the tight seat to face her.

"Cat, look at me." Thankfully, she did, and he gently pushed his warmth and affection along their Bond. "What you did, Cat, was a miracle. I don't think anyone, Dany, Marco, me, or even Elaric, has even the smallest thought that you didn't do enough."

"Yeah." Onnie nodded but quickly turned to look back out the window.

"Alright, come on. Let's go," Gabe said and got out of the car. He walked to her side, helped her out, and closed and locked the car.

"Gabe? Where are we going?" Onnie said, looking around them. "Is there anything here?"

"Nope. Nothing at all," he said and retook her hand. "Come on."

Ever since Gabe had gotten his license, he used to come to this overlook when he'd had a bad day or needed to escape his small town for a little while. On the mountainside, on the opposite side of the road from them, there was a great spot to look for fossils during the day, but the cliff side was genuinely spectacular at night. The turn-off had room enough for a few cars to park and enough space for them all to enjoy the view, but he'd never seen anyone else. Not that he was complaining. In his opinion, the solitude made it an even better place to think.

The night was quiet as they trudged through the gravel to the guard railing where a few benches were lined up. He knew the minute Onnie saw the view that she understood why they were there.

"Oh my gods, it's amazing!"

She broke free from his hand, ran up to the railing, and looked over the dark valley. Below them was a sea of mountains covered in a soft blanket of trees. Scattered amongst the trees were sparse and sporadic house lights. They twinkled like stars in the sky as the soft breeze repeatedly moved tree branches across the light sources, blocking them and then revealing them once again. If you looked past the mountains and trees, you saw nothing but inky blackness in the distance as the sky went on forever before it wrapped around and up above them, where it was filled with stars.

He'd seen it many times over the years, but it still took his breath away every time he saw it again.

"Beautiful, isn't it?"

Onnie's eyes were wide as they continued to roam over everything, and her smile stretched ear to ear.

"I've never seen anything like this."

Gabe walked up behind her and braced his hands on either side of her on the railing. She leaned back against his chest, and he kissed the top of her head. Neither of them said much, simply enjoying each other's warmth as they looked out over the sea of trees and shadows. They stayed like that for a long time, Gabe content to hold Onnie as she tried to absorb the beauty like a sponge. When she shivered, he rubbed his hands up and down her bare arms, and when he felt her goosebumps, he sat on a bench behind them before pulling her into his lap.

"Do you feel better?"

Onnie snuggled further into his arms and nodded against him. "Yes. Thank you, and you were right. I did the best I could, and even that was a miracle. Looking out at all of that proves how small we are. How, even though I feel like our problems are the worst in the world— they aren't."

Gabe chuckled. "Well, except for the prophecy, but yes, I agree."

Onnie snorted and gently pinched his stomach. "Okay, you got me with that one, but for some reason, even that feels less...complicated now."

"What do you mean?"

"I'm not sure how to explain it. If I look at the prophecy in parts instead of as a whole, it's much more digestible."

"Was there a part you were having a hard time digesting?" Gabe said, teasing her with her own words.

"I mean, besides all of it?"

Gabe chuckled but left her room to talk.

"Really though, I mean all of it. The fact that it exists at all is overwhelming."

He ran his fingers through her hair and rested his forehead on the back of her head, the smell of her rose-scented shampoo mixing with the fresh breeze and evergreen trees around them.

"There's so much at risk if I fail," Onnie said so softly that Gabe nearly missed it.

"There is," Gabe sighed, "but you won't."

She shook her head against him. "Don't say that. You can't know that."

Gabe ran his palm along her cheek and tipped her face up so she could see him. "Yes, Cat, I do. Even if we put aside your capabilities, you're still you, Onnie."

Her eyes flashed blue for a second, and they widened at his use of her name.

"You won't fail because magic or not, you are incredible. You may have needed magic and the Bond to bring back Elaric, but you figured out how to do it on your own. Your stubborn determination and intellect are what made it possible. You made a plan, found who and what resources you needed, and then carried it out. *You* did that, Onnie. Not the Keeper, magic, or even all that damned tea."

She chuckled at his comment about the tea, but he cut off her laugh with his mouth. It was only a second later that she wrapped her arms around his neck and shifted to straddle his lap and kiss him deeper. He pulled her closer, and when they both needed to breathe, he kissed her nose and rested their foreheads together.

"I love you, Onnie."

She sniffled and nodded against him, "I love you, too, Gabe."

"I promise we'll find a way to end this with ice, not blood."

Onnie stilled in his lap and sat back to glare at him. "Oh, no. There will be blood, Guardian. I just don't want it in the sky."

Gabe swallowed roughly at the steel look in her eyes and managed to nod.

She softened again and sighed, "I just hope none of it is ours either."

"I know, Cat."

He pulled her back to his chest, and they held tightly to one another. Gabe squeezed his eyes closed and reached for Mal.

We need a plan.

We do. She okay?

Yeah, but I don't want to wait for that bastard to make the next move. Help me?

Course, dude. Are we telling her?

Not yet. I ran into the city earlier to pick up a weapon order.

Care to share?

Double-ended switch blade staff in Cat's size.

Mal's soft laugh made Gabe smile. *My dude, you sure decided on one hell of an engagement ring.*

Gabe struggled not to laugh aloud and let Onnie in on his private conversation with the feline. *It's not a bad idea, actually. Do you think she'd go for a crossbow?*

This time, Mal's amusement swirled along their Bond, and Gabe pushed his face into Onnie's hair to hide his increasing grin.

My man, you give her a crossbow as a proposal, and I think she'll tack you to a tree.

Likely, Gabe said affectionately.

Now, Dany, on the other hand....

That time, Gabe wasn't able to hold back his laugh, and he pulled away from Onnie to laugh into his palm. All he felt was her confusion as she stared at him with a smirk.

Onnie Moore

Onnie felt infinitely better. Asking Gabe to go for a drive had been just what she needed, not to mention the pep talk he'd given her. That also helped.

His eyes glowed blue as he spoke, and she couldn't look away from his determined yet pleading stare. His words were honest and direct, almost authoritative, but his eyes...his eyes were pleading with her to understand.

He was just as frightened as she was of the prophecy. Logically, she'd assumed that, but seeing it in his eyes, the way his jaw tensed, and how the tips of his fingers had pressed a bit harder into her flesh when he'd been speaking, she'd underestimated how frightened he truly was.

"Hey, Gabe—"

Onnie winced, and Gabe stiffened. She quickly checked their Bond and found nothing unusual, nor with Mal's or the other's.

"Cat?"

She pressed the tips of her fingers to her temples and squeezed her eyes closed.

"One sec."

She could feel that he was starting to worry when they heard Mal along their Bond, *Onnie, one of the wards activated.*

Yeah, I know. First Keeper, any idea what happened?

It was brief, like the other morning. Whatever it was has already subsided. It was near the tunnel again.

I guess that means Gabe and I are headed back.

Before Mal could answer, Gabe spoke up. *Mal, would you and Elaric be able to check it out while we drove back?*

Works for me.

Selfishly, she wasn't ready to head back yet, but she knew she didn't have a choice. Or she thought she hadn't.

"Gabe?"

"What? It will take us some time to get back, and if it were *that* much of an emergency, you'd have already relocated us."

His logic was correct, and she didn't want to argue, so she sighed and reached for Elaric to add him to their conversation.

Elaric?

What's up?

Would you mind checking the wards for me? Gabe and I aren't back yet, and something triggered one of them. Mal will go with you.

Of course. Mal, meet you at Marco's. Give me a minute to tell Stephan I'm headed out.

Thanks, you two, Gabe said before she could. Then, a small blush crept into his ears, and he smiled at her. "Sorry, did I overstep?"

Onnie shook her head, and the corners of her lips turned up at his cute blush. "No, it's fine, and you're right. Besides, I guess I won't always be able to do everything."

"Not on your own," Gabe said with a grin.

She could feel how happy he was along their Bond, and it was probably because she figured out what he'd intended to prove without him having to say it.

"Remember, Cat, you may be the only one named in the prophecy, but a Keeper is a packaged deal. At a minimum, it implied you have Mal and I, too."

She tilted her head, momentarily confused over his statement, but it didn't take long for it to make sense. Onnie gently put her two warm hands on his cheeks, and the contrast with his night-chilled skin made him shiver.

"Thank you, Gabe. You're right. I needed the reminder."

She smiled and pressed her lips to his, and Gabe didn't hesitate to reciprocate. He pulled her closer and deepened their kiss until she relaxed again. In his arms, surrounded by darkness and stars, feeling his pulse under her palms and hearing her own in her ears, she remembered. She had Gabe and Mal.

When she finally let him pull away, she pressed her forehead to his neck. Their breathing echoed in the quiet night, overshadowing the crickets and owls in the distance. But more than that, it mingled with her own, proving she wasn't alone once again.

Elaric Rickson

Elaric climbed the stairs in the back area of the Day Night Cafe as he headed up to the apartment he shared with Marco—the same Marco who was behind him and brooding.

"You're positive you don't want me to join you?"

"Yes, you're working tonight. Besides, Onnie wouldn't have asked me to go in her place if it was dangerous."

"What about taking Dany with you?"

Elaric stopped, his hand on the apartment's doorknob, and he turned and looked down at Marco, still a few steps from the top.

"Marco. I'm fine. I'm just going to the tunnel and back. Mal's going with me."

Marco stared at him for a few seconds, but then he sighed and nodded. "You're right. I'm being ridiculous."

"Yes," Mal said suddenly from where he was seated beside Elaric's feet. "You are."

Elaric looked down at the feline and smirked. *Thanks for the assistance.*

"Fine, I fold," Marco whined. "Just promise you'll *both* be safe?"

"Damn, here I thought we'd run there, scissors in our hands and barefoot," Mal sassed.

Elaric was worried Mal's ballsy attitude would piss off Marco, but to his relief, the sanguiste laughed and bent down to pet the feline.

"If you can figure out how to hold scissors in your paw, Mal, then I'll shut up and let you do it." Marco scratched under Mal's chin and then stood up. He met Elaric's stare and then nodded. "Alright, see you when you get back." With that, Marco turned and returned to the restaurant below.

Once he and Mal were in the apartment, the front door closed, and Marco was back out on the busy cafe floor, Elaric groaned. "Seriously, thank you."

Mal pointed to Elaric's shoulder with his paw, and Elaric quickly grabbed his jacket from a hook by the door and nodded. Mal appeared on his shoulder a second later.

"It's fine," Mal said lowly. "I understand his concerns, but you were right. Onnie would have gone herself if it were more than just recon."

"That's what I figured."

Elaric left the apartment and walked them to the bottom of the stairs and out of the door tucked in the back of the hallway that led to the backside of the building.

"If it were anything I didn't think we could handle, I'd have asked him for backup, not to mention she'd appear at our side in a split second."

Mal snorted. "I'll be impressed if she doesn't anyway."

"True." Elaric smiled and walked to the far side of the small parking lot behind the cafe.

Mal's head turned, and he looked around. "Wait, how *are* we going to get there?"

Elaric smirked at the furry friend on his shoulder, and then he stopped at a motorcycle tucked out of the way in the corner of the lot. He watched as Mal's eyes went wide, and then he was no longer on his shoulder and, instead, sitting on a fence post ten feet away from Elaric and the bike.

"Nope, no way. I'm not getting on that thing," Mal said, shaking his head.

Elaric crossed his arms. "Why not? Scared?"

"Yes!" Mal said, unashamed.

Elaric hesitated. He'd planned on teasing Mal more, but after his honest admission, he felt it would be in poor taste.

"Alright, look," Elaric said, pulling a helmet out of a nearby storage compartment and hanging it on the bike's handlebars. "We're not going far or fast, so why don't you try it? Worst case, you can leave me behind and relocate, and I'll meet you there."

"And where do you suggest I sit? I don't see any basket for Toto on the front."

Elaric snorted. "Toto was a dog. Besides, I grabbed my larger jacket. Come on."

He pulled his zipper up partway and then pulled the coat away from his body, leaving a gap between it and his shirt, plenty of room for Mal.

Mal continued to side-eye him for another moment, but eventually, he hung his head.

"I swear, the things you people make me do."

While he continued to complain, and not even slightly under his breath, he jumped off the fence and made his way up onto the seat of Elaric's bike.

"You'll be safe, I promise."

Elaric helped the cat climb into his coat and zipped him in securely.

"See, comfy?"

"Actually...yes, but don't you dare tell anyone I said that."

The leather jacket muffled Mal's voice, which also meant he couldn't see Elaric's struggle not to laugh at the tough feline act as it slipped to the floor like silk.

"On my honor."

Elaric pulled on his helmet and threw his leg over the bike. Once he'd settled them both in safely, he put the key in the ignition and started the engine.

Mal, if you need me or want to know what's happening, just let me know. Alright?

Will do. Just please, I want to get home at the end of the night. There's a salmon filet in the fridge that's sushi-grade.

That time, Elaric laughed loudly and revved the bike before heading out of the parking lot and onto the streets toward the town's entrance tunnel.

Mal, you never cease to entertain me.

Don't make me claw your nipple, man.

Knowing the Link wasn't bluffing, Elaric held in his laugh and focused on getting them to their destination safely.

As the wind whipped past his body, Elaric realized he'd missed riding his bike in the last few months. Body-less time and before, included. He'd been an early adopter of motorcycles in the early nineteen hundreds and had one ever since. He loved the feeling of the air rushing past his skin, the loud purring of the engine, and the freedom that came with a small and quick mode of transportation. He'd never had many belongings since he rarely stayed in one place for too long, so whatever he could fit on his motorcycle was all he needed.

In the dark of Alku's night, Elaric sped down the empty road. Trees rushed past them as the infrequent street lights burned out his night vision just as it recovered—over and over.

How you doing, Mal?

Actually...I'm fine.

Good! See, I told you you'd be okay.

Where we at?

Nearly there, another minute or two. Do you want me to park on the Alku side, and we can walk through the tunnel?

Sounds like a plan.

As predicted, Elaric pulled up to the tunnel two minutes later and slowed down to barely a crawl.

Mal, gonna be bumpy for a second. I'm gonna leave the bike off the road a bit. I won't be going faster than this.

Got it.

Elaric walked his bike to the hillside, off the paved road, and onto the dirt and gravel. He turned off the engine and pocketed the keys before pulling his helmet off and hooking it on the back of the bike.

"Come on out," he said as he unzipped his jacket.

Mal slowly rolled out of it before disappearing and reappearing on the floor beside a nearby tree.

"Shall we get this over with?" Mal asked, and Elaric got off his bike and grabbed a flashlight from a small compartment.

"Let's do it. Wanna lead?" Elaric clicked on the light and lit the ground in front of him.

He followed behind Mal, who would flit in and out of the flashlight beam, his dark fur wrapping him in the shadows as soon as he left the portion of illuminated asphalt.

First Keeper?

Yes, Elaric?

Sorry, I don't mean to bother you.

You are never a bother to me. What can I do for you?

Mal and I are checking out the ward by the tunnel. Anything we should know that we don't already?

Hmm, unfortunately, I don't think so. All I know is that the ward was triggered. It reacted quickly and then was quiet again.

So, whatever triggered it changed its mind and left quickly?

Or was swiftly taken care of.

Got it. Thank you.

Elaric swept the flashlight up and around the arch of the tunnel's interior walls and was relieved to see it looked in excellent repair. Then he began to worry.

"Hey, Mal?"

"What's up?" Mal asked, glancing over his shoulder as he walked.

"What do you think about Onnie pulling this thing down?"

"What do you mean? Do you think she can't?"

Elaric chuckled. "Ah, no. At this point, I don't think there's much that woman *couldn't* do if she put her mind to it."

"Agreed. So, why are you asking how I feel about it?"

"I guess I'm not really sure. I think I'm just trying to process everything. It's been an interesting few months."

"Understatement of the century, my man."

"Perhaps," Elaric smiled.

"Ah, we're here," Mal said as they exited the tunnel, one of the few lamps bathing them in yellow light. 'Wanna go right, and I'll go left? Not sure which side of the road it was on."

"Sure."

Elaric crossed the road and stepped into the trees, sweeping his flashlight on the ground as he walked. He meandered in and out of the trees, around bushes and rocks, and ducked under branches. The forest was quiet, and he shivered. He'd spent many nights under the stars, just him and his bike against a tree, but in recent years, it had gone from being quiet, introspective time to himself to achingly lonely. Something he hadn't realized until just then.

Anything? Mal asked.

Nope, nothing yet.

Elaric stepped over a large boulder in his path, but his foot slipped on the other side. In the split second before he fell, he decided he'd rather land on his ass than try to awkwardly catch himself over the rock and probably do more damage to his wrist.

As expected, his tailbone hit the forest floor, and he winced.

"Ow."

He was lucky there was a thick layer of leaves beneath him, or he'd probably be really sore in the morning. He got to his feet, looked at his palms, and could feel sticks and tiny stones embedded in his flesh, but it was too dark to see anything.

Be careful. I just fell on my ass.

You good?

Yeah, nothing too bad. Slipped on a damn rock.

Elaric stuck the flashlight's backside in his mouth to examine his palms, but he immediately spat it out.

Hurry, found it.

Mal was beside him instantly, and he'd perched himself on the boulder that had taken Elaric out only a minute before.

"What's wrong?"

Elaric held both of his bloody palms out for Mal to see and then quickly rubbed them as clean as he could in a soft patch of moss a few feet away.

"I thought you said it wasn't that bad?"

"It's not mine." Elaric nodded towards a nearby shrub where an arm was sticking out.

Mal's eyes followed to where he'd pointed. "Yipes!" Mal jumped when he saw the bloody appendage, and the next second, he disappeared and reappeared at Elaric's feet. "Damn it, man, you could have warned me."

"Trust me, freaked me out, too." Elaric carefully picked up the flashlight and cleaned it off with the hem of his t-shirt.

"Alive?" Mal asked, creeping closer but staying behind Elaric's feet.

"Not sure, but I highly doubt it." Elaric carefully reached out and touched the body's wrist but felt nothing. "Nope, no pulse."

"Gross," Mal said and stuck his tongue out.

Elaric squatted down and carefully hefted the body from beneath the branches by its armpits with a grunt.

"Yeah, this is the one we want. The body hasn't gone stiff yet."

"Dude," Mal said with disgust, "why do you know that?"

Elaric just stared at Mal and raised one eyebrow. "You don't think I'd pick shit up over the centuries?"

"Blegh," Mal said, shaking his head. "Alright, let me look."

Mal walked over to the body, slowly sticking his nose toward the man's face, but he quickly jumped back and sneezed.

"Damn. If the wards hadn't gotten him, the alcohol would have."

Elaric sniffed the air and coughed. "Hell, how did I not smell that before now? What, did he swim in it?"

"No idea, but either way, I don't think we have anything to worry about. The wards did their job, and whoever this was, they were probably just unlucky enough to wander around drunk near the wrong town."

Elaric got to his feet and shined the flashlight around the small clearing. "Actually…why were they wandering around?"

"Who knows?"

"No, really," Elaric started to walk back toward the road. "Where's their car?"

"Maybe they walked?" Mal said, and Elaric looked down at him with the best, *really?*, face he could manage. "Alright, probably not, but what's the alternative?"

"Jakob?" Elaric asked.

"I don't know. It sounds a little out of his MO, but what do you think?"

Elaric groaned, "I'm not sure. Why don't we report the body to the cops and see what they find?"

"How upstanding of you," Mal teased as they returned to the tunnel entrance and made their way back to the other side.

"Can it you," Elaric teased and pulled out his cell phone. "Let me call, and then we can head back. I want to wash my hands."

"Go for it," Mal said and then licked his lips. "Yummy, salmon. Here I come!"

Elaric chuckled and called Alku's small police department while his furry companion made lip-smacking noises beside him.

Chapter 22: Chats in the Sun

August 2022 - Alku | Onnie Moore

Onnie held Gabe's hand as he led her into Alku's police station, a small building connected to the town's equally small fire station. She'd not yet needed to enter either building, but considering the fire station stood in front of the town's library, she'd passed them multiple times a week for months.

Alku only had both response teams for show—or Outsiders.

If there was a fire in town, elemental witches were far faster and more effective than a human fire truck. Gods forbid there was a fire at one of the more remote homes. A fire truck wouldn't even be able to reach them, considering many didn't have roads leading to them at all.

They did, however, respond to issues involving Outsiders or in situations like the one Onnie was there for—incidents that happen just outside of the tunnel.

"Gabe, nice to see you, man!"

Onnie watched as a tan-skinned uniformed cop stood up from behind one of the handful of desks within the small space and held out his hand to Gabe.

"Nice to see you, Dillon."

The man was younger than Onnie had expected, but that didn't matter to her. From what Dany and Gabe had said, he was a standup guy, and they'd gone to school together when they were younger. Apparently, Dillon was a mechanite, a sub-race of humans who could speak with mechanical things. And he was brilliant.

His chocolate eyes were warm when he smiled broadly at Onnie, and he slightly lowered his head of dark hair in a bow-esk gesture.

"Keeper. Nice to finally meet you. Dany and Gabe have told me a lot about you." When he met her eyes again, his seemed to sparkle with mischief. "Including that, you hate being called Keeper, so consider that my formal cop introduction." He held out his hand to her. "It's nice to meet you, Onnie."

Gabe snorted, and she glared at him playfully but took the man's outstretched hand, his grip strong but warm and calloused.

"Nice to meet you, too, Dillon, and thanks, I appreciate it."

He stepped back and riffled through a few loose papers on his desk before finding the one he wanted and holding it out to her.

"Elaric mentioned you'd come by today when I spoke with him last night. This is what I know of the victim so far. It's not much."

Onnie took the paper and mentally read it to Kushima as she went.

Male, mid-thirties, no identification or wallet. Only a few loose bills in his pocket, all hundreds. Caucasian, stocky, shy of six feet tall. Highly intoxicated before death, far above the legal limit. Death caused by blunt forced trauma to the rear of the skull from impact with a rock after an assumed fall.

Kushima interrupted, *The wards. He was probably knocked off balance hard enough for that wound to be fatal.*

Onnie agreed but continued. *Officer was called to the scene by a hiker who found the body located just outside the Alku tunnel, among the trees. Victim lost a lot of blood at the scene but was likely dead within minutes of the impact and unconscious from the bleed out. Officer contacted local police departments outside of Alku and found a missing persons report from a ride-for-hire driver who had driven the victim to Alku but was asked to stop outside the tunnel. Victim wandered off into the trees prior to paying his fair, and when the driver attempted to follow after him, he was unable to do so in the dark. Driver waited for twenty minutes, but the victim never returned.*

Onnie handed the paper to Gabe and asked Dillon, "Why would the driver submit a missing persons report?"

Dillon smirked. "He didn't. Not at first. He was pissed, rightfully so, that he'd been stiffed his payment, so he reported it to his dispatch and headed back into the city. It wasn't until later in the evening that he had cooled off and did the right thing. He said his father used to go hunting in the forests of Montana and that he didn't want to be on the hook if the guy ended up dead—mauled by a bear or something. So he reported it."

"Makes sense."

She watched as Gabe's eyes skimmed the information she'd just reviewed, and when he finished, he passed it back to Dillon.

"Okay, so what do we do now, Cat?"

"Dillon, is his body still here?"

"Yup, in a drawer. City morgue is in our basement, not at the clinic. Doc comes here when we need him."

Onnie shivered. "Convenient, but ew. Yeah, can I see it?"

"Follow me," Dillon said.

He led them across the space to a single elevator, which he keyed open and gestured for them to head inside. When the doors closed, Onnie saw there wasn't a button to select a floor, but she assumed there were only two, so it didn't need instructions. When the doors opened again, they were led through two heavy double doors and into a highly chilled room straight out of a cop show.

Stainless steel everywhere, all spotless. Large tables stood in the center of the room, and three walls were lined with drawers to hold bodies and supplies. The room smelled of antiseptic and death, but all were hidden under a veneer of sterile order. Or at least they tried to be.

"Things seemed to have slowed down for you guys recently," Dillon said. "Dany hasn't called me to deal with one of your roaches in a few weeks."

Gabe squeezed Onnie's hand before he nodded. "Yeah, not sure if it's a good thing or not, but at least it looks like there are fewer victims."

"Yeah. I won't lie, the angels were highly interested in what was happening here. I stuck to the story Dany gave me, but you know, angels," Dillon frowned at Gabe.

"Dicks."

Dillon nodded and then approached a drawer. He paused with his hand on the handle and looked at Onnie. "You ready?"

"Yes, thank you."

He pulled out the draw in one quick motion, and Onnie was relieved to see that the man's body was beneath a clean white sheet and appeared to be sleeping peacefully. She shut her eyes and sought out the man's Bond, its color dimmed and undoubtedly signifying his passing. Without opening her eyes, she reached out, rested her fingertips on the fabric covering his forehead, and searched for his soul.

"Soul intact. Doesn't look damaged or tampered with."

Kushima, what do you think? Feels like an Outsider with bad luck to me.

I can't help but agree.

Onnie removed her hand, opened her eyes, and saw both men staring at her, their faces impassive.

"I think he was a random accident."

"What are you going to do about his soul, Cat?"

"Leave it. I don't want to cross into the angel's domain if I don't have to. Besides, as an innocent, he deserves better."

"You're sure?" Dillon asked before rolling the drawer closed again.

"Yes, thank you. As much as I agree we should be cautious, I don't want to start down the slope of messing with innocent souls just to be careful."

"Understandable," Dillon said, an approving smile on his lips. "Anything else you two need from me then?"

"I don't think so," Gabe answered.

"Alright, well, keep me posted on how things are going." Dillon led them to a door on the far side of the room. "Here, this will take you up a small ramp to the street. I've got a few things to do down here still."

"Thank you, Dillon, and it was nice to meet you." Onnie held her hand out to him again, and he shook it gently.

"Ditto. I'll try to stop past the shop one of these days and in civilian clothes. I haven't picked up anything new to read in far too long." Dillon smiled and held the door open for them.

"Please do," she said as Gabe squeezed the man's shoulder.

"Later, man, and thanks again for the help."

"Happy to, even if it weren't my job."

With one final head nod, Dillon went back inside and closed the heavy door behind himself.

"Nice guy," she said, walking with Gabe up the shallow ramp and to the sidewalk.

"Always has been. Shocked us all that he became a cop."

Onnie chuckled. "Shouldn't the nice guys be the cops?"

Gabe gave her a sassy look like she was a dreamer, but then he pulled her against him and kissed her sweetly.

"I'll see you later?" he asked without releasing her.

"Yeah, I'm going to meet Dany at the cafe."

Gabe nodded, kissed her once more, then let her go and walked backward down the sidewalk away from her. "Have a good day, Cat."

"Love you."

"Love you, too."

She stood there a few minutes watching his back until she couldn't see him anymore. Something drew her eyes back to the morgue door, but she shook her head and began walking to meet Dany.

Onnie and Dany sat on the patio at the Day Night Cafe, absorbing the warm sun as if they were plants. A pitcher of iced tea was between them on the table, and a few empty plates had crumbs left from their lunches.

"How does Vanessa come up with these recipes?" Dany asked,

rubbing her stomach. "It really should be illegal to make food this good."

Onnie grinned. "I know. I go home to cook and end up chewing—sadly."

Dany mimicked Onnie's groan before leaning back in her chair with her eyes closed. "How was your drive last night?"

Onnie felt her cheeks redden. "It was nice. He took me to an overlook, and I swear, I don't think I've ever seen anything more spectacular."

"Ah, I bet I know where he took you," Dany said with her eyes still shut. "He always used to disappear to that ridge when he was stressed or had a lot on his mind."

"Well, it helped, and I'm grateful that Elaric was able to help with the warding issue so we didn't have to rush back."

Dany's head snapped up. "What warding issue?"

"Oh," Onnie said with a tilt of her head. She'd assumed he'd have told Dany. Or Mal would have. "There was a drunk who activated the wards near the tunnel. I asked Mal and Elaric to check it out since it seemed pretty benign."

Dany crossed her arms haughtily. "The rogue?"

Onnie shook her head. "No, apparently just a drunk. Elaric called in the body, and Dillon confirmed it. Gabe and I saw the body this morning. I guess the man's hired car from outside Alku also called in a missing persons report after their belligerent customer stumbled off into the forest on foot."

"How odd," Dany said, her brows knit together in thought.

"What is?"

"Why did the warding kill them? Seems a bit extreme, doesn't it?"

Onnie shrugged, "Depends on the level of their destructive intentions. You know that. Besides, Elaric said it looked like an accident."

"That's one hell of a coincidence," Dany said skeptically.

"I guess, but the ward repelled them, and Dillon said the man slipped since he was so trashed. He hit his head on a rock on the way down."

Onnie wasn't sure of the exact actions the wards had taken, but either way, they did their job, even if it was a brutal outcome this time.

Dany frowned, and Onnie knew she was still digesting the entire situation, and nothing would pry her focus away until she'd mulled as much as she wanted to mull.

"I'm sorry we didn't tell you. It wasn't intentional. I hadn't realized you didn't know."

Onnie was trying to be more honest with her friends, but she knew she'd broken some trust and had some rebuilding to do.

"It's fine, I guess."

"Dany…" Onnie groaned. "I swear, we weren't trying to keep anything. Gabe didn't want to return to Alku yet and asked Elaric and Mal to check for me since whatever happened seemed low risk." Onnie looked away and picked at one of her nails in her lap. "Gabe wants me to rely on you guys more often. Not try to do it all on my own."

Dany sighed. "Yeah, he's right. I get it. I'm not mad." Dany smiled, and Onnie was relieved to see it was genuine.

"Okay, thank you, and sorry again."

"No big," Dany said and waved her off.

Onnie nodded, but her eyes were drawn behind Dany to the front cafe doors as they were pushed open. "Sam!"

The young-looking day walker, who had been close friends with her grandfather and grew up, kind of, with Dany and Gabe, turned and smiled a big toothy grin.

"Onnie!" He looked down where Dany had bent her head backward to look up at him. "Dany!"

Dany laughed and righted herself. "Come join us, troublemaker."

Sam scoffed but did grab a chair and pulled it up to their cafe table. "What're you two ladies up to?"

"Lunch," Onnie said.

"Ruining future food for ourselves forever," Dany added, and Onnie chuckled.

Sam grinned. "I know what you mean. Vanessa's food is almost so good it could be used as torture."

Dany winced. "Ooo, that's a horrible idea."

"What she giveth, she can taketh away," Sam said with a silly accent.

"I agree with Dany," Onnie added. "Horrible. Remind me not to piss you off. Ever."

Sam smirked but said nothing.

Onnie stared off into the distance, watching people mill around the center of town. For the most part, Alku did look like a typical town filled with ordinary people. Until you looked closer. There were people you never see outside their homes after dark, people with glowing amber or lime-green eyes, or someone always covered in dirt, even first thing in the morning. The diversity was impressive, and Onnie was lucky to have become a Keeper in a town that could educate her just by existing around her.

"Hey, Onnie?" Sam said, and Onnie looked over and cocked her head at his tone.

"What's up?"

"I um," Sam sighed. "I just wanted to say thank you...and I'm sorry."

Onnie stared at him, fully confused. "For...what?"

Dany rolled her eyes. "Elaric. You space."

"Oh!" Onnie blushed. "Sam, I'm not sure what you think you need to apologize for, but for the other, you're welcome. I guess. I don't need thanks for that either."

Sam groaned, put his arms on the table, and buried his face in them. Onnie reached over and ruffled his blonde hair affectionately.

"Hey, wanna come over this weekend and help me make cookie dough? My freezer supply is almost empty. I'll send you home with some...."

Dany laughed. "Not above bribery, are you?"

"Not in the slightest. Sam, really though," she poked what little she could see of his cheek, "you have nothing to be sorry for. We were all tense and upset."

"You have to know I've been avoiding you," Sam said, muffled by his arms.

Onnie sat back in her chair and twirled the end of her long braid around her finger. "So?"

Sam's head shot up, and he glared at her. "What do you mean so?"

"So what? How are you *this* old and don't get this," she grinned at him.

"What's that supposed to mean?" Sam said, sitting up and crossing his arms while Dany laughed into her palm.

"You're not going to like everyone all the time. It's okay to be angry, hurt, or whatever. People need space sometimes. I knew you'd come back once you were ready to talk."

"And here you are," Dany said, elbowing him in the ribs as she sipped her tea.

Sam was still frozen in his defiant state for a moment, but then his shoulders dropped, and he rubbed the back of his neck.

"You're right. How am I *this* old and don't understand that?"

Onnie smiled. "You do now."

Sam laughed and sat back in his seat, finally relaxed. "That I do. Thanks, Keeper."

Onnie narrowed her eyes at him and glared. "I'll allow it, but just this once."

The three of them sat and talked for a while. It was nothing heavy, and they flit from light topic to light topic. She had missed Sam, but she'd seen his aura from afar one day and knew he needed space to sort himself out. When he did and was ready to talk, she'd be there.

"Excuse me," a middle-aged man called to them from the street.

Onnie looked around at the patio, and though they weren't the only ones on it, no one else seemed to respond to the man. That was probably because he was looking straight at their group, though.

"Can you help me?" he asked.

"Uh, sure. What do you need?" Onnie asked and sat up in her

chair. She immediately checked the stranger's Bond and aura, and while he wasn't a cheery man, he didn't look like the type that the rogue usually manipulated.

The man rubbed the back of his neck roughly. "Ya' see, I'm a bit lost. Would you mind pointing me in the direction of the local bed and breakfast?"

Onnie looked closer at the stranger but kept a friendly smile on her lips.

"Sure. We can give you directions. Dany, you know the streets better than I do. Would you mind?" Onnie looked over, and rightfully so, Dany was confused but any indications of it were gone a second later.

Checking something. Would you mind? Onnie said privately to Dany.

Dany flashed her friendly smile at the man, drawing his attention. "Sure. So, first, you'll want to go...."

Onnie lost track of what Dany was saying as soon as she began scrutinizing the man as discreetly as possible. His clothes were rumpled, and his hair looked messy, but there was nothing suspicious past that. It looked like he'd recently woken up from a nap or something, but nothing was alarming with that on its own. She couldn't check his soul without physically touching him, so she'd need to rely on his outward appearance and mannerisms.

"Thank you, Miss," the man said, drawing Onnie back to her surroundings. He waved to them, turned on his heels, and left.

Once out of earshot, Dany turned and hissed across the table. "What's with that? Find what you were looking for?"

Onnie shook her head, "Nope, nothing. I was just being paranoid. Sorry."

"After everything happening around here," Sam said, "I think you're allowed to be a bit twitchy."

"What he said," Dany agreed, indicating in his direction with her thumb.

"Thanks," Onnie smiled, relieved they weren't annoyed with her over-cautiousness.

"So, Sam, I wanna know more about the cute girl you're working with."

Sam's cheeks actually reddened slightly, and Dany sniggered. This was just what Onnie needed—a relaxing day, just friends, no rogue or roaches.

After a few hours of conversation, much more tea, and copious amounts of sun-warmed skin, Dany got to her feet and stretched with a squeak at the apex.

"Alright, I have to run to the library for a bit."

"Sounds good. I'll head back to the shop in a few minutes." Onnie glanced at Sam, hoping he'd catch her intention to stay and talk with him for longer.

"Thanks for lunch, Sam."

"Course," the kid stood to hug her, and then he and Onnie watched Dany head toward the library and away from them. When she was significantly out of earshot, Sam spun to look down at Onnie and crossed his arms.

"Alright, what was that look for?"

"Sorry, I want to talk to you, but I don't want Dany included."

"Why not?" Sam snapped defensively.

His protectiveness of Dany made Onnie happy, and she was relieved that he looked out for her so fiercely.

"Because I want to talk about her father."

Sam's eyes widened, and a few seconds later, his brain caught up, and he dropped heavily back into his chair. "Fine. That's a pretty good reason."

Onnie smirked. "Thanks for your approval." Her comment broke the tension, and Sam's smile returned.

"Anytime, I'm glad to be of service." His smile faded quickly and was overwritten with a sour expression. "What do you want to know?"

"Anything. You knew him. There's no way you didn't. What should I know that might help us?"

Sam rested his head back on the chair, his face to the sun above him, and he closed his eyes. When he finally opened his mouth to speak, his phone rang, and they both jumped and laughed at their twitchiness.

"Hey, Elaric, what's up?" Sam said, answering it.

Onnie couldn't hear Elaric's side of the conversation, but Sam's gaze flicked to her, and then he got up and walked further away from her.

She could still hear his response when he said, "Sure." Then he nodded before wincing and slumping forward. "Fuck. Yeah. Got it."

He mumbled a few more things that Onnie couldn't make out, then hung up and sulked back to her.

"Are you alright? Is Elaric?" Onnie carefully brushed her Bond with him and found his temperament was typical, so she backed off.

"I'm fine. Give me a minute, and I'll be right back. Need anything?"

His eyes glanced at her glass, and she downed the last few sips of the iced tea and cautiously passed it to him.

"Sure? Thank you."

Sam nodded, and she quickly looked at his aura before he left. It surprised her that he was tense and anxious as he left her on the patio and returned to the cafe.

Kushima?

Yes?

Have any idea what that was about?

I do not.

Elaric okay?

Yes, seems to be.

Onnie frowned, closed her eyes, and tilted her face to the sun just as Sam had a few minutes prior.

It's warm today—the sun.

Kushima's soft laugh made Onnie's smile return.

Enjoy it for both of us, then.

Do you miss it?

The sun?

Being...alive.

Kushima surprised Onnie when her joy washed over their Bond. *I do not. Not any longer.*

What changed?

You.

Onnie's eyes popped open, but her attention was drawn to Elaric and Sam exiting the cafe with drinks for the three of them.

"Hey, Onnie," Elaric said, setting her glass on the table in front of her. "Sorry, hope you don't mind if I crash your party. Felt a bit stir crazy in the apartment today."

"It's fine, you're always welcome."

When Sam retook his seat, she narrowed her gaze at him and found his aura was the same as when he left. He felt her scrutiny and pointedly looked away from her.

"Alright, you two, what's going on?"

Elaric sighed but smiled still. "Reading his aura, I assume?"

"Wait," Sam glared at her. "You can do that? How?"

"Long story, but yes. To both of your questions. Did I make you uncomfortable with my question?"

"Yes," Sam said and then returned his stare to anything but her.

"I think I can explain," Elaric interjected. "Jakob was an ass, and that's beside the point that he abandoned his duty. It's just a touchy subject. You didn't do anything wrong, Onnie."

This time, it was her turn to look away. "I'm sorry. I didn't mean to open old wounds. I hoped that if I knew more about him, it might help us."

"I get it." Elaric's voice was gentle, and his aura and mood were even.

Onnie could tell there was more, but if he was going to that much trouble to hide whatever it was, she was willing to let it go.

Elaric, I'll drop it. I trust you to tell me if it is important.

Thank you, Keeper.

Onnie rolled her eyes but then figured tit-for-tat was fair play. *You can stop covering your emotions and masking your aura. I can tell you're hiding something anyway.*

Elaric went pale, quickly picking up his glass of ice water and drinking nearly half of it.

Honestly, Onnie, he laughed along their Bond.

Sorry.

No. Don't be.

Elaric sighed, this time audibly. "I'm sorry. I'm so used to covering for Marco, I didn't even realize I was doing it."

Sam raised one eyebrow at his comment but said nothing.

"I understand. I don't want you to feel like you need to censor yourself in front of me, and if you ever do...just talk to me first?"

Elaric scootched his chair around the table and pulled her into a hug. "I promise."

"Either of you gonna share with the rest of the class?" Sam said finally, a goofy grin back where it belonged.

"If you're good," Elaric said, ruffing the kid's hair.

Sam glared playfully at him, and Onnie hid a laugh behind her palm. When Sam started poking Elaric's side, he was swiftly put into a headlock.

Onnie watched the two of them quietly. She enjoyed watching them, and if she stopped to think about it, she could imagine her grandfather in the middle of their chaotic roughhousing.

I'm glad everyone is moving on, Kushima. We all miss him, but....

Moving on is a part of life, and...the dead are not offended but rather relieved.

Onnie could feel the pain behind Kushima's words, but that was only the thin top layer. Beneath it was joy, amusement, and thankfulness that kept Onnie smiling, even when thinking of such weighty things.

Chapter 23: Surrounded

August 2022 - Alku | Onnie Moore

The typical chill was in the air within the First Keeper's library, and Onnie couldn't suppress the inevitable shiver. Her arms had goosebumps under her sweatshirt, and not for the first time did she look at the large bowls of blue flames, wishing they gave off some amount of heat.

"Thank you again for your help the other day, Elaric."

Elaric was seated in one of the chairs across the table from her, his nose buried in an old lore book about transmogromorphs. Her voice pulled him from the passage he'd been reading, and he placed his finger on it and looked up with his head tilted.

"What's up, Onnie?"

Onnie had manifested Kushima, who sat beside her, laughing softly and drawing both their gazes toward her.

Don't mind me.

Onnie glared at her. "As if. What do you find so funny?"

Young one, if you thank Elaric one more time, I won't blame him were he to plug his ears.

Elaric sniggered, and Onnie's own ears heated as she looked away. Kushima was clearly correct in her observation, and his laugh was enough evidence of that.

"Sorry."

"It's fine, Onnie, and you're welcome. Again."

Onnie sighed and poured herself a cap full of tea from her thermos.

Onnie, you had wanted to know my thoughts on the final room within the mountain, did you not?

"Yes, I'd honestly forgotten about it, though." Onnie slurped her tea, which echoed in the stone room, and she quietly apologized—again.

"It's fine," Elaric grinned and then addressed Kushima. "I assume you're talking about the one in the room with glass walls?"

Indeed. I requested that we wait to discuss it. If you're comfortable with it, I'd also like your input, Elaric.

"Wait," Onnie snapped, and Kushima and Elaric looked at her in surprise. Onnie frowned at Elaric. "Are you okay with that? I know it's not...easy to talk about."

"It's fine," Elaric's smile was genuine, and he carefully closed the book he'd been reading and set it aside. "How can I help?"

The day Onnie and the others retrieved your body, Onnie was violently ill before she came here. I believe I know the cause, and I believe you do as well, even if not consciously.

"Why are you being so cryptic?"

It hadn't taken Onnie long to learn that she should worry if Kushima's comments were so cagey. It was rarely a good thing.

Young one, you have seen a fair amount of the dark side of the magical world, however....

"It gets worse," Elaric finished and rubbed his forehead. "Much worse."

"Alright, so educate me. Why was that room, the air, all of it, so...ick." Onnie pulled a face and shivered, and Elaric chuckled at her.

"Correct response," he sighed. "I think you're correct, First Keeper, though I don't want to admit it."

Blood magic.

Onnie's stomach sank, and she suddenly felt like being physically sick again.

"That's..." she shook her head. "No, of course, that's real, too." She forced herself to swallow and took a quick sip of her tea. "Okay, explain. Please."

Let me start at the beginning. Many millenniums ago, there was a civilization beneath that mountain. You found part of it the day you ventured into it. They were a mining settlement and were the ones responsible for most of the cobbled streets within the town. Though that's not what the stones were originally used for, but that's not relevant currently.

"Okay, so we had dwarves?" Onnie blurted.

Elaric snorted. "Not exactly, but if I'm following the history correctly, it's a good enough parallel for a zwerkalt."

Like all others, they became greedy, and they wanted more. They turned to blood magic.

"For what gain?" Onnie looked at Elaric, who shrugged.

"Sorry, I'm old, but not that old," he looked at the First Keeper and frowned. "No offense."

Kushima laughed softly and shook her head. *None taken. I wasn't yet located here when that settlement was active.* Kushima switched to address Onnie's question. *Truthfully, they wanted all of it. They wanted wealth, power, and extended lives. Their desires overtook them, and they committed some incredibly vile atrocities.*

"Blegh," Onnie groaned.

Elaric's voice was somber, and he put his head into his hands. "You think Jakob tapped into what they left behind?"

I do.

"That would make sense. His capabilities to reanimate corpses if he had their souls, looking through other's eyes, hell, even the fog beasts."

"Fog beasts?" Onnie asked.

The black mist you saved Miranda from.

"And what you threw back at him that day in his lair."

Onnie nodded, "Ah, yes."

She looked down at her hand, which had caught the dark mist and later was covered in raw, damaged skin as if it had been eaten by acid.

"Bastard hurt like hell."

Elaric's head shot up. "What?"

"The one I caught. Before..." Onnie cleared her throat. "My hand was raw like the skin had an acid burn. I also removed it from Miranda the morning after the storm. My throat was raw too, but Xayn's magic helped with that, along with everything else I'd forgotten."

Do not fear. She is fine. The little one is as well. Those beasts were remnants left over from that civilization that had been buried long ago.

"He woke them up," Onnie stated, and both Kushima and Elaric nodded. "Okay, so what does that mean?"

"A problem for another day," Elaric sighed. "But one we'd better not forget."

Agreed. For now, stay out of that room. There's no telling what remains within.

Onnie frowned and traced the stitches in the blanket on her lap. When she finally connected all the dots, she groaned and roughly yanked on her braided hair.

"Shit. Gabe can't smell it because Jakob used his own blood. Didn't he?"

Kushima's pride nearly knocked the wind out of Onnie when the woman grinned and nodded.

Elaric scoffed. "Of course he did. Why didn't I think of that?"

"I mean, you were just a *bit* preoccupied," Onnie razzed him. "So, what does all this mean for us right now?"

Not a great deal. I merely wanted you to be aware and take the correct precautions. I believe the mountain will be fine if left on its own until after this current issue has concluded.

"You sure?" Elaric asked shakily. "I mean, it is blood magic we're talking about—"

Before Elaric could finish his thought, Kushima's projection winced, flickered, and then disappeared entirely.

"Kushima!" Onnie shouted and stood up so quickly that she knocked her thermos and blanket to the floor.

"Outside!" Elaric growled and pulled her behind him as he rushed over and shoved open the door for them both.

When Onnie's first foot hit the hardwood outside the library, she hissed and crumpled to the floor, Elaric instantly at her elbow. Mal appeared at her feet, and while Onnie held her pounding head, she threw walls up around herself and the shop along the Bond. She had no idea what was happening, but blocking everyone out and containing whatever was happening to her and Kushima's Bond was the safest first step.

Kushima? What's going on?

The wards.... I'm sorry. It was so sudden.

What happened?

"Onnie, what's going on?" Mal said, trying to see her face as he stuck his concerned head under her chin. "Elaric, what the hell happened?"

Don't tell about...her...please.... Onnie begged, knowing she was forcing her friend to lie once again.

"Not sure. I think the shop told her to come back out. Her first step, this happened."

Thank...you....

Onnie's eyes were tearing, and she looked up, her teeth gritted. "Wards."

Elaric must have understood her meaning because he immediately relayed the information to the others.

Something happened to one or more of the town wards. It affected the shop, and Onnie also looks like she's in pain. Gabe?

I'm on my way, stay with her.

Obviously. Mal's here, too.

Onnie pushed the other's conversation aside and focused on Kushima. *What happened?*

I'm not sure, but if I had to hypothesize, the intention ward coming into the town is being overwhelmed. Never in my years have I seen anything like this.

He's trying to brute force the wards now?

Precisely. Jakob's prior attempt was just a test.

Was it at the tunnel again?

No. It's not coming from one place.

Shit, divide and conquer.

I think that's likely.

Onnie looked up at Elaric, who had his arm around her, practically holding her up, considering she felt like a limp noodle that was being shaken violently.

"You back?" he asked.

She nodded. "Mal, go to Dany. Tell me when she's ready, I'll go get her. We can't wait."

Mal disappeared, and Onnie jumped when Gabe ran into the room. She hadn't felt him enter the shop, and that alone deeply unsettled her.

"Cat!" He rushed over to kneel in front of her and began surveying her body for injuries.

Onnie, we're ready. I'm in the back room at the library, Mal prompted her.

Be back, Onnie told Elaric and Gabe before she relocated to the library without waiting for their response. She was still on the floor when she got there, and without Elaric's support, she began to fall over.

"Shit," Dany rushed over, grabbing her shoulder to keep her upright. "What's going on?"

"Mal," Onnie said, and he nodded, so she relocated her and Dany back to Abbot's.

"For fuck sake, Onnie!" Gabe hissed but rushed to the other side of the room to where they'd appeared, and he took her from Dany's grasp. "You can't just disappear."

"Stop," was all she could manage, her head still pounding "Minute."

She closed her eyes, shutting out four concerned sets of stares.

Kushima, I have to block this out. I can't stand much more. Any ideas?
You must block your Bond to the wards as you've done to the others.
But what about you? Won't you still feel it?

Kushima laughed quietly. *Young one, I cannot feel pain. You needn't worry about me.*

"Don't lie to me," Onnie growled aloud on reflex and added, *I know you feel pain. You felt it every time I pulled too much power. When Abbot died, and you were attacked. Do not lie to me.*

Kushima was quiet for a moment before she sighed. *Do it anyway, Keeper. I can only stay here and try to hold and strengthen the wards. I need you to deal with the physical aspect of the problem.*

Onnie hated it, but she was right. *That makes sense, but we will discuss this further after this is over. I refuse to have this happen again.*

Good. Now, do it.

Onnie pulled up the Bonds around her and found the brightest Bonds that ran from her and the shop and then merged into one multi-colored rope, its components of different thicknesses, strengths, and ages—a millennium of powers and Keepers compounded into one massive set of wards.

At the section between her and where it joined with Kushima's, Onnie ground her teeth and cut off the flow of power to and from the Bond. It flickered and went nearly dark. She left just enough energy to keep it lit, and she immediately felt better when the pain coursing through her body subsided.

Kushima?

When there was no response, Onnie began to panic, but then she felt Kushima press on their Bond, but it was incredibly faint.

"Damn it!" Onnie said and opened her eyes. "Dany, ibuprophen, four of them. We can't waste any time."

"Cat, explain," Gabe asked as Dany rushed to do what she asked.

"Short version. The wards are being attacked."

Gabe paled. "The tunnel?"

"No, all around us. He's trying to split us up, and the roaches have circled the town."

Dany handed her a few pills, and Elaric tossed her a water bottle that had been on the desk.

"We need to split up. I have nearly nullified my connection to the wards. I can't do anything while in that much pain, but that means the shop is feeling all of it instead of us both carrying it."

No sooner had Onnie finished her sentence than the ground beneath them began to shake.

"Earthquake?" Dany asked, and Elaric shook his head.

"No, we need to hurry," Onnie said and struggled to her feet, Gabe swiftly clutching her elbow and stabilizing her. "I'm going to go back to his base in the mountain." Onnie watched Dany shiver, and Elaric's eyes darkened. "I won't ask anyone to go with me, but from the glass room, I should be able to see nearly the full circumference of the wards and direct you where to go."

"Smart plan," Elaric said, pulling Dany into his side and rubbing her arm.

"Cat, I don't want—" Gabe started, but Onnie held up her hand.

"I'm not asking," she said firmly.

Gabe's frustration flashed in his eyes, and she lowered her walls from around the group, only keeping up the one between her and the wards.

"Keeper," he growled. "I'm not arguing. I'm agreeing."

She blushed and immediately felt guilty for jumping to conclusions. "Sorry, I'm just—"

"Scared, we know." Gabe pulled her into his arms, and she took a deep breath. "I'll go with you. You need someone at your back, and there's no way he won't send someone up there if he can."

"He's right," Dany said with a weak smile.

"We need more help," Onnie stated.

"Leave it to me," Elaric said. "You and Gabe go find their locations. Mal and Dany can go to the first one and do some recon, and I'll go talk to Sam."

"Good call," Mal said and appeared on Gabe's shoulder, his tail rubbing the back of Onnie's head every time it moved.

The ground shook again, this time more strongly, and Onnie squeezed her eyes and fists shut as she heard a few books clatter to the floor.

"We need to go. Dany, Mal, I'm sending you to the tunnel. Maybe he hit there again. I'll go see where else and let you know if you need to move."

"Understood," Dany said, opening her arms for Mal to relocate into a second later.

"Elaric, I'll send you to Marco's," Onnie said, and when he nodded, she did it immediately. "Dany, Mal, you're up."

"Stay safe," Dany said, and Onnie agreed and sent them to the tunnel.

She turned and looked up at Gabe. "You ready?"

"Are you able to go to the gym fir—" he asked, and they were in his office before he'd finished his sentence.

"Hurry," Onnie said as he dashed into his cabinet and pulled out two carved staves.

He held one out to her, "Send this one to Dany."

Dany, incoming staff, Onnie informed and sent it.

Thanks, she replied before going silent again.

"Ready?" Onnie asked, and Gabe grabbed a smaller staff from the back corner of the cabinet and then shut it.

"Yes."

The instant they were in the abandoned lair room, Onnie coughed and doubled over from the effort. She'd used a lot of power, and though she'd been careful and was confident the shop hadn't suffered, she'd taken the beating herself. Her hands were shaking, and her joints were starting to ache along with her head. She should have taken more pain relievers, but it was too late at that point. Thankfully, the noxious air from the last time she'd been in the mountain was faint. Probably contained behind the door they'd yet to open.

"Take this," Gabe said and opened her hand to give her the small staff. It was only about three feet long, and the center foot was wrapped with leather. "There's a release here and here," he showed her two small bumps in the leather wrap. "They will trigger the lock mechanism, and a blade will come out from each end. Be careful."

"I'll ask you more later, but thank you." She kissed his cheek, her shaking unhideable. "Do not go into the room over there or even touch the door. I'll explain later."

"You got it. I don't plan on leaving the room unless absolutely necessary."

Onnie nodded and turned to the floor-to-ceiling glass wall overlooking the valley that Alku was nestled at the center of. She shook and stumbled but caught herself against the glass before Gabe noticed.

Dany, check-in.

Instead of Dany, Mal answered. *You were right. There's one here, but they're dead.*

What? Onnie asked and closed her eyes to bring her view of the Bond up.

Yup, a human. Head smashed in like a pumpkin. A tree fell on them.

Onnie shoved the back of her hand against her mouth to hold back the urge to vomit. *Where's Dany?*

Currently throwing up her lunch beside me.

Onnie swallowed down her own. *Understandable. Elaric, hold on for a few minutes. I have a hunch we may not need much help after all.*

I've already got Sam and Vanessa with me, and we're heading toward the West side of town. Want us to turn back?

No, but warn them of the first one we found.

Onnie opened her eyes but let the Bond stay visible over the valley she overlooked. "Gabe?"

"Here," he said from a few feet behind her, his back brushing against hers. "What's up?"

"I can see…" she quickly counted the bright spots around the town's ward that were within view. Judging by their spacing, there was probably one or two groups on the other side of the mountain out of her sight. "Four groups of three, and if I'm right, they'll all be dead. If their pattern holds, another two groups will be on the backside of the mountain."

"The rogue do this?"

"No, the wards. That's how it protects Alku."

Gabe sucked in a breath. "It kills them?"

"Yes, in this instance. The wards adjust to the situation. If the threat were a belligerent drunk, like yesterday, it would confuse them and turn them back towards the highway and away from us. That person likely not intending to cause harm. They simply would by virtue of the situation. Last night, the man was unlucky and slipped after the wards repelled him."

"But these people are *actively* trying to destroy," Gabe said, resigned.

"Correct, and I'd bet it knows they're roaches."

Onnie, update? Mal asked so everyone could hear.

Sorry, yes. Beyond the lone one that Dany and Mal found, I see six groups of three beings a piece. I'll guide you along the ward line to the next group. Keep your guard up. We have no idea why he's sending roaches to their death.

We'll be to the boundary shortly, Elaric replied.

Mal, when you and Dany are ready, go North along the tree line, and you'll find a group. I'll keep an eye on you and let you know if you go wide.

Dany groaned. *Yeah.*

Onnie took a deep breath and carefully checked the barriers blocking the ward's backlash. She lowered it slightly and exhaled when there wasn't any searing pain.

Kushima?

I'm here, young one. Everything's fine.

Are you hurt?

Not badly. A few books on the floor, but that's the extent of it.

Onnie sighed in relief. *Thank the gods.*

Ready for directions, Elaric stated.

Continue along the border South.

Onnie watched as the five glowing points representing her friends trudged slowly through the trees in the valley of Alku. Each time one of the teams found a group, it was the same as the last—all dead. There were various races, with nothing on them or around them to provide any clues as to who they were. Not one of them was still alive, and none was able to be saved, but Onnie was too exhausted to get to each and every one of them to retrieve their souls anyway.

By the time they'd located all the bodies, it was late afternoon, and Elaric took Vanessa and Sam straight home. Mal walked Dany home since that was the closest house to where they had been searching, and Elaric promised to meet the pair there later.

As soon as they'd finished, Onnie's knees buckled, and Gabe lifted her into his arms. Then, she relocated them to their living room.

"You okay, Cat?"

Gabe settled her onto the couch and squatted down in front of her, his palms on her knees.

"Yeah. Thank you."

She handed him her staff, and he took it from her with a smile and got to his feet.

"Gabe, I need to talk to the First Keeper for a while. Could you make some tea?"

"Sure, would you mind letting me listen in, though?" He brought over the quilt her mom had made and draped it over her lap.

She smiled, though it was weak due to her exhaustion. "Of course."

Gabe leaned down, kissed her forehead, and headed into the kitchen to make tea.

Mal, I'd like the four of us to discuss the wards and what happened today. You up to it?

Onnie had only included Gabe, Mal, and Kushima in the conversation and left the others to rest and do what they needed to do after such a long and traumatic day.

I am. Gonna stay with Dany until she sleeps, which won't be long by the looks of it. I'll come home once Elaric gets here.

Thanks, Gabe said, speaking the words before Onnie had the chance. *Can we start with what happened before I got to the shop?*

Yeah, Onnie said, snuggling into her quilt and closing her eyes. *While Elaric and I were in the First Keeper's library, something felt off, and we left. Once we crossed the threshold into the study, overwhelming pain hit me. I closed it off to everyone else as quickly as possible but stayed connected to the shop.*

I was also experiencing a similar…pain, for lack of a better explanation. Knowing that Onnie would be unable to act in her current state and, I, without the ability to assist physically, told her to close her connection to the wards and focus on solving the issue.

That's why the earth shook, Gabe stated.

Yes, Onnie agreed. *Thankfully, whatever happened was relatively quick, so the shop is alright.*

Good, Mal said with a sigh of relief.

Agreed. I was disconnected from Onnie for only a few minutes before the wards calmed. My prediction is it lines up with when all of the intruders were eliminated. At the time, however, we were experiencing the attack as it was happening without knowing what or how long it would continue.

Onnie heard the kettle beep in the kitchen, and she sat back up, ready for Gabe to return.

Don't think I'm letting you off the hook for lying to me, First Keeper.

Oh, snap, Mal said. *I know that tone…good luck, Master K.*

Kushima laughed softly, but Onnie felt her apology. *Yes, well, I did break our promise. I will not do it again.*

Better not, Onnie scolded.

Gabe drew the conversation away from the First Keeper with his concern along their Bond, making Onnie shiver. *What about the bodies, Cat?*

You mean their souls?

Yes.

I…I just can't right now. Maybe I could free a few, but not all of them. I think we will have to gamble that it will be alright and leave them for the angels.

Gabe was quiet, and she could feel him ruminating.

Big guy, Mal prodded.

I don't like it.

Gabe exited the kitchen with a steaming mug of tea in one hand, a bowl of cut fruit and cottage cheese in the other, and a bottle of water tucked under his arm.

Neither do I, but it's where we're at.

Unfortunately, I agree with Onnie, the First Keeper said. *Neither of us has the strength right now to see to them all.*

Gabe handed Onnie her tea and then sat beside her, placing the bowl on the coffee table for when she was ready.

He sighed and cracked open the water bottle. *Alright. I trust your judgment.*

Was there any lasting damage? To the wards, I mean, Mal asked.

No, thankfully, the wards are still in place, the First Keeper confirmed. *For today, I believe everyone needs rest. Tomorrow, we can talk further.*

Of course, thank you. Onnie pulled away from their conversation, Kushima's warmth flowing along their Bond before she, too, rested.

"Drink your tea and eat, Cat, and then we'll shower and call it an early night, okay?"

Gabe pulled one of her feet towards his lap and began rubbing her ankle. She nodded and sipped her tea, spacing off into the distance. Her headache was mostly gone after the medication had kicked in, and the tea seemed to be chasing the last of it away. Unfortunately, her muscles still felt like noodles.

When Gabe interrupted her brain's wandering, she jumped, a blush creeping up her cheeks.

Gabe smirked at her before asking, "Can you confirm something for me?"

"Sure, what's up?" Even her voice sounded exhausted and strained.

"It's safe to assume he's now outside the wards, right?"

"The rogue?"

Gabe nodded.

"Yeah, I'd say that's a safe bet. Not sure why, but my random guess is it was an accident."

"So, how'd he get past them before?"

"Once again," Onnie shrugged, "I'm guessing, but I don't think he had to. I think he was already here."

Gabe's eyes widened, and he paled. "You mean in Alku? For how long?"

"I have no idea, but either he never left, or when he initially came back, he didn't have any ill intentions. Something must have happened."

Gabe's brow furrowed. "What about his roaches?"

"Same thing? I don't know. He was a Guardian, he had knowledge of the wards, and maybe all of his roaches were recruited as Elaric was. Within the city, then twisted and manipulated."

After a few minutes of thinking, Gabe's quiet laugh broke the silence.

"Abbot once told me, "We all have the capacity for darkness within ourselves. Our strength comes from being tested and resisting the seductive hand it extends to us." I almost wonder if he knew."

Onnie sighed. "Knowing him, I wouldn't doubt it."

Chapter 24: Under the Veil

August 2022 - Alku | Gabriel Vansand

He and Elaric leaned on a stack of mats in the Alku school gym, watching Dany train Onnie to use a staff weapon. Both women moved sluggishly, but if you looked into their eyes, you'd see only determination and icy fury.

"How's she doing?" Elaric asked.

"Exhausted. Cat slept, but I think it was just too much too quickly yesterday for both her and the shop. I got her to drink some tea this morning, but she barely ate and then nearly dragged me out of the house in my pajamas to come train."

"She can feel it, Gabe."

"So can I."

Gabe knew whatever they were waiting for was close. The end was coming, and with it, his father's last chance to get what he wanted. It was guaranteed that whatever he did would be big, and after two attacks on the wards in a row, the man was definitely growing impatient.

"How's Dany? You went to her place after dropping Sam and Vanessa off at home, right?"

Elaric crossed his arms and nodded. "Yeah. She's...fine."

Gabe glanced sideways at the man beside him, but Elaric's stare never strayed from Dany.

"I think she may still be in shock, to be honest. If the bodies she and Mal found were like the ones we did...."

"Yeah."

Gabe ran his hand roughly through his hair and sighed. Of all the people who should have been dealing with gruesome corpses, it should have been him, not his sister. They watched Dany step behind Onnie and put her arms around her, demonstrating how she should grip the staff better.

"Gabe, your sister is amazing."

"I know," he snorted. "She reminds me constantly. Often without ever having to say a word."

Elaric smiled, and Gabe could see the love in the man's face for Dany. Not for the first time in recent weeks was Gabe grateful for Onnie and what she did for Elaric. The man himself aside, she'd put Dany back together when no one else could.

"Thanks for watching out for her," Gabe said. "Truly. Where I used to be able to watch out for both of them...I don't think that's possible anymore. I feel better knowing you're with her."

"As long as she'll have me, but even after that," Elaric smiled.

"Gabe! Come show Onnie the blade switch," Dany called over to them.

"Coming," he smirked at Elaric. "Guess I'm up."

Elaric nodded, and Gabe pushed away from the mats with his foot and crossed the gym to where the two women were in front of a standing bag, working on form and technique. Onnie lowered the practice staff as he approached, and both women looked up at him.

"I think she's got the basics," Dany said, bending to grab a water bottle from the floor. "At least enough that if she needed to use her staff, she might not only flail around."

Cat groaned, "Ug, I suck."

Dany giggled. "You do, but you picked it up for the first time today. Sorry, Onnie. Bond can't help you here."

"Yeah, yeah." Onnie gently shoved Dany, who lightly punched Gabe's shoulder then she wandered over to Elaric.

"How are you feeling, Cat?"

"Sore and exhausted, but fine," she rolled her neck. "I'm not sure how much more I can do, but Dany thought you should at least show me the staff's switch so I don't accidentally trigger it and then cut someone when I can't figure out how to retract them."

Gabe chuffed. "Can't say she's wrong." He walked a few paces away to where her smaller, bladed staff was leaning against a wall. "I'll show you how the mechanisms work, and then we can take a break for lunch. You didn't actually eat breakfast."

"Sure," she said, verbally waving him off before drinking half a water bottle.

When she was ready, Gabe held the staff out horizontally to the floor. "See how the center section is wrapped?"

"Yeah."

"Use that to orient yourself if you can't look at your hands. If you don't feel leather, or when you extend a finger, you feel wood, you need to re-grip."

Cat nodded. "Makes sense."

Gabe rotated the staff so it was in the correct position for him to hold it properly. "If you want to use the blades, try to have it rotated like this." He watched as she bent forward to see where his hand gripped the weapon.

"This part," she pointed to just beside his thumb.

"Perfect," he beamed at her. "See how my thumb is in a small divot? That's so you can reach a bit further," he slowly stretched his thumb toward the end of the staff, "and press this raised bump."

When he pressed it, and nothing happened, her eyebrows wrinkled, but she quickly moved to examine where his other hand would have also been holding the staff.

"There are two."

"Yup," Gabe said with a smirk, placing his second hand on the staff. "Both releases are in the center of the staff. That way, you can either grip the center with one hand, and when you squeeze, it will trigger the blades, or, if you have it held in two hands, then you can use both thumbs, but if you accidentally press only one of them nothing will happen."

She nodded and stood back up straight. "Alright. Makes sense."

"Here, you try," he passed her the staff.

"It's...not much heavier than the practice one."

Gabe shook his head. "Nope. Partly because the practice one was weighted so you could train with it for this specific staff, but also because I tried to get it as light as possible. Unlike me, and to a degree, Dany, you won't be able to rely on brute force and body weight to put power behind your swings. You need to be more precise. Surgical."

"Wait to strike until I'm confident it will matter," she said, looking up at him.

"Exactly."

"Okay," she sighed. "Let's get started then."

Onnie Moore

"Thanks, Gabe," she stepped onto her tip toes to kiss his lips briefly.

"Of course, Cat," he smiled. "Go home and shower and get some food."

"Yeah, I will." She looked at Elaric, "Hungry? You're welcome to join me for lunch."

"Sure," he smiled, and she didn't miss Gabe's grateful nod to Elaric, even if they thought it was outside of her peripheral vision.

I'm too worn out to care about Gabe's scheming, she said to Kushima.

Remember why he does it, young one.

I know.

"I'll call you after the game, and we can see what you feel up to tonight." Gabe handed her another water bottle and took the staff from her.

"Sure," she nodded and followed Elaric to the gym door.

Love you, Cat.

Love you, too.

You did a good job today.

Onnie chuckled. *Liar, but I appreciate it.*

You'll get better, Gabe said as she and Elaric exited the gym.

"Shower first, but do you want to pick food up on the way or something else?" Elaric asked.

"There are leftovers from the other night at home if you're up for it."

"Works for me."

They began their walk, and Onnie stared at her feet with each step she took—one in front of the other, over and over.

"We don't have much time left. Do we?"

She heard Elaric sigh. "I don't think so. You can feel it too, I assume?"

Onnie switched to the Bond. *Yeah, we both can.*

Indeed, Kushima replied.

All we can do is be as ready as possible.

Truthfully, I'm a bit relieved, Onnie admitted. *I'm ready for this to be over.*

I'm sure you are, Elaric acknowledged.

We all are, young one. Just be sure you're not rushing through precious time to prepare and miss the opportunity to do so.

Yeah, I know.

As they walked, Onnie watched the people of Alku going about their days around her. People she'd never met, flitting in and out of shop doors. Coffee in some hands, a snack for the road in others. Everyone was happy, just as they always were.

Something caught her attention across the street, and she saw a young couple arguing. She couldn't hear them, but their auras were vibrant and passionate, drenched in their anger.

Then Onnie shivered.

"Elaric. Did you feel that?"

He looked down at her. "Feel what?"

"Guess that's a no," she shook her head. "Sorry, I just got this feeling."

"What feeling?"

"Like...as if a veil was shifted to the side for a split second, and what was below it wasn't good."

"The wards?"

She shook her head. "No. As far as I can tell, this wasn't magical. It was...instinctual."

Elaric frowned and tipped his face to the sky. "Well, that can't be good."

"Agreed," she paused. "What happened to the bodies from yesterday?"

"Dillon and the fire department picked them up. They are in the morgue until the angels can come to handle their souls, and then their bodies can be picked up by the human police. Why?"

"Oh, actually. Um..." she glanced around them, "any idea why the angels never came for the other souls?"

"Oh," Elaric frowned.

It is the warding, young one. That is why they needed to be notified by your law enforcement. One of Alku's wards makes it difficult for them to see deaths within our borders. We must inform them.

Elaric's eyes narrowed. *Interesting. I had no idea.*

It is simply a side effect of another ward. The other Sanctuary Cities are the same or similar.

Too many wards, densely covering a single area? Onnie asked.

Precisely. A lot of interference.

That is interesting, Onnie agreed with Elaric's earlier statement.

Chapter 25: You Understand Nothing

August 2022 - Alku | Onnie Moore

"Onnie, one of these days, we should connect you with a mechanite," Stephan said with a refined chuckle and a smile hidden behind his wine glass.

"I'm not that bad…" Onnie glared at Elaric, who shrugged and failed to suppress his grin. Marco's face was firmly in his public persona mode, and he just smiled politely, though she saw his eyes glitter with amusement. "Fine! You've made your points," Onnie laughed.

"It's fine. In fact, I think it's a good thing. You shouldn't be amazing at everything," Elaric teased. "It's reassuring to know you break something just by looking at it."

"Oy!" She playfully shoved his shoulder. "They don't break. They just…give up."

"I've honestly never seen someone who repels technology quite like you do," Stephan smirked, and Onnie picked up her wine and proceeded to pout dramatically.

The laughter and chatter around their group of four at the Day Night Cafe was delightful, and the low hum of it felt soothing. It had been a few days since the wards had last been attacked, and everyone had recovered for the most part. Both she and Kushima were still slightly overextended but nearly back to normal. Onnie hadn't felt like staying cooped up at home, so she'd called Stephan to see if he was free for dinner, and she ended up with three for the price of one. Dany was busy with Gabe, and Marco had the night off, so he and Elaric joined her and Stephan for dinner and conversation.

"Where are Dany and Gabe tonight?" Marco asked, and Elaric answered before Onnie could.

"School. Dany needed to let off some steam after the other day. Gabe offered to beat her up," Elaric smirked.

Marco laughed. "And what was Dany's response to that?"

"Exactly as you'd expect, "as if," or something like that," Onnie said with a smile. She loved watching Dany and Gabe's sibling interactions, and neither was ever malicious or cruel. Even the most sassy and snarky comments were said in jest.

Onnie was about to ask Stephan about Sam when she saw his face harden, and he seemed to go even more paler than he normally was.

"Stephan, what's—"

A searing pain flared through her body, and this time Onnie knew what it was. It was the same pain she'd felt a few days prior.

The wards are being attacked!

She shouted to everyone reflexively. Stephan, being the only one unable to hear her, only saw her hiss and then clutch her head as the pain brought tears to her eyes.

Cat, where are you?

Elaric answered for her as Stephan swept her into his arms and rushed into the kitchen, Marco and Elaric behind them.

Day Night Cafe with Marco, Stephan, and I.

Stay there. We're on our way, Gabe said quickly.

No! Go to the tunnel, Onnie forced out. *We'll meet you there.*

Cat—

Before he could argue, she directed the pain of the wards to him for only a fraction of a second, and everyone heard his reaction when he felt it.

Don't. Argue, Onnie snapped as Gabe acquiesced. Understanding rippling through their Bond before he receded to focus on getting him and Dany to where they needed to be.

Stephan sat on one of the stools at the small table and held her to him like she weighed nothing. His eyes searched her face, and she knew he was trying to decode her aura, which was, no doubt, a mess.

"What can I do?" he asked Marco and Elaric.

Explain everything to him, please. I need to talk to the First Keeper, Onnie told them.

She immediately shifted to talking to only Kushima. *Can you tell me anything about the attack?*

Young one…I think…I think we only have one option left to us. They are attacking from both within and outside the wards.

How did they get in?

I know not, but we both must be strong enough for what's coming next. You are correct. It's time to go to the tunnel.

Do it. I'll tell the others and get us there.

Onnie spoke via the Bond and aloud for Stephan's benefit. "We're lowering all the wards."

What! Dany shrieked, the shock evident in her mental voice.

"They are attacking from inside and out. We can let them break through and weaken us before we confront them, or we can lower the wards now. That will preserve the strength we need to hold them back, and then we will be able to face them as strong as possible from the beginning."

Onnie looked at Marco, whose eyes were nearly all darkened pupils. His body was so still that he looked as if she'd frozen him in place. She shifted her attention to Stephan, whose body language was nearly identical. When she looked at Elaric, he nodded once, his understanding of her unspoken question immediate.

"Dany and Gabe, meet us at the tunnel. I'll bring Elaric and Marco with me," she said aloud and via the Bond again.

"I'm coming with you," Stephan stated.

When she looked up at him, he smiled, but she shivered and feared that she was seeing a truly out-of-control sanguiste for the first time.

"Do not worry, Onnie. I'm still in control. You are safe. You have my word."

He's very old, Elaric said privately to her. *You can trust him. He may look out of control, but he's very much still in the driver's seat.*

Thank you. Onnie relaxed against Stephan again. *And Marco?*

He's also fine. Mostly. But you and I both know he'd harm himself before you.

She swallowed roughly, then addressed the other two. "Once the First Keeper servers the warding and my brain doesn't feel like it's going to—"

The pressure in Onnie's head relaxed as if someone had suddenly let go of the stranglehold they'd had on her brain, and she sagged further into Stephan and exhaled.

"Ah, so much better."

He stared down at her, but after a few seconds of studying her, he helped her to stand on her own two feet, and she straightened her clothes.

You alright? she asked Kushima.

Yes, but you should hurry.

"Wards are down. Meet you there."

Cat, be safe. I'm sending Mal to you.

Thanks, Onnie said as Mal appeared on Elaric's shoulder.

The feline looked her up and down, then looked between Stephan and Marco before nodding to her.

"You four ready?" she asked. "We have no idea what will be waiting for us."

"Realistically, no," Elaric answered, "but yes. Let's do it."

Marco only nodded, but Stephan's response had Onnie shivering again.

"There are some debts, long overdue, to be repaid."

Onnie swallowed roughly but then took a deep breath. "Alright, Stephan, Marco, close your eyes and count to five. Then open them."

Onnie glanced around the kitchen and realized people surrounded them. There were cooks, waitstaff, and everyone in between. They all seemed anxious while they continued doing their jobs, giving the Keeper and their boss a wide berth, but they were still paying attention.

"Pay them no mind," Stephan sneered, but likely not in response to his staff. "They are all trustworthy and of our world."

Onnie nodded. "Close your eyes."

When she saw both men do as she'd asked, she relocated all five of them into the street a few hundred yards ahead of the tunnel leading out of Alku. In precisely five seconds, both sanguiste opened their eyes, and Mal jumped to the ground from his perch on Elaric's shoulder.

"Watch my back. I need to connect Stephan's Bond."

Elaric nodded, and Onnie quickly found her friend's Bond, making him shiver beside her as she connected it to her own, forgoing gentleness for expediency.

Stephan is here as well, Onnie said to everyone.

She saw when Stephan's grin turned unquestionably terrifying, and she was glad he was on their side.

Less than ten minutes out, Dany said.

"Elaric weapon?" Onnie asked.

After only a few heartbeats, his eyes widened in understanding, and he shook his head. "Fists, thank you."

We have company, Marco growled along their Bond, and the group shifted into a formation, back to back with Mal at Onnie's feet.

She had a sanguiste on either side of her, and as she pulled the Bonds nearby to be visible over the real world, she glimpsed that their Bonds were nearly stationary. Typically, there was a slight pulse or waver in a Bond, almost like a metaphysical heartbeat, but when she looked at Stephan and saw he was as still as stone, she realized his Bond reflected his body.

She diverted her attention back to the treeline before her and struggled to keep her face expressionless as she counted the Bonds of their foes.

There are over two dozen on this side, she said to everyone and immediately felt Gabe's anxiety rise.

Nearly the same on the other treeline, Stephan added.

Half as many are coming from the tunnel direction, but they seem larger than your average roach, Marco provided.

Shit, Onnie hissed. Even she hadn't expected that the rogue would have converted that many people to his control so quickly.

They seem to be waiting, Stephan noted. *Keeper?*

What are they?

Stephan was quiet for a few seconds before he growled, and the hair on the back of Onnie's neck raised.

A *mix of races and species. However, not all of them are entirely…* alive.

Fuck, Gabe cursed.

Onnie took a deep breath, steeling herself. *Well, that honestly makes this easier. First Keeper, you ready?*

As you will it, daughter of mine blood.

Onnie growled, *"As you wish."*

She closed her eyes and reached for the Bonds of every stray pebble on the road around them and lifted them into the air, roughly four feet off the ground. With a mental push, she sent them flying at the speed of bullets out from their group's center, into the trees, and down the tunnel.

The sounds of grunting and a few bodies hitting the floor rang out in the quiet forest night. Onnie watched as two Bonds on her side went dark.

"Two down on this side."

Stephan threw his head back and laughed. *I see. I understand now.*

It was Onnie's turn to laugh, and she opened her eyes and turned to look at her friend.

You understand nothing. The blue of her eyes, reflected in his inky black ones, stared back at her. *I'm just getting started, Stephan.*

When she saw a sanguiste, so deep into their predator instincts, shiver in response to her, she couldn't help but feel slightly proud.

She turned back to those hidden within the forest.

"Shall we play again?"

Like before, she reached for the Bonds around her, grabbing loose sticks and twigs this time. With a push on their Bonds, they whizzed off into the trees, and this time, there were a few auditory responses as she pierced and punctured their attacker's flesh.

"Three more down," she informed.

Gabe and Dany incoming, Marco warned.

Onnie turned toward Alku as Gabe's car skidded to a stop relatively far down the road from them. The instant she saw his car shift into park, she relocated Gabe to stand between her and Stephan, and Dany between Elaric and Marco. Thankfully, both had weapons in their hands.

As if they'd been given orders to wait for the whole group, their attackers ripped apart the quiet night when the remaining four dozen roaches howled and swarmed the seven of them.

The first casualty was a young, twenty-something-looking human roach who was probably trying to prove he was tough shit. Instead, he rushed directly at Onnie, and before Gabe could step in front of her, she relocated behind the man, gripped his neck, and ripped his soul from his body with such force that he hit the ground completely unmoving. She quickly hid away the soul as she had in the past, the movement quick and seamless.

"You bitch!" a woman shouted from behind Onnie.

She didn't even waste time turning around. Instead, Onnie opted to freeze the woman before casually walking behind her to remove her soul as forcefully as she had to the younger man's.

After their group had eliminated a dozen of Jakob's forces in less than three minutes, the roaches began weaving around Onnie. Instead, they focused their attack on the rest of the group.

Onnie saw that Stephan had a sanguiste in his grip, and she watched as he cracked the man's neck, and his body hit the floor at Stephan's feet. Dany and Elaric were back to back, and her Sister spun and kicked a lumbering human in the chest, which sent him flying away from her at the same time that Elaric snapped the neck of a waif-like undead woman and dropped her body.

"Cat! Focus!" Gabe snapped, and Onnie flinched as he swung his staff at her left flank, which impacted a middle-aged man covered in dirt smudges instead of Onnie.

Onnie's eyes went wide, and she ran back to the center of their group, where she closed her eyes and filtered through all of the Bonds and chaos around her.

Kushima, can you tell me if the wards are being targeted even though they're down? Or if anyone crosses them while they are inactive?

It's possible, but either no one has, or I cannot.

Crap, he's not here. Jakob, he's not with this group.

Perhaps he's still outside the border.

Onnie opened her eyes and checked her surroundings. Their group seemed to be holding their own, and other than what looked like a few scratches, no one was overly injured on their side. However, Onnie was surrounded by a ring of her friends, who were then surrounded by a ring of bodies at their feet, which were beginning to hinder their fighting ability.

Everyone, watch out. I'm going to clear some of the space around us.

Onnie used the Bonds of the corpses to force all of them out and away from her allies. A few of the bodies impacted active foes and took their feet out from under them, but either way, it cleared some room to maneuver better. It also cleared more space for being attacked.

A low, rippling laugh emerged from the darkness, rolling over Onnie and the others.

"You still think you have a chance. How naive."

When the rogue completed his taunt, Onnie gritted her teeth as all the roaches they'd taken out by that point struggled but got back on their feet.

"Fuck me!" Gabe hissed.

"You've got to be kidding me," Dany groaned.

Onnie looked closer at those who had returned to their feet but noticed a few roaches were missing.

Mal, find the ones whose souls I took. Confirm they got back up.

On it, Mal said and disappeared from her side.

Onnie, Elaric said, his mental voice shaking. *I recognize this one. This man was one of the bodies from the attack two days ago.*

Onnie clenched her teeth and fists and felt her body shake in rage. *I see. So that's how he did it.*

The bodies that you couldn't remove souls from? Gabe asked.

Exactly. That's how they got inside the wards. The wards allowed the dead to pass through, and then Jakob reanimated them, or whatever, once they were inside. We collected his soldiers for him.

Onnie heard Marco hiss from beside her, his revulsion blinding her with the strength of his aura.

Less than a minute later, Mal relayed, *Those without souls are still down. Keeper, there are too many of them. Don't even think about it,* Mal scolded before Onnie had a chance to comment.

She sneered and tsked. *You underestimate me, Maldwyn.*

Onnie, don't do it. There's no point bringing down his army if you're out cold by the time the rogue shows up, Dany said with her characteristic logic.

How many can you take down and still have enough strength, Keeper? Stephan asked. *Realistically.*

A third, maybe slightly more, Onnie replied honestly.

Gabe stepped in front of her and swung his staff at an incoming roach, and the sound of their skull cracking echoed over the fray. Once their body hit the ground, Onnie knelt and gripped their neck, removing their soul and stowing it away.

Cat, we need to do this the right way. Pick the biggest obstacles, not just the low-hanging... he swung his staff to the left, and the end connected with a woman's stomach...*fruits.*

Fine. If someone is struggling, tell me, and I'll come to you. Don't be a hero, Onnie lectured.

Hell of a pot you are, Miss Kettle, Mal snapped.

Hush you. Go see if you can skirt around in the forest and find the rogue. He's not here. Try outside the tunnel on the outer side, Onnie instructed, and then the feline was gone.

I can't help but think that none of these pests are particularly difficult to deal with, Keeper, Marco voiced, his elbow smashing into the eye of a man with glowing golden irises.

Agreed, Elaric added. *Diversion?*

Hmm…as far as I can tell, this is the only attack front.

Onnie closed her eyes, but judging by the Bonds, everything looked the same as before.

Kushima, anything?

Unfortunately, no.

Ug, we need a better view—oh, he's gonna kill me, Onnie said with a wince. *Gabe, trust me. I'll be back within thirty seconds. Don't panic.*

With that, Onnie relocated herself to the mountaintop and into the glass room of Jakob's base.

Cat! Gabe shouted. *Mal, find her!*

Onnie closed her eyes and quickly scanned the valley below her. *Nothing, damn it,* she hissed to Kushima.

You should return. At this rate— Kushima began until Mal appeared at Onnie's feet.

What the actual shit, Onnie? Mal hissed.

I'm already done. Let's go back, she nodded and relocated them both back to the group. *As far as I can tell, this is the only place we need to worry about.*

Onnie pointedly ignored Gabe's flesh-burning scowl from beside her and glanced down at Mal. *Did you find him?*

No, but there's something odd just beyond the tunnel.

What is it?

Hard to explain….

"Onnie!" Dany screamed as the man who'd asked them for directions the day they'd had lunch at the Day Night Cafe reached for her and yanked on her hair, pulling her backward.

Onnie relocated to the back of the man, ripped his soul out, and checked on Dany. "You okay?"

Dany nodded with a wince and reached up to rub the back of her head. "Yeah, thanks."

"Of course."

Onnie began flitting from place to place, collecting souls and pocketing them until she had double digits hidden within her Bond. Then she returned to Mal's side.

We can't win this battle of attrition, Mal said to everyone.

Onnie saw Elaric and Gabe make eye contact for a split second, and then Gabe said the words she'd been dreading.

Lead them to the tunnel. Keeper?

I'm ready. Let me make a path.

Onnie grasped the Bonds of the roaches and froze them in place. "Go!"

No one hesitated. Instead, they all sprinted toward the tunnel and past the roaches as they slowly began to shake and break free of Onnie's hold as she'd expected them to. It didn't matter. It had been enough of a delay to allow everyone to escape the conflict without fighting through them. She released her hold over everything and relocated to her friends at the tunnel's entrance.

Mal, show me what you found. Gabe, come with us.

The three of them ran through the tunnel to the other side, leaving the rest of the group to hold off the swarming minions.

There! Mal said, and they skid to a stop.

Onnie squinted and noticed what Mal was referring to—a black haze hovering a few feet off the ground a few yards past the tunnel. It reminded her of the blood beasts Jakob had used to attack them in the past, but this was less mist and more…nothing.

Understanding hit Onnie like a truck. She tried to examine the haze's Bond only to find there wasn't one, and she couldn't manipulate it at all.

Kushima! Is that what I'm thinking?

Without a doubt, though how, I have no idea.

What is it, Cat? Gabe asked her and Mal.

Void.

Excuse me? Mal said, his little kitty jaw dropping. *How is that even possible?*

We have no idea, but there's no doubt. That's what it is.

Gabe shifted and continued to scan the area around them. *What do we do with it?*

Onnie shook her head. *I have no idea, but now I understand why we couldn't relocate into the room with the well. It was warded to react like the First Keeper's library.*

Heads up, you've got two incoming, Elaric warned.

Mal and Gabe shifted to guard Onnie's back. Onnie looked over her shoulder and saw a tall man with dark hair and red eyes running straight for them. Behind him was a more petite woman, and as she got closer, Onnie saw how young she was and remembered Ana from when she was Gemini.

Onnie stepped around Gabe and relocated her staff to her via its Bond. Just as Gabe was going to rush past her, she held her right hand out to her side and opened her palm. The staff appeared in her upturned hand, and she triggered the knives as he'd taught her. She growled and lunged for the man headed straight for her.

While he was undoubtedly larger than she was, she had the advantage of surprise, and his eyes widened as she sliced downward on his right arm. She used the Bond on her knife to augment her lesser physical strength and pulled the blade down and through the joint, cutting the appendage clean off. The man dropped to his knees and howled in pain, clutching his bleeding shoulder. Onnie ignored him and ended him quickly by relocating behind him, gripping his neck with her left hand and pulling his soul free. At the same time, Onnie repeated the severing process on the neck of the woman, who was still sprinting toward her, too stunned to stop her forward-rushing momentum to dodge Onnie's staff in time.

With the threat gone, Onnie sucked in lung-fulls of air, the adrenalin rushing through her veins. She calmed her heart rate and calmly bent to retrieve the woman's soul. When Onnie turned around to return her focus to the unexplainable void, she forced herself to ignore the terror Gabe and Mal openly wore on their faces. Her fingers were sticky, and she knew the evidence of her deeds had marked her clothing, skin, and even deeper, but now was not the time to unpack that.

"Cat—"

Onnie watched as the void rippled and a robed figure began to emerge from within its center.

"Move!" she shouted, relocating Gabe and Mal behind her.

"Hello, Keeper of Prophecy. Shall we end this?"

The man who used to be Jakob and used to be a Guardian slowly lowered his hood and sneered at the three of them. His face was sallow and pale, but his eyes were black, endless, and a flame flickered within them. He looked no older than forty, but all that was lost on Onnie as she stared at his fangs.

"It's time to show you how much of a child you truly are."

Then, he was gone.

Chapter 26: The Prophesied Keeper

August 2022 - Tunnel outside Alku | Gabriel Vansand

Before Gabe had even registered that the man who used to be his father was standing before them, obviously a sanguiste, but also something far sinister, he was gone.

The world seemed to slow around Gabe, and his first thought was that Cat had manipulated time again, but when the rogue guardian was suddenly between him and the Keeper, Gabe's brain snapped out of its stunned fog. It didn't matter though. He was too late, and he knew it. He'd never make it to Onnie in time.

A gust of air rushed past Gabe, nearly knocking him forward into the back of the rogue and then into Onnie. Instead, Onnie was pushed backward into Gabe's arms as the rogue was thrown to the side.

"You will not lay a hand on my Keeper," Stephan hissed from where he now stood between them and the rogue.

Onnie shook her head, and she probably saw stars for how hard she'd hit Gabe's torso when he caught her, but he didn't have time to check.

"Oh, how unexpected," the rogue said sarcastically, standing tall again, not phased at all by their exchange or by being flung across a street with little effort. "Stephan."

Stephan hissed again, and Gabe even shivered, the sanguiste's instincts and effects unavoidable even though he completely trusted the man.

"I see. I wondered how you were able to cause so much trouble, Jakob. You found the Original."

"Oh no," the rogue smirked. "They found me. See, they needed someone to help bring about the Prophecy, and who better than a former Guardian who knows the inner workings and secrets of the Keepers?"

We're being forced back to you. There are too many of them, Marco told everyone.

And the bastards keep getting back up, Dany said with annoyance.

Bring them. It's time to pull the tunnel down, Onnie stated with determination. Then she stepped away from Gabe and stood on her own.

Acknowledged, Elaric replied, and then all was quiet again along their Bonds.

Gabe peeked down at Mal, whose back was arched, and he hadn't taken his eyes off the rogue. Onnie stood firm, her blue eyes glowing almost white as they roamed their adversary.

"You play with things you do not understand," Stephan growled, genuine disgust dripping off his every word.

The rogue laughed and threw his head back. "Oh, how ignorant can you be? It is you, *child,* who does not understand. I understand it all." Flames flashed within Jakob's eyes, the red glow harsh against his black pupils.

"Why you thought I would stand by and allow this, I do not know," Stephan said.

When the former Guardian spoke again, his voice was deeper and felt as if it reverberated off of everything around them.

"I did not. You weren't even in my thoughts, for I knew you'd pose no threat—he who's taken a vow. You've built yourself a false reality since you left us, Stephan. I think it's time you were woken up."

Gabe could only see Stephan's back, but it was easy to imagine how endless his eyes must have been by that point.

"It is you that still dreams, not I."

I will keep him distracted. Deal with the others, Stephan told them all, and before anyone could argue, he'd lunged at the rogue again. They both became a blur until they disappeared into the forest's darkness beyond the road, the sounds of trees rustling and crunching, splitting the night.

Gabe pivoted to look back down the tunnel as Dany and Elaric sprinted to his side and hunched over, wheezing.

"Where's Marco?" Gabe asked.

Be ready, Keeper. You've got twenty seconds, Marco answered, and Gabe's gaze snapped to Onnie.

Her eyes were closed, her palms up turned at her sides, and a faint gold glow was beginning to build around them. Gabe had no idea what she was planning, but with that much power, he knew he needed to get the others out of the way.

"Elaric, take Dany!" he pointed away from the tunnel. "Mal, check on Marco!"

Five, Marco said as everyone scurried behind Onnie and watched the tunnel's entrance.

Gabe reached for his Bond with Onnie and found it blocked, unsurprisingly. She'd been doing that far too often lately, and that would be something he would bring up with her when all of this was over.

He swallowed.

If they survived.

The glow in her palms had extended and now reached up to her neck and had begun to pulse. In those last three seconds, he prayed to whoever was listening that she would be fine—that everyone would be.

Marco burst from the tunnel, disheveled, with dirt on his cheek but safe. The tremors began when he was barely two feet from the tunnel's exit.

Gabe widened his stance to retain his balance as the shaking increased. When he checked on the others, only Onnie and Mal were stable. The rest of them were attempting to keep their balance just as he was.

The roaring came next, and Gabe turned back to the tunnel only to see the ground ripple around Onnie's feet before it pushed forward and into the darkness within. The roar stopped, and there was a handful of heartbeats of silence.

Then the tunnel came down—all of it.

Rocks crumbled, and the cement arch collapsed. Rebar snapped, and trees crashed to the asphalt from their homes above the opening. The forest's silence was gone, replaced with the grinding of rock, the groaning of wood, and the screams of wildlife as it fled from the disaster occurring around it. The air smelled of ozone and freshly soaked soil.

The entire thing only took a few seconds, but all that was left was a cloud of dust that floated out from the thoroughly impassable rock wall where a tunnel had once been.

"Cat!" Gabe turned away from the destruction and had expected Onnie to be struggling with the amount of power she'd just used. Instead, her head turned slowly to look at him and smiled.

"I'm fine."

Gabe gasped, her eyes no longer Keeper blue but a blinding white.

"Onnie!" Dany cried as she rushed to stand in front of her and then gripped her shoulders. "Are you alright?"

When Onnie nodded, brushed past her best friend, and walked over to the tree line where Stephan and the rogue had disappeared, Gabe's brain caught up.

"Keeper!" He bellowed and reached for her wrist, but when he touched her skin, his palm felt like he'd been gripping coals, and he recoiled reflexively.

She looked down at his hand, then her arm, and then up to his face.

"Silly Guardian."

"Keeper," Marco said from where he stood, further away from them. "You've done well. Now, you need to release her. Come back, Onnie."

Onnie cocked her head to the side, the movement robotic and doll-like with the erie smile and white eyes. "But I have not gone anywhere, sanguiste."

That…that's not Onnie, Mal said to presumably everyone except her.

Indeed. That is the Keeper of Prophecy, Stephan said as he stumbled back into the street lights and out of the trees.

What the hell are we supposed to do now? Dany asked frantically.

Stephan slid to the floor against a tree as Marco rushed to his side. *We pray.*

"Rogue! You have waited so long for this. Why do you act shy now?" Onnie—no, the Keeper of Prophecy said in a voice louder than natural. There was no response from amongst the trees, and Gabe looked over at Stephan, who seemed unharmed, just worn out, which terrified Gabe almost as much as what was happening with Onnie.

Mal, any ideas? Gabe asked.

None. Prophecy is Prophecy, man. We…we have to watch it play out. You and I have done our part.

The Keeper of Prophecy scoffed. "Well, if you're not willing to come out to play, how about I *drag* you out the way you did me." The woman's voice nearly growled as she raised her arm toward the trees, where it remained stationary.

The thud of trees falling, rocks cracking, and birds fleeing filled the quiet night for a second time. It grew louder and louder until the rogue's body was ripped from the trees and thrown to the opposite side of the road, his body smacking the rubble now blocking up the tunnel. The impact of bone against rock, and the air rushing from the man's lungs was deafening, and even Gabe winced. Rogue or not, that had to be agonizing, and when he slid a foot lower down the stone, a streak of blood was left in his wake.

"*You* wanted this Prophecy to happen. *You've* been trying to reach me—to *use* me. I do not understand your hesitancy to see how this play ends."

The Keeper of Prophecy slowly stalked her way over to where her target had landed in a heap at the base of the blockage once she'd released him.

Gabe chanced a glance around him and saw Elaric and Dany slowly circling away from Marco and Stephan to the opposite side of the road, leaving Mal and himself behind the Keeper.

"You…are brilliant," the twisted creature said with a sneer, then spat a mouthful of blood to his side. "Everything I hoped to achieve."

"Tell me, has everything gone to plan? Did it happen the way you expected it to? Lived up to your…*standards?*" she mocked. She lifted him off his feet via his Bond to hover half a dozen feet from the ground again.

"I know why you summoned me, once honorable Guardian. Why you've changed this Keeper in ways irreversible. Did you truly think I would assist you? That I would choose you over myself?"

Does anyone know what she's talking about? Gabe asked.

No, Elaric, Marco, and Stephan all said a bit too quickly.

"And what about you? I know you lurk within him. I can see your mark upon his Bond. Your poison, twisting and corrupting this once savable soul."

The man said nothing, and the Keeper tsked.

"Come now, cat, got your tongue?"

Is she fucking playing with him? Mal hissed.

Just like earlier, a different, lower voice rolled from within the body hanging before them. A maniacal, cackling laugh that made Gabe's skin crawl, and judging by the other's reactions, it wasn't just his.

"Oh, yes. You are perfect. I have waited endlessly for you, Keeper of Prophecy."

Stephan, any ideas here?

Trust her.

Gabe swallowed. Hard.

"You have lost your mind if you think I will ever bow to you, [*undefined]."*

Gabe shook his head clear and wanted to rub his ears after whatever she'd said both hurt and tickled his eardrums. *What the hell did she just say?*

"I will not need you to bow. There are other means of—"

"Keeper!" Stephan said sternly. "It's time."

To his surprise, the Keeper of Prophecy slowly turned to look at Stephan, and with her back to Gabe, he could only watch. Stephan made eye contact with her while Marco's eyes were wide beside him. Then Stephan nodded.

The deep voice laughed again from within the rogue. "Oh, Stephan, you still think you can reach the child. How—"

"Enough!" the Keeper of Prophecy shouted. Then she held up her hand, and it began to glow like it had before.

Two different voices screeched from within the single body she held captive, and then both were silent. Then, only Jakob was left, breathing heavily while an orb of red flame burned within the Keeper's palm.

"I tire of you," she sneered, clenched her fist, and the flame went out. Red powder slipped to the floor from between her fingers until her palm was empty.

"Keeper, you've accomplished your goal," Marco said, his voice steady. "Return her to us now."

Stephan held one of Marco's wrists within his grip, and Gabe could see both men's hands were shaking slightly.

While Marco tried to reach Onnie, Gabe risked a glance at the man she still held aloft. To his surprise, the rogue—no, his father, looked past the Keeper and met Gabe's eyes. Gabe had given up on the man named Jakob long ago, but for a fraction of a second, he swore the darkness had left him, and he was just his dad again. Then it was gone.

The rogue began to laugh, his body coughing and shaking as he did so. Gabe had been so focused on him that he'd taken his eyes off of Onnie, and when he looked back at her, his mind went blank.

The Keeper of Prophecy turned her head and met his gaze, unbreaking and unblinking. "Guardian. You've done well. I thank you."

Mal hissed at his side, and Gabe felt the urge to do the same. The Keeper's stare reminded him of a sanguiste's predatory intimidation, and Gabe was thoroughly ensnared.

"Cat," Gabe forced out and then took one step toward her, willing to try anything to get through to her.

He could move no closer, though, and when he tried, he fell to his knees and looked around for the others. Elaric clutched his chest, Dany talking rapidly at him, though Gabe couldn't hear what she said. Marco and Stephan were doubled over, and their jaws were so tightly clenched that Gabe could see their muscles flex from the strain, even as far away as he was from them. Mal was last, and the cat lay on his side beside Gabe's knees, breathing heavily, fear in his glowing blue eyes.

Gabe...the...sky... Mal said.

Gabe looked up into the reddest sky he'd ever seen, a full white moon shining eerily above them.

Realization hit Gabe, and he squeezed his eyes shut and then looked back at the woman he loved. Or rather, the being she'd become. Onnie, the strongest person he'd ever met...had given in.

Marco was right. This was the Keeper of Prophecy. Not his Cat. She was gone.

Gabe could only watch as the Bonds of the people and things around him flickered into vision in the real world. Their blinding lights began to draw into Onnie's body as if she were a black hole before going dark. She didn't distinguish between friend and foe. She took it all. Tree, stone, Jakob, even Gabe himself.

The rogue laughed again, and then Gabe saw his Bond go dark, and Gabe squeezed his eyes shut. She'd done what she'd promised. Jakob was gone, and all of them were safe, but at what cost?

"Onnie! Stop this!" Dany screamed.

Gabe's eyes shot open to see his sister sprint to Onnie's side and try to talk sense into her. She looked unaffected by Onnie's draw and fucking pissed. Gabe realized Dany was the only one of them without magic, and he managed a soft laugh. At least his sister would survive for however long the world lasted after the Keeper of Prophecy had drained it of all magic.

"Snap the fuck out of it!" Dany screamed in her face. "Did you get Elaric back to kill him again?" She forcefully pointed over to where Elaric was barely conscious, his eyes connecting with Marco's, and then returned to Dany's. The Keeper looked at Elaric and then back to Dany, her face still blank, devoid of emotion.

"What about Marco and Stephan? They came here to help *you!* Can't you see what you're doing to them?"

Again, the Keeper of Prophecy looked between the two individuals, but nothing seemed to register. Dany screamed and paced in a tight circle, her hands clenched in fists at her sides.

"What about Gabe? And Mal? You are *killing* the man you claim to love. Can you do that? Will you be able to live with that guilt when this is over?"

When the Keeper looked at him, Gabe knew the answer to Dany's question. It didn't matter. He didn't matter. To her, he was a stranger—simply a power source.

Dany...go...get...ou... Elaric said but lost consciousness.

Gabe watched his sister register what was happening and how close Elaric was to being killed for a second time, and this time, without a way back. Her head snapped back to Onnie, and she put her palms on both of Onnie's cheeks. Then Gabe heard his sister along the Bond.

Fine, you don't seem to care. You don't seem to feel. *Well, if you can't...I WILL!*

Gabe went from hearing and feeling nothing from Onnie through their Bond—no emotions, no real thoughts, just a thirst for power—to seeing her flooded with Dany's fear.

The Keeper of Prophecy's eyes went wide, and she shrieked the most blood-curdling scream he'd never wished to hear in his lifetime. Dany didn't let go as Onnie's nails tried to claw Dany's hands from her face, but Dany didn't let her pull away. His sister's fear rippled and rushed into Onnie's Bond, and Gabe wondered if what Dany was doing was survivable. A person could only handle so much before their body gave out.

No sooner did he think it than the night was silent except for Dany's heavy breathing. Onnie had stopped shrieking, and Gabe felt as if the world around them held its breath.

Dany sobbed and then yanked Onnie into her arms, and they slumped to the ground together. He met his sister's gaze and said thank you with his eyes. Then it was Gabe's turn to scream as he was slammed with magic and power as it burst forth from Onnie. He coughed, and his eyes watered, and then he was knocked to the ground and flat on his back.

The sky above him was the last thing he saw before he lost consciousness. The red had begun to recede, and blue mixed with it until the stars shined.

The glittering, icy blue color brought a smile to his lips as he gave in and passed out.

Chapter 27: Far too Young to Die

August 2022 - Tunnel outside Alku | Elaric Rickson

Elaric groaned, and when his eyes opened just a fraction, he re-shut them. His head pounded, and he swallowed what tasted like dust, ash, and sand.

"What the hell happened?"

"The Prophecy, that's what. You have one impressive girlfriend, E." Marco's voice said from above him, and Elaric chanced to open his eyes a second time.

Immediately, Marco was forgotten, and Elaric's eyes went wide when he saw the sky above him was twinkling as waves of blues washed across it, small sections of red threaded through. It looked like the Aroura Borealis, and it was beautiful.

"Thank you, once again, for activating the blood link," Marco said with a smile, and Elaric refocused on his friend whose lap his head was currently resting on.

"I'm not sure you're the one who should be doing the thanking," Elaric smiled. "Fill me in, but first, is everyone alright?"

Marco nodded. "Yes, everyone will survive. Minus Jakob. All thanks to Dany."

"Tell me," Elaric said and closed his eyes again since it relieved the pain in his head.

"When the Keeper of Prophecy pulled the last of the rogue's life force and power into herself, I think Dany realized what was happening. When she saw you lose consciousness...well, she tried to reach Onnie through guilt. She screamed and shouted at her, trying to get through to her. I'm not sure what happened after that, but she grabbed Onnie, and then...the Keeper screamed." Marco shivered. "It was...unnatural. Like an animal cornered, desperate, in pain. I've never heard anything like it."

Elaric reached up, took one of Marco's hands, and squeezed it.

"Next thing I know, Stephan and I, who were very close to following you into oblivion, watched Onnie collapse, and then all of the power she'd been draining and pulling into herself released. Gabe and Mal are still out cold. So is Onnie. I think the only reason Stephan and I could hang on so long was due to our being sanguiste and the length of our second lives. We had more to take than she had time to siphon."

"Why am I awake then?" Elaric opened his eyes and asked, confused.

"Not sure, but I'd imagine the blood link. Your body rebounded faster because of it."

"Ah, okay," Elaric closed his eyes again. "Where's Dany?"

"With the others. She asked me to watch over you while she and Stephan dealt with them."

"Makes sense."

Thank you, Dany, Elaric said to her, hoping their Bond communication still worked without Onnie being fully conscious.

I love you, stay with Marco. I'll come to see you when—

I'm fine. Take care of Gabe and Onnie. They need you more than I do, and I love you, too.

Make sure Marco's alright, too. He said he was, but we both know he'd lie through his teeth to everyone but you.

Elaric chuckled, and Marco looked down at him, one eyebrow raised. *You're not wrong,* he replied and then spoke to Marco.

"Dany wanted me to check on you. She said, and I quote, "he said he was fine, but we both know he'd lie through his teeth to everyone but you.""

Marco rested his head against the tree he was leaning on and laughed. "I repeat, one impressive woman."

"So…" Elaric pressed him with a smile. "Are you fine?" With the blood link activated again, he could have checked Marco's aura, but he knew the man too well and didn't need a lie detector. That didn't mean he couldn't make Marco say it aloud.

Marco smiled and nodded. "Yes. I promise. I'm exhausted and need a shower, but overall, I'm alright."

"Alright, thank you." Elaric smiled. "What are the others doing?"

"Pretty much the same as us. Dany's with Gabe, and Stephan has Onnie in his arms with Mal on her lap." Marco looked off into the distance. "They seem fine."

"That's a relief," Elaric shifted and groaned again. "Okay, I'm a bit sore. This form isn't the most robust." Marco snorted, and Elaric turned on his side, facing Marco so he could press his forehead into the man's hip and close his eyes. "Mind if I rest my eyes a bit?"

Marco squeezed Elaric's hand, which he'd never relinquished. "Please do. You're safe." Marco was quiet, but with Marco's sanguiste hearing, Elaric heard him whisper, "Finally."

"She seems well enough that we can move back to town in a few minutes," Dany's voice said from above Elaric's head. "Gabe's still out cold, but Onnie insists she's fine enough."

"What do you think?" Marco asked, and Elaric shifted so Dany knew he was awake. Marco already knew by Elaric's change in breathing, so there was no use in pretending.

"Hey," Dany said, much closer to him.

Elaric opened his eyes and smiled at the two most important people in his world.

"How are you feeling?"

Elaric shifted and sat up before answering her. "Fine, actually. How's Onnie and Stephan?"

"Mostly fine, somehow, and all back to normal. Though he looks like hell," Dany chuckled.

"Never seen him other than in a perfect suit, huh?" Marco asked, and Dany laughed and shook her head.

Elaric looked over at Onnie, who was sitting up, her back to him while she was talking to Stephan.

"What's the plan?" he asked.

"Onnie's going to bring us back to her house. I've already called Xayn to bring some supplies, so he'll meet us there." Dany said. "Oh, Marco, would you mind driving Gabe's car home?"

"Not a problem. Keys are still in it, I assume?"

Dany snorted. "Yeah, we're lucky Onnie let him put it into park."

Marco got to his feet. "I'll go talk to Onnie then."

"Thanks," Dany said as he walked away from them.

"How are you doing, Dany?"

Elaric took a good look at her, and other than a few cuts and scrapes, she seemed fine, but her eyes and aura said another thing entirely.

She looked at him and smiled softly. "I'm tempted to lie."

"I know, but please, don't." He reached up and held her cheek, caressing it with his thumb. "What do I need to know right now? The rest can wait."

Dany leaned into his palm and closed her eyes. "I'll need some of Xayn's time, a very long bath, perhaps some wine, and a really long cry." She opened her eyes, but they seemed pretty calm. "That said, I'm thankful everyone is alright, he's gone, and it's over."

"Well, once we get everyone home, I'll make sure you get everything you need. Sound good?"

"Sounds amazing." She leaned forward and kissed him softly. Elaric shifted to hold her more securely, but when she hissed, he dropped his hands and sat back.

"Sorry," she said, carefully touching the back of her head. "I think my scalp will probably be sore for a while."

Elaric frowned but kissed her cheek. "Then I won't do that again. I'm sorry."

"Not your fault."

Dany looked over at the others, and he followed her gaze. Marco stood over Onnie and Stephan, his arms crossed, and Elaric could see the tension in his body.

"I wonder what they're talking about?"

Elaric sighed, "No idea, but Marco isn't happy with whatever it is. He's probably scolding her for being reckless and ignoring the danger she put herself in. I'm trying not to eavesdrop."

Elaric could have heard their conversation but was too exhausted to focus on it.

"Oh, I remembered something from the day I..."

"What is it?" Dany asked before he needed to explain further.

"Onnie's eyes. I swear there was a second in that room that her eyes went white."

Dany frowned. "Like..."

"Yeah. Keeper of Prophecy white. It was only a flash, and I'm not sure she even realized it."

Elaric watched as his brilliant girlfriend's mind tried to work out the cause and implications of the information, and he brushed his palm over her cheek.

"You don't have to solve the mystery now."

Dany scoffed but smiled. "I think my brain is too tired anyway. Thanks for telling me, though. I'll talk to Onnie about it. Eventually. She's going to need some time to sort all this out."

"I imagine so. She used a lot of power today, and from what I can tell, it wasn't her normal everyday Keeper powers."

"Oh, no," Dany groaned and pressed the heels of her hands into her eyes, "I bet Abbot's is a *nightmare.*"

Elaric chuckled. "Actually, I think it will be fine this time."

Dany peaked through her fingers at him, and her brows knit together in confusion.

First Keeper, how did Abbot's and you fair?

We are well. Onnie, for all her rashness, had the forethought to shield the shop before she...lost control.

The entire shop?

Unbelievably, yes.

Huh, alright, I'll come to check on you soon.

Take your time. We're fine. Thank you for everything, Elaric.

"Yeah, I um," Elaric apologized in his head to Dany and then made a small white lie. "Overheard Onnie the other day. I think she had a plan to minimize the fallout."

"Wait, really? That would be a relief."

Dany's shoulders slumped, and she relaxed. Elaric pulled her gently to him, and she leaned into his chest and sighed. He was careful not to touch the back of her head, but he took comfort in holding Dany in his arms and knowing they were all safe.

Elaric? Onnie asked along their Bond.

Hey, he replied, seeing that Onnie hadn't turned to look at him and that Marco and Stephan seemed to be having a well-animated conversation.

Are...are you alright? Onnie's voice was laced with regret, and when he checked her aura, it reflected it.

I am. You did well, Keeper. Please, don't feel guilty.

Onnie was quiet for a few seconds. *Ah...so it was bad enough for you to activate the blood link.*

Elaric hadn't realized she didn't know that yet, though when he thought about it, she was probably trying to conserve some of her energy.

I did, but not because of you. I did it when we first encountered the roaches. It had nothing to do with you unless you count my desire to be more...durable when protecting you all.

You swear?

Elaric sighed. *Don't believe me?*

It was quiet for another minute, and Onnie finally responded. *Thank you.*

Tell me how you are. I'll be honest. I know why Marco, Stephan, and I rebounded so quickly, but you're usually out longer than this, right?

Actually, I'd like to talk to you and Marco about my...theory, but let's give it a few days. Is that alright?

Onnie, you take whatever time you need. I'll always be here. All of us will be. You're stuck with us now.

Instead of replying, Onnie looked at him over her shoulder, and he watched as her aura softly changed into a shade of pink, her gratitude and unconditional love blinding. He smiled, and she returned it before staring at Marco and Stephan again.

"Dany?"

"What's up?" she said, looking up at him.

"Would you mind if we moved over to the others?" He was ready to go home and get everyone cleaned up.

Dany shook her head. "Not at all. Let's go." She got to her feet and lowered a hand to help him up.

When he was on his feet, he pulled her closer, kissed her again, and whispered in her ear, "I'm so ready for that vintage movie."

Elaric watched as the tips of Dany's ears blushed, and she nodded.

Then he kissed her again.

Gabriel Vansand

When he started to become aware of his surroundings, the first thing Gabe noticed was the throbbing beat directly behind his eyes. There was a softness beneath him, and he could smell the familiar scent of his soap mixed with laundry detergent. The subtle smell of earth and pine also tickled his nose.

Xayn.

Gabe tried to open his eyes and search out his best friend, but even moving his eyes behind his lids hurt, and he groaned.

"Gabe?" Xayn said at his side, and then he felt the man's rough hand was holding his own.

Gabe squeezed his hand weakly, but it was enough, and Xayn's grip relaxed.

"What...happened...."

"You're at home. Everyone is alright, but I need you to try not to move. You hurt your shoulder, and if you agitate it, my remedies won't be enough. You need to go to the clinic tomorrow for an x-ray."

"Cat? Dany?"

"Fine, both fine. A few minor scratches. They are in the other room with Elaric and Mal."

Gabe swallowed and felt Xayn release his hand and lean over him. When he sat back, one of his hands slipped behind Gabe's neck, and he helped him tip his head up a few inches.

"Water. Don't move more than your neck."

Gabe followed orders and took a few sips from a straw. The tepid water soothed his throat, and he didn't think that water had ever tasted so good. When he finished, Xayn returned the cup to the nightstand and retook his hand.

"Lights?" Gabe asked, his voice far less raspy.

"Sorry, yeah, let me get them."

The immediate loss of Xayn's weight on the bed sucked, and Gabe admitted to himself that he was far more freaked out than he'd thought. When he heard the lights click off and Xayn returned to his side, Gabe forced his eyes open to escape the images of a blood-red sky and searing white eyes.

He turned his head just enough to see Xayn, and Gabe's stomach sank. He looked terrified.

"Xayn?"

The glowing lime-green eyes of his best friend glanced at him before looking away.

"Xayn, what's wrong?"

"Nothing."

Gabe pressed his pointer finger against the inside of Xayn's wrist. "You are a shit liar, and you know it. Talk to me."

Thankfully, Xayn laughed and then took a deep breath.

"The sky…I…as soon as I saw it, I knew. Grandma and Elanor… they…we stood on the porch. When Onnie…." Xayn swallowed roughly. "They are fine, but it took a lot out of them."

"I wasn't sure how far she pulled from," Gabe admitted.

"There wasn't a place she didn't."

"What?"

Xayn nodded. "Stephan called a few people. I overheard him. The sky turned around the globe, not just here. The humans are spinning it as a solar flare or rare aurora, which seems to be working."

"Good gods," Gabe hissed.

"From what it sounds like, no one was hurt, and the five of you were the only ones affected so strongly."

"How are you?"

"Fine. Tired, but fine."

Gabe shut his eyes and reached for Cat along the Bond. She felt it when he brushed against her. Her hesitancy and fear rippled through him before he could return it with love and gratitude.

I love you, Onnie said timidly.

I love you, too, Cat. Are you alright?

Fine. Take…stay with Xayn.

Gabe felt her pull away from him. Even though he wanted to press her on what had happened, he could feel her reluctance and how skittish she was.

"So, what's wrong with my shoulder?" Gabe asked Xayn.

"Sprain, I think. I gave you something for the pain, topical for the bruise, and a tonic."

"Okay. Thank you." He tentatively tried to move his arm to test how bad it was but couldn't.

"I bound it to your chest. Sorry, I didn't want to risk you moving it in your sleep."

"Got it." Gabe looked up at Xayn and gently tugged on the man's hand until he looked at him. "Thank you."

He nodded, but Gabe saw his eyes shimmer.

"Xayn?"

"Sorry." Xayn sniffled and looked away again.

"Dude, what aren't you telling me?"

Xayn adamantly shook his head. "Nothing."

Gabe sighed but dropped it. "Fine. Come lay down. You look exhausted."

"It's fine, I should go, you—"

When he tried to release Gabe's hand and get up, Gabe held tighter and practically growled at him.

"Knock it the fuck off, Xayn. Unless you're genuinely worried about Elanor and Grandma, get your ass in this bed and keep me company."

Xayn froze, and Gabe could feel his best friend's inner turmoil radiating off him.

"Dude, we've slept together hundreds of times. What's going on?"

To his relief, Xayn's eyes widened, and he rushed to answer. "No, it's not that."

"Then what the hell has you so closed off?"

When Xayn finally looked back down at him, tears pooled in his eyes, and one ran down his cheek. He opened his mouth to say something but then snapped it shut again.

Gabe sighed but smiled up at him.

"Please? Every time I close my eyes, I see the sky, and…" Gabe shivered and then hissed when his shoulder screamed at him.

Xayn immediately shot back into herbalist mode.

"What is it? Shoulder?"

"Yeah, it's fine. I just moved too abruptly."

Xayn leaned over to inspect the bandages and ensured they hadn't loosened. Once satisfied, he sat back, and Gabe saw his walls crack. The sound of Xayn's shoes being pushed off with his toes thudded in the quiet room, and then he shifted lower on the bed so he could lie beside Gabe. Now that their faces were at the same level, Gabe used his free hand to dry the man's cheeks.

"Thank you, Xayn."

Xayn's eyes were squeezed shut, but he nodded.

Gabe closed his eyes. When he saw a pair of emotionless white eyes staring at him, he found Xayn's hand and squeezed it until the inside of his eyes were black again.

He'd begun to doze off when he heard Xayn's soft whisper.

"I can't lose you, too, Gabe."

Understanding filled Gabe, and he tugged Xayn's hand closer to his side.

"Right here, man. Can't get rid of me if you wanted to."

The last thing Gabe heard was Xayn's soft sobs go quiet, and his breathing evened out as sleep took him.

Then it took Gabe.

Chapter 28: Altered

August 2022 - Alku | Onnie Moore

It had been a week since their confrontation with the rogue guardian had reached its boiling point. Everyone in their group was together again for the first time, lazing around the fire pit on Onnie's back deck. The only difference was that Stephan was also with them tonight.

After the prophecy was triggered and the sky turned red, everyone, including the other residents of Alku, recovered.

Gabe's left arm was in a sling from when he collapsed and hit the ground wrong, but thankfully, it was only a sprain and not something more serious. It was a wound to his pride for sure, considering he'd ended up the most hurt of the group, and Mal constantly teased him about it. Especially since the injury wasn't from their fighting but from when Gabe passed out after Dany had saved them all. Gabe was a good sport about the teasing, mostly, but every once in a while, Mal would appear in Onnie's lap after dodging something Gabe threw at him in retaliation.

Marco and Stephan had come out unscathed and recovered the fastest, both back to normal before she'd even woken up that night. When she did, Mal was on her lap, and she had been in Stephan's arms, and he'd been humming softly under his breath. She'd stayed still, listening to the soothing words in a language she couldn't identify, and even when he knew she'd regained consciousness, he'd continued for a while longer. It was only after Kushima had assisted Mal and he'd woken up that Stephan stopped.

Elaric had also rebounded quickly thanks to his blood link with Marco. Onnie knew he'd lied to her about when he'd activated it, but she let it go. She carried enough guilt over the entire situation and what had come after it that if he wanted to try and lessen some of it for her, she'd gladly take him up on it.

Being the only one with zero magic, Dany hadn't been affected like everyone else. It was only after everything had calmed down that Dany admitted she'd felt the barest of tugs on her Bond, but she'd been running on so much adrenaline that it hadn't been difficult to ignore it, and it was a hell of a good thing she did.

Dany had saved them all.

Kushima and the shop had been nearly unaffected as well. Only a few things had fallen from shelves before Onnie had put shielding up. It was still foggy to her when she actually put the shields up, but she had a feint memory of covering the surfaces in the shop in defensive barriers. Kushima had described them like the layer of bubble wrap people would wrap around their furniture before moving it. Thankfully, Onnie had done it before she pulled the tunnel down, and they hadn't dropped until after she had lost consciousness.

As for her, well, Onnie had been back to her feet so quickly after it all that everyone knew something was up and wanted answers. She had initially thought she would only want to tell Marco and Elaric, but Kushima, ever the voice of reason, had pointed out that Onnie herself had wanted to be more honest with Gabe and the others. So, instead of hiding it, they were all under the prophecy-colored sky, drinking wine and cider, eating takeout from the Day Night Cafe, and relaxing.

"There's one piece I still don't understand," Dany said from where she sat on Elaric's lap, passing a bottle of cider back and forth between themselves.

Onnie snapped out of her daze and sipped her wine. "Hm?" Mal shifted on her lap, and she scratched under his chin.

"The prophecy mentioned souls of the willing. What's with that? Was that...us?"

Onnie's hand froze with her glass halfway back to her lap, and she knew she'd gone pale when she looked at Elaric and then Marco, who were both stone-faced.

I'm scared, Kushima.

You've faced worse. What do you think they will do?

"Cat," Gabe said from beside her on the bench they'd pulled up to the circle, "I know that face. If you don't want to talk about it, you don't have to, but...."

Onnie took a deep breath and shook her head. "No. It's time. Just, uh...give me a second."

Without thinking, she drained the remainder of her wine, nearly half a glass, and placed the empty vessel on the bench beside her. As expected, everyone except Elaric and Marco's eyes were wide at her uncharacteristic alcohol consumption. Then she took a deep breath.

"The First Keeper and I have talked about it, and I believe that the prophecy refers to the souls I had...extracted that night."

Dany looked about to say something, and Onnie held up her hand to stop her.

"It's not that simple. Let me finish."

Dany closed her mouth and frowned.

"First, I need to go back before that night. I, um, have not been releasing the souls I've taken from the roaches. I've been keeping them."

She paused and closed her eyes, waiting for the outrage, the scolding, and the disappointment. After nearly a minute, she cracked one eyelid and saw that everyone was still looking at her, but no one looked anything but curious. Onnie glanced at Gabe, and he took one of her hands and smiled.

"I assume there's more. Keep going," Gabe encouraged and squeezed her hand.

She cleared her throat and continued. "Yeah. So, after I released the first soul and the man returned to attack us again, I was more careful. I noticed that when I let go of the soul, it was being dragged back to Jakob, and I couldn't redirect it, no matter what I tried."

Stephan shook his head. "No matter how low one falls, there is *never* an excuse to reanimate an unwilling victim and, even worse, to enthrall them."

"I agree, so I stopped giving him the opportunity. Every time I gained one, I um…hid it within my Bond at the ah…fiber level so no one would find them."

Onnie looked down at her hands, but Mal's face popped into her view.

"Wait, you did what?" he said, and she winced. "No, explain. I want to understand."

Elaric cleared his throat and spoke up before she could. "Ah, I think I can help with that answer a bit."

"Wait, you knew?" Dany asked in shock.

Elaric nodded. "Yes, and so everything is on the table, Marco knew, too." Everyone turned to look at Marco, though his face was still expressionless. "And so does the First Keeper."

Gabe sighed and shifted his sling on his shoulder. "Alright. So, everyone except Dany, Mal, and I."

"Please don't take this the wrong way when I say this, but didn't you all do the same thing to Onnie regarding the prophecy?"

Onnie's jaw dropped, and when Gabe and Dany started sputtering rebuttals, Onnie laughed.

Thank you, she said to Elaric privately.

"I am not criticizing any of you or your choice to keep that from her," Elaric clarified. "I just want you to have the same perspective. You can be mad, but at the end of it all, the Keeper decided that some secrets are better kept for the benefit of others."

Gabe turned to look at her, and she looked away.

"Cat, please. Keep going?"

She turned back to him, and after checking to see his aura, he was still receptive and open to hearing her out, so she nodded.

"Elaric's right. I won't hide anything anymore. It wasn't easy to do any of this—keep them safe or lie to you all. Every day, those souls weighed on me. Physically and mentally, but...it was our best option. So, rather than burden you with something you could not control, effect, or frankly, help with, I decided to do it alone."

Mal smiled and shook his head. "The fiber level? Really, Onnie? None of us would have been able to see them at the thread level. Overkill much?" Then he sighed. "I understand why you didn't tell us. Don't like it. But I...get it."

"Thanks, Mal," Onnie scratched the top of his head. "So, yeah. Going back to the other night. When I took the souls then, I hid them again."

Stephan smirked and chuckled lowly. "So, that's why those ones did not get back up. Had you released the souls instead?"

"Yup, they would have been pulled right back to him."

Dany groaned and smacked her forehead, the sound cracking the night. "Souls of the willing. Not us. *Them.*"

Onnie smiled at her brilliant best friend and the literal savior of the world. "Got it."

Gabe sighed, "That's...insane."

"You have no idea. There are, ah...there are a few more things though," Onnie said before everyone got too distracted and she lost her nerve.

"Damn girl, I can't take much more," Mal said dramatically, and she snorted and tickled his belly.

"Behave, you wanna know or not?"

He grinned at her, and she shook her head at his dramatics.

"You're so spoiled. So, yeah. The souls I kept safe before that night are in the First Keeper's library."

"Does that mean you still have the other ones with you?" Gabe asked, and she slowly shook her head.

"Excuse me," Marco said, abruptly leaving the group to walk to the end of the deck and as far from her as he could get without actually leaving.

Elaric watched Marco's receding back, and then he refocused on her, and she sighed.

"He's...disappointed in me. I think." She stared after Marco and frowned. "There's no easy way to say this, but the souls of the willing were used as fuel by the prophecy. They were burned up before I began pulling from you all."

Dany spoke up first. "Wait, why is he putting that on you? He knows as well as any of us that the person in control at that time wasn't you."

Onnie shook her head. "No. It was still me at that point. Um...and...the wards...."

"I hesitate to ask," Dany winced.

"Where do you think I got the power to pull down the tunnel? Though the ward part ended up being a good thing, they aren't ruined, just...drained."

After that, everyone was quiet, and Onnie let them sort out their feelings and judgments while she watched Marco at the end of the dock.

Marco....

Not now, Keeper.

She sighed and left him alone, her heart aching. Looking at Stephan, she saw a complex mix of emotions in his features and quickly looked away from him.

"Um, one more question...." Dany said softly.

"Sure, you can ask anything you want," Onnie said, hopefully sounding less wrung out than she felt.

"Is that why you were okay and awake so quickly afterward?"

"Ah...no, well, not directly."

"So, what's up, girl? You beat me in recovery, and I'm not technically even real," Mal teased.

"Hey!" Onnie scolded and flicked the tip of his nose gently. "Take it back. Right. Now."

Mal's eyes flashed blue, and then he nodded. "Alright, alright. I take it back."

"Good," Onnie pouted. "Don't say that again."

"I won't."

"So, how, Cat?"

"Well, when I pulled in all that magic, it wasn't just raw power. The prophecy mentions the final Keeper, didn't it?"

"Yeah, so what does that mean?" Gabe asked, his brow furrowed.

Onnie searched everyone else's faces, and they all looked equally confused.

Should I show them, Kushima?

Do you think you need to go that far?

I…honestly don't know. It might make Gabe less…overbearing in the future.

Or worse, Kushima chuckled.

"What color are my eyes?" Onnie asked and looked at Gabe.

"Normal, green," he answered.

"And…" Onnie sent power to one of her new, still dim, Bond threads, and she shifted her eyes to the white of the Keeper of Prophecy, "Now?"

Gabe's eyes went wide. "What are you doing?"

She turned and looked at Elaric, then Dany, and then Stephan. Elaric snorted and called out to Marco.

"Marco, come here. You're going to want to hear this."

Much to her relief, Marco listened and began walking back over to them.

"Wait, I don't get it. What are you doing that requires that much power right now?" Dany asked, concern in her voice.

Onnie shook her head as Marco retook his seat next to Stephan. Marco saw her eyes but quickly looked away again.

"I'm not doing anything, or rather, I'm not using any power. Let me try another example."

"Keeper…I know where you're going with this. Is that truly

necessary?" Elaric said, and she froze, her hand upturned, an athame now resting in it.

"Let her do it," Marco said curtly, and she frowned but nodded in agreement.

"You know I'll be fine, don't worry so much."

Gabe must have figured out what she was about to do because he reached for the knife.

"Cat, what are you—"

She cut him off by relocating to stand on the other side of the fire and out of his reach.

"Stop, Gabe, trust me."

Just like before, she sent power to a different dimmed Bond thread. Then she ran the tip of the blade down the inside of her arm in a three-inch, shallow line.

Gabe and Dany were both on their feet and rushing to her side instantly. Elaric shook his head, a small smile on his lips. Marco frowned, the first real emotion she'd seen from him all night, and Stephan's eyes were wide.

"Onnie! Why would you do that!" Dany said, grabbing her arm to inspect it as Gabe reached for the knife. Onnie let him take it from her, and she waited for them to calm down.

"Cat, why the hell—"

Gabe started to scold her, but Dany grabbed his uninjured wrist without looking away from Onnie's.

"Gabe, stop. Look."

They both looked down at Onnie's forearm as the skin knitted together within seconds. Dany cleaned off what little blood there had been with her shirt sleeve and revealed Onnie's unmarked skin.

"I see," Stephan said quietly. "Well, judging by your ability to experience the sun still, I imagine not all of the sanguiste traits were permanent. Fair to say for the transmogromorph or other races as well?"

"Correct," Onnie said, pulling her arm back from the others. "The last few days, I've noticed a few skills, or benefits, or...restrictions that I've acquired from each race."

"You did not heal fast enough to be considered an elder sanguiste," Marco stated.

"That's what I thought. I don't think I have the full...strength of that trait, just enough that it's sped up compared to a human or other races."

"Onnie," Mal said, appearing on Gabe's good shoulder, who was still beside her.

"What, Mal?"

"I understand now. Are you okay with this?"

Onnie opened her arms, and Mal appeared in them, and she squeezed him gently.

"Honestly? No, but there's nothing I can do about it now. I...I just have to make the best of it."

"Is this what you wanted to talk to Marco and me about?" Elaric asked, gently pulling Dany back into his lap by her wrist.

"Yes."

Mal relocated into Dany's lap, and she snuggled him.

Marco stood and walked over to Onnie. He stopped before her and studied her with his characteristic stone-faced gaze. She watched him searching her and guessed he was probably reading her in his own way. Then, the real Marco came to the surface, and he pulled her into his arms and hugged her tightly.

"M-Marco?" she stuttered, confused as she hugged him back.

"I've said this before, but it means something more now and needs a minor adjustment, so I'll repeat it. I will never be able to repay you for bringing E back, but I will spend the rest of *my* life trying to do so."

"Marco?" she struggled to keep her voice even.

For as long as you will have me beside you, I will be here, Onnie. He kissed her cheek and stepped away.

Thank you.

Marco nodded, walked a few paces from the group, and looked out into the darkness. His aura was remorseful, but there was relief and joy she could see him trying to suppress. Onnie glanced at Stephan, who was watching Marco with a neutral expression, though his aura showed his concern.

"Can someone please fill me in?" Gabe said gruffly.

"Um, ditto," Dany agreed.

Onnie wasn't sure how to explain to the others, but Mal pulled himself from Dany's grip and relocated back to Onnie's arms. He gently flexed his claws on her arm before she could speak.

"She's the last Keeper because she has the sanguiste immortality," he explained for her.

It took less than a second for Gabe to recoil from her. Onnie felt his shock and then fear pulse along their Bond.

"Wait…that's…that's not possible…."

Onnie saw the fear in his eyes, and she squeezed her own shut and turned away.

I knew he'd make this difficult, Onnie admitted to Kushima.

Give him time to process and grieve. He will need time to adjust, Kushima said.

Then Elaric added, *He's just learned the love of his life will never age, will never die, and will outlive him. Give him time.*

Marco added, *We'll do what we can to help him understand.*

"Onnie," Mal said, and she looked down at him. "Let's go for a walk."

She glanced at Gabe, then turned away and walked away from the group and into the darkness.

When they were far enough away that no one would overhear them, she whispered, "Mal, will he forgive me?"

"There's nothing to forgive. You've done nothing wrong, Onnie." Mal pointed to the tree line. "Come on, let's take the trail."

Onnie sighed. "He'll be mad I left without him. Going off on my own again."

"Then let me accompany you," Stephan said from behind her. She turned to see him emerge from the darkness and fall in step beside her and Mal.

"Besides, Onnie, you can take care of yourself. We all know that, but he feels like it's his job to protect you," Mal said.

"Isn't it?"

"It may have been. In the past, Guardians were needed for a Keeper's survival, but can you tell me that you truly need him anymore?" Stephan asked.

Onnie stopped and glared at him. "Of course I do! What kind of question is that? I'm only human, and I'm not infallible. Everyone needs someone to guard their back."

"Keeper," Mal said, "you are not *only human* anymore."

"But he is," Stephan said, slipping his hands into his pants pockets.

"Oh shit," Onnie said with a groan. "I understand."

Stephan rested his palm on her shoulder and nudged her back to walking. "Onnie, do you remember what I told you about how the sanguiste came to be?"

"I do. Why?"

"I owe you an explanation from the other night."

"You don't need to tell me anything you don't want to," Onnie said genuinely.

"Naw, I wanna know. Spill it," Mal said.

Stephan laughed and scratched the top of Mal's head.

"I told you very few know the true origin story of the sanguiste. We tried very hard to cover up the truth. To rewrite history."

"We?"

He nodded, and she saw the corners of his lips turn up.

"Yes. Myself and my brothers and sister. Keeper, I am of the Original." He stopped walking. "My Second Father was the human who danced with the devil and sold his and his kin's souls to the demons for the rest of eternity."

Onnie's eyes went wide, but Mal spoke before she could.

"Damn, man, I knew you were old, but you may literally be the age of dirt!"

"Maldwyn!" Onnie scolded, and Stephan laughed so hard he clutched his side.

"Mal," Stephan said, still chuckling, "You're going to have a very long life now. Never change, my friend. Somehow, I think eternity just got a lot more interesting."

"I aim to please."

"Um," Onnie said, looking away and hoping she could cover her aura well enough to fool Stephan. "I don't remember what happened after the tunnel came down. Would you tell me about Jakob? The sanguiste part, I mean. That's what he was, right?"

You do not want them to know you were aware while she was in control? Kushima asked.

No. They would worry and begin treating me like glass again. There is nothing we can do to change it, so I'd like to keep it between us. For now, at least. Is that okay?

Of course, young one.

"What he was, was freaking creepy," Mal said, and Onnie tugged gently on one of his ears.

"Of a sort," Stephan said, gesturing for them to continue walking. "I can tell you he was not my blood sibling, so I do not think he was entirely a sanguiste. I believe his abilities were a combination of a blood link and something worse, but truthfully. I don't know."

"The second voice…."

Stephan nodded. "Correct. My Second Father."

"Are you alright?"

Stephan stopped walking again and turned to look at her, his expression rapidly flitting from confusion to shock, to understanding, to respect, and then affection. His aura matched each change as he went through them.

"You're worried about me?"

Onnie looked down at Mal and grinned. "Would it be rude to smack my elder?"

Both Mal and Stephan laughed loudly, and Stephan put his palm on her cheek. "You needn't worry for me. I'm fine. However, had you not, you wouldn't have been Onnie."

Mal bonked his head under her chin, and Stephan removed his hand. She nodded, and they continued their walk.

"Ah, and about Marco...."

"He'll be fine. Give him time. I do not think he's angry with you."

"Yeah, why's he being so broody then? Well, more than normal," Mal asked.

"There are two types of sanguiste in this world, little Maldwyn—those who respect life and those who don't. A sanguiste's soul is not destined for reincarnation. We must go to the demon to whom we owe our souls."

"So, he's mad that those souls are gone for good?" Mal questioned.

"Partly. Marco was not given a choice to become a sanguiste. It was done without his knowledge or consent."

Onnie squeezed her eyes closed. "Oh, Marco."

When she reopened them, Stephan's aura and face were filled with regret, and he nodded.

"As I said, there are some who do not respect life. I think Marco feels those souls were also not given a choice." He quickly looked at her. "The choice was taken from them by Jakob, not you, and as I said, I think he understands that."

She looked down at Mal in her arms and traced the edge of his ear with her eyes.

"Thank you, Onnie," Stephan said.

"For?"

Stephan's voice was sad when he spoke again. "For caring about Marco as you do. While I am not his true second father, and he sees me more as a meddling boss most days, I consider him mine. Vanessa, Sam, and I, we all do."

Onnie chuffed. "Stephan, he's not difficult to love. Truthfully, none of you are." She sighed. "My life before coming here, meeting all of you...let's leave it at I don't miss it. I have my brothers, my Mom, and Lewis, but they are separate. Apart."

"Not of your world," Stephan finished for her.

"I love them. With everything I am, but the truth is, they will never understand all of this, and now...."

"Yes. I know."

"But, I have you. And Marco and the First Keeper, and the others. A chosen family. One who understands."

"You do. While you will never forget your family, there will come a time when you're more grateful for your chosen one than your blood."

Onnie squeezed Mal, "Would I be horrible if I said...I'm already there?"

"That's not horrible, Onnie. It's honest," Mal said, "but don't waste what time you do have with them. We'll all be here. Waiting for you."

They walked further in silence, and Onnie tried to focus on her footsteps.

One after the other.

Ever forward.

Except they were not the only steps, she heard.

She was not alone.

Chapter 29: Let me Take You Home

August 2022 - Alku | Gabriel Vansand

Gabe watched as Onnie and Mal walked away from the group— away from him.

Stephan stood up and followed her quietly, and Elaric broke the tension among those still around the fire.

"Gabe, sit down. Let's talk."

Gabe turned and looked at Elaric, then Marco, and finally Dany, the latter who looked just as shell-shocked as he did. She and he were now the only people at the fire destined to die after a human life span. Then he realized that Dany already had to have come to terms with Elaric outliving her, and he scolded himself before doing as Elaric requested. Gabe walked back to a vacant chair and sat down heavily.

"What do you want to know?" Elaric asked.

Gabe's brow crinkled. "I…I'm not even sure."

"You're afraid," Marco stated, and Gabe nodded without looking up.

"That she'll be hurt?" Elaric asked.

Gabe made eye contact with him but quickly looked at Dany and then back to Elaric. The man understood, judging by his slight smile.

"Dany, I think he needs to talk to you. Not us." Elaric kissed her cheek, shifted her off his lap, and stood up. "Come on, Marco, show me what you were brooding over earlier."

Marco got to his feet, and they both left to stand at the end of the dock. Dany turned and looked at Gabe, and when she saw his face, her eyes softened.

"I get it," she looked over at Elaric and glared at his back. "I see why he wanted me to talk to you." Then she sighed, the sound weary and heavy. "I've been there, Gabe. I am there." She shifted to sit closer to him and hold his free hand.

"How am I supposed to protect her when she'll outlive me?"

Dany snorted. "Do you really think she needs your protection anymore?"

Gabe yanked his hand back and winced when he pulled his injured shoulder.

"What the hell does that mean?"

"Gabe, she doesn't need you to protect her anymore. You know that. That's why you didn't argue with her or try to stop her just now when she walked away and into the dark. Alone."

"Dany, be very careful what you say next," Gabe said through clenched teeth.

Dany rolled her eyes and crossed her arms. "Truth hard to hear?"

"Stop it."

"The prophecy mentioned the last Keeper, not the last Guardian. She'll probably just replace you."

Gabe stood up so quickly his chair slid back and groaned along the wooden boards. "Enough."

Dany stood to face him and poked him in the chest with her finger. "That's what you're thinking. Isn't it?"

"How would you know what I'm—"

"Because I've already done it!" Dany shouted. "I've already thought all of that. With Elaric."

Gabe froze and realized what he'd been doing to his sister. He shut his mouth, letting her yell at him.

"Why would I bother staying with him? He doesn't need me. I'm going to die anyway. He can find someone else, go back to Marco, hell, be alone, and just *not* have to deal with others' lifespans. Do you know what he said to me?"

Gabe shook his head.

"Why was I so worried about tomorrow when today wasn't even over? He may not need me tomorrow, and I will leave him in the future, whether we like it or not, but we can do nothing about that. Right now...right now, he needs me by his side. *Wants* me by his side."

Gabe ran his fingers through his hair. When he spoke, he sounded like a child. "I'm sorry, Dany."

"Do you really *really* think Onnie doesn't still need you? That a Keeper can be her own Guardian?"

"No."

"So, why are you being an idiot and making her feel like she did something wrong?" Dany snapped and then sat back down and looked away from him.

"She did nothing wrong."

"Correct," Dany said without looking at him.

"I am an idiot."

"Correct again."

"Dany?"

"What?" she said, still without turning toward him.

"Thank you."

When she grunted, he bent and kissed the top of her head before he walked away from the fire and into the nearby woods.

Mal, where are you?

Nearly at the clearing.

Is Stephan still with you?

No, he left a few minutes ago.

Thanks. Do you mind if I have a few minutes with Cat?

Why the hell are you asking me for permission? You hurt your arm, not your head, dude.

Gabe chuckled. *Alright, asshole. I get it.*

You better. Hurry up. I'm hungry. Maybe Dany will make pasta.

You just ate! Gabe laughed as he began to jog, his arm aching from the jostling.

So? I'm leaving. Hurry up.

Gabe sped up, gritting his teeth at the pain in his arm, and he was thankful he knew the shortest route to the clearing from their house. He slowed down as he got nearer and tried to make some noise so he didn't scare her. When he stepped into Wayward Clearing and saw Onnie sitting on a rock in the center of it, he felt a sense of deja vu.

"What are you, a wild animal? All that thrashing about." Onnie tsked, but he saw a small smile in her silhouette.

He slowly walked up to her, and when he stood at her side, he looked down and into her eyes that couldn't hide her emotions.

"Will you let me take you home this time?"

To his relief, she smiled. "Only if you promise you'll stay. Forever."

Gabe sat beside her and gently held her face in his palm. "I promised you I'd never hurt you, didn't I? I haven't done very well with that lately, but I will do better."

Onnie nodded, and he kissed her lightly. She smelled of jasmine and vanilla, and he wanted to wrap himself in the fragrance. He sat beside her and closed his eyes, taking a deep breath. The scent of pine and damp leaves was comforting, and he thought of his childhood chasing Xayn and Dany through the trees. His sister had always been by his side, the two of them supporting each other when their parents didn't. Now, they were truly without family.

Gabe looked at Onnie's profile and smiled. They may not have a blood family left, but they sure as hell had a chosen family.

"Hey, Gabe," Onnie said rather suddenly.

"Hm?"

She looked down and fiddled with a stick, peeling the bark off of it in curling ribbons. "Are you okay? With what happened, I mean. With...your dad...."

He chuffed. "Of course that would bother you." Gabe placed his free hand over Onnie's, stalling her nervous fidgeting.

"What does that mean?"

"It means you're too caring for your own good, Cat."

She laughed softly, "Funny, Stephan just said something similar."

He smiled at her and kissed her cheek. "Please, don't worry about this on mine or even Dany's behalf. Our dad died for us long ago."

"If you're sure."

Onnie tilted her head back and gazed through the tree canopy at the stars. The sky hadn't fully returned to normal, the blue still streaking across the black with a tinge of red and forming delicate swirling patterns.

"What are you thinking?" he asked his ever-pensive girlfriend.

"Do you know what that is?"

Gabe looked at the sky again with her. "The colors?"

"Yes. See how it's whispy and almost cotton candy-like?"

"Sure."

Onnie sighed and lowered her gaze, and he hated the wrinkle of self-doubt that crossed her forehead.

"Those are Bond threads."

"Oh," Gabe hadn't really thought about it, but it made some sense, or at least wasn't any more strange than anything else they'd gone through. "Is that a bad thing?"

"Not exactly, I just, I still feel guilty. I was unraveling people's Bonds with their magic, their race...their *self.* If Dany hadn't stopped me, I would have unmade the magical essence of our world."

Gabe pursed his lips. He understood why she was beating herself up, but he didn't have to like.

"How did Dany get through to you?"

"Fucking brilliantly. Honestly," she turned and looked at him, a grin from ear to ear, "she's too smart for her own good."

Gabe smirked. "Don't let her hear that. It'll go to her head."

He teased his sister, but he agreed with Cat. There was no one quite like Dany and how her mind worked.

"She'd deserve it. Do you remember when we told her Jakob was still alive?"

"When she popsickled us all? Yeah, why?"

"She'd been researching how it happened and if it was controllable. Well, she figured it out. Dany overwhelmed me with her fear." Onnie rubbed her chest with the heel of her hand. "My heart gave out."

Gabe tensed. "What did you just say?"

Onnie met his eyes, and still, the woman managed a soft smile. "Yes. Dany would have killed me if I hadn't had the sanguiste regeneration."

Gabe clenched his jaw and looked away. How was he supposed to process that? His sister would have taken Onnie from them— murdered a Keeper. Killed her best friend and the woman he loved.

"Gabe, stop." Onnie clasped both his cheeks and turned his face back to her. "First off, I'm fine. Second, she did the right thing. In fact…" Onnie sighed, "She did what I asked."

"What does that mean?"

His own heart felt like it was the one that had stopped beating, and he involuntarily held his breath, knowing whatever she said next, he wasn't going to like it.

"Gabe, your job, your role, is to protect me. Mal's is to guide me. I asked the others to make the hard decision…if it came to it. The world or me—they would choose the world with my blessing."

He felt his jaw pop from how hard he was trying to keep himself from exploding. His emotions were too high, and he wanted to reign it back in, but he had to admit he was struggling.

"To be clear, I don't think Dany *intended* to harm me. Just snap me out of it."

"Does that even matter!" Gabe snarled and then took a deep breath. "Sorry. I, um, give me a second."

He stood up without waiting for her reply and walked to the edge of the clearing, his back to her.

Mal, did you know Onnie asked the others to…kill her…if needed?

Mal sighed and then appeared on his shoulder. *I did.*

Why didn't I? Gabe growled, and he heard Cat's intake of breath from the other side of the clearing. Clearly, his emotions were not under control.

Man, what good would it have done?

What does that mean?

No one, Onnie especially, wanted you to have to be the one to make that choice if it came down to it. Would you have sat back and done nothing if you'd known the others were watching her, evaluating, judging if she'd crossed the line and were ready to remove her from the equation?

Of course! Gabe clenched his fists, his injured arm protesting from the tension.

That's a lie, my friend, and you know it is. Mal bonked his head against Gabe's temple. *But that's fine. No one wanted you to have to be the one to do it if it came to it. None of us wished that on you. We'd have lost both of you.*

Gabe… Dany said, and he sighed.

Cat?

Yeah, she said that she told you about our conversation before the tunnel. Please, Gabe…don't…don't think worse of us. I agreed to her request as much for you as I did for her, and only after hours of her pleading her case.

I'm exhausted, Gabe admitted to Dany and Mal.

Who wouldn't be? Mal said. *Come on. Let's take Onnie home. I think we could all use some cuddles in nice, warm blankets.*

Hey, Gabe. I'm going to sleep at home tonight. These three will walk me home. Okay?

Yeah. Call me tomorrow?

As if there's a universe where I wouldn't—multiple times a day.

Gabe smiled and scratched Mal under the chin. "Fine, you win." He turned and found Onnie was still near the boulder they'd been sitting on, but she had her eyes closed. Even this far away from her, in the dark, she was breathtaking.

"Cat, come here. Let's go home."

Her eyes snapped open, glowing blue for a few seconds before returning to their original color. She crossed the clearing and smiled at Mal.

"Hey, Mal."

"Make with the magic mumbo jumbo. I wanna cuddle."

Gabe snorted, took one of Onnie's hands, and then kissed the top of her head. "For once, I agree with the loudmouth. I could use some snuggle time, too."

Onnie giggled and nodded. "Your wish is my command, good sirs."

Gabe squeezed her hand, and then they were home, and never had it felt so good.

Epilogue

September 2022 - Alku | Onnie Moore

Onnie grabbed a sweatshirt from the back of the couch in Abbot's study and followed Elaric and Dany to the door leading into the First Keeper's library.

"Dany, need one?" she asked, pausing by the trunk in the corner where she stored extra clothes.

Dany's blood-red hair bounced as she nodded. "Please. Hot enough out that I didn't bring a jacket with me."

I'm not going to summon you today, Kushima.

I assumed as much. Do not worry, I'll be fine.

Onnie tossed one of Gabe's sweatshirts at Dany while Elaric pulled the door open for them.

"Dude, I wondered where this went," Dany laughed as she pulled on the hoodie and zipped it up.

"Oops," Onnie grinned. "I steal one of yours?"

"Nope, but I used to snag this one when he wasn't looking."

Onnie passed Elaric, who still held the door, and saw him smirk.

"Should I be concerned for my wardrobe?" he asked.

"Probably," Dany stated, kissing his cheek as she passed him and entered the frigid room.

Onnie shivered, and she went straight to the table where her quilt was and folded herself into it. Elaric shook his head, but he smiled at Dany's back as she walked across the room to sit beside Onnie before he pulled the door closed. He joined them and snagged a chair before spinning it backward and sitting across from them.

"So, what exactly are we doing?" Dany asked as she pulled a corner of Onnie's quilt over her lap.

"Few things," Onnie smiled. "First, I'd like to ask you for a favor."

Dany snorted. "Duh. Whatever."

"Elaric is going to…" Onnie looked at him, "Actually, you wanna do this? Or do you want me to?" Onnie saw Dany's aura shift to one of panic, and Onnie groaned. "Sorry, that made it sound like a bad thing. Dany, it's not bad. Please, don't worry."

Dany took a deep breath and nodded. "Yup. Fine. All good."

"Hey," Elaric said gently, holding his hand out to Dany, who took it and smiled. "She's right. Onnie is going to let me take the forms of some of the souls she's been protecting. That's all."

"Yes, but obviously, some of them you've seen before, so I didn't want you to panic if you saw them in the future. I've already warned Gabe and Mal, but," she glanced at Elaric, "Well, we wanted you to help us, so I asked you to come with."

"Oh." Dany looked from Elaric and then back to her. "Okay." She took a deep, steadying breath. "Alright, I'm fine. Sorry."

Elaric shook his head. "Nope. We understand."

"So, what's the favor part?"

"It will take me a bit of work to retrieve each soul. Once I do, Elaric and I will look at each of them so he can decide if it is one he wants to take. Either outcome, I have to tether them into my Bond so we can give them to Dillon after we finish so the angels can come to get them."

"Will you help us while we're in the void?" Elaric cocked his head. "Well, more void."

"Sure, but what can I do?"

"A few important but basic things, and then I'd like you to help me get them to Dillon."

"First of those basic things..." he smiled at Dany. "Onnie will get tired, cold, and worn out the more she does this, and since I'll likely be occupied, would you mind making sure she has tea and blankets and is fine in general?"

Dany rolled her eyes. "Really? Of course. Why are you two being so squirrely?"

Damn, this woman is far too intelligent, Onnie said to Elaric and Kushima.

She's your Sister. You should not be surprised.

Onnie grinned. "Well, there's one more part."

"Yeah," Elaric said, taking his hand back from Dany and sitting back in his chair. "Well, my kind...well, family...um, we're forbidden from sharing not just our base form with others, but also the actual form creation."

"I'll be too busy caring for the souls and watching over Elaric. Would you watch what you can and learn how it works?" Onnie said, saving Elaric, who was clearly squirming.

Dany looked at him and narrowed her eyes, "You're sure?"

Elaric nodded.

"We don't plan on sharing anything with the wider world, obviously, but truthfully, as Keeper, I don't like not accurately understanding how it works. We are going to store the process in the archive. Even if it's never seen or used, it'll be here just in case."

Onnie looked down at her fingers in her lap. *Dany, if I had known how it all worked, I might have been able to save his forms, too, but I didn't.*

She felt Dany's hand clasp hers and looked up to see her best friend smiling. "I get it. I'll do what I can."

"Thank you," Onnie said with a smile, but she had to resist the urge to sniffle. "Oh, have you heard from Dillon?"

"Yeah," Dany squeezed Onnie's hand and released it. "He's fine. Whatever they hit him over the head with the day of the attack didn't do permanent damage."

"That's a relief," Onnie said. "I feel so bad that he got hurt."

"Onnie," Elaric said sternly. "You said so yourself the day the wards were attacked. You wouldn't have been able to collect their souls. We had no way of knowing that Jakob would reanimate them all in the morgue."

"I know."

Dany agreed with Elaric, "It was bad luck, Onnie. They wouldn't have bothered with Dillon if he hadn't walked into the morgue. He was just in the wrong place at the wrong time."

Onnie nodded but said nothing more. They were right, but it still sucked, primarily for Dillon, who ended up knocked out cold on the sterile floor.

Dany wiggled her way out from under the blanket and stood up. "Alright. Well, now that I know what you want from me, let me get us all tea and something to take notes with." She glanced at Elaric, "Is that alright? We can leave them in here if you're worried."

Elaric smiled and shook his head. "Not worried. Please, and thank you."

"Okay. Two teas for us, and what do you want, Elaric?"

"Tea's fine, thank you."

He stood and quickly kissed her, and then she nodded once more at Onnie, shoved the heavy door, and left to gather what she needed.

"You doing alright?" Onnie asked Elaric as he retook his seat.

"Yeah. I just don't want either of you to be put in danger because of me."

"I know," Onnie smiled. "I'll make sure she understands how important it is to be careful with this, but I meant what I said. There may have been something I could have done if I'd known how—"

"Don't go there, Onnie. I told you, my life was more than enough. Forms can be replaced."

Onnie looked away. "Not all of them."

Young one, Kushima said to both of them, *do not forget that what you did was near to a miracle and not to be taken lightly. While I know Elaric misses his other forms, the fact that you accomplished what you did was enough.*

Exactly, Elaric agreed. *Thank you, First Keeper.*

Onnie sighed but smiled. *See, you're ganging up on me already?*

Kushima laughed softly. *Never. We merely have the same perspective.*

Fine, Onnie said, rolling her eyes. *I believe you. I'll drop it.*

"Thank you, Onnie, truly. You did more than I thought possible, and I will forever be grateful to you for it. Ignore the rest."

She nodded.

They both looked toward the door as Dany pulled it open, a notebook and pen in her hands. "Water's on."

"Thanks."

Dany sat down her note-taking supplies on the table. "Actually, Onnie, I have a question."

"Sure, what's up?"

"Did you get anything from the transmogromorph race?"

"Oh," Onnie saw Elaric's aura shift to discomfort, and she hesitated to say anything without knowing why the question put him on edge. "Not sure yet. Why?"

Kushima, do you have any idea why Elaric's so uncomfortable?

I'm unsure.

"Curiosity, mostly. How do you find out what each one gave you?"

Dany leaned on Elaric's back, becoming a human backpack. Her silliness made him smile, and his aura returned to something more positive.

"Well, we've figured out there are a few different types of...threads. Sanguiste immortality and healing, for example. I will weave that one into my main Bond, and then it will stay active permanently, so I don't have to pay attention to it. I may be able to tweak it, but I have no idea yet."

"Are you planning on doing that to everything?" Elaric asked.

Onnie shook her head, "No. For things like green witch hearing...let's just say I have a new-found respect for Xayn and Marco."

Elaric snorted, "Yeah. You and me both."

Dany's brow crinkled, and Onnie knew that look. "What's wrong, Dany?"

"Nothing. Not really. Just trying to absorb it all."

Sister, I believe your kettle has come to a boil, Kushima informed them.

"Oh shit!" Dany dashed to the door and out of the room before Onnie and Elaric even had time to laugh at her.

"Never dull," Elaric teased fondly.

Onnie snorted, "Nope. Never."

Are you ready to retrieve the souls, young one?

"As I can be," Onnie frowned. "At least I know it will be easier to remove them from the flames than to hide them."

Elaric smirked, "Honestly, Keeper."

Onnie crossed her arms. "Hey, none of that."

Elaric's smile fell, and his aura darkened again. "Onnie, how are you doing with all of this?"

"I assume you mean all of it, but the eternity part specifically?"

He nodded.

She sighed and dropped her head into her hands, her thumbs rubbing her temples. "I'm fine. It's not really me I'm worried about."

"Gabe?"

"Yeah."

Give him time to adjust, young one.

"Is there enough?" Onnie asked quietly.

"Enough what? Time?" Elaric asked.

She nodded.

Elaric placed his palm on her knee. "Onnie, I'll be honest, it will be difficult. On both of you. All of you, really."

You must trust your Guardian, Keeper. Perhaps all young Gabe will need to accept the situation and adjust, is time. However, you must understand his perspective, and not just as your Guardian.

"Meaning?" Onnie asked, lifting her head and looking at the ceiling.

"Your boyfriend knows that his girlfriend will have to watch him die."

Precisely. None of this will be easy, and I believe he will have the most challenging time of it, but I stand by my decision. Gabriel is your Guardian and will be able to fulfill his duty.

"Forever?" Onnie said softly.

Elaric looked away, and then Dany opened the heavy door and returned with thermoses of tea in her arms.

"We ready?" Dany asked.

Onnie nodded weakly, not missing the lack of an answer from Kushima, and Elaric's aura filled with sympathy.

Maybe that meant there was a way.

Onnie sat up straighter and took her thermos from Dany. "Yes. Let's do this."

Onnie had brought Elaric back, and she could see the Bond as no one else in history ever had. She'd survived the prophecy. If Gabe wanted to stay by her side, she'd find a way to make it happen.

The woman who had been used, ignored, and felt the need to hide had been human, but she wasn't.

She was the Final Keeper—everything had changed, and as far as Onnie was concerned, anything was possible now.

Eliza Leone

Eliza Leone is an author from the Pacific Northwest who specializes is chronicling the stories of her imaginary friends. As a kid, you could find her on the playground with a few kids acting out the stories they'd made up. When she got older and discovered there were entire worlds hidden within the pages of endless books, chances are her nose was in one. Over time, Friday nights were reserved for bookstore runs with her mother and together, they'd resupply for a week of adventures.

Writing had always been a far off dream, her ability to spell and do that grammar thing correctly, severely lacking. It wasn't until her mid-twenties that she decided if she was only writing it for herself, then no one would care about her lack of proper punctuation. Ten years and over a dozen books later, her family, human and fiction, convinced her to finally share her stories with the world.

From short stories and micro-fiction to the entire urban fantasy universe of Alku and its people, Eliza can't wait for you to giggle, sob, and throw your book across the room with her. Just...please don't throw the e-readers.

You can find Eliza Leone on: Discord at https://discord.gg/DvfMefpJAP, Instagram @ElizaLeone_author, Twitter @ELeone_author, and at ElizaLeone.com.

Leave feedback, read exclusive bonus content, and support this project at www.campfirewriting.com/explore/ElizaLeone

www.ingramcontent.com/pod-product-compliance
Lightning Source LLC
Chambersburg PA
CBHW030913050726
47498CB00003BA/721